SWORDS & SORCERIES

Tales of Heroic Fantasy

Volume 8

OTHER ANTHOLOGIES AVAILABLE

from

PARALLEL UNIVERSE PUBLICATIONS

SWORDS & SORCERIES: Tales of Heroic Fantasy Volumes 1 - 7
Presented by David A. Riley & Jim Pitts

KITCHEN SINK GOTHIC 1 & 2
Selected by Linden Riley & David A. Riley

THINGS THAT GO BUMP IN THE NIGHT
Selected by Douglas Draa & David A. Riley

CLASSIC WEIRD 1 & 2
Selected by David A. Riley

SWORDS & SORCERIES

Tales of Heroic Fantasy
Volume 8
Presented by

David A. Riley

Jim Pitts

PARALLEL UNIVERSE PUBLICATIONS

First Published in the UK in 2024
Copyright © 2024
Cover & interior artwork © 2024 Jim Pitts
To Wake the Hunter © 2024 Tais Teng & Jaap Boekestein
Moonfinger and Gift © 2024 Andrew Darlington
The Quality of Mercy © 2024 Geoff Hart
Employment for Magical People © 2024 Monica Goertzen Hertlein
The Hero's Path © 2024 Jeffery A. Sergent
Little Lives Rounded by Sleep © 2022 Matt McHugh
First published in *Strange Wars: Speculative Fiction of Coalitions in Conflict*, April 2022
Wardark and the Pirate King © 2024 Craig Herbertson
For the Heart of a Spearslayer © 2024 R. K. Olson
The Stone Heads © 2024 Scott McCloskey
The Troupe © 2024 Andrew Graham
Lair of the Mutant King © 2024 Adrian Cole

All rights reserved. No part of this publication may be reproduced, stored in a retrieval system, rebound or transmitted in any form or by any means, electronic, mechanical, photocopying, recording or otherwise, without the prior written permission of the author and publisher. This book is sold subject to the condition that it shall not by way of trade or otherwise be lent, resold, hired out or otherwise circulated without the publisher's prior consent in any form of binding or cover other than that in which it is published.

ISBN: 978-1-7393674-4-2

Parallel Universe Publications, 130 Union Road, Oswaldtwistle, Lancashire, BB5 3DR, UK

Dedicated as always to the memory
of writer, editor,
and publisher,
Charles Black
who inspired this anthology series

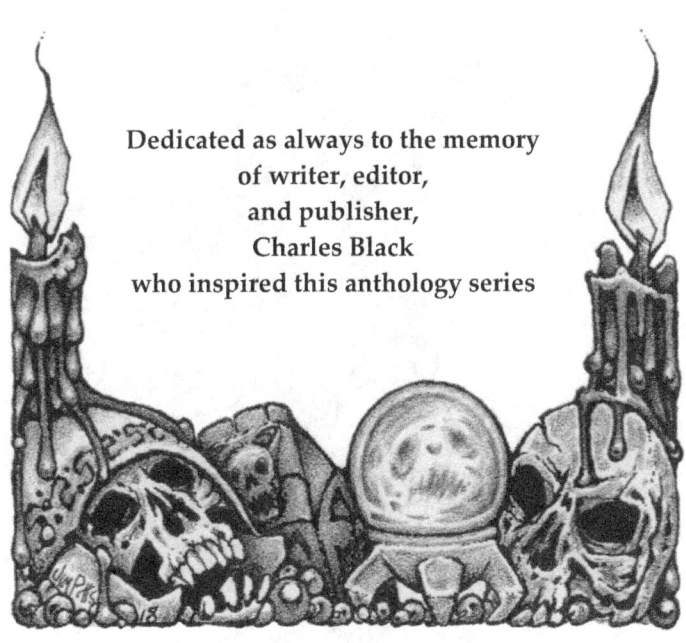

CONTENTS

INTRODUCTION	9
David A. Riley	
TO WAKE THE HUNTER	21
Tais Teng & Jaap Boekestein	
MOONFINGER AND GIFT	55
Andrew Darlington	
THE QUALITY OF MERCY	71
Geoff Hart	
EMPLOYMENT FOR MAGICAL PEOPLE	85
Monica Goertzen Hertlein	
THE HERO'S PATH	112
Jeffery A. Sergent	
LITTLE LIVES ROUNDED BY SLEEP	134
Matt McHugh	
WARDARK AND THE PIRATE KING	162
Craig Herbertson	
FOR THE HEART OF A SPEARSLAYER	192
R. K. Olson	
THE STONE HEADS	213
Scott McCloskey	
THE TROUPE	257
Andrew Graham	
LAIR OF THE MUTANT KING	283
Adrian Cole	

 # INTRODUCTION

Welcome to our eighth volume of swords and sorcery stories.

Opening this collection is a collaboration between Tais Teng and Jaap Boekestein.

Tais Teng is a Dutch sf writer and illustrator with the quite unpronounceable name of Thijs van Ebbenhorst Tengbergen, which he shortened to a humble Tais Teng to leave room for exploding spaceships.

His drawings range from talking teapots to quite beautiful bat-winged ladies with a naughty character.

SWORDS & SORCERIES

In his own language, he has written everything from radio plays to hefty fantasy trilogies. One was even a mythos novel with Paul Harland: *Computercode Cthulhu*. To date he has sold seventy-five stories in the English language, while Spatterlight recently published his SF novel *Phaedra: Alastor 824*, set in the universe of Jack Vance. Teng is a great admirer of Clark Ashton Smith and the last years he has been writing stories set in his Zothique, the last continent of Earth, under a dying sun. His Dutch publisher published them as a collection titled *Gekleed in soepel mummieleer* (*Clad in Supple Mummy Leather*) with 21 interior illustrations.

A second Sword & Sorcery series is set in the alternate Arabian Nights universe of the Inland Sea. You can find samples of both of the series in *Swords & Sorceries*. His most recent S & S sales are to *Cirsova*, *Carpe Noctem* and *Strange Aeon 2024*.

The following information about Jaap Boekestein has been provided by his co-author Tais Teng: "Jaap Boekestein (1968) writes science fiction, fantasy and horror since the late 1980's in Dutch and English. Over 500 stories and about a dozen of his novels and novelettes have been published. Although his stories can be pretty wild, he lives a very normal life in the coastal city of The Hague where he works in IT as an evil servant. Uh… civil servant. Definitely a civil servant.

SWORDS & SORCERIES

"He has written several Dutch Sword & Sorcery novels set in the universe of Kadhal, featuring three dancing girls who have to survive in a city filled with dark magic and crime.

"His current project is a series of stories about a galactic conman and investigator. So far the word count is 700k+. Some of those words are pretty decent. Some of them are pretty and indecent. Together with Tais Teng he started a few years back the only indigenous Dutch SF genre: ziltpunk, which are stories about positive, grandiose, idea rich futures of the Netherlands after huge and diverse climate changes. Futures where tornados are herded for their energy, where the Netherlands are flooded by an ice sea, or the Dutch tame the seas with living dragon-dikes and armies of crabs."

Andrew Darlington: "Since my previous appearance in this wonderful series of books I've been furiously involved wearing my other guise as music journalist for 'RnR' magazine, interviewing such luminaries as Kiki Dee, the Magic Numbers, Kelly Jones of the Stereophonics and Passenger (who did classic song of regret and remorse,  'Let Her Go'), while writing a series of books for SonicBond publishers, one on the Hollies, another about the Human League, and one detailing the full history of the Small Faces. I also write on diverse topics for the 'IT: International Times' website, and have written lyrics for the new album by U.V. Pop, a long-standing but recently revived association with musician-friend John White. I also find time for walking in the wild and wuthering West Yorkshire landscape, along the network of canal towpaths that extends and interconnects forever, Victorian infrastructure for coal and wool to feed their industry, it fell into disuse early last century, but is now renovated for slow house-barges and rambling towpath walkers. There are squirrels and heron. And I walk there in a slight morning mistiness, thinking of new 'Eternal Assassin' tales for a forthcoming collection."

Geoff Hart is a Fellow of the Society for Technical Communication (STC) with more than 35 years of experience as a writer, editor, information designer, and French translator. During this time, he's published more than 450 articles, most available via his Web site (*www.geoff-hart.com*), as well as the books *Effective Onscreen Editing*, *Writing for Science Journals*, and *Write Faster With Your Word Processor*.

A popular speaker at the STC annual conference and STC chapter meetings, Geoff has given presentations and workshops in North America, the U.K., India, and China on topics ranging from writing and editing to information design, cross-cultural communication, and workplace survival skills. He currently works as a freelance French translator and scientific editor, specializing in authors for whom English is a second language. In his spare time, he writes fiction and has sold nearly 72 stories. Geoff won the 2023 Kepler Award for his short story *The Ninth Tentacle*. Visit him online at *https://geoff-hart.com/*.

Monica Goertzen Hertlein is an accountant, sociologist, and aspiring author. She always wanted to write, but never thought it was a real job. After career and family, she returned to her passion of fiction writing. Her stories have been published in *The Lorelei Signal*, *Another Realm*, and *Every Day Fiction*. Three of her short stories, including a first-place contest entry, are included in the Saskatoon Writers' Club anthologies: *Fact, Fiction and Fantasy* and *Bridges of Imagination*. Her entries to the Writers of the Future contest, including an earlier version of this story, won Silver Honourable Mention and Honourable Mention. She is a member of the Saskatchewan Writers' Guild, Saskatoon Writers' Club Inc., and Women's Fiction Writers Association. She grew up, resides, and writes in Saskatoon, Saskatchewan, Canada, on Treaty 6 Territory and the homeland of the Métis.

Jeffery A. Sergent lives in a small town tucked away in the hills of southeastern Kentucky. He has taught at the local high school for thirty-three years now and has been a fan of science fiction and fantasy much longer than that. For

twenty of those years at the high school, he taught a class in SF & F Literature. His work has appeared in *Lost Worlds*, *Alienskin*, *Fiction Vortex*, *Swords & Sorcery Magazine*, and *Tales from the Magician's Skull*.

Matt McHugh was born in suburban Pennsylvania, attended LaSalle University in Philadelphia, and after a few years as a Manhattanite, currently calls New Jersey home. His fiction has appeared in *Analog*, *The Saturday Evening Post*, and *The First Line*. His story "Burners" won the 2019 Jim Baen Memorial Award and "Jennifer Gives Her Heart to Radioland" is PARSEC's 2021 Short Story Contest winner. In 2022, he was a grant finalist for The Speculative Literature Foundation.

Craig Herbertson was born at home in Edinburgh, Scotland in 1959. Obsessed with fantastic worlds from the moment that he bought *Tarzan and the Forbidden City* in a second-hand bookshop, his bookshelves are still lined with journeys from Lemuria to Hyperborea.

SWORDS & SORCERIES

His first mainstream publication was a novelette in the *Pan Book of Horror Stories* in 1987. Nearly fifty short stories, two collections of horror stories and two dark fantasy novels have followed. His dark fantasy, *School: The Seventh Silence*, has been compared to Franz Kafka and Lewis Carrol but Wardark the Reiver has simpler motives. Doomed by the sorcerer Xianthus to a perilous quest, he has appeared twice in *Swords & Sorceries* and returns now to battle the Pirate King.

Check out Craig's website *https://heavenmakers.com* for reviews and observations on fantastical worlds.

After a 30-year technology marketing career that sent Bob (R. K. Olson) to every continent but Antarctica, he retired to pursue a writing career last year. His sword and sorcery character, Dar the Spearslayer, was featured in six of Bob's short stories published within the last year in magazines such as *Crimson Quill Quarterly* and *Dark Horses*. In December

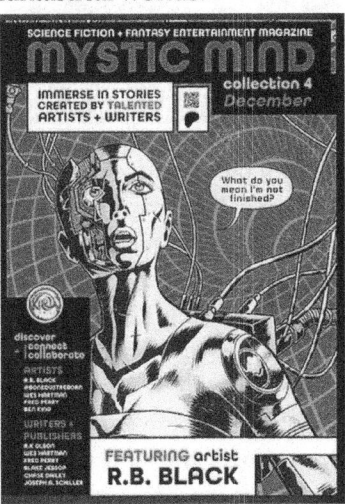

2023, one of Bob's stories was voted by readers of *Mystic Mind Magazine* as the 2023 Short Story of the Year Award Winner. The launch of his first novel is planned for later in 2024.

Bob lives and works near the Atlantic Ocean in the New England region of the United States.

Scott McCloskey counted the dead with Crom across many ragged copies of *The Savage Sword of Conan*

throughout much of the 1980s. Though the issues are now but tarnished steel, the influence on his writing is as pure as a platinum blade. Today he stands beside his wife and daughters on the eastern coast of the United States with a gaggle of Russian Wolfhounds to mind, but hooves still beat in time to the endless ride across the scorched sands in his heart.

Scott's work in swords, sorceries, and the supernatural has been featured in publications such as *Paying the Ferryman* by Charon Coin Press; *The Cellar Door 3: Dark Highways, Negative Space 2: A Return to Survival Horror,* and an upcoming anthology of his own horror short stories by Dark Peninsula Press; and of course, *Swords and Sorceries: Tales of Heroic Fantasy Volume 6*, by Parallel Universe Publications. His heroine, the Ysir warrioress Dracht Kar, continues her adventures in volume 8. Cursed by her own kin to roam the land in a state between life and death, the Blood of Ten Thousand leaves her shattered homeland — crossing the sea to face new and fantastical threats.

Andrew Graham is a writer new to fantasy from the north of England whose only previously published story, *Sorceries in Assabarr*, appeared in *Swords & Sorceries: Tales of Heroic Fantasy Volume 7*.

Adrian Cole is a native of and lives in North Devon, England. In a career which spans 50 years of publication in 2024, Adrian has had some three dozen novels published and close on 200 short stories. He works in several genres, including Heroic Fantasy, Sword & Sorcery, Horror, SF, Mythos and supernatural crime. He has appeared in a number of *Year's Best* anthologies and in 2015 his *Nick Nightmare Investigates* won the prestigious British Fantasy Award for best collection.

His latest published work is *Germanicus. Lord of Eagles* (DMR, US), the second in his epic *War on Rome* trilogy, set in an alternative Romano/Celtic Europe in the days of Rome's emperors.

Further new works to appear this year include a reprinting of his Sword and Planet saga, *The Dream Lords*, a compendium volume of the initial three volumes with new material, and a new volume, the sequel, *Dream Lords: Legacy*, both books from Cirsova Press, US. His Elak of Atlantis stories, which bring back into print Henry Kuttner's celebrated Sword & Sorcery Atlantean king, will be collected and published with new material in a trilogy from Parallel Universe Publications, each fully illustrated by award-winning. British artist Jim Pitts.

Also due this year will be a special edition of the magazine, *Weirdbook*, to which Adrian has been a regular contributor, going back to its earlier incarnation in the 1970s. *The Adrian Cole Special* will include exclusively Cole material, with some eight new stories, plus an interview and a comprehensive bibliography.

And, as usual, this book is favoured with the amazing artwork of Jim Pitts. As well as being busy on the collection of Elak of Atlantis tales by Adrian Cole, Jim is regularly featured these days in the pages of *Phantasmagoria Magazine*, *Lovecraftiana*, and *Schlock! Webzine*, and elsewhere.

These then are the authors and artist whose work appears in the pages of this, our eighth volume of sword and sorcery stories. We hope you enjoy them.

David A. Riley
Oswaldtwistle. 2024

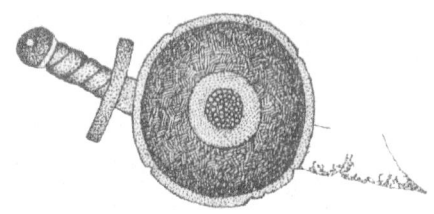

TO WAKE THE HUNTER

An Aztec Noir Tale
Tais Teng & Jaap Boekestein

When our Lord Tlaloc arrived the sky turned black as jet, with two tiny suns hovering in the north, one the colour of a quetzal bird's breast feathers, the other wan as a dying ember.

The Great Lord howled his hunger and drank the blood of one-fifth of Tenochtitlan's citizens. Next; he closed his nine eyes and fell asleep, his snore rumbling across the lake. Our priests keep him fed since that day, pouring a never-ending stream of fresh human blood for his proboscises to suck and putting still-beating hearts in his maw.

Our Lord awoke only once during these centuries when the pale men from beyond the Great Sea invaded his sacred hunting ground to their everlasting sorrow.

--The Annals of Moctezuma

The window of Xulab's office oversaw the Castilian district: wooden shacks with sagging straw roofs and prune trees, adobe churches. In the distance, the Central Temple rose, a stepped pyramid, crowned with the unearthly silhouette of the Sleeping God.

It rained. It always rained in the shadow of the pyramid, something to do with the god's aura according to the priests. No matter. The rent was low here, the fattened marmosets for his evening's meal cheap. No decent Maya or Aztec wanted to live among those unclean foreigners.

Xulab sat behind his desk and cleaned his Castilian gun. His desk had started out as a sacrificial stone but blood and the scrape of obsidian knives had worn down the screaming face until it was impossible to see if it had once belonged to the Lady of Snakes or the Stormgod.

Xulab took a healthy swig from his jar of triple-distilled mezcal. It tasted as bad as ever but left his tongue pleasantly numb.

Good, the cylinder rotated smoothly again. Now insert the cartridges: bullets of petrified wood for slaves and foreigners, iron for citizens, and silver for the aristocrats.

"Good to see you at least take care of your weapon."

The voice was the kind of husky that stiffened his member instantly. A goddess's voice. He turned around. Her face was as beautiful as her voice, a true jaguar face, spare and elegant with obsidian tresses streaming down her back. Aztec, he saw, high-born with the characteristic eagle nose and perfect sloping brow. Not at all like his own pug nose and a head round as an egg.

She wore a mantle of jade beads and blood-stained flamingo feathers. An ornament in the shape of a two-headed snake circled her neck. It opened all four eyes. A living snake. *Shit.* "You are a priestess of Coatlicue?"

"Such is the case." She smiled. "Just like your sister."

"I doubt that she sent you here. We are..." he shrugged. "Not exactly on speaking terms."

"She warned me that you are excitable, uncontrollable as an avalanche, but rather shrewd. Doggedly determined, she called it. Following every trail like a Castilian bloodhound."

"High praise indeed."

She pursed her lips. "And then she said that only a desperate fool would ever hire you."

"She is right. The last two weeks even the trickle of desperate fools dried up."

She looked him up and down. "A yokel. No one would ever think you a high-born warrior."

Why did all beautiful girls consider him a farmer's boy, only one step above an ape or a Castilian?

"That is what my officer decided, too. Even when I saved our whole company by killing that Apache noble. We were outnumbered ten to one but with him gone his braves lost all interest in killing us."

"Spare me your excuses. Their leader would have made a most splendid sacrifice. Dead he was just meat."

"I…"

"No matter. We need your help. Your, eh, dogged persistence, because we are stumped. An egg was stolen from the feeding cave. A living egg."

"And you want me to get it back? Catch the thief?" He nodded to the wall. "My rates are up there. Three ounces of silver every…"

She shook her head, her hair a breathtaking ripple of living obsidian. "Find the egg and we'll reinstate you. Even better, make you an officer."

"And if I fail?"

"You'll have to stay here, with your friends the cockroaches. Offhand I can't think of a worse fate."

"I see. Say, what exactly was your name?"

"Exalted Lady of the Two-headed Blood-coral Snake will do fine." The message was clear. He didn't deserve to know.

*

On the street, children were playing "Stamp on the Cities". The oldest girl took the part of the Sleeping God because the Sleeping God was female, well, kind of female, with him laying eggs.

"Crush Cortés' fleet and all of New Spain!" the chorus sang, with the god-girl splashing through a rain puddle. "Wade the Great Sea! Don't leave a single stone a-standing!"

The girl stepped stiff-legged. Long ago, after the god had awoken, he had crossed the ocean on legs as long as a hundred masts. That had been one of the most horrible surprises: leaving the pyramid he had grown monstrously huge. Big enough to walk across the ocean. Killing the priests that fed the god his blood had been Cortés' greatest mistake: it had cost him not only his life but also his country.

"Burn their orchards, tear down their walls!" the choir yodelled and then they enumerated the Castilian cities now gone forever. "Mighty walled Madrid! Fair Malaga! Grenada of a thousand pillars! Wide-harboured Marseilles! Ancient Rome and beautiful Paris!"

How eagerly the girl trampled the cities of all of Mexica's enemies under her calloused heels. It didn't matter that they had been the cities of her own ancestors. These children were Tenochtitlans now, Xulab understood, part of Eternal Mexica with the Sleeping God their patron.

He felt a warm glow: even these pale wretches were part of the empire now, worshippers of the Sleeping God.

The priestess snorted. "They think it is ancient history. Well, if he discovers one of his eggs gone, he might stamp on a city again. This city."

Tenochtitlan housed more than a million inhabitants. It would take days, but history had learned that only very few would escape.

"But a single egg? He must be laying hundreds each year!"

"Yes, and he always sucks them dry before they hatch. The Sleeping God doesn't want any rivals."

Xulab felt his stomach knot. It had sounded like a splendid opportunity: just find that stupid egg and he would be a warrior again, back on his life road. But the stakes were much higher: not only his career but a return to the days of His arrival. *Let's start as quickly as possible*, he thought. His sister had called him a bloodhound. Well, a dog had to sniff the trail.

"I need to see the feeding cave."

"First we have to visit the Central Temple. You'll work with our best agent." She silenced him with a look before he could object. "Do you imagine we would trust a disgraced warrior who showed so little self-control that he killed a prime sacrifice?"

Old sins were never forgotten. Xulab looked down at his feet. He had learned to control his temper. A commoner has no honour to defend. "Of course, Exalted Lady."

"Good. Our agent, she is on sacrificial duties today. We will meet her on top of Tlaloc's Body."

She? That could become interesting.

Behind them, the children were chanting again. "For He is a hunter. A hunter of men and even a billion hearts won't take the edge off His hunger."

*

The Central Temple dominated the city: huge and dark, wearing a nimbus of swirling thunderclouds. The only way up was climbing the three hundred oversized steps, pushing against the wind that roared down, the rain turning to hail before you came halfway.

Xulab used to dream about his final march up these stairs. A warrior. O yes, proud as a rooster, while maidens sang about his mighty deeds, his fearlessness.

At the top awaited the greatest honour a warrior could strive for, to have his living heart ripped from his body and offered to the Sleeping God. His essence would descend to the Underworld, A second, perfect Tenochtitlan was promised to such a stalwart soul: her streets paved with gold, her channels running with the blue and green blood of defeated demons. He would stand on the walls of the ultimate city with his comrades, there to fight monsters on the side of the very gods. All warriors longed for that Great and Glorious Battle, the reward for a life well and fearlessly lived.

It was like climbing a waterfall, he soon found out, the stones ever more slippery with blood and algae. Although he had kept himself in shape, Xulab's lungs laboured while the Exalted Lady took the gigantic steps with nimble ease, almost dancing, her feathers waving in the gusts.

Xulab bit down on his lower lip and ignored the stitches in his sides. He had been a panther warrior, and panther warriors would rather die than show the slightest weakness!

Halfway up the stone stairs transmuted into the unearthly flesh of the god. Scales sprouted from the stones, and veins throbbed under Xulab's feet, transporting blood that glowed like living gold.

Tlaloc towered above them, his feeding tubes dangling, his faceted eyes mercifully hidden under lids as corrugated as a rhino's hide. His flesh was five times as heavy as lead and the pyramid might have buckled under his weight, if it hadn't been for the scales. Each scale made everything it contacted light as thistledown.

SWORDS & SORCERIES

When Cortés took Tenochtitlan for the second time he had tried to fling the statue of Tlaloc down the stairs, the usual way the Castilians dealt with idols. He had been unable to budge it. As Bernal Dias, one of the few survivors, noted in *How We Lost New Spain*: "The idol must have been cast from lead or anchored in the stone, Cortés decided. Even when our leader took three horses to the top of the pyramid it didn't shift a single hairsbreadth from its pedestal."

The god hadn't noticed the Castilians' effort, as a man might disregard a dozen ants tugging at the sole of his sandal. What he did notice was the halting of the steady flow of blood and hearts. He awoke and assumed his true shape once more: no longer a statue three man-heights tall, but a veritable mountain of writhing flesh.

The snake priestess had not looked back even once: she clearly expected him to keep up. Only at the top did she pause for a moment. Was there a malevolent gleam in her eyes?

A crowd of priestesses and sacrificial victims had gathered in front of the Sleeping God's head. They had arrived in time to witness the daily ritual: not the lowly, but essential, blood offerings of Castilians, criminals, or prisoners of the Flower wars, but the ripping out of hearts of truly heroic warriors, the very best artists, the most beautiful sons and daughters of the noble houses. *Blood from the slaves, hearts from the braves.* A crowd of priestesses and sacrificial victims had gathered in front of the Sleeping God's head.

It could have been no coincidence that a panther warrior stepped forward to be sacrificed just at that moment. A less than subtle reminder of what he once had been, and what he could be again if he succeeded in finding the sacred egg.

The Exalted Lady nodded to the snake priestess who stood in front of the panther warrior. She wore only a jade mask and held an obsidian knife in her left hand. "Our sister will supervise your investigations."

The supple body of the priestess was covered with blood, her breasts full, her nipples erect. Despite the rain and the long climb, Xulab felt his body react. What was it with snake priestesses? The combination of lust and death? Some secret spell or pheromone?

A little snort sounded, but when Xulab turned the Exalted Lady of the Snake, the priestess was looking at her colleague.

The warrior stood, arms open to accept the honour. Rain soaked his muscular body, and his eyes were turned to the heavens. The gaze of panther warriors could inflict mortal fear in the hearts of their enemies.

With a savage ululation, the masked priestess plunged the obsidian knife into the warrior's chest and turned the stone weapon around. Blood flowed hot and red, ribs cracked, but the warrior did not cry out, still held himself erect.

The masked woman reached with both hands into the gaping wound, her nails sharp as knives. Her hands found something and she pulled. Flesh tore and she lifted the beating heart to the sky.

The crowd whooped with joy. The warrior smiled, bowed his head, and elegantly sat down to die. Rumours said panther warriors only died when they wanted to, but Xulab knew that was nonsense. The rigorous training gave the warriors an almost magical control over their body. They could move, speak, fight with wounds that would immediately kill any other man, but ultimately panther warriors remained merely mortal.

For a moment Xulab closed his eyes, honouring the warrior for his strength and control. *If it had only been me.*

The masked priestess threw the warrior's heart into the dark pit of Tlaloc's maw.

"May your sleep be deep," the other priestesses sang. "Let it be everlasting."

Seeing his sacrifice was accepted, the panther warrior smiled for the very last time and expired.

The nude woman walked over, her hips and breasts swaying. The priestesses of Coatlicue took lives and created lives. All of them were skilled in the man-woman arts, the dance of the snake and the butterfly. Even if they granted their gifts to only a few.

She won't deny me her body. Not when we are together on a god's business. Quite explicit pictures filled his mind. Surely the lady would be pleased with his efforts, would she not? He kept his face in check, but could not resist a little wink, a custom he had picked up in the Castilian district.

"I am sure you two will fit together like a boxer's fist in a clawed glove," the Exalted Lady of the Snake said. "Because you know each other so well."

The naked priestess who was covered in the blood from the man she had just slain, lifted her mask. It was a face Xulab had known and hated all of his life.

"Hello brother," his sister Third Hummingbird said. She smiled. Her teeth had been filed to points, just like Xulab's own.

*

A memory instantly surfaced.

They were playing 'Rip out the Heart' in the backyard with a whimpering stray dog and as usual they were quarrelling. How old had they been? He eight, she seven?

"I will go live with Tlaloc," Third Hummingbird screeched, brandishing the toy knife that was so dull they had to hammer it between the ribs of the dog with a stone. "I am going to be a priestess of Coatlicue and after cutting ten thousand throats and ripping out a thousand honoured hearts, I will join the Sleeping God."

"No way!" Xulab shouted. "I will become the greatest warrior ever, capturing a hundred thousand enemies whose blood will feed Tlaloc until he burps. Oceans of blood! It will be my heart that the priests will rip from my chest, not yours!"

Only one child per family could be sacrificed to Tlaloc, that was the law. Of course, that law did not apply to non-citizens like those ugly pale Castilians or foreigners, but their hearts would *never* be offered to the great Tlaloc anyway. Only their blood, if they were exceedingly lucky.

Third Hummingbird did not argue, she just punched him in the face, with predictable results.

Mother had to separate them, and father trashed them both soundly afterward and sent them to bed without dinner.

Xulab smiled. Those had been the good times, filled with hope and endless sunlight.

*

The Feeding Cave had been carved deep into the bedrock, not far from the banks of Lake Texcoco. A massive wooden gate formed the single entrance: Hinji ironwood reinforced with bands of Damascene steel. Twenty Serpent's Teeth, lesser snake priestesses, armed with carbines and traditional macuahuitls slung across their backs, guarded the place.

"Your weapons," their officer ordered. Xulab handed over his gun and was padded down. The Serpent's Teeth were clearly professionals: they found the thin steel knife that was hidden in a seam of his woollen mantel and even recognized his necklace with the blood coral beads and shark teeth as a provisional knuckle-duster. When they were finally satisfied that he was truly unarmed, they unbarred the gate.

The plumed officer put a hand on Xulab's shoulder.

"When I asked for your weapons I meant all of them. Had you come without your sister you would be lying on the ground now, your throat cut."

Xulab shrugged. "I carry so many weapons it is easy to overlook one."

The officer snorted. "Commoners shouldn't be allowed to carry any weapon at all!"

*

A golden glow suffused the cave, all eggs pulsing with the heartbeat of their distant progenitor. Hundreds of them, varying in size from a man's head to eggs as big as the hump of one of those imported desert horses. Each lay in his own bowl of fresh blood, contently feeding.

A shiver ran down Xulab's spine. These were the children of Tlaloc. If those eggs were ever allowed to hatch, they would devour the whole world, an unstoppable forest fire of appetite that would leave only bones and an empty sea.

"All priests on duty were tortured, of course, but they revealed nothing," Third Hummingbird told her brother. "They hadn't seen, heard, or smelled anything unusual."

Xulab nodded. No doubt the corpses of the unlucky guards had been fed to the dogs.

He looked around. The artificial cave was as wide as the Great Ball Court.

"Why are the eggs stored here? Isn't it easier to collect them from the inner chambers of the pyramid and feed them straight to Tlaloc? Why move them here, keep them stored and in the end carry them back?"

"You know why I recommended you?" Third Hummingbird asked.

"Well, why?" Xulab suppressed a sigh. So his sister wanted to play games instead of giving answers to straight questions.

"When you succeed, I will be the one who pointed the high priestesses to you and that will increase my status. If you make a mess of it, it will hurt my status a bit, but I will have the pleasure of seeing you fail beyond redemption. Death will be too good for you. They will probably cut off your manhood. Yes, and sell you to the roaming tribes of the Great Plains to serve as a man-whore for apprentice warriors."

"I certainly want to elevate your status, dear sister," Xulab lied, "I will try my best to succeed. So answer my question, why all this?" He gestured at the feeding cave.

"The Sleeping God only kills his children when they are about to hatch. We think he prefers mature godlings. You know, like ripe fruit."

What do we really know about what the Sleeping God likes?
"And they 'ripen' here?"

"The conditions are just right."

Yes, he now noticed the two sunlamps hung on the ceiling, one, as the annals said, *the colour of a quetzal bird's breast feathers, the other wan as a dying ember. A recreation of the terrible homeland of the Sleeping God.*

He felt his sister's gaze on his neck while he investigated the cave, like the rub of a pointed icicle. Xulab inspected the walls, the ceiling, and the floor.

"No secret passage," he told her. "No hidden doors. The guarded gate was the only way in or out."

"The missing egg was lying over here," Third Hummingbird pointed to a rack made of fossil ivory. "Ready for transport. It was that close to hatching."

"Now who would want to steal one of the God's eggs, dear sister? Are there any suspects?"

His sister remained quiet for a moment. She clearly still found it difficult to aid her brother in any way.

"Too many suspects. Any of the other temples might have taken it to undermine our position. Even if the egg is found in the next two days it will make us look like fools. Unworthy to serve the Sleeping God. Maybe those bitches of Coyolxauhqui, the Moon goddess. They would be happy to replace us and become the new servants of the Sleeping God.

Our spies are trying to find out who is behind this all, but that doesn't concern us. Our task is to recover the egg. Before one of the others brings it back triumphantly."

Temple politics, it never ends.

Xulab squatted next to the big ceremonial pond in the middle of the cave and tasted the water. It was brackish, which meant it was connected to the lake.

He took off his sandals and mantle, removed his heavy jade earrings.

Third Hummingbird frowned. "I understand that you feel unclean in such a holy place. Still, this isn't the right time to take a ritual bath."

"I have to go down there. This is the way the thief arrived and left with the egg." He pointed down. "This well wasn't dug. It is a natural pipe, a sinkhole."

"You'll drown. After five meters you'll be blind.'

Xulab opened his hand. "This necklace is made of glow-stones. When I crush them I'll be able to see for at least twenty heartbeats."

Glow stones were made of crushed eggshell: put them in contact with blood and they started to shine. He searched the cave and finally took up a large gold mask in the shape of a bird skull. It was almost impossible to lift, half a man's weight with the edges of the beak razor sharp and he had to stumble to the edge of the well.

Three Hummingbirds frowned. "Paying your way into the underworld?"

"It'll afford me a quick dive. Sinking like a stone, eh? An old pearl-divers trick."

*

Panther warriors can keep their breath for at least five minutes but they aren't pearl-divers. In the end, they'll gasp for air and find only water.

The waters closed around him, frigid as a snow-witch's breath. Around him, the light ebbed, became twilit, then stygian. Twelve man-lengths, twenty, and then the mask smashed into the bottom with a singular crunchy sound.

Bones. They must have used this well to drown virgin sacrifices before the Sleeping God arrived. He let go of the mask, and crushed the glow-stones in his fist until he felt the shards slice the mouse of his thumb.

A golden radiance instantly surrounded him.

Algae had covered the skeletons. Those blobs must be skulls. All looked rather small, tiny. *I was wrong. Not virgins but the firstborn of noble families. Probably to cajole the Grain-goddess. Wait, that looks like footprints. Recent footprints.*

The alga mat had been marred in four places.

SWORDS & SORCERIES

Someone had passed here. Two prints where he came down, and two where he pushed off to ascend to the cave. He must have used a weight like me, only much heavier because the prints are so deep. Yes, there it lay. An anchor, of all things. An inverted mermaid formed the centre part, with her spread arms turning into hooks. Clearly Castilian. Aztecs wouldn't have bothered to decorate so profane a piece.

He looked up: two dark holes in the ceiling. *I came from the right. That leaves the left, even though it looks rather narrow.*

He rose in a cloud of silt and swam up into the tunnel to the left. Xulab moved in the sea-snake way: undulating and using his whole body. Castilians swam like frogs or windmilled their arms, frothing the water in a way that was sure to attract sharks.

Up in the darkness, a soft glow appeared. It wasn't distinct at all and could be just a wishful illusion. He put on a last effort and the light brightened. It was blue, sky blue and then he knew it couldn't be true, just a final lie to ease his death.

His face broke the surface and he gulped down air, filling his lungs.

He had emerged in an underground cave, another sinkhole. A rope was dangling down the shaft and to the left, a mummy had crumpled on the gravel. The skin was a loose sack, so translucent he could see the bones. *Sucked dry. They must be fools, who didn't know the first things about the egg they set out to steal.* Handling an egg without gloves made from cast-off god skin was lethal. The eggs were hungry and quite able to feed themselves when the flow of fresh blood ceased. The moment a basin ran dry they slyly put out hair-thin cilia which fastened on anything warm-blooded. When he looked at the corpse again, he felt his eyes rotate away and refuse to focus. An elusion spell, making the wearer close to invisible. That was Hinji *alchemy*, nearly spent if he was able to look at the dead thief at all.

*

The next item of interest was a strange kind of helmet with a crystal front plate. An extremely long and flexible hose connected the helmet to something that looked like an oversized bellows. It was the kind Castilian blacksmiths employed, Xulab saw: you needed at least two apprentices to pump them. The floor of the cave was too pebbly to bear footprints, but the bank of grit looked disturbed. So there had been at least three thieves and two had fled with the egg when their comrade had been sucked dry.

The lamp finally was one of the newfangled Arabian ones, he saw, the kind that shone almost forever but slowly poisoned the bearer. The Tuaregs used them in their silver mines. Well, their slaves did.

Such a confusing hodgepodge of clues. A Castilian anchor, a Hinji spell, and an Arab lantern.

He used a part of the hose to fasten the helmet to his belt and started to climb.

*

Xulab emerged in the backyard of a bone glue factory. Sweating Han people ran from boiling cauldron to cauldron, stirring the broken bones and flaccid hides, adding lime from glass amphorae. A leg bone rose from a boiling pot, with the hoof still attached, and beckoned Xulab. The stink was overwhelming, worse than a slaughter-field at high noon.

"High-born sir?" A fat man waddled in his direction,

clearly an official to go by his tasselled hat. "You come to inspect, yes?" He bowed and added: "Most esteemed and terrible panther knight?"

Xulab felt a flash of pride: even with all his regalia taken away he clearly still had the bearing of a panther knight. But no, in the eyes of the Han all Aztecs were panther knights. Even if he wasn't an Aztec, but a Maya.

"Where am I?" he asked. "What is the direction of the Great Temple? No, just the exit would suffice."

The man pointed with a trembling hand.

"You no inspect?" He reached for his money belt.

"No need to bribe me. Keep your yuans for a real inspector."

The man shuffled backwards and bowed again. "May Monkey lead your way and the goddess of mercy smile on you."

*

"If you find a man dead with the knife still piercing his heart," he later told Three Hummingbirds, "trace the knife first."

"The helmet you mean." Three Hummingbirds was a Why-don't-you-say-what-you-mean girl. "It was handmade. Look at these less-than-elegant blobs of solder, the scratches in the bronze. A smith's prototype. Clearly his first effort." She rose. "Let's find and torture him until he tells us the names of his co-conspirators and where they hid that stupid egg."

"But the spell and the lantern?"

"Hinji sorcerers sell their knowledge to anyone who offers a handful of emeralds and you can buy a lamp on the markets if you are foolish enough. No, the anchor and the helmet point straight to the Castilians."

*

Foreigners had their own districts in Tenochtitlan. The haughty Incas, the treacherous Apaches, the mercantile Hawaiians, the Tuaregs with their hunting condors: they didn't mix well.

It soon became abundantly clear that Third Hummingbird had never visited the Castilian part of the city before. With disdain she looked at the pale urchins running across the muddy streets, the bearded men leaning in the doors and the women dressed in long robes, straw hats, and veils. "You really live here? This place is like a prairie dog's burrow."

Xulab didn't deign to reply. He carried the strange bronze helmet in a canvas bag. With his free hand, he checked under his mantle for his gun. Few high-born Aztec women ever visited this district, and they usually wore far more than just a loincloth and a blood-stained feather mantle. There would be trouble soon. And indeed, only a moment later one of the young Castilian bravo's whistled and called out: "Hey little chicken, you wanna meet a real big white cock?"

Third Hummingbird turned sharply and inspected the Castilian. He and his mates were grinning and he made a gesture that left little to the imagination. Clacked his tongue, which was a mistake in any language.

She will kill him and I will have to shoot at least one of them, Xulab thought while he cocked his concealed gun.

His sister walked up to the grinning young man, her smile gentle, enigmatic. It also quite effectively concealed her filed teeth.

"You clucked at me like a turkey? Called me a chicka?"

Before he could react, she punched him square on the chin and immediately kicked him between the legs. With a shuddering cry, the Castilian went down on his knees and Third Hummingbird kicked him again until he fell face first in the mud.

"I am a snake priestess of the Sleeping God and I devour little cocks like yours by the bushel." She turned to the other men who were backing away. "Any others who can miss a few teeth?"

They all turned and ran, leaving their friend wailing in the mud.

Xulab had put away his gun before his sister turned around. A true jaguar warrior fought hands-on, with weapons only a last option. Her scorn would be withering. "You haven't changed much, dear sister. Not anything at all, actually."

"Bring me to those metal workers so we can pull some nails. Gouge out a few eyes!"

Not changed a bit...

Conveniently, all Castilian smiths were located in the same street.

When the great fleet in Tlaloc's wake returned from the devastated lands, the white slaves were all housed in the same quarter. The artisans with useful skills were put to work: smiths, candle makers, and glass blowers. All the others served as unskilled labor, working the fields and mines, and quenching the never-ending thirst of the Sleeping God.

"I'll do the questioning, in my own way. Thank you very much."

Third Hummingbird snorted. "What would a mere

man know about the finer points of torture? Panther knights swing their maces, hack off arms and legs!"

"Torturing a dozen valuable smiths will raise too many awkward questions," Xulab stated. "We don't want the other priests to prick up their ears, now do we?"

"Well, we'll try it your way first. But if we fail to get results soon, I will call in the Serpent's Teeth. Or even my sisters."

*

The fourth smith recognized the bronze helmet. "That looks like Morano's work." The huge man pointed at a mark inside the helmet. "Look, that is the Saint Mohammed cross with the feathered snake. Morano puts that on all his work. I always use the flower of Xochiquetzal-Magdalena."

Those Castilians had truly bizarre customs. Why would an artisan want his work to be recognized as his own? They were slaves, without honour. But in this case, it came in handy.

"And where do we find that Morano?"

"A little down the street. The house with the bronze mask above the door."

*

For a Castilian Morano was a small man, only half a head taller than Xulab. He had extremely broad shoulders and big arms. Almost as wide as he was tall, he looked like a dwarf from a North Castilian tale.

In his left ear, the smith wore a gold ring and he looked at the world through ovals of clear glass that perched on the bridge of his nose. Was it something religious or merely a strange piece of jewellery?

"That helmet? I can't quite recall, dear Lord and Lady. Now anyone can put a mark on a piece of metal, can't they? It doesn't prove anything." Morano the bronze smith had started trembling, though. A tiny river of sweat snaked down his brow and Xulab felt a stab of annoyance. *How does this barbarian dare to lie to a panther knight!*

"I guess we need your Serpent's Teeth, after all, dear sister."

Third Hummingbird's smile bared her sharpened teeth. "Yes, let's see if his memory improves when he sees his wife and children flayed alive."

Morano instantly fell on his knees. "Dear Anansi-Jezus! Not my family! I beg for mercy."

Third Hummingbird laughed out loud and Xulab heartily joined in. *Mercy? For a low-born Castilian? How ridiculous!*

"It all depends on what you tell us." He had not the slightest intention to call the Serpent's Teeth. They were rabid butchers. Drowning everything in blood was not the most effective way to investigate.

The white man wrung his hands, and fell on his knees. When he looked up the snot was streaming from his nose.

"Yes, yes! I made that helmet. It was a commission. I actually fashioned four of them. They are like the helmets of the undersea knights of Han. Inca rubber and airtight bronze. A man can walk underwater without drowning."

Amazing. Those Castilians may be mad and theologically insane, but sometimes they come up with the strangest notions. "Why would a man want to walk across the sea bottom? Men are no fish!"

"I..." The smith hesitated and looked at Third Hummingbird who ogled him like a snake a helpless chick, eager, hungerly. "It was to get the sunken gold of Cortés' fleet! When Lord Shaitan-Tlaloc destroyed the fleeing fleet of Cortés the Cursed, all the gold sunk to the bottom of the sea. It is too deep for divers, but underwater knights could get to the gold." He spread his arms. "They paid me half upfront. The rest would come once they dived for the treasure."

But those underwater knights did not want any gold, they wanted an egg of the Sleeping God. "Who commissioned the helmets?"

"Dear Lord and Lady, I don't know! He came late at night and always wore a mask."

Something didn't ring true. The way he said "mask." Hesitant.

"I can't tell from what race he was, except that he paid handsomely. And I didn't dare refuse."

"His face," Xulab said. "You said mask but what you meant you couldn't look him in the face. It was like your eyes wanted to turn away."

"Exactly lord! It was as if he was a ghost, a reflection in moving water."

"The Hinji spell must already have been working," Three Hummingbirds said. "This man is worthless and we are wasting our time here." She sighed. "We can't even offer this dog to the Sleeping God. Great Tlaloc would be offended by his lying blood."

"No doubt. Morano, you piece of offal: listen. I might consider sparing the lives of you and your family if you point us to the man who paid for the helmet. Who is he? Where can we find him? There must be something you noticed even if you couldn't look at him."

"I don't know. I truly don't know. We signed the deal with our blood. Yes, on my oath-stone, I made the helmet and he paid me. That was it."

"You signed the deal in blood? Yours and his?"

"Uh… yes, Lord." He fingered the mouse of his left thumb where a recent cut had been expertly sutured.

"Hand us that oath-stone."

He stumbled to the drawing room, the place where Castilians received their honoured guests.

The oath stone was a slab of slate, inset with a cross and a stylized spider. It must have come from across the Great Sea, from the Castilian homelands.

"You are going to kill me, eh?" the smith said. "Even if I have told you everything I know?"

"That is correct. Dead men tell no tales, as you Castilians say."

"Give us the location of the egg!" Three Hummingbirds snapped. "Maybe we'll let you go then."

"That last is a lie." The face of the smith had become a serene mask: he had accepted his death like a true warrior and wouldn't plead anymore. Only hate was left. Xulab approved: this one would ascend to Valhalla, feast in Odin's halls, and swing his sledgehammer like Thor.

"An egg, you said." In the last seconds of life all things become clear and the light of truth shone from the smith's eyes. "So they stole an egg. They'll nurture it, feed it their very own blood and it'll become their god, their war-lord. They'll return to Tenochtitlan and the young bull will fight his aged rival." The smith nodded, still in his prophetic trance. "The Sleeping God didn't descend from the stars to conquer the Four Corners of the Earth. He fled, a refugee from some…"

"Blasphemy!" Three Hummingbirds shrieked. Her nails slashed across his throat, opening the jugular vein. Xulab stepped back when blood fountained.

"That was a bit premature," Xulab said.

"'He was just guessing. He knows *nothing* about any

conspiracy." She looked down at the corpse. "His family?"

"A waste of time." Xulab didn't want any detours while the trail grew cold. And there was no honour in killing mere slaves.

"I'll call the Keeper then. We need her to bring us a cage of trackers."

*

Hummingbirds were the best trackers in the Four Corners of the Earth, far superior to Castilian bloodhounds. They could smell a blooming hibiscus flower from miles away. Or, trained in the right way, the blood and sweat of any particular human.

The Keeper of the Hummingbirds arrived in a cloud of miniature birds, a hawk perched on each shoulder.

"You!" Xulab gaped at her.

"The very same," the Exalted Lady of the Two-headed Blood-coral Snake said. "But better call me Keeper. Commanding raptors and deadlier birds is my true talent."

"No more chit-chat. Let's start." Three Hummingbirds held the oath-stone high and the birds zipped past, licking the congealed blood with their nimble tongues.

"Now go find them."

The hummingbirds circled the body of the smith and then two alighted on his upturned left hand, pecked the recent cut.

"Not him!" Three Hummingbirds yelled at her namesakes. "The other one!" She turned to the Keeper of the Hummingbirds. "Tell them, sister."

The Keeper of the Hummingbirds nodded and set a malachite flute to her lips. A note sounded, just on the verge of Xulab's hearing. The hummingbirds rose and sped away, assuming a pointing arrow formation.

"They are following the scent of the conspirator now," Keeper said. She was as beautiful as before: sleekly muscled and now wearing a splendid mantle made of quetzal feathers. Her cheeks were pierced and set with emerald knobs. Great Quetzalcoatl would return and the sky rain summer wine, though, before she would lie with a disgraced panther knight. That was still abundantly clear.

*

The stink warned Xulab, even before they turned the corner. They were back at the glue factory.

The gate still stood open, an advertising sign in front: "Bring us your reeking carcasses, your crumbling bones and sun-dried hides. We pay top prices!"

Inside hung an eerie silence: no voices shouting, only the bubbling cauldrons, the hiss from a badly sealed high-pressure line.

Behind them, the gate clanged shut. Soldiers emerged from behind the cauldrons. They wore lacquered cuirasses, shields made of the discarded scales of the Sleeping God.

Xulab recognized their officer: the portly overseer who had tried to bribe him. *So that was a ruse. They knew very well that the sinkhole connected to the depot.* The man raised a crossbow and Xulab had to make a somersault to avoid the hissing bolt. Two soldiers went down a heartbeat later, skewered by Three Hummingbird's throwing knives.

Xulab ducked behind a cart with fly-covered horse hides and raccoon carcasses.

"We have had our fun, right?" he heard Keeper call.

"Certainly," Three Hummingbirds answered, launching her last throwing knife and uncoiling her garrotte. "Back to business."

The Keeper put her flute to her lips and the hummingbirds descended, swift as so many arrows. They speared eyes, bored their sharp beaks into soft cheeks. Two, three seconds later the soldiers started falling down, foaming at the mouth.

"We modified them some more," the Keeper declared. "Not only sensitive to blood but they have poison-sacks, filled with sea-snake venom." She nodded. "I ordered my birds to kill them all except the officer."

Xulab walked up to the spasming victims, plucked an obsidian scimitar from a stiffening hand, and started cutting throats.

Their officer was left alive, a swarm of hummingbirds circling him. He still seemed a fat official, ineffective, but his eyes no longer looked watery. A steady gaze met Xulab's own and the chin was lifted high in defiance. The only way that head would bow was when it was lopped off.

"You are days too late," the officer said. "We showed them the entrance to your hell-hole and they carried the egg away."

"We can torture you?" Three Hummingbirds said.

"You'll have to be fast then, my dear lady. You have only about three heartbeats left." He closed his eyes and slumped down like a marionette with all his strings cut.

She looked down at the corpse. "A bird pecked him after all?"

"No way," Keeper protested. "My birds, they are very disciplined and obedient."

"I heard about the Han," Xulab said. "They can stop their heart at will and they don't fear death like the Castilians. No Heaven or Hell. They'll just get reborn and if they die in the right way they might return as a prince or even a minor godling."

A quartet of hummingbirds descended the sinkhole, emerged three minutes later and set out across the yard. Just outside the gate, they assumed the arrow formation again.

"So the one who smeared his blood across the oath stone wasn't the mummy down in the cave," Xulab said. "Good to know."

*

It felt strangely right, walking these streets with his sister. They had always been rivals but often fellow conspirators, too. Like the night they set out to steal a baby crocodile from the sacred pool. They had walked hand in hand, under a dazzling full moon and they knew that what they were doing was dead wrong. Which made it all the more delightful. *Three Hummingbirds and me, we two against the whole world.*

He had given his sister a leg up, and she was reaching down for him from the top of the wall. The feel of her calloused hand in his, her grip as strong as his own had made him realize that they should be a team. If they could ever stop their bickering, they would be unbeatable.

He looked at his sister, striding so confidently next to him, and felt a stab of... Not love, not exactly respect, but something more bittersweet. Regret for opportunities lost perhaps?

*

The gate of the Hinji quarter was flanked by two gigantic statues: an elephant with a human body and a six-armed woman warrior, wearing a skirt of hacked-off arms and a necklace of tongues. He saw his sister nod approvingly: this was the kind of female she could respect.

Inside Xulab encountered a rat's warren of winding alleys and dead ends, nothing like the straight boulevards and palazzos of Tenochtitlan proper at all. *But so much easier to defend. It would be like storming a labyrinth. Fire a musket and the bullet would ricochet right back in your face. Cortés wouldn't have stood a chance.*

*

"Sayid Masura Hinji, Miracle-worker, and Holy Seer by the grace of Allah and Shiva," the sign stated in curly, gold-plated letters. "Beloved family members raised from the death and unfaithful lovers cursed! Inquire inside for our surprisingly fair prices."

Xulab pushed the door open with the point of his boot, and raised his recently acquired scimitar.

Sayid stepped from behind a counter. He had the spare face and burning eyes of an ascetic, one who sleeps on a loam floor, a stone his pillow, and prefers a crock of glacier water to an amphora of sparkling wine.

"Customers?" He frowned. "I somehow doubt it." He snapped his fingers. "I got it. The egg seekers!"

Keeper raised her flute, but the sage spoke a single word and all hummingbirds fluttered down like dead autumn leaves.

"No need to reach for further weapons, my dears. I'll tell you all you want to know. Mexica isn't well-loved, you know. Castilians and Han, even my own countrymen, they all conspired to steal your egg." He raised his hands. "I am a simple monk and abhor violence, especially against my own person." He opened a drawer and took out a small hand mirror.

Xulab glimpsed a galleon sailing down the Grand Channel in the glass. He burned the picture in his memory: golden letters in Castilian script. *La Reina Isabella*.

"Not that," the magician said, clearly annoyed and the mirror next showed a glade, under a sky filled with thunderclouds. The mirror grew huge, the height of a man and he stepped inside.

The mirror instantly snapped back to its former size.

How Xulab hated magic! It was a rare day when a hero got to lop off the head of a perfidious necromancer. Most of the time he ended up with his bones turned into seaweed or his trusty maquahuitl changed into a reed stalk.

"Do we follow him?" he asked.

His sister shook her head. "Into a mirror no bigger than my palm? Anyway, I think he spoke the truth. They paid him for an invisibility spell and that was it."

Xulab took the mirror. It still showed the glade but now from high up and no bigger than a thumbnail. Even if they could open the gate they would fall down for half a mile. *Forget it.*

"I know where the egg is," Xulab said. "I glimpsed it in the mirror."

*

The Grand Canal reached all the way to the Gulf of Mexica, tunnelling through mountains, stepping down to sea level through a hundred locks. The Grand Canal was the logical way to go when you wanted to escape with contraband.

Arriving at the quay it took some time to find the harbourmaster. Three Hummingbirds snorted when she discovered him lying in his hammock, snoring, with his helmet perched on his ample belly. She cut one of the ropes and the worthy fell down. Xulab's sister put a foot on his heaving breast, and looked down on him. "Know that the Sleeping God is always thirsty. Your choice. The Great Pyramid or you tell us where we can find La Reina Isabella." It was clear that she wasn't speaking about any honourable tearing-out of the heart but that the official would be drained like any lowborn Castilian.

"I know!" the official cried. "She left! Early last evening. I signed the papers myself."

Three Hummingbirds folded her arms. "What kind of crew?"

"Such a motley troupe, great lady! Han officers, Castilian sailors, a Tuareg mage to command the albatrosses." He frowned, scratched his chin. "Yes, the navigator wore a red turban. He must be a Jain. Hinji."

"Where did they go?'

"Down the Grand Channel, past Tlaxcala. Then the Great Sea. I didn't think to ask what their final destination was." He now clearly regretted that oversight.

*

"We have to arrive at Cempoala before them," Three Hummingbirds said. "That is the last harbour and if they reach the Great Sea…"

"They have such a huge head start," Keeper said and then her face cleared, became one huge smile. "We can take a condor! I have always dreamed of flying them."

*

Panther knights were supposed to be fearless. Xulab

had to bite his tongue not to whimper when his bird launched from the platform. It didn't help that Keeper was whooping with joy twenty yards to the left of him. He lay in a sling below the mighty mechanical bird which was beating her wings as steady as metronome. It was Hinji clockwork that controlled the wings, a Tuareg accu driving them.

Monstrously far below him Tenochtitlan had become a toy, the Sleeping God no more than a muddy blob. In the west the sun was sinking fast, painting Lake Texcoco blood-red.

"Just follow me," Keeper had said. "The left handle swings you to the right, the right to the left. Just like paddling a reed canoe, eh? Down makes you go faster, Up stalls you. As easy as... As peeling a sweet potato."

"I get it," Xulab had nodded, although he had never peeled a sweet potato in his life.

*

A moonless night and they flew under a sky filled with unwavering stars. They soared so high up that Xulab was panting to fill his lungs. If the servants hadn't clad him in a leather coat and put a helmet with goggles on his head, he would be frozen stiff by now, his eyes frosted marbles.

"Tlaxcala!" Keeper pointed. "See the lights?" She had left the surviving hummingbirds behind and was now escorted by a trio of hawks. No doubt they were more winter-proof than the hummingbirds.

Below them, the Grand Canal was a ribbon lit by orange amber-force torches.

Such a pity, he mused, *that the emanations of the Sleeping God made any form of far-speaking impossible. In the Castilian Protectorates, we could just have sent an order to the Cempoala guards to board the Isabella the moment she arrived. Well, that was the price one paid for hosting the single living god on Earth. And the god had hated the semaphores as well. Freak storms had pulled down the towers until the engineers had gotten the hint: nothing faster than a message pigeon was allowed in the Empire.*

*

Xulab must have dozed because the night had been replaced by the first scattered sunlight in the eastern sky. In the distance, the land became strangely flat, with a steely gleam. That must be the Great Sea, a place he had only heard about and never quite believed in. *Such an incredible expanse of water! A thousand, no, a million Lake Texcoccos.*

He reached for his Han spyglass. A hundred ships were sailing down the Canal, their navigation torches still blinking. Only three were galleons big enough to be the La Reina Isabella. He zoomed in: none was the Isabella.

Xulab maneuvered closer to his sister. "No trace of the Isabella. What should we do?"

"We fly on. She must be somewhere at sea."

Xulab frowned. "How do we land on the deck of a moving ship?"

"We don't!" Keeper replied. "We just crash-land in front of the ship. The condors are very light and will float for a time. Long enough to climb aboard."

"And then? I will be the three of us against a crew of how many? A hundred? I know a snake priestess is supposed to be worth at least three men but this is ridiculous."

"We won't be alone." Keeper jerked a thumb upward.

A squadron of at least three dozen living condors was following them. A veritable army of raptor birds and that wasn't even counting the hawks who trailed behind.

SWORDS & SORCERIES

*

The sixth ship was the Isabella. The Coast of Mexica had become a grey ribbon, with the sea dotted with white and red sails.

Xulab swooped low, the condor having become a part of him. These were his wings he flapped, his very own tail feathers to steer with.

Despite the Castilian name the sails were painted with huge Han characters and the mermaid on the bow lifted six arms, all of them bearing swords or maces. He glimpsed a row of bronze bombards, but none were manned. Strange, they must have seen them because the crew was running across the deck, milling around like a disturbed ant heap. He frowned. Some were climbing the rails, jumping in the sea?

The deck buckled, broke open and a dozen tentacles emerged, each ending in a toothed sucker. *The fools. The egg must have hatched and is no longer satisfied with mere cups of blood.*

It went horribly fast. The tentacles were like the tongue of an anteater, a dozen sticky tongues, cleaning out an ant heap.

Nine heartbeats and the decks lay empty in the clear morning light, with the last sailors plucked from the topgallant and the single launched sloop.

A whirlwind dropped down from the sky, split up like a cat-of-nine-tails in as many dust devils.

He is a weather god. Of course, he can control the winds.

Each tiny tornado touched a sail, touched it with exquisite care and the ship jumped forward, shot across the waves, fast a skipping stone. There was no earthly way they could ever hope to catch up.

Xulab felt a surge of joy, of pure happiness. *He'll conquer his own land, feed on the blood of ten thousand strangers, and become their god. And then he'll return to challenge the Sleeping God.*

He saw himself standing next to his splendid sister, clad in the full regalia of a panther knight. Three Hummingbirds would become his war comrade, no longer a rival, for they would be standing on the walls of Tenochtitlan, defending their city and their god against monsters. *I won't have to wait for a priest to tear my heart out and cross over to the Land of the Dead. Three Hummingbirds and I'll soon fight the Great and Glorious Battle, right here and now. A Castilian would call it God's Kingdom on Earth.*

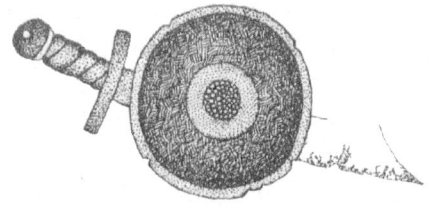

MOONFINGER AND GIFT
Andrew Darlington

She shocks alert, up out of sleep.

Her blade of finely tempered iron sheathed beneath her, instantly ready.

She glances across to where Gift Anstar lies in an untidy straggle of straw-coloured hair. Yes, she's fine.

Then Moonfinger Antherica is on her feet, her hair flaming and sparkling in splendid disarray.

The huge silver moon, goddess of the night, is on her side, illuminating the frozen forest darkness.

She sees the dead thing that shambles in shadows, lurching its clumsy, devouring menace.

In a rush of blood she grips the sword-hilt in both hands. It fits her grip well, and she braces her feet ready for ten long heartbeats, focusing her tough and self-reliant strength.

But the beast comes at her faster than she'd expected; she takes a step back and whirls the blade around her head. She sees maggots crawl within its eye-sockets. The wisps of white hair that cling to patches of skin along the visible skull curvature. The rasp from lips cracked black and stretched in mirthless grin, drooling an obscene gurgling that emanates from its ruptured throat. The charnel house stench that invades her nostrils. She curses beneath her breath. The curse freezes into icy mist. Her brass-studded jerkin catches light, as though prematurely splashed in gleaming blood.

She poises her sword, aims, strikes in a liquid blur.

The blade first gleams with a flash of energising white moonfire, then bites deep with an explosive burst of savage anger. It gnaws deeper, taking the top off the cadaver's head. The revenant spasms and falls like a stone. Its foul sounds dribble away.

Her blade slimed with the hue of death she watches the severed section of brain matter. Waiting. Then the slug wriggles free, casting a grotesque writhing shadow. Waving this way and that, like a caterpillar on a leaf, wondering which way to turn next.

Her mouth floods with saliva. She spits her disgust, and grinds her boot-heel down onto the mind-slug, feeling its surface-tension resist for less than a moment, before it squelches and splatters.

She holds her blade in readiness, surveying the frozen trees, expecting more. The dead tend to move in packs.

An owl disturbs foliage high above. A shimmer of falling snow. Nothing more.

Then movement. A shambling shadow. Another. The forest crawls with menace.

Fear clogs her mouth and throat.

She kicks out at where Gift Anstar has woken, and is watching her fearfully, swathed in furs.

"Time we were gone," snaps Moonfinger. "It's not safe here anymore."

They mount, jerk the reins of their horses, and ride side-by-side into a blood-red dawn-rise, as though death rides at their heels. Their urgent mission takes them south, ever-south.

After two full day's ride they approach a lake of lead beneath drugged clouds.

There's a small, ragged community of fisherfolk in a

huddle of smoky huts on the shingle shore.

Yes, they grudgingly admit they know of the entity the two women seek. It is said to inhabit the ruined tower, although none claim to have glimpsed it in a generation.

The ancient tower is isolated on a headland overlooking the frozen lake. Its configuration conforms to what they've been told about the Eternal Assassin's lair. It is approached by a treacherously narrow track of frost-crisped grass, between a tumbled wilderness of fractured rock where snow lies thickly on the stones, uneven underfoot through ice-drenched thickets. They pass empty tombs where once had lain the skeletal remains of warriors situated around the stone-buttressed walls, until the two arrive at a smashed door of weathered oak and bronze, ponderously hung on a single hinge. There's no response when they call through cupped hands. Now the daylight falls through glassless windows as they slow-pace inside. Moonfinger Antherica has her blade poised, and moves warily one pace ahead, fearful of being watched by some unseen menace. Gift follows her, a pace behind. But there's nothing more than a disturbed flurry of bats high in the vaulted ceiling. At first it seems the tower is abandoned, the air smells dank and unwholesome. Until they climb a curve of worn stone steps into a high gallery, to discover a confusion of dusty retorts, frosted phials, a ceramic kiln sided by cobwebbed bottles of green glass in clumsy disorder. Tomes of profane lore from arcane minds of antiquity.

A telescope assembled from an artfully framed arrangement of lenses. And a slumped figure in silver armour, in the lax posture of death. He sits as though frozen, or ensorcelled, closeted within the shadowy realms of his necromancer apparatus.

The two women halt in hushed silence. Gift Anstar peers in delighted wonder.

Moonfinger Antherica is more cautious. "Adsiduo Sicarius?" she says, her voice pitched a little above a whisper, her hand on her sword-pommel.

He barely shifts. A statue carved from ice. As though he's sat there unmoved for ten years.

"We're too late," says Gift, "he's dead."

"He's eternal," snaps Moonfinger. "He cannot die. That is the curse placed upon him."

They circle the unmoving statue. Yes, it breathes. Barely. A man with a bloodless face of bone. He's aware, he peers distractedly. A dark expressive face masked in elfin abstraction.

Moonfinger stands back, hands on her hips, and addresses the frozen figure. "We seek your aid. We travel from the far north."

"You lie. There's nothing but ice to the north." His voice a rasping croak.

"Yet that is from whence we come, from where to journey. From where fire fell from the sky, a star with a comet's tail, to create our valley, Where the dead rise to inflict vengeance upon the living."

He barely moves his hand, in a palm-up gesture of indifference, trying to force his thoughts into coherent shape. He barely senses the soft sighing of his own shallow breaths as he inhales and exhales. Can barely hear the slow determined pulse of his heart. Slivers of ice wrinkle and fall in shiny flakes. "It means less than naught. Leave me. I'm done with this world."

"We understand how these transactions operate. It's well understood. You're a paid assassin with the necromantic powers our tribe need. We have nothing to offer by way of reward." She lowers her gaze, as though uncertain. She nudges Gift Anstar forward, reaches up to unfasten the straps and toggles of the girl's enveloping furs. The garment falls to reveal her lush nakedness, the cascade of straw-coloured hair rippling down across her bare shoulders and full breasts. "But if you help us in our hour of need, she is your slave to do with as you please. This is the contract we offer."

A bitter laugh. "What need have I of slaves. Slaves are an encumbrance I do without." He coughs an accumulation of phlegm. "Naturally, you are both welcome to stay long enough to eat or drink."

"Thank you." The tall naked girl looks at him acutely and speaks slowly, her voice deep and soothing, yet still her words bite. "But the time for such courtesies, for meaningless phrases and observations is past, time is now fleeting, vital." The final word ever-so slightly drawn-out and emphasised.

"I say what I must. I'm incapable of intellectual dishonesty." His voice a thin cold blade of menace.

Gift pulls her furs back around her body, as though suddenly self-conscious.

"You're a devious creature. I swear you even deceive yourself at times." Moonfinger Antherica flings back her auburn rage of hair. A tinge of hopelessness in her tone. "The armies of darkness walk the face of the world. Yet you don't give a damn what happens to us. You just sit around getting aesthetic pleasure from our pain. But you're not apart from the world. You must be a part of it."

Just as he moves in a more decisive way. "You say fire fell from the sky to carve your realm from the icesheet?"

She appears to regain control of herself. "You enjoy goading us. It's not pleasant to be analysed, prodded and checked up on as though we are one of your thaumaturgical experiments."

"Wait…" He holds a forbidding hand, leaning forward. "Tell me, and I may yet return with you…"

Off-balance, Moonfinger Antherica is unsure how to respond. Suspecting some fresh kind of taunt. "I know only what's commonly known among my people. It happened just before the coming of the ice, a fireball from the night ripped a gaping volcanic wound deep into the Earth leaving lingering heat that allows us to dwell within its realm. Until the dead began to rise. Why does that make a difference?'

He rests his chin on his gauntleted fist in a contemplation of mutilated concepts and fragments of ideas. "It might. It might make all the difference I need. I need time to sit. Time to think things over."

He speaks with effort, his throat dry, his tongue swollen. He's been submerged in a placid lake of semi-awareness while eternities slipped by. He yawns and stretches. His hands nurse his aching head as he stands with great effort, scarcely capable of movement until long neglected energies flood back to possess him. He's rigid, stiff and sore, bracing his legs wide apart, breathing unsteadily. A lengthy pause. "Yes. I ride north with you…"

He gathers instruments from his shelves into a backpack. There's no horse in the hold, so the mismatched trio leave the shadow-haunted tower and descend to the village of hovels on the lake shore. Moonfinger Antherica notices the Assassin's initial stiffness eases the more they walk. At the lake's edge he smashes the ice, and carefully undresses, unstrapping his armour piece by piece and laying it on the ground carefully beside the backpack. They watch as, once naked he steps into the water, to wash hibernation from his mind and body. Slender to the point of emaciation, hairless, the ripples of water wash a scum of dried sweat and secretions from his body. Strength pours back into him with each shock of cold as he cleanses, his movements becoming more lithe and agile. They watch the ponderous sway of his penis as he emerges dripping, and dresses.

Then with increasing animation, Adsiduo Sicarius barters for a mount. The fisherfolk have no steeds, only a number of clumsy work horses. So he strikes a deal. The two women are sufficiently relaxed in his presence by now to laugh at the spectacle of the legendary assassin astride the lumbering heavy horse as they ride up through the treeline and head north.

They retrace the earlier trek taken by Moonfinger Antherica and Gift Anstar. They cross the huge white plain of a frozen sea where immense ribcages protrude through the ice like temples, the bone stripped clean by gulls.

He catches glimpses through his previous lives of the days before the glaciation when this sea was ice-free and traversed by trader-ships with painted sails on voyages between bright young coastal cities. Before the world's periodic axial tilt caused the ice to spill south and crush those cultures back to scattered scavengers. A doomed cycle of hopelessness which combined with his own essential loneliness to force him into the long soul-crushing lethargy that has consumed him for decades. A long bleak hibernation in his tower, deliberately slowing his metabolism to a pulse, while the world around him froze into endless white wilderness.

They spy activity on ice-shelves that is likely seals, and on ice-floes that resemble extracted teeth. Solitary birds circle.

They cross an ice-bridge that spans a bottomless chasm.

They skirt huge treacherous expanses of jumbled foothills, then head through a narrow valley that runs as a knife-cut between towering peaks, emerging onto the broken rocks and jutting pinnacles of linked upland plateaus. There are the howls of circling wolves that keep their distance, and tracks in the snow that betray the presence of other predators. At each nightfall they bivouac at the glisten of cave-mouths or within the pitiful shelter provided by ruined trees. Igniting a fire and eating frugally from the panniers carried by the horses. Adsiduo Sicarius feels the pangs of ravenous hunger as his body adjusts after its long hibernation.

The night sky is filled with frostily scintillant stars. Moonfinger takes direction sightings, mapping from star to star.

"Tell me of this star-begotten stone," he says.

"It is of no consequence. It means nothing." Moonfinger's eyes are a spit of defiance against the night.

"It may hold every consequence," he insists.

"Our people have suffered long and long," she explains patiently.

"But this new blight afflicting you, animating the dead is different."

"What can death mean to you? You can't die." Her words are an accusation.

"No, that's the curse. I can die. I die too frequently. And each time it hurts more than the last. I know that each death is not the end, merely a transition into another state of existence. That I am but part of an ancient lifeform. Aware of what it knows. Feeling what it feels."

"Don't you ever get tired?"

"I've been tired forever."

She stares hard at him, uncomprehending. Then moves away to sit with Gift.

For the rest of the day, the next, and succeeding days, they ride wild and hard northwards beneath the heatless sunlight glare, snow kicking beneath their heels. Clouds pile thicker and the cutting wind whines, its freezing breath rasping harsh against their lungs. They watch cloud spread in a pall of gathering dark, until a blizzard ice-storm falls upon them with shattering violence, whirling crazy up out of nowhere. They ride into the blizzard, with spiked starglitter caught in its ferocious gusts, as they huddle into themselves. They pace their mounts, walking at their side, or riding alternately.

"I wasn't always called Gift," says Gift, walking close to him. Her voice just audible above the howl. "And Moonfinger wasn't always called Moonfinger. I was named Elm. She was named Snow. We were renamed by the Matrikas in accordance with our mission to seek you out, and to cajole you into assistance. To be Gift, and to be rejected could be seen as an insult. And yet, your strangeness makes such a reaction irrelevant." She looks into him and sees only the black emptiness and silence that lies inside his mind. "You are eternal? You saw the very dawn of time? That's magical."

A bitter laugh. "Not quite the dawn of time. And it's biology, not magic. There is no magic, only imperfectly understood sciences."

"You're wrong. Magic is all around us. Life itself is magic. Waking up each morning to see the sunrise is magic. Planting a seed and it grows into a tree is magic. Becoming pregnant, and a new person emerging from your body, that is magic."

He almost smiles as he inclines his head. "That is certainly a point of view."

As the storm lessens, they see the loom of black peaks

that climb above them, ominous and hostile. The sky meets the peaks in wild tides around feet of granite that will stand against the elements until the world grows old. Moonfinger shivers at the sky's redness, their backs to the chill wind that comes up the slope behind them. They pass over the high saddle of a frowning cliff, through a narrow throat, to tip over into the wilderness interior that is their hidden valley. Evening sidles up on them as they descend a steep slope towards misty swamp as the sun descends through beaten gold and copper behind the high crater ridge of mountains.

The deeper they get, the more lush the vegetation thrives. Until they find themselves riding through bowers of forest alive with birds and aswarm with insects. He feels a stirring that he thought had long died, a sense of intrigue about this lost valley hidden away from the rest of the world. To the women this is increasingly familiar terrain. They urge their mounts forward through a final barrier of trees to a village of huts built on stilts. It is placed on the shore of a bubbling lake from which ghost-trails of steam burp and hover in a warm mist.

Moonfinger drops from her horse in a single smooth movement, crosses to the nearest hut and climbs to its floor-level. There's already a suspicion that the village has been abandoned. Throwing aside the sacking draped over the entrance simply betrays the chaos inside, smashed pottery, a huge cooking cauldron and bedding cast in sad tatters. She stands for less than a moment, passing her hand over a forehead moist with sweat. This was where she had been born and spent her childhood years. She knows every part of this place. This is where the Matrikas coven had given her and Gift their mission. Were they too late?

She heard a cry from outside, and stooped back out through the entrance. Gift was wielding a blade uncertainly as three grotesque cadavers advance from out of the forest shadows. Adsiduo Sicarius sits astride his heavy horse with an amused expression. Moonfinger vaults back down to the ground, her sword already in her hand. She takes the nearest shambler down from behind, as Gift skewers another through the skull. At the same moment a crossbow bolt impales the third through its empty eye-socket, and a group of villagers emerge from concealment.

It's only now that Adsiduo Sicarius takes an interest. He dismounts and strides across to the twitching bodies, indicating for the others to stand back. He kneels beside the closest corpse and uses a knife to neatly sever the skull in half. Moonfinger advances as the foul mind-worm squirms free from rotting brain-matter, spitting her disgust as she raises her boot to crush it. The Assassin holds a forbidding hand, stopping her.

"It must die," she protests.

"Crush it now and we learn nothing," he answers over his shoulder. "It is only through knowing that we gain power over it, and its vile kind."

Instead, he extracts a clear glass flask from his pack, forks the translucent slug onto the knife blade, and in a single motion inserts it through the open neck of the flask before corking it tight. He holds the flask up to the light, watching the trapped entity squirm within its transparent prison.

As he stands he acknowledges the circle of villagers who have gathered around them. Four crones in dirty hooded robes, three women – one of them nursing the crossbow that had taken out the shambler, and a cluster of ugly ape-like males. He recognises that a form of sexual dimorphism has happened here, where the males have devolved as a result of the community's isolation. That, too, is intriguing.

"You are the Eternal Assassin?"

He switches his attention to the crone addressing him. She's pushed her hood back from a shock of white hair and a face of worn leather.

"Some have addressed me that way. I make no such claims."

"You answered our call? You're here to rid us of this pestilence?"

He brandishes the flask at her. "Allow me time to study this specimen. Then I may know."

"You have until the full moon. The night of silver that governs the tides of time and the rhythms of our being. You have no longer…"

As afternoon gives way to sullen evening.

*

The moon is a skull-head.

Shadows of the grave wrap around them.

Plunging deeper through a dark tunnel of trees, in long shafts of brilliant moonlight he sees a tumbled mass of ruined masonry in stony pinnacles, wild tortured shapes of fallen columns, shattered pillars, piles of scattered roof slates, inhabited by scuttling bugs, and algae-covered heaps of smashed stone and mutilated rose-coloured marble strewn every-which-way. So either Moonfinger had lied, or had been poorly informed about the origins of this hidden realm? It was either older than she'd imagined, or the destroying fireball had obliterated a thriving pre-existing civilisation. Yet this is where the plague of cadavers had begun. This is where his analysis of the extracted mind-slug had led them.

"All our knowledge of these revenants is theoretical,"

he warns. "When we apply what knowing we have for the first time, things will go wrong. Any precipitate action could lead to quick disaster. That is the nature of speculation. The point is, will we be able to improvise our responses."

"What do we know…? We know everything and we know nothing," snorts Moonfinger from her storm of red-gold hair.

"We know that we cannot kill what does not live," says Gift.

"The corpses are animated by the slugs," he says. "They can be destroyed."

Colour fades into a thick humidity that presses down on the three travellers. He hears the trees breathe in a sharper blackness than before, a scene not lacking in its own weird beauty. His footsteps hasten along the slanting stony path, slithering down the steep declivity through the place of graves. Where the dead are interred. It's a tomb-smelling place where stone walls drip and bones turn underfoot. A horde of agitated rats slip and dart beneath their feet. And the first few lumbering corpses emerge.

He hacks his way through a gathering wall of predatory corpses. Gift and Moonfinger a pace behind, to left and right, their blades soiled with dead flesh. Leaving a welter of severed body-parts and glistening viscera in their wake. Hideous shapes slither across his line of vision, they writhe and twist like agonised souls in torment, their shapes continually shifting, like whispers from another world. The feelings of unease are fleeting, but leave an unsettling aftertaste. He can't continue to ignore them. So he opens himself to absorb them, and feels a sense of being drawn.

Glancing sideways he sees that both women are even more intensely affected. They shift as one, with single-minded resolve, and strike out through yet lower terraces of crypts. He follows their lead. The dead appear to be holding back to allow their passage. He licks his lips and grips his gore-wet sword tighter. They emerge on the rim of a boiling pool of magma-heated water, definition lost in a haze of warm droplets. Moonfinger and Gift walk as if in a dream, slow, retarded by a force beyond understanding.

An involuntary shudder, half physical and half instinctive distaste. The alien hostility of the swamp creeps apace with moving shapes half-glimpsed through the cloying mist, and the grotesque sounds of hideous squelching. Gift can smell threat in the air, she swallows, feeling the dryness in her mouth, her thoughts paralysed, as if this was to be her last moment alive on the earth. There are things worse than death or the fear of dying, for this was no natural sound, she'd heard nothing as foul as this before. She bites her lower lip in fear.

A blustering breeze disturbs the haze, and they see the beast hunched beneath the massive turret of a weed-infested crypt, its obscenity overflowing the limit of its pillars. A towering tentacular mass, translucent, oozing vile sticky fluids, undulating and sentient, eyeless, yet he knew it was aware of his presence and was reacting, as though it was watching him. This is what was drawing them. There was movement, faint pulsations to it, a twitching and quivering of the tegument that never ceased. As he gazed, transfixed in horrid fascination, he sees the nest of squirming tentacles swelling and budding, casting off wriggling worms that take on grotesque life of their own. His ripple of revulsion is answered by a quivering that passes through its vast glutinous mass, as the vile jelly spins new tentacles that coil in around his legs.

The moon was gone. Time died. Every nerve tense. Transfixed in terror, and incapable of movement,

Moonfinger and Gift rip screams from their throats as a mass of mind-slugs slither across their feet and slip-slither up their legs. There's nothing left. After this, there can be no sanity left.

His legs are engulfed in writhing mucous, he allows it to happen, as the translucent fingers grip tighter, as if examining its strange prize. He was drawn, unresisting into the maw of the viscid mass of horror, sending impact waves across its monstrous carcase. Sensing its evil thought-energies as clear-cut as knife blades probing into him, hurting him, seeping into his bones. There's nothing resembling a mouth, nothing to indicate the presence of sensory organs. Yet at its very core, the shadowy suggestion of a cerebellum. He fights the instinct to struggle as he sinks deeper into the living mass. Ingested to the waist, his torso sinks deeper into the writhing horror, drawn beneath the quivering yielding surface, the pulsating mass of energy. He was drowning inside its protoplasmic mass, its constriction contracting his muscles, threatening to squeeze his heart to a standstill. A silence that hurts his ears with its weight. Unable to breathe. Yet holding.

Being torn slowly and painfully apart, he maintains his fierce grip on his blade even as the monster invades his thoughts. He opens himself. Drinking in its story. Hoping. Yearning. It's a primordial dark-dwelling sentience immured in the bowels of the Earth, only shocked to the surface by restless seismic magma-flow. Incapable of independent movement itself it sought out cadavers sufficiently intact that it could activate them to provide the mobility it lacked.

It had not arrived on the comet impact. It came from within the world itself.

He was flooded with dark despair. The hatred and

desolation built within him. He wrenched the blade with both hands and drove it down through layer after layer of slime, powered by a raging anger. The entity was screaming inside his head. It was screaming even as it died. Even as its tentacles cease whipping and the mind-slugs die and fall away. Even as the animated corpses fell and moved no more. Even as it deflated and collapsed in upon itself, dissolving away into slime. And he stood there, messy blade dripping ichor, gripped in both hands. It took a long time before his heart stopped pumping noisily.

"That vileness reached out and froze us," says Gift, blood trickling from her bitten lip. "Yet its influence did not affect you."

He looks away. Uncertain of his response. "It was touching your humanity," he breathes softly. "There is part of me that is not human. That is what I was seeking here. Another self. It betrayed that promise."

Gift takes a pace towards him, and wipes slime from his face. 'I am still Gift," she says with an intense large-eyed gaze.

He looks beyond her. His face as expressionless as ever, but for the faintest tightening of his thin lips. "I only feel alive when the flames ignite and burn the world," he whispers.

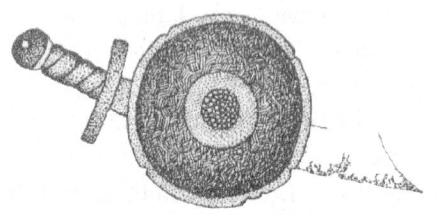

THE QUALITY OF MERCY
Geoff Hart

Even after several centuries, I wake, covered in sweat, to the same dream. The Prince Who Must Not Be Named makes an abrupt crushing motion with his fist and Devora disappears in an eye-searing burst of light that leaves afterimages. In the dream, I still pray she's been cleanly consumed by her own powers as he pushes her beyond the limits her mortal shell can bear. But in her place, there stands a beautiful young piglet that squeals and flees back through the dimensional portal before any of us can muster breath to shout her name. Since that day, I've never eaten pork. The mere thought sends me gagging to the privy, spewing my stomach's contents.

My remaining companions and I struggle, but his spell holds us tight. We can breathe, but naught else other than keep our feet.

With his only serious threat eliminated, he turns to me. "You know what you must do." It's not a question.

I feel a chill hand brush my spine and I shiver, despite the heat that has sweat trickling down my sides and soaking my helmet liner. Devora and the others followed me here. They trusted me to keep them safe and bring them home alive, whatever else might come to pass.

I failed them.

Had we been on the plane that gave us birth, I could have raised my thrice-blessed sword and called for aid from my goddess. I try, but my voice is never heard, and my sword's no more useful than any other sword. I nod, and feel his spell relax about me. I go to one knee.

"Promise you'll spare them, and I swear to serve you."

He nods. "I promise their suffering shall be brief." With that, he draws a finger across his throat, and before I can draw breath to scream a denial, my brothers and sisters in arms, closer to me than any family could ever be, burst into flame so intense, I see it through the gauntlet I've instinctively raised to protect my eyes. They're gone leaving only afterimages and aching memories. And so I learn my first lesson about the Prince: he does not lie, but he chooses convenient wordings that are literally true but never hold the comfort of honesty.

*

I wake to sweat-soaked sheets. In hindsight, trying to take down a demon prince in his own stronghold was rankest folly. *I'd* been an utter fool believing myself justified to enlist my found family on this quest. They'd been fools to trust me. But we'd been young, at the peak of our abilities, and working together, we'd never before been defeated.

There's always a first time.

*

It took years, but I eventually came to appreciate this about the Prince: though his logic might be convoluted, often beyond my mortal ability to grasp, he always lived up to the letter of his side of the bargain. My family was, indeed, all dead before they knew it, and undoubtedly had not suffered. As for me? What he did to me was far worse. He made me live. Far beyond the human span, he made me live. And his words wrote themselves upon my soul in letters of fire:

"The terms or your oath are these: You shall serve me only for as long as you survive, and then I'll release you." He paused to let me dwell upon his meaning. When he saw focus return to my eyes, he continued. "Moreover, apart from the occasional minor favor, I shall require you to honor that service no more than once per year. Should I need you more than that, you'll be compensated."

It was a measure of my grief and despair that his words seemed merciful, though even then, so early in our relationship, his subtle smile warned me against excessive hope. Only one service per year? How bad could that be?

I soon discovered how bad: I could not be killed, though I could be sorely wounded and forced to spend painful years recovering my health. Once I learned that lesson, the terms of our contract became painfully clear. Had I but the span allotted a mortal, I would perhaps commit one or two score sins by obeying his commands. But as the first century passed, I realized how many sins there would be. So many that I confess to forcing myself to stop counting. Each sin weighed upon me, and would do so for eternity, but at least I would not punish myself by tallying their number.

You take your victories where you can.

*

Some uncounted number of years into my servitude, I sat in a rural tavern, a structure that justified its name only because it served fermented fruit and vegetable mash that could be literally (if charitably) described as liquor. The man, in whose guise the Prince had appeared, sat across the table from me, sipping wine from a crystal goblet that had never seen the interior of this hovel. He cast no shadow I could see, though the tavern's rushlights flickered so badly in the thick air it was uncertain whether any man's shadow could be traced to its source. The slight whiff of sulfur that came from him might have been from the match-stick he'd used to light his thin cigar, whose glowing tip cast wraiths of smoke that writhed disturbingly before vanishing into the thick air. At my side, my sword moaned its quiet disapproval; it continued to serve me, though why I could not say, but it did not like working for the Prince.

"To summarize," I proposed before taking a sip of my drink. "You want me to slaughter a convent full of nuns and novitiates?"

He nodded and sipped his drink.

"What have they done to offend you?"

"Does it matter? A year has passed since your last service. Do you propose to withdraw from my service by refusing me?"

Through the long years, I'd wondered what might come to pass should I refuse him. I had not yet mustered the courage to attempt that rebellion. "I wish nothing more than to withdraw from your service." I sipped my "wine" again, holding a forefinger aloft to forestall his reply. "But I can guess the cost."

"You would be a great many years paying the cost. Years beyond mortal count. More to the point, you continue to entertain me and serve me well after all these years. I'll not easily release you."

"Since the *service* is never a challenge too trivial for me to quibble over, I can only assume that the service—"

"Will test you to destruction. Perhaps." He nodded, and drew a sheet of parchment from his sleeve and held it a moment just out of reach. "Or perhaps not. In this case, the service will be among the rarest kind: one that you, and that unpleasant sliver of steel at your hip, might approve under other circumstances. Trust me on this."

"*Trust you*? Do you jest?

He frowned. "I never jest."

It was true. Nor did he lie. At least, he did neither in a way that my mortal wit could parse before it was too late to help me and the true meaning had been laid bare.

He cast the parchment on the table. "Follow this map until you find them."

"What if there are two convents at my destination?"

His frown deepened. "Now it's you who jest."

The Prince had a subtle sense of humor, but it never encompassed my jests. Nor did it lead him to tolerate derision. I averted my eyes.

"When you find them, kill them. Let none who dwell within survive, no matter how innocent they might seem. Should any survive, I shall deem your service unfulfilled. And I will be very much displeased." With that, he dissolved into the shadows, taking with him the faint whiff of sulfur. The parchment hung a moment, then fell to the table. I seized it before it had time to stick.

I beckoned to the tavernkeeper. "More wine," I said. "Leave the bottle."

*

The convent stood at the top of a long ridge that overlooked a small town. Most of the town's buildings were wood-framed, with thatched roofs, but the keep was of local stone with high quarried-stone walls, and looked well-maintained. The convent of the *Soeurs de La Miséricorde* was a wood-framed building, unwalled and with the massive timbers crudely squared. It was larger than the keep, larger in fact than the town seemed sufficiently prosperous to sustain. But it perched close above the road that led into town, about a day's travel on foot from the nearest town of any significance and just before a steep descent that would encourage weary travelers to stay the night instead of daring that descent if they arrived too near dark. It showed signs of having been enlarged several times over the centuries. To one like me, who had lived those centuries, the different architectural styles were familiar, and their mixture was not entirely uncomfortable.

Above the double-door at the front of the building, a wooden sculpture hung like the figurehead of an ocean-going ship: a sturdy woman of middle years, holding a long, triangular dagger two-handed, the point angled upwards between her breasts. The eponymous weapon had a wicked reputation, even in this age of wickedness, for it brought both surcease from pain – and death. An inauspicious omen given my purpose in coming here.

I approached and raised the heavy knocker, producing a surprisingly loud boom that must have resonated throughout the halls. I readjusted my sword on my hip, more by reflex than out of any premonitory fear. After a few moments, an inspection port shot open with a wooden *clack*, and a mild voice called through the hole.

"How can we be of service, weary traveler?"

"I seek shelter for the night, a meal, and perhaps companionship to while away the hours before sleep.

The portal closed with another *clack*, and after a moment, I heard the sound of a bolt being withdrawn. The leftmost door swung open. I noted, without comment, the sturdy bar that rested against the rightmost door, ready to be dropped into rests that would withstand anything short of a ram. A bar that would take two strong men to lift. An odd precaution for such a venerable religious order, but perhaps it explained how they'd survived whatever challenges the centuries had thrown at them.

"Follow me." My guide was a young woman, barefoot and wearing a shapeless shift that covered her from chin to toes. She glanced only briefly at my sword and my lack of armor or any baggage beyond a thick blanket in which I'd wrapped my few possessions. "I'm named Helena. And you?"

I declined to answer. After a moment, she shrugged and led me deeper into the convent. As we passed a dining hall, she paused. "Come here for your evening meal when you have settled, then again in the morning to break your fast." Then she led me to my room, a simple cell with a bed that would be too short for me and a chamber pot that had been polished so clean its brass shone in the faint light from the oil lamps in the hallway.

"I'll leave you here." She bowed and left without meeting my eyes, her shift brushing the floor with each step. I took a moment to inspect my chamber, which in addition to the chamber pot, held only a pallet with a straw-stuffed mattress and pillow. I deposited my blanket and scant possessions on the bedding, hesitated a moment, then placed my sword atop the pile. It made a faint querulous noise, but made no attempt to stop me as I left. It had been a long walk, and I was hungry.

In the dining hall, I stood a moment in the doorway, appraising the situation. There were perhaps a dozen acolytes, dressed in thick red robes adorned with the gold-stitched shape of their order, and half again that many novitiates in unmarked shifts. Many eyes turned my way, as

SWORDS & SORCERIES

I was a stranger and, as I'd expected from what I'd learned of their order, the only man in the room. One of the older women approached me, met my eyes, then laid a callused hand on my shoulder. "You have come a long way to our convent, haven't you?"

"Farther than some; not as far as others."

"I wasn't referring to your physical journey." She paused a moment. "Come sit with me privately." She took my elbow and led me to a small table, separate from the others. "I am Selene." She paused and when I did not reciprocate, nodded. "And you shall be *Guest*, then, until you choose to share your name."

I met her eyes. "I have reasons not to use my name."

"Here or anywhere, yes. I saw as much." She beckoned to one of the novitiates, who stood fast enough to topple her heavy wooden chair, then rushed to the kitchen. "Sit, please!"

I sat, and shortly thereafter, the novitiate returned bearing a large bowl of stew and half a loaf of bread. I hesitated, and when Selene smiled and nodded, I muttered a grace—one of my recurring small acts of rebellion against the Prince—and began eating. She sat in a companionable silence, waiting for me to finish. The food was simple but tasty, and far superior to most of what I'd eaten on the road that led here. I soon finished it and mopped up the dregs with what remained of the bread.

"I thank you, Mother."

"Not a mother. Our members have taken no vow of chastity," her hand fell upon my knee. I gently removed it. "But we take measures to ensure that none conceive a child."

"Part of your teaching?"

She nodded. "Upon accepting the robe and the misericord, we vow to bring no new lives into this world of tears, but rather to help those in need to leave the world and move on to the next one when their time has come."

"Mercy, then."

"Of a kind." She sat back. "Sister Helena tells me you came bearing a sword. A mercenary, then?"

"Once a knight, but no longer. I do what good I may, whither I may, but serve under no man's banner."

"No *man's* banner."

I frowned. "You're perceptive."

She ducked her head. "Some of us have the gift. It helps us know the kind of healing that is most appropriate."

"*Healing*, you say, or *mercy*?"

"The quality of mercy depends on one's perspective and the needs of the wounded."

"The misericord has no reputation for healing."

"And yet, our goddess assures us that in ending suffering, it too can heal. Guidance that perhaps you should consider to ease your own suffering."

"I have my own supernatural guide who might well appreciate that philosophy, if not the healing." I declined to elaborate on the nature of that guide.

"So I have seen. I feel certain that your guide and mine have interesting discussions when they compare the nuances of their theology."

"You believe they come together to discuss?"

A bright smile appeared on her face, and erased many years. "Most sentient beings enjoy discussion, even with those who strongly oppose their ideology. Perhaps more so. I too enjoy theological discussion. Wish you to retire to your cell and compare our theologies?"

I yawned, for it had been a long walk. "Perhaps another time. Now the healing I need most will be best provided by sleep."

"Ah, I see now you are exhausted, both physically and spiritually. Can you find your way back to your cell, or will you need help?"

"I won't get lost."

"Then I wish you a long and restful sleep."

As I left, I noticed that several of the sisters now openly appraised me, and wore what they must have considered secret smiles. I did not wonder at their meaning. But as I felt no premonition of peril, I shrugged and made my way to my bed. I was asleep almost before I stripped off my clothing.

*

I woke in the night at the sound of clothing falling to the floor, and before I could fully throw off the veil of sleep, felt a warm body slide under the covers beside me. A warm hand fell upon my chest.

"Each man needs a different mercy," said Helena, "and Sister Selene sent me, fearing you might prefer a younger woman. I have been sent to offer you what surcease I can." Her hand slid down across my belly, causing me to shiver. Her lips followed along the path it had blazed. And for the rest of that night, we compared our different theologies using the common language men and women have always shared for such discussions.

When we were done and she slept, I whispered a spell that invoked profound sleep in those who were weary, and when her breathing gentled, I carried her outside the walls. I tied her limbs to a cedar tree that had seen nearly as many summers as I had, then gently placed a gag in her mouth, ensured that she was able to breathe, and re-entered the convent.

*

In the morning, I woke to find myself clad only in a clean shift, lying atop a cold stone slab in a high-ceilinged room. High up, its windows were ornamented with stained glass that showed scenes of women, each bearing a misericord. I sought to rise, but found that my limbs would not obey me. Yet I felt no fetters, and from what I could see, I had not been tied with visible bonds.

"It was administered while you slept." Selene's voice sounded sad, but not unduly so. She saw my incomprehension. "The drug that binds your limbs."

"Ah. And why do my limbs need binding?"

"Because not everyone embraces the mercy we offer."

"Some have mercy thrust upon them?"

"Indeed." She leaned across me and kissed my brow. From a sleeve, she withdrew a long dagger with a triangular cross-section. It glinted coldly the light of the multitude of candles that lined the walls.

"And what if I choose not to accept that mercy?" I reached for my sword with my mind, and felt its eager reply.

"Our goddess would take it amiss if her gift were rejected. As you undoubtedly know, it's unwise to displease such higher beings."

She turned at the sound of something cutting through the air, and my sword smacked hard against my palm, as it had done so many times before. "Then I fear I shall have to apologize to her when my work here is done."

Despite the shock of my sword's sudden appearance, she reacted swiftly. Before I had shaken off the effects of the drug, she thrust her weapon into my chest, passing between my ribs with the skill of someone who'd done this many times before. The blow would have killed a mortal man. I wasn't mortal. When she withdrew the blade for a second thrust, I knocked it from her hand with my sword, then without pausing, took her head from her shoulders with the return swing—a difficult feat, but my sword was unnaturally sharp and had certain advantages against foes it deemed to hold a different theology. I had time to register the shock on her face before the screams of the others echoed from the high walls. I hadn't noticed their presence until that moment, as they stepped from the shadows cast by the candles.

I threw myself from the slab, landing on my feet, sword between me and my assailants. The nuns bore misericords, which were as ineffective against an armed and standing opponent as the diverse assortment of bludgeons born by the novitiates. Neither posed a serious threat, as they were not a combat order and violence was not the core of their religion, only an occasional tool. Soon their cries of fury became screams of terror. I tried to ignore one novitiate's look of betrayal when I pulled my sword from her chest, and largely succeeded; I'd had many opportunities to practice. The part of me that once welcomed the chance to prove myself against evil quailed at my actions, but the larger part, the man I'd become, continued the distasteful work of slaying each of the women. I'd done so much worse in the past. Yet that other part of me still prayed they would find mercy, not knowing whether my prayer would be heard.

When the last body had fallen, I lifted the bar into place across the main door and hunted through the building in search of survivors. I found none. I returned to the door, unbarred it, and left. Then I turned, touched my blade to the door, and sent it a command. Instantly, it burst into flame, a more-than-natural flame that ignited even the thick beams of the walls. Within moments, the convent was aflame. I waited by the open door until it was clear that none could have survived. Then I turned and began to walk away.

A voice came from behind me. "You've done well, my servant. Save only one thing."

I stopped, hesitated a moment, then turned. The Prince stood amidst the flames, the hellish wind from the fire tossing his hair but otherwise having no effect.

"I live to serve, Master."

"Say rather that *you serve to live*."

"I have no need of reminder."

"And yet a reminder sometimes proves salutary when you disobey my command."

"I disobeyed no order. All who dwell within are now dead."

"And the one you bound to the hedge?"

"She no longer dwelt within."

He shook his head ruefully. "You've learned well from your master. Too well, perhaps. In future, I'll be more careful in my wording."

You take your victories where you can. Through force of will, I repressed a smile, but I'm sure he felt it.

"Still, all but one are now dead, and that must needs suffice."

I ground my teeth. "They truly deserved this fate?"

"How many men, women, and children have they slaughtered over the years in the name of mercy? In the service of a bloodthirsty goddess?"

"I can't begin to imagine."

"Then it's probably best you don't try. I'll see you in a year, my servant."

I turned without a word and went to unbind Helena. "Go free, child," I whispered in her ear, then said the words that would let her wake in good time. Then I walked away. Behind me, there came a crash as the ceiling beams gave way beneath the heat and collapsed.

Author's note

Despite my choice of name for the antagonists of the story, the *Soeurs de La Miséricorde* (Sisters of Mercy) bear no resemblance to their namesakes in our real world. I chose the name solely based on the nature of their symbol in the story, which is a nasty piece of work that resembles a rondel dagger, designed to slip between armor plates or eyeslots in a helm and end a fallen knight's life. Whether or not the victim was suffering or sought such "mercy".

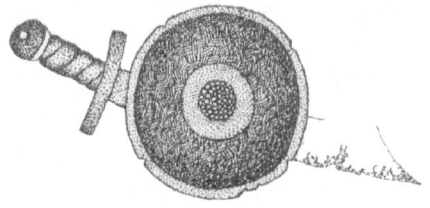

EMPLOYMENT FOR MAGICAL PEOPLE
Monica Goertzen Hertlein

An icy gust swept over the frozen fields, flipped back the hood of Moraeg's oversized cloak, and took her breath like the wrath of God. Gasping for air against the winter wind, she used her gloved hand to yank the hood back over her tangled red braids and held it tightly beneath her chin.

This storm is not God's vengeance. God would forgive her. He would even forgive the Baroness, though she deserved damnation.

Moraeg brought her trembling hands to her mouth and blew on them. The ripped glove she had found did little to shield her numb fingers from winter's blast. She wished she knew a spell to block out the wind. Or thicken her cloak. At least the freezing detracted from clenching hunger pains.

Behind her on the road, a carriage approached. She shuffled to the side in the mud-scarred snow, as close to the roadway as she dared without being in the carriage's path.

A man stuck his head out the side window. "Hey, there. Need a coin, lassie?"

Moraeg nodded.

A silver piece flashed through the air. Moraeg dove forward, arms outstretched. The coin landed in her cupped palms.

The horses and carriage continued on their way. The wind picked up again, swirling around her now-uncovered head and arms. But Moraeg stood motionless, unable to take her eyes from the silver glinting in her hand. It sparkled like the coin that had grown colder as she imbued it with dark magic until a tinge of frost glittered around its edges. Bile curdled in her stomach and the back of her throat.

But this coin was only a mundane coin, and she was no murderess. She caught her breath, one hand on her heart as its beat returned to normal, then tied the coin into a fold of her skirt.

She pulled the cast-off cloak around her again. Beneath the lace-trimmed sleeves of her chemise, her skin had reddened. She rubbed her arms, nearly as numb as her stiff fingers.

A few minutes later, stable stench tainted the frosty wind. She saw a thin line of smoke bending from a rooftop ahead. Her footsteps picked up speed.

The building was a two-storey inn with wooden stables behind, thatched roofs dusted with snow. Along with the hearth fire and horse-stink, she smelled roasting meat. Her empty stomach clenched painfully. How quickly it had grown accustomed to regular meals.

A clamour of voices, rattling dishes, and creaking wooden benches spilled from the tavern's door along with the scents of roast mutton, sour beer, and smoke. Inside, the noise and smells thickened around her along with a heavy warmth that throbbed in her ears, nose, and hands, increasing the pain even as it pulled her in.

She leaned against the door to close it behind her, her hands too painful to push. A few patrons at the wooden table nearest looked over before returning to their beer and stew. Another man, huddled beside the hearth, arms wrapped around his stomach as if in pain, looked up. His hopeful expression fell when he saw Moraeg. He bent over again with a groan.

From the kitchen, a woman with an apron tied across her bulging belly hurried in. Seeing Moraeg, her welcoming expression faded and her heavy jowls drooped in a frown.

"Our tables be full, child, but ye can set beside the fire long's you stay outta the way and don't be botherin' me customers." The woman turned to go back to the kitchen.

"Wait a moment."

Moraeg's frozen lips felt puffy and her words slurred, but the woman stopped and looked over her shoulder.

"I'd like to buy a bowl of stew. I can pay." Moraeg had sense enough not to flash the precious coin in a roomful of strangers, but her hand drifted down to the knot in her woollen skirt.

The heavyset woman's eyes followed the girl's hand, then she nodded. "Alright." She disappeared into the kitchen.

Moraeg sidled further into the room. Shoulders hunched, she took a seat on the floor beside the hearth, near the man doubled over in apparent pain. She wished she could help him. If only the vast library at the barony had contained healing spells as well as spells to punish poachers and capture thieves.

But her tingling, aching fingers would be near-useless anyway until the frostbite was painfully thawed out of them. And she was weak with hunger. She pulled off her worn glove and laid it near the hearth.

The kitchen woman came back with a steaming wooden bowl, a hunk of brown rye bread, and a mug of beer. Moraeg's eyes watered with gratitude. Though a silver coin would pay for a meal and lodging besides, the woman could not have known Moraeg had more than a copper or two.

"Thank you." Moraeg's hands shook as she reached out.

The woman's rounded cheeks reddened. She pushed the food and drink into Moraeg's clumsy hands before hurrying away.

Ignoring needles of pain in her fingers, Moraeg used the bread to shovel stew into her mouth, then devoured the bread, sopping up every last drop of gravy from the bowl. Finally, she downed the beer, not putting aside the mug until it was empty.

A stabbing pain in her gut as it adjusted to the sudden input doubled her over with a groan, echoing her hearthside companion. But she recovered quickly, tamping down the fading hunger pains with a touch of magic.

Fed and warm for the first time in days, she pulled off her cloak and folded it beneath her. Then she wrapped her arms around her knees and leaned her head back against the charred stones of the chimney and sighed.

She had barely closed her eyes when an angry shout roused her. A scrawny man wearing an apron headed towards Moraeg.

At his heels, the kitchen woman tugged at his rolled-up sleeve. "Said she could pay."

"Then let her pay." The man came to a stop, hands on his narrow hips, staring down at Moraeg. His face would be handsome except for the frown tightening his lips. "Well, lass. Where's the price for the meal? We don't take trades from strangers. It's cash or we call the constable."

Moraeg's blood ran cold. Her stiff fingers rushed to unwrap the silver coin and hold it out. "Here's for the meal and a night's lodging."

The woman gasped.

The man's gaze narrowed further. "Where'd the likes of ye get silver? You stole that? I should send for the constable anyway." But the man reached out and snatched the coin from her.

Heads craned in her direction. A ripple of quiet shushed conversations like a wave going out from where she sat on the floor, staring up at the skinny innkeeper.

Fear set Moraeg's heart racing, along with indignation. "I didn't steal anything. A man gave me that coin."

"A beggar, then." The innkeeper frowned down at her. "We don't want ye around here."

His wife tugged his sleeve again but he ignored her.

"I paid you for lodging." Moraeg's conscience shifted uncomfortably at the label of beggar.

"Not a beggar. Look at those fine boots." One of the gentlemen at the table nearest the hearth pointed at her feet. "Dyed blue and a perfect fit."

"And her blouse." His companion nodded his chin toward Moraeg's white blouse.

"Lace trim. Quality handiwork." The man tugged at his own wide sleeves where lace spilled from beneath a linen coat with brass buttons.

Her stomach flipped. She should have kept her cloak on, warm room or no. They would never believe the clothes were hers, the only garments she had when she fled.

The skinny innkeeper frowned deeper. "How'd you get them fancy boots and shirt and silver coin?"

His wife stopped tugging on his sleeve and watched Moraeg with an expression of mingled curiosity and suspicion. Every eye in the suddenly quiet room fixed on her. Even the man beside her stopped groaning.

"A nobleman riding in a carriage threw me the coin."

She poured the truth of her tale into her stare, though fear rippled through her, huddled on the floor staring up at her accusers. "He would have passed by here just before me. He was headed this way."

"Doesn't explain the fine clothes, even if that were true," the gentleman with brass buttons said.

Several others nodded.

"Her hair's red." A shrivelled-looking man with a patched brown tunic and grey whiskers stared at her. His voice quivered. "And she's got a witch's mark on her arm."

Moraeg clamped a hand over the purple birthmark on her left forearm, bared by the lace of her chemise.

The innkeeper stepped back, one arm out as if to protect his wife from Moraeg. "Ye a witch, girl?"

She opened her mouth, her mind blank. How could she answer without being guilty of lying? How many sins dared she heap on her soul?

If they grabbed her, she was unable to defend herself. The thought of conjuring curses made her stomach heave. She swallowed hard to keep the stew from boiling up her throat.

Before she could gather her scattered thoughts, the inn's outer door swung open and closed again. An elderly woman, grey hair wrapped beneath muffling layers of cloth wound around her head, paused on the threshold.

Her frosty eyebrows rose at the scene near the hearth. "Have I missed some excitement? I was told my patient's situation was not urgent."

The man beside Moraeg groaned in pain.

Everyone else looked from him, to Moraeg, to the new arrival.

"She's a witch." The old man in brown lifted a shaking, skeletal wrist and pointed at Moraeg.

The elderly woman's brows rose further. She began unwrapping the cloth from around her head. "And?" She turned her gaze toward the innkeeper. "Has she performed some curse? Jinx? Hex?"

The thin man scowled. "She had a silver coin."

Her face entirely free of the heavy scarf, the woman chuckled. "If that were a crime, there's many a rich man headed for the cells."

"She might have stolen it."

The newcomer looked at Moraeg. "Did you steal the coin, child?"

Moraeg shook her head. "A man gave it to me." *Please believe me. Please convince them. I'll leave and not come back.*

The woman looked at the innkeeper. "Do you have evidence to belie her story?"

He scowled. "No."

"Where is the coin now?"

A sour expression compressed the innkeeper's thin lips further. He unclenched his palm to show the silver.

"That is payment for..." The woman looked enquiringly at the innkeeper's wife.

"Supper and lodging," the kitchen woman replied.

"Just supper." Moraeg was *not* staying here.

"Then I believe you owe her the difference."

The grey-haired healer brushed past the innkeeper, whose mouth opened and closed before his scowl deepened. He spun and headed for the kitchen, followed by his wife.

The healer knelt beside the groaning man. She set down a satchel that smelled of lye and mint.

The innkeeper's wife came back, poured a handful of copper coins into Moraeg's open palm without getting closer than necessary, and hurried away again.

Moraeg wrapped her fingers around the coppers. The

gentlemen returned to their roast and wine. The others bent their heads together over their ale and stew. Even the old man returned to his beer, though his eyes repeatedly darted in Moraeg's direction.

The healer had mixed a tincture and was helping the groaning man to drink, bracing his head with one hand and pouring a noxious-smelling liquid down his throat with the other. He gagged, but swallowed and looked at her gratefully.

"Shouldn't take long," she assured him.

"Thank you," the man croaked before resting his forehead on his knees.

"Thank you," Moraeg echoed. Her words were woefully inadequate. This woman had saved her from the constable. Or worse. If they sent her back to the Baroness...

"Take this." Moraeg held out the coins.

"That's generous, child, but I suspect you need it more than I." The healer's grey brows drew together over hard brown eyes. "You look like you haven't eaten or slept well in some time. Do you need a place to stay tonight?"

Tears pricking the back of her eyes, Moraeg nodded. "I have enough to buy me a night at some other inn." As far down the road as she could walk before cold and hunger caught up to her again. She kept back a few pence and offered the other coins. "Take the rest. I don't need it. I can..."

There was really nothing she could do to earn a living. She could sew, but not well. She could cook, but no better than any other woman. Her only hope was to find a market for love potions and luck spells, not that she knew many of those.

"Keep the coins, child. You don't owe me anything." The healer's wrinkled hands wrapped around Moraeg's, closing her fingers around the treasure. "But if you want to express your gratitude for my assistance clearing up this recent misunderstanding, you can help me carry this satchel back to the city."

The healer pointed to her bag. It looked heavy, slumped to the plank floor.

"My old bones don't do as well in winter's chill as they did before." With a pat on the back for the man who was resting rather than groaning, the healer pushed herself to her feet. She put one hand in the small of her back and rolled her shoulders. "Can you do that?"

Moraeg leapt to her feet, snatching up the satchel and throwing it over her narrow shoulder. "Yes. I'd be happy to."

The healer raised a brow. "I suspect you want to wear your cloak."

Embarrassed, Moraeg bent to throw her outsized cloak around her shoulders and put on her single glove once more.

The healer patted her shoulder and smiled. It was the first smile Moraeg had seen on the elder woman's face. It took the hard glint from her brown eyes. "I'm Gwenyth."

"I'm Moraeg."

"Let's go, then."

*

The quarters Moraeg shared with Gwyneth were cramped and smelled of lye, tucked among a row of wooden shacks huddled inside the city wall. A hearth in the middle added to the heavy autumn heat.

"Hand me the St. John's wort, please." Several long strands of grey hair had come loose from Gwyneth's headscarf and stuck to her wrinkled cheeks as she stirred a steaming pot.

Though Gwyneth herself lacked magic, she was an excellent teacher in healing arts. And being able to diagnose a patient's suffering made it easier for Moraeg to direct a healing spell, when Gwyneth's vast knowledge was insufficient to cure an injury or illness.

If only her meagre collection of writings saved from disintegrating books resembled the endless shelves of carefully preserved tomes the Baroness had collected.

Moraeg dismissed that thought. Better an assistant's bed in this shack than a suite of rooms at the barony's grand estate.

Gwyneth poured sour-smelling goo into a jar and passed it to Moraeg. She closed her eyes and felt for the healing properties in the liniment used on the king's injury, using her magic to give the medication extra strength.

Did the king know his treatment was enhanced by magic? If he did, would he demand her skills to punish thieves and poachers? Inwardly, she shrank at the thought.

"Pack my bag, and make sure we have a good stock of willow bark." Gwyneth tapped her stir stick on the edge of the pot, set it down, and wiped her hands. "We have errands in the city before we stop at the palace to check King Edward's shoulder wound."

Moraeg began packing stoppered jars and sharp-smelling, cloth-wrapped bundles into a leather case slung from her narrow shoulder.

Gwyneth patted Moraeg's back. "You make an excellent healer's apprentice."

Her rare smile sent a warm feeling of pride through Moraeg's chest but she shook her head. "You don't need my help."

"I appreciate your hard work and caring heart." Gwyneth ruffled Moraeg's red plaits. "You're a good girl."

Guilt clawed at Moraeg's thoughts. She was not good. But she had spared the Baroness, who deserved death.

They stepped out the door.

After all these months, the busy streets retained their wonder for someone from north of the craggy isles. The colour and variety of clothing from brown wool tunics and orange skirts to purple silk gowns; the mounds of cabbage and onion to heaps of glittering buckles and needles for sale; was so much more than the northern country estate of Moraeg's childhood.

The sheer number of people cramming the maze between crowded structures, elbowing each other aside, shouting insults at those who walked too slow or too fast, fascinated her. She had once seen a person with his head wrapped in cloth, hair entirely hidden, and a woman with skin so black it was difficult to look at.

Moraeg was pulled away from her gawking by a desperate tug on her arm.

"Please!" a woman begged, "The healer! I need help."

"What is it, dear?" Gwyneth asked.

Sobbing too hard to answer, the blacksmith's wife tugged on Moraeg's arm.

When they entered a wooden dwelling attached to the smithy, the woman pointed to a man's body, stiff below blankets soaked with sweat. "My husband."

Gwyneth went to the cot. Her remorseful expression told Moraeg it was too late, there was nothing she could do for the blacksmith. "I'm sorry."

"No," his wife whispered. She buried her face in her hands.

If she had no family to take her in, her lot would be

dismal. A widow was dependent on the charity of the church and that was unreliable at best.

As Gwyneth laid a sympathetic hand on the distraught widow's shoulder, Moraeg was drawn to a tingle of magic emanating from the blacksmith's body. A faint aura of luminous green traced from his right hand up his arm and across his chest.

Bile curdled the back of her throat at the hallmark of curse magic. Magic drawn from hatred, terror, and a wish for vengeance that felt familiar and made her stomach turn.

*

Throughout their visit to the palace, while Gwyneth worked on King Edward's shoulder wound, Moraeg tried to hide her shaking. When asked to hand her mentor remedies or supplies, her clumsy fingers trembled. Her stomach clenched repeatedly, sending sharp pains through her chest as she waited for Gwyneth to accuse her of causing the blacksmith's death. Every time the king's cold, blue eyes turned her way, she braced herself for an arrest order.

But there was no accusation and no arrest.

Not that day. Not the next.

By the end of the third day after the man's death, Moraeg was ready to confess and get it over with rather than bear the guilt. She opened her mouth.

"Remove those pots from the hearth." Gwyneth pointed.

Trying not to spill the cooling liquids despite her shaking hands, Moraeg carried each pot to the work bench and set it down. By the time she had finished, Gwyneth was seated on the plank bench, watching her.

"Sit down," her mentor said.

Moraeg's planned confession fled her thoughts. She sank onto an upturned barrel facing the elderly healer. *I'm sorry. Please don't send me away. Don't let them arrest me.*

"Tell me what's bothering you."

Tears welled up more quickly than words. Gwyneth's face blurred, then Moraeg dropped her face into her hands and sobbed.

After a while, she felt a gentle hand under her chin, lifting her face.

"Magic caused the blacksmith's illness, didn't it?"

Moraeg nodded.

"I felt something, kind of a tingle, along his arm," Gwyneth said. "You sensed it, too."

Moraeg blinked the moisture from her vision to focus on Gwyneth's warm brown eyes. "I killed the blacksmith."

Her mentor blinked, then sat back and folded her wrinkled hands in her lap. "Tell me more."

"I cursed the coin." The confession tumbled out, incoherent and interrupted by choked sobs.

The Baroness coming to her family's hut, smiling, asking to see the little girl with magic power. Her jewel-studded wig of silver-blonde curls had twinkled in the early spring sunlight. She smelled like roses.

The soft bed and clothes trimmed with lace. The library. The workroom.

The curses. The sick feeling in her gut. Her growing despair that her work for this elegant woman with the kindly smile was not justice against poachers and thieves, but the tyranny of a vengeful despot.

The day Moraeg said no, red jewels had decorated the Baroness's wig and her sleeves were tied with red ribbons. Her rose perfume smelled overly sweet, aggravating the upset in Moraeg's gut. "I won't create a death curse."

The Baroness did not smile. "How is your family, dear?"

Icy dread touched Moraeg's spine.

"I understand there was a delicious smell of venison stew from their hut the other day."

Deer meat was forbidden to peasants. Terrified for the safety of her parents, grandparents, and siblings, Moraeg escaped the castle two nights later. She crossed barley fields and skirted villages to reach her family's hut.

By the time she arrived, her father had been thrown in prison and her grandfather's hand cut off for poaching. Her mother lay on a pile of blood-soaked bedding, one eye swollen shut, cheek bruised and bloody, right arm broken, the normally-neat hut in shambles around her.

Through broken teeth and a throat raw from screaming, she gasped that thieves had come upon her, unprotected, with three young children, her maimed father, and elderly mother. The bandits attacked them, then ransacked the hut.

Moraeg had buried her grandmother, consoled her grandfather, pacified her siblings, and healed her mother as best she could. Then she returned to the Baroness and promised to enchant the coin with a death curse once her father was released from prison.

"He broke the law, dear." The Baroness smiled. "However, mercy is greater than justice."

Moraeg poured the hatred she felt for her benefactress into the curse. Cold vengeance that frosted the edges of the silver coin as it infused the metal. *Justice.*

When the curse rebounded, striking the Baroness instead of her intended victim, she knew what Moraeg had done. Her blue eyes had glittered with a faint echo of Moraeg's loathing and fear as she bargained a cure for herself in exchange for the safety of Moraeg's family. But Moraeg was to leave with nothing but the clothes she wore and never return.

At the end of her confession she sat, head bowed, waiting for Gwyneth to call a constable. Despite her vow to cause no further harm with her magic, to never take a life, not even from the wicked Baroness, her curse had killed the blacksmith.

Gwyneth leaned forward and grasped her arm. "How did the cursed coin work?"

"When the Baroness wished harm to the person she paid with that coin, she would fall ill." But Moraeg had cured the Baroness after their bargain, so how could anyone else have suffered?

The Baroness was clever. And vindictive. She had turned Moraeg's bid for freedom into a weapon.

Moraeg's hands flew to stifle a whimper. She had a horrifying vision of a series of victims, lined up and pointing, calling her a murderess. She should have forgiven the Baroness, should have tempered the strength of her curse. She should have found another way to freedom and safety.

Gwyneth's voice sharpened. "Moraeg, look at me."

Hands clasped to her mouth, Moraeg raised her eyes to her mentor.

"The curse is triggered when a victim pays someone to whom they wish ill, is that right?"

Moraeg nodded.

"We'd best visit the blacksmith's wife."

*

The smithy had been taken over by the dead man's brother, who seemed unconcerned with the fate of his sister-in-law. A neighbour directed them to a nun who had given the woman shelter.

When they finally found her in a tiny chamber of the convent, she was desolate, barely acknowledging their presence and ignoring their questions. She lay curled on her side, hair matted, facing a bare wooden wall.

Gwyneth sat on a corner of the cot, holding the woman's hand. "Dear, this is important. Is there anyone your husband owed money to that he may have had reason to dislike?"

"I wasn't involved in his business dealings."

Moraeg's heart sank.

"You don't know anyone he may have paid before he fell ill?"

The woman turned slowly to look at Gwyneth. Moraeg held her breath.

"The rent was due on Michaelmas."

Only a day before the man's death.

"Did your husband harbour any ill will for his landlord?"

The woman shrugged and turned away again.

Gwyneth squeezed her hand. "God be with you, dear."

It took them another trip to the smithy to determine who the landlord was.

The man was alive when they arrived at his home, but his household was in chaos.

"Thank goodness, I was about to call for you," a housekeeper breathed when she saw Gwyneth on the doorstep.

The landlord lay in bed, tossing and turning, curly hair damp and tangled, eyes shut. Visible to Moraeg's magical senses, a green aura traced from his hand up his arm. It had not yet spread to his chest.

His wife stood beside the bed, cradling a sobbing toddler with blond curls.

"Please, give me a few moments of privacy to examine this man," Gwyneth asked them.

With a hesitant glance over her shoulder, the wife left the room.

As soon as they were alone with the unconscious patient, Gwyneth turned to Moraeg. "Use what you need from my satchel."

For a moment, Moraeg was unable to move, guilt freezing her limbs. Gwyneth gave her an impatient glare.

Hands clumsy in her haste, Moraeg mixed a poultice of bishopwort, garlic, wormwood, and helenium and spread it on the sick man's arm. Then she took his right hand and began an incantation. The aura flickered. The colour of the luminescent traces changed to yellow and then faded. His labouring breaths smoothed. He stopped tossing and his eyelids flickered.

She slumped to her knees on the floor in relief, murmuring a prayer of thanks. Gwyneth patted her hair and then left to give the recovering man's family the good news.

The wife returned, followed by the housekeeper who now held the sniffling toddler.

The wife grasped her husband's hand, the one Moraeg had clutched to enchant the counter-curse, in her pudgy fingers. She looked over her shoulder at the healer. "You're sure he'll be all right now?"

"Yes."

"You say there was a contagion on the money he got from the blacksmith? The one who died of plague?"

"Yes." Gwyneth's expression remained calm. Not even her eye twitched at the lie.

Moraeg stared up at her mentor with awe, gratitude,

and remorse for putting her in a position that required falsehood.

"Where is the money now?" Gwyneth asked.

"We paid our taxes." The wife looked down at her husband and patted the hand she held.

A frisson of fear shivered down Moraeg's spine. The coin was in the king's possession?

"Is there any chance he was happy to pay tax?" Moraeg asked, her heart in her throat. If the cursed coin had gone into the king's coffers along with any ill will…

The wife grimaced. "We're proud to do our part, if only King Edward would put that money to good use instead of squandering it on roads and fancy buildings. The old king would never have countenanced such waste."

Gwyneth gave Moraeg a grim look.

*

When they returned to Gwyneth's small hut, Moraeg sagged onto the bench next to the table and let her head fall onto her crossed arms. The familiar smell of lye enveloped Moraeg when her mentor sat on the bench beside her.

"I need to know precisely how this curse works," Gwyneth said.

"I don't know what else to tell you," Moraeg mumbled into her crossed arms.

Her mentor huffed impatiently. "Is only the owner of the coin affected by the spell?"

Moraeg lifted her head. "I'm not sure."

"How specific does the wish for harm have to be? Do you have to know the person you pay or can it be a miserly reaction to having to part with money?"

Disturbed by how much of the spell she had left vague,

Moraeg clenched her fingers together on the table. "I don't know."

What would happen now? Would the king's tax collector die? Had she cursed the king? She had sworn never to take a life, not even when it was deserved. Now her hatred was a living contagion, spreading through the kingdom.

"Is the curse activated if you send money through a third party, but intend for the beneficiary to come to harm?"

She hunched her shoulders and buried her face in her hands.

"What if you never personally touch the coin, but wish harm to the person who receives it? If the king harbours ill will for someone and money from the royal coffers comes into their hands, will His Grace be cursed?"

Horror clamped Moraeg's chest. Would her curse spread to other lands, other families, other rulers? How many murders would be on her conscience?

Her mentor turned on the bench to place her hands on both Moraeg's thin shoulders. "King Edward may be at risk. We'll have to tell him about the coin and the curse."

Moraeg managed to nod, though tears overflowed and dripped down her cheek.

Gwyneth shook her. "You have to permanently neutralize the coin."

The fear and hatred she had channelled and moulded engulfed Moraeg. Once she held that enchantment in her hands, before sending its energy back to the darkness she had twisted it from, she would have to face her fear. Her hatred. She would have to forgive.

Her body shaking, blood rushing in her ears, Moraeg stared at Gwyneth.

*

Moraeg waited, stomach in knots and hands clasped behind her back. Even seated, King Edward's gaze was on a level with hers, his blond hair smooth beneath a narrow golden band adorned with purple gemstones and a matching medallion around his thick neck. She could smell the liniment he rubbed into his wounded shoulder.

There was no sign of a glowing, green aura tracing his arm.

The hard-eyed ruler glanced suspiciously at her. "So you cursed the coin?"

Moraeg nodded. "I enchanted it to make the Baroness deathly ill when she tried to curse someone with it. She knew it was my work. She glared at me from her sickbed when her servant brought me there." Moraeg's shoulder twitched at the memory of the bruises his hands had left. "I bargained a cure for my freedom and assurance that my father would be released. She agreed. I brewed an antidote, then she banished me."

There was a moment of silent stillness. The only movement was the king's thick finger tapping the carved arm of his gold-painted throne. "I assume the thieves who attacked your family were bully boys sent by the Baroness?"

Shocked, Moraeg stared. The Baroness could not have... But she could. She would. With a smile.

The dark pit of loathing deepened. That woman was evil. She deserved to die. Moraeg should have left her to perish, then her family would have truly been safe.

"Have the clerk bring me the tax rolls," the king commanded.

He rubbed his shoulder while they waited in the Council chamber.

When a bewildered clerk brought the requested tally sticks, Edward examined the records.

"Have there been any expenditures of silver since we received this payment?" He held up a notched stick.

The clerk wiped his palms on his embroidered tunic and shook his head. "No, Sire. Cook has enough coin on hand to cover daily purchases."

"Take us to the treasury."

At the king's command, the clerk led them past rooms full of tally sticks, to a guarded chamber with chests and bags piled on shelves from floor to ceiling.

"Find it and remove it." With a rustling swirl of saffron coat, Edward spun on his heel and left.

The clerk squinted at Moraeg curiously.

"I need to examine you," Gwyneth said to the clerk, "and I need a list of anyone who touched the money paid by the blacksmith's landlord. We have reason to believe one of the coins was contaminated with a deadly contagion."

The clerk's squinty eyes widened. He hurried out, muttering about lists.

Moraeg stared after him, hands clenched. *I can't do this. I can't forgive her.*

Gwyneth caught her gaze. With a final encouraging nod, she left the room.

Moraeg sank to her knees in front of the first chest. She passed her hand across the pile of coins but nothing appeared amiss. One by one she examined each coin from the top layer. Nothing. Same with the second chest and the third.

As she put her hand into the fourth chest, a jolt went through her. Heart pounding, she picked up a coin but nothing more happened. When she held up another coin, haze shrouded the air around it. It made her sick to her stomach, as though she had swallowed rotten meat.

Closing her eyes, Moraeg tested the enchantment, feeling its strength and depth. Renewed terror and hatred for the Baroness flooded her memory, deeper than she remembered. Her mother's anguished voice was fresher. The smell of blood sharper. Her grandmother's shrunken body heavier as she dragged it to a shallow grave. Her grandfather's sobs were louder.

Moraeg's hand tightened on the coin. She was not the murderess. She was not responsible for the blacksmith's death. It was the Baroness who had loosed this curse into the world, knowingly and with self-serving purpose.

She would get this coin to the Baroness again, then wait for the curse to activate. She would stand and watch that smile wither as the glowing green aura encapsulated her, as sweat soaked her embroidered sheets and her breathing harshened. She would teach that woman to fear the way Moraeg had been afraid.

There would be no bargain this time. The Baroness would die. The dark pit of panic and hatred widened, begging Moraeg to seek vengeance for every death the Baroness had incited, every hour of suffering she had caused.

And another death would result from Moraeg's magic.

She forced her shaking fingers to open, bracing her right wrist with her left hand. The coin lay in her right palm. Breathing deeply, she prayed for the strength to forgive. To let go of her hate.

The dark pit that demanded vengeance shrank slightly. She pushed aside fear and anger and guilt flavoured with a childish wish for the world to be fair. She concentrated on grabbing hold of the curse.

Once she had hold of the source, she cast the spells that would drive out the black magic. When the curse broke, she had an impression of thick black ooze running out and sinking through the floor, dispersing into the earth.

Inside, she felt light, at peace. Kneeling on the smooth stone floor in front of the chest, she bowed her head and prayed for the blacksmith's wife, the tax collector, and anyone who had touched this coin. She prayed for the servants at the barony, and the Baroness herself.

Then she got to her feet, shook out her skirt, and went to find the king.

*

Moraeg stood again in front of the hard-eyed king, staring down at her from his throne. Gwyneth stood off to the side, her expression as heartening as the king's was threatening.

"It's done?" the king confirmed.

Moraeg nodded.

"No more curse?"

She shook her head.

No one spoke. The king's jewelled finger tapped against the arm of his throne.

"You were proficient at creating these talismans?"

Moraeg nodded at the floor. Her earlier peace seeped away as nerves writhed in her stomach.

"What did the Baroness use them for?"

"She punished poachers and thieves."

"Her estate is in the lowlands? On the other side of the rocky isles?"

"Yes."

"Were there that many thieves on her property?"

Moraeg frowned. Occasionally one of the peasants and servants risked poaching or stealing. Including her father. "It happens, yes."

"In my experience, punishment does little to deter theft.

Desperate people have no time to consider consequences when their children are hungry. Perhaps the lady should be reminded of her duty to protect those sworn to her service."

Moraeg blinked up at the king's hard face, wondering how someone who had never worried about his next meal could understand.

"What other spells do you know?"

Heart pounding in her throat, Moraeg stared into the king's blue eyes. "I've learned how to discourage pests from eating the crops and to make animals fertile. I can brew love potions and luck spells. I've practiced some fortune-telling." She grimaced at the last. Even with her power, knowledge of the future was imprecise and unreliable.

The king raised his brows beneath the gold band that circled his brow. "I understand there is high demand for such services, though I cannot claim to find it a useful talent."

Embarrassed, Moraeg broke their gazes to look down again at the worn stones beneath her feet.

"If you can ensure healthy crops and animals, however, I would find great value in those capabilities."

Scarcely daring to breathe, she lifted her head slowly. Was King Edward offering her employment?

"All my information, and I assure you I have multiple sources, advise that your gift is powerful. If you use it in my service and refrain from enchanting illnesses and punishments, I will keep your belly full and provide you a warm, safe chamber to call your own."

"Can you make sure my family is safe?" Moraeg bit her tongue trying to recall the words. She had just been offered the fulfilment of all her wishes and she was asking for more.

The king appeared surprised but not offended. "I will ensure they are protected."

"And the blacksmith's widow needs a place to live." This time she did bite her tongue.

Edward's brow furrowed beneath the crown but his lips twitched. "I've made suitable arrangements."

"Thank you." She tried to think of better words to express her sincere gratitude.

The king brushed aside her thanks with a flap of his jewelled hand. "I may also be able to arrange access to our small collection of magical texts."

This time, she was unable to voice her thanks. She hoped she did not look as foolish as she feared with her slack jaw.

The king merely sat back in the carved throne, a twinkle in his blue eyes despite his stern expression. "You must put those resources to appropriate use and dedicate your best efforts to making this kingdom's people prosperous."

"Yes." Her voice croaked. She cleared her throat. "Yes, I'll do everything I can to help. Thank you, Sire." Her curtsy was an awkward wobble.

"I'd be more impressed if you could make this blasted shoulder wound heal quicker." The king rolled his left shoulder.

Moraeg looked at Gwyneth in panic. There was little more she could do to speed the king's recovery.

"The king knows it was your touch that eased his ache much sooner this time than the last two," Gwyneth said. "Perhaps in future he will avoid such injuries knowing he is no longer as young as he used to be."

"None of us are as young as we used to be, even this child." The king waved a hand in dismissal. "You must have work to do, and this one needs to consult with my clerk to begin her new role."

Gwyneth gave a more graceful curtsy than Moraeg,

even though she had to brace one hand on her back as she straightened with a grunt.

In the corridor outside the throne room, Moraeg put one hand on Gwyneth's arm. "I can't work for the king." A hard knot of disappointment lodged in her throat at the idea of saying no to his generous offer.

Her mentor stared in surprise. "It's everything you asked for, everything you wanted."

"I can't leave you alone."

Gwyneth's sharp eyes fogged with moisture. She put her hands on Moraeg's shoulders and leaned close. "Child, I appreciate your concern, but I can find another lass to fetch and carry. You can help more people by learning to use your magic as it was meant to be used than you can following me around."

The thick knot in Moraeg's throat expanded as tears gathered in her own eyes. "But you…"

"I've managed quite well on my own for some years now." Gwyneth straightened, though she still held tightly to Moraeg's shoulders. "My gift is to heal those few God chooses to put in my path. Your gift, child, is to learn all you can about magic and use your talent to make life better for an entire kingdom."

Could she finally explore her power? Use it to feed people and heal sickness?

Gwyneth gave her a little shake. "You're a good girl."

The lump in Moraeg's throat choked off her words of gratitude but she nodded.

"Now go. I'm busy." The healer turned Moraeg and gave her a little push to where a clerk in an embroidered tunic waited.

He showed Moraeg to a workroom twice the size of the one the Baroness had provided, with piles of books and packed shelves that smelled of formaldehyde, while describing a potato blight plaguing the northern towns.

Moraeg gaped; breath caught in her throat. She could learn so much here. Then the clerk squinted at her and she pulled the nearest book closer and flipped through, looking for spells effective for potatoes.

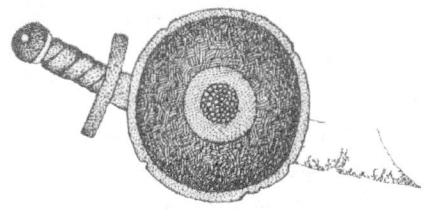

THE HERO'S PATH
Jeffery A. Sergent

I

Mouse had a bad feeling about this one. The place *felt* bad.

His eyes were drawn once more to the figures carved around the cave's yawning mouth. They may have been people. Demons, maybe. He couldn't tell. Body parts were elongated and grotesquely misproportioned, and a few sported what looked to be animal heads and genitalia. They had either to be the work of an ancient primitive or an unskilled artisan.

Gooseflesh raced up and down his arms and along the back of his neck as the uncomfortably chill air rolled out of the gaping entrance, carrying with it the sharp odour of rot.

Brom, as usual, was calm, focused. "Light torches," he said. "Leave the rest."

"Yes, *Sayin*." Mouse removed the heavy pack which carried their equipment and food. "Water?"

Brom shook his head.

Mouse set both skins next to the pack.

The warrior then handed his young companion his double-bladed axe. Mouse tucked it into his belt, positioning it for easy access but also keeping it from interfering with drawing his own dagger should the need arise. The need never had, thankfully, but Mouse preferred to be safer than sorry. Just out of habit, he touched the pommel of the knife he carried on his other hip.

Brom unsheathed his broadsword and let the scabbard fall. Mouse hurried to pick it up as the swordsman began his preparatory ritual, a series of slow, methodical exercises which loosened his huge muscles and awakened his combat reflexes.

Mouse watched the warrior's movements in awe. He had never seen another person like him. He stood a half head taller than Mouse, whose lanky frame reached nearly six feet, and his shoulders were as wide as a door frame. No one knew from where he had come, but, judging from the titbits of information he'd revealed during their infrequent conversations, Mouse believed it was from somewhere beyond the northernmost wastes. But even more unnerving than Brom's mountainous stature were his cold grey eyes, which were as lifeless as a statue's. Those eyes had unnerved many opponents before a single sword stroke had been made.

Brom even terrified Mouse at times, but not because of his size or his ferocity and skill in combat. Nor was it because of those cold, pitiless eyes. No, it was because of his unwavering focus. Once Brom had settled upon a course of action, he moved like an unstoppable force of nature.

"Maybe he provides them a service?" Mouse wondered aloud. He was piling up rocks and branches around the equipment to conceal them as much as possible from a casual glance.

"No," Brom said.

In Tarkush, certain guilds demanded payments for their 'protection.' This, at least, could explain a village willing to pay tribute to this sorcerer. It wasn't right, but it made sense. The guilds actually protected what they considered their own interests after all, so why would these villagers pay if the sorcerer didn't provide something in return. They hadn't seemed to be afraid of him when he and Brom had been among them. At first, Mouse thought they were paying him to avoid being cursed or killed, but they hadn't really seemed to care about the sorcerer one way or another.

And what did the sorcerer get out of the arrangement? A sheep? Grain? The village wasn't near any major road. What was worthwhile about it? It didn't even have a name. It was a mystery Mouse would've loved to have explored more, but Brom wouldn't, or rather, couldn't wait.

The unstoppable force was on the move.

As Mouse swept away the footprints around the lip of the cave with a leafy branch, a glint caught his eye amidst the dirt and gravel. He bent to brush away more with his hand. It was a stone tied to a leather cord.

He picked it up.

As he began rubbing the grime away, he saw it was quite an unusual one: It was green with black streaks, maybe a couple of inches long and half as wide, and in the centre was a black slit like a pupil. It looked like a cat's eye.

"Look," he said, holding it up for the swordsman to see.

"It is not part of the path we follow," Brom said, continuing his exercises.

The path – it was always the path.

Brom called it *The Hero's Path*. The giant warrior saw his life as following a single purpose, this Hero's Path. He claimed it led him wherever he needed to be and provided whatever he needed to survive, so he would take nothing that did not come from a vanquished foe. Brom could have been disgustingly rich during the time Mouse had travelled with him, but none of the treasure was 'part of the path we follow.'

It bothered him, too, that he kept saying 'we,' as if Mouse had chosen this path as well. Even more disturbingly, the further along the 'path' they travelled, the more steadfast

Brom became, which concerned Mouse greatly. He reckoned there was only one end to the Hero's Path.

True, all heroes fought for glorious causes or strove toward grand purposes. All heroes became the stuff of stories, legends, and myths. But, in the end, all heroes died, and Mouse wasn't ready to march toward that end yet.

"Leave it," Brom added as he finished.

"Yes, *Sayin*."

Mouse knew the stone had to be worth something, for he had never seen anything like it before. And he had seen a lot of stones during his years on the streets. One like this would've bought him a considerable amount of comfort in Tarkush, so as soon as Brom had turned his back, more out of instinct than thought, Mouse slipped the necklace around his neck and tucked it beneath his jerkin and shirt.

It was oddly warm against his skin.

Mouse quickly lit the torches and handed one to the warrior, who carried the broad blade in the other: He could wield it as easily with one hand as two.

Mouse shivered again. Cold sweat rolled down the back of his head. His jerkin, shirt, and pants couldn't keep the chill out either. He wondered how the loincloth-clad Brom stood it.

"The Path calls," Brom said, as he always did.

A shiver ran down Mouse's spine, but he suspected it wasn't from the cool air this time. Mouse was no hero; nonetheless, he followed Brom into the gaping darkness.

II

Darkness pressed against their fragile bubble of light like a living thing, and the flickering of the torches cast bizarre shapes upon the walls that followed the pair inward like shadowy stalkers. The tunnel showed evidence of being worked by long dead masons, and the cavern floor had been worn smooth by centuries of use. There were no sounds save the blood pulsing in Mouse's ears. The rotten stench became more pronounced, but mingled with it was the sharp garlic-like pungency Mouse had only ever encountered near the smithies in the city.

After what seemed an eternity, a ghostly light appeared ahead of them. It was, at first, faint and orange like a dying ember, but once Mouse's eyes fixed upon it, it was all he could see, drawing him steadily forward, mesmerized by the dancing light of a whisperwill, until their path abruptly widened into a chamber bathed in a lambent glow.

The stone here had been crudely worked into a rectangular shape about the size of the great room of the last inn where Mouse and Brom had sojourned several nights ago. Braziers of dying coals stood in each corner, but even with the addition of their torchlight, parts of the ceiling remained concealed in utter darkness. A stalagmite stood in the centre of the room with a spherical growth at its tip like the pate of a bald man. A prismatic sheen swirled along its surface.

Lining the walls to their left and right were an assortment of tables and cabinets of varying sizes and styles. Atop some of these were strewn strange vessels, containers, and black candles. One table was covered with scrolls, beneath which shone the glint of silver and gold and the gleam of precious stones. Mouse wondered if there were any more stones like the one he'd found outside.

"There could be a fortune here," he whispered, but Brom quickly shushed him.

Something stirred behind them.

Both spun, Brom ready to face whatever horror lurked in this sorcerer's lair, Mouse out of reflex. But there followed only a sob.

A rusty kennel had been slid between two tables with boxes stacked upon it. It was about the same height as the neighbouring furniture, maybe five feet wide and three or four deep. Something crept in the shadows within, but it was no animal. When the two brought the torches to bear, they saw it was a girl.

Her red hair was dirty and matted to her scalp, and she wore what looked like a rotted flour sack. Wet, filthy straw filled the bottom of the pen. She had curled into a far corner.

"We have to get her out," Mouse said.

"She's not part of the path we follow," Brom replied. And with that, he moved toward the two exits on the far side of the chamber. The torchlight writhed and danced within the crevices of an ancient, arcane script carved into the dead rock. "She could be an unnatural," he added.

Mouse lingered at the cage.

"Hey," he whispered. "We'll get you out after we finish with the sorcerer."

She rubbed at her eyes as if she was ashamed to have been crying.

Mouse smiled for her. She didn't seem unnatural. Nothing about her did, but that could be the whole point of such creatures, he supposed. She was young, too: she couldn't have been more than Mouse's age, probably a year or two less.

She crawled toward him.

"You going to kill that bastard?" she asked. There was a hint of excitement in her tone.

"Yeah." He tried to sound confident.

"What if you don't?"

He nodded toward Brom. "He's a great hero."

She cast a glance at the large warrior then looked back to Mouse. "Shouldn't you free me first? Just in case?"

Mouse turned slightly. Brom was still studying the openings, trying to decide which way to proceed. He didn't blame her for wanting to get out; the only thing unnatural here was the reek. She was obviously not even released to relieve herself.

He paused a second to study her. She didn't *feel* unnatural. In fact, he couldn't help wonder how pretty she might be underneath the filth. Either a smudge of dirt or a dusting of freckles ran across her nose. He wasn't sure which, but he found himself wanting to find out.

"Hello?" she said, snapping him back to the moment.

"Sorry."

"Tell your friend it's the right one," she said. "There was another girl here three days ago. He took her that way. He always goes that way."

"What happened to her?"

"I don't know."

There was a pause as both seemed to share the same thought: If she wasn't freed from this place, a similar fate awaited her.

Finally, Mouse asked, "Do you know where the key is?"

"No." She stuck her face through the bars and extended a hand. "My name is Catja." She smiled. It was a pretty one, one that wouldn't lead you to believe she was in mortal danger.

"Mouse," he said, shaking it.

"Mouse? What kind of name is that?"

"The only one I've got." Which was true. He had been born and raised on the streets of Tarkush. It was all anyone had ever called him as long as he could remember, and the one time he did ask about it, Muro, the master cutpurse, had simply answered it was because Mouse was always getting into everything.

"Here." He handed her the torch. The light danced within her captivating green eyes.

From his belt, he pulled two slender pieces of metal. The lock appeared to be nothing he couldn't handle, but it would take a little time. "You'll be off to your parents in just a –"

"Bugger that," she said. "My parents sold me to him. I'm not going back there."

For several heartbeats, Mouse couldn't form a thought. He couldn't believe what she'd said. He didn't want to. All of his young life, he had dreamed of having parents, a family, unconditional love. Joy and happiness – that's what he'd always imagined families were about, what he'd craved. How often had he watched families leaving their homes or shopping around the stalls. Brothers and sisters playing games. Fathers carrying their sons through the streets. Mothers welcoming their children home with open arms.

How could it be true?

Brom called sorcerers evil, but sorcerers did what they did. What they always did. It was their nature. Parents were not supposed to sell their children. *That* was unnatural. *That* was evil.

"Come," Brom said.

"Just a moment."

"Now."

"But –"

Mouse felt a twinge of guilt. He wanted to help Catja – and he would. After he helped Brom.

He slid the picks back into their concealed pouch and sighed. "Yes, *Sayin*."

To Catja, he whispered: "I have to go."

"What? You're going to leave me here?"

"On the way back. I promise."

"Dammit, you can't leave me!" Tears brimmed her

large eyes, despite the fierceness of her tone.

"I promise." He took the torch and rushed to Brom's side.

"Mouse," she whispered. "Please."

"I promise."

"Coward!" She spat the word in his face then crawled back to the far corner of the cage. She didn't look at him when she added, "You are a mouse! Just a frightened, little mouse."

Her words cut him more deeply than any blade ever could.

"We go this way," Brom said, indicating the left passage.

"But –" But Brom had already gone.

The words 'this is the path we follow' floated from the darkness.

Mouse had been stashing some things for himself the past few months, some coins here and there, a few stones, the necklace. Part of it was old habits from his life on the streets, but part of him knew he'd have to go off sooner or later. He'd just been waiting for the right time and the right place.

Maybe this was it?

And there came the guilt again, and that's what kept him from running off even when the path they followed seemed to lead into increasing danger. He felt he still owed Brom.

Mouse sighed and looked back at Catja once more, but he couldn't see her. "Promise," he whispered, then hurried to catch up with Brom.

III

Their path narrowed and snaked back and forth. Something lingered in the air, something different from the pungency of the prior chamber, a deep, earthy aroma.

Mouse kept looking over his shoulder, back toward Catja, even though he knew he wouldn't be able to see her. Brom, however, moved forward, like an inexorable force drawn toward the violence and bloodshed he craved. Mouse sometimes wondered if Brom loved to fight and kill more than following his hero's path or if fighting and killing was what being a hero was all about.

And there was that twinge of guilt again.

It had been seven or eight months ago since Brom had caught Mouse trying to filch from his purse. When the guards had arrived ready to strike off Mouse's hand, however, Brom offered to take him away from the city to 'work off' his punishment in the form of indentured servitude. Given the choice, exile was better than what was essentially a death sentence. What good was a thief who couldn't thieve? And that was even *if* he survived the dismemberment.

During their time together, Brom had never offered to touch him, which was Mouse's initial fear, nor hit him, nor let him go hungry. The food wasn't always good or a lot, but it was always there. Life hadn't been bad at all. And the sights! Mouse had gotten to see what lay beyond the hills surrounding Tarkush's walls for the first time in his life. That alone had been worth it. He felt he owed Brom for simply giving him a chance to see things he would never otherwise have seen, for allowing him to actually live instead of merely existing, caged within the city's walls.

Still, Mouse wasn't the wide-eyed youth he'd been when he'd left Tarkush; nor was he awestruck by Brom's abilities as he had been. Over the past few weeks, he'd begun to think he'd paid his debt. Plus, he didn't want to be a party anymore to what he realized was Brom's obsessive pursuits.

But he'd think on it more later. Now, he had to think

about staying alive so he could help Catja.

The corridor gradually widened; bones lay scattered along the edges of the wall.

Brom handed Mouse his torch then motioned for him to be still. He wrapped both massive paws around the hilt of the great sword, moving in slow circles with the ease and stealth of a great wolf ready to lunge on its prey.

As silent as a whisper, the thing reached from the ceiling.

It was like an earthworm stretching down, except this one was wider than a man's arms could reach around. Its 'head' slammed to the floor where Brom had been standing just an instant before. Mouse stood with the two torches, frozen, as it pulled itself up. As if sensing their heat, it turned toward Mouse, and its mouth irised open, revealing a series of serrated teeth the colour of a festering wound. It reared back like a snake ready to strike. It made no sound except the stretching of its slime-coated hide as it arched for the attack. Mouse couldn't take his eyes from the horror. In their travels, he had seen many strange and ghastly things, but nothing had stoked the fear in his belly like this faceless fiend. Everything else he'd seen had been men, evil and depraved and barbaric, yes, but they had been men. This was something he could not name.

Before it struck, Brom appeared at its side slashing with the broad blade, blazing like a falling star in the torch light. The sword sliced through the thing's viscous coat and into its skin. In the span of a heartbeat, he struck again. As he fought, he swore in the name of his people's god, a name unknown in these lands.

Mouse moved to the wall, out of harm's way but still able to provide the necessary light for Brom to see. The monstrous worm snapped twice at the barbarian, but each time, the big man was somewhere else. He had an agility and grace that belied his massive form. After rolling beneath one such attack, he rose and thrust the great blade into the creature, piercing it to its hilt. It tried to withdraw into its hole in the ceiling at that point, but the fighter's sword barred its retreat. Purple gelatinous fluid flowed from the slashes and punctures as it silently writhed.

Without a word from either, Mouse dropped one of the torches, drew the axe from his belt, and tossed it to Brom. The warrior rolled beneath the wriggling form and caught the axe in one hand, and in a single fluid motion swung the weapon, digging the blade deep into the thing. He swung again and again like a logger attacking the trunk of an old tree: Each hit was clean and true. In seconds, the thing was dead, its flaccid body hanging from its hole. The 'head' of the beast lay on the floor.

Brom was prodding the severed end with his foot when Catja's scream raced down the tunnel toward them. It was a soul shattering sound, filled with desperation and primal fear.

Mouse would have sworn he'd heard his name called. He turned, futilely holding the torch toward the black corridor behind them.

"He knows I am close," Brom said.

In all the time of his service, Mouse had never directly disobeyed Brom, had never thought about it. He didn't think about it this time either. He ran. He couldn't stand the thought of something happening to that poor, caged girl. Mouse knew Brom would be angry, very angry most likely, but for the first time also, he didn't care.

IV

The door was open, the kennel empty.

Mouse hesitated, unsure what to do.

A shout issued from the right passage, one that sounded more like defiance than terror, but when Mouse turned to follow it, he couldn't move. In that instant, it was as if ice has been poured into his veins, and as his heart grew cold, it seemed to sink to the pit of his stomach. Cold sweat rolled down the back of his scalp as he struggled to take one step forward, but try as he might, he couldn't force his foot to cross the threshold of the passage.

Maybe it was better this way. Catja wouldn't see him for the failure he was before . . .

No, Mouse was no hero. He knew that. He hadn't even been able to open the cage quickly enough to save her, so how could he hope to go toe-to-toe with monsters and sorcerers? It took a special kind of person to do that: someone like Brom, someone he was more and more convinced wasn't human at all.

Mouse felt a scream building within him, one of fear, frustration, and powerlessness, and when he could no longer contain it, a massive, heavy hand clamped onto his shoulder.

"This is my task, boy," Brom said. He spoke with a gentleness Mouse had never before heard in the barbarian's voice. It was almost as if Brom not only acknowledged his effort to go save Catja but also admired him for his attempted bravery. Maybe Mouse was just fooling himself, but for whatever reason, it made Mouse feel like he'd done something at least, something most people couldn't have, and that warmed his heart enough to follow the hero once more into darkness.

Their path narrowed, snaked back and forth, up then down, and on the last sharp turn, led to a chamber filled with flickering light and dancing shadows. Somewhere from within, a deep, throaty voice chanted something in an inhuman tongue.

Mouse's senses were overwhelmed. He'd heard descriptions of the abyssal pits somewhere in the past, and this place was surely one of them. Braziers burned in each corner of the room and to either side of a giant, grotesque head that had been carved from the dead rock. It may have been a depiction of a god or demon, but like the ones outside, the features were a mockery of anything decent and civilized. Mouse began to think the carver hadn't been unskilled at all but rather quite mad.

Before the grotesque façade, a large stone had been worked into a crude altar. At either end stood two creatures, man-sized and man-shaped but definitely not men. They looked as if their skin had been flayed from every inch of their blood-oozing bodies, and their heads were stretched so that it was the size of two stacked atop one another. Their fingers and toes were taloned, and needle-like teeth pointed in odd angles from their circular mouths. Between them, Catja lay naked upon the cold stone, shackled by wrists and ankles.

Brom tossed the torch to the floor and entered, raising his axe in one hand. "Sorcerer." He spoke with a chilling calm.

The sorcerer stared at Brom. "So barbarian, you finally come."

"You will not escape this time, Bol-lag."

The sorcerer barked something that sent the two bloody things leaping toward the warrior.

Mouse watched the first few heartbeats of the battle. It was fast and ferocious. The two things attacked in tandem like a single beast, yet Brom was able to deflect and dodge each blow and bite. Bol-lag watched with the intensity of a proud owner of a pit-fighter. And in that moment, Mouse realized he'd either not been seen or had been considered unimportant by the sorcerer. He immediately dropped his torch and ran to the altar to begin work on Catja's shackles.

"Don't move," he whispered.

The locking mechanisms of the shackles were primitive and simple. He had one foot free in seconds.

The chains rattled as she strained to watch. Her smile defied the gloom surrounding them; it's glow warmed Mouse as he worked.

"I knew you'd come," she said.

He hadn't been so sure. He glanced to Brom. One of the creatures was dead already. Its head and left shoulder sliced away. But when Mouse looked to the sorcerer this time, their eyes met. A smile snaked across his thin, parchment-dry lips. He pulled something from the sack at his hip as the second lock popped open.

Catja strained to look at what held Mouse's attention. "What is it?"

Mouse poised to dodge, expecting a knife or dart or something arcane, like a flask or powder, but instead, the sorcerer pulled forth a freshly severed hand. He pressed it to his lips like one gently kissing the hand of royalty, then tossed it onto Catja.

When it landed between her breasts, she screamed. "*Pahka*! What is it?" She flailed her legs wildly. "It's on me! Get it!"

"I got it," Mouse said, but when he moved to knock it away, the appendage rose onto its fingers and spun toward him, following his movements like a wary spider. He dropped the picks atop the altar and drew his dagger from its sheath. The hand crawled onto Catja's trembling stomach and raised itself up to hiss from a slit in its palm that created a malformed mouth.

"It's alive!" she screamed. "Get it!"

The hand-thing watched Mouse with three eyes that bulged from between its knuckles.

With an uncanny speed, it dashed and leapt from Catja's squirming body. The hideous mouth snapped open and shut as it flew toward his face, but despite covering his eyes with one arm, he managed to swat it down to the floor with his weapon hand. Where he'd knocked it to, he couldn't tell. He strained to detect its movement, but all sound was lost in the din of Brom's battle and the sorcerer's chanting.

When he glanced to find Brom, something grasped his ankle. Mouse began hopping around and kicking with his leg as if performing some macabre dance, but its fingers only tightened their grip. And he could feel that awful mouth chewing at the supple leather of his boot, trying to reach the flesh beneath. He smashed at it with the pommel of the dagger to no avail, then tried to pry it loose with his fingers. It immediately jumped to the altar and began crawling up Catja once more.

"It's here again," she shouted. "Get it off me!"

It scampered up her body and raised itself with pinky and thumb to hiss into her face.

She arched her body and kicked with her legs, trying to jostle it from her chest.

By that time, Mouse was there, smacking it away again. It landed but immediately bounded straight for his face once more. Mouse swung with his dagger, catching it mid-flight on his blade. It made a sound, a scream perhaps or another hiss, but the blade had entered its mouth and emerged from its back. As its fingers curled around Mouse's fist like the legs of a dead spider, he let the weapon drop and kicked it away.

He hurried back to the altar to find his picks to finish freeing Catja. When he looked to find Brom this time, the warrior stood over the second creature, the head of which had been split in twain. Brom and Bol-lag stared at one another over the corpse of the demon-thing.

Brom, however, looked as if he was straining against invisible chains. His muscles bulged with effort, yet all the sorcerer was doing was holding his open palm toward the big man.

"You meddle with things you do not understand," the sorcerer said.

"Your evil ends this day."

"Was I evil when I served the same cause as you, northman?" The sorcerer laughed. "Who are you to say what is good and what is evil?"

"You betrayed us." Brom spoke with more emotion than Mouse thought him capable of. "Taniel died!"

"Her cause was lost from the beginning. I simply chose not to follow her to its end."

"It was the path we were sworn to follow."

"I follow my own path, hero." The sorcerer spat the last word as if it was bitter or venomous. He then began drawing a symbol in the air with a finger that looked more a skeletal claw, and not only was it was longer, having an extra joint, it ended in needle-like points. Finished, he slid a bone dagger from his belt and sliced the back of the hand that held Brom at bay. Drops of blood coursed around his wrist and fell to the ground and seemed to hiss like fat falling from a spit. The air in front of the wizard shimmered, then three glowing symbols appeared, one atop another.

Brom shouted to his god but still could not move. His hate-filled eyes glared at the wizard. Mouse expected the sorcerer to laugh maniacally or gloat. Instead, Mouse would have sworn Bol-lag looked upon Brom with what may have been regret or pity.

"Mouse?" Catja's voice startled him back to his task.

He had one hand free, and as he began work on the other, he heard the wizard speaking in another strange tongue, one almost like a chant, but one that was dark and fuel for night-terrors. As the last restraint popped open, an anguished bellow filled the chamber, shaking Mouse to his bones, but he refused to look.

Catja slid from the altar into his arms. At any other time, he would have wanted the moment to last forever. She felt so soft and warm and alive, but he knew they had to get out quickly. Grabbing Catja by the wrist, he turned. The sorcerer glared at them. In one hand he held the bone knife; it and his arm was covered with blood up to his elbow. In the other hand, he held a blackened heart, small and shrivelled.

Brom lay dead on the floor behind him.

"Where are you going, little mouse?" His words were colder than ice.

Mouse placed himself between the sorcerer and Catja.

"Give me the girl," Bol-lag said, "and I promise you a painless, natural death."

"Go to hell," Catja shouted from over his shoulder.

"I wasn't talking to you, girl" he said without emotion. "How can you hope to win, boy, when that northern savage could not?"

Mouse could think of nothing to say.

The sorcerer barked a word and raised the heart toward Mouse, squeezing the remnants of the blood onto the stone floor. His first thought was to dive away and run for the exit. But, this time, he had someone else to think about.

"Run, Cat!" he shouted, grabbing the hilt of his knife.

As he did so, something struck him in his chest, right over his heart. It grew cold where it had struck and tried to force itself inside of him, but the iciness did not penetrate through his shirt. A moment later, it passed around him like icy water. If this was the same spell he used against Brom, he wouldn't be able to move. Then he too would die.

At least Catja had a chance.

The wizard approached, chanting, raising the bone dagger. Instinctively, whether to quell his fear or to provide a sense of security, Mouse's grip tightened on his knife hilt.

Did it?

He squeezed again. Yes – he could move! The spell, for whatever reason, had not worked.

The wizard approached and smiled.

"You had your chance. Now you will suffer a hundred lifetimes before I release you to spend eternity in the abyss as a hellfly, forever eating the dung of demon lords."

It took every ounce of Mouse's will *not* to move at that moment.

"Let him go," Catja said from somewhere behind him. "I'll stay. Willingly."

Mouse's heart sank. He'd hoped she'd fled when she had the chance.

"Too late for bargains," the sorcerer said.

Bol-lag used his bloody hand to pull open Mouse's jerkin and shirt and poised the bone dagger to strike. As he began chanting, his eyes fell to Mouse's exposed chest. "What!"

He stepped back, his eyes widening as if he'd glimpsed his own fate in the abyssal pits.

"The Eye of Kaleet! Where –" He reached for the bag at his hip. "How –"

Several things happened simultaneously in that instant

that kept Bol-lag from discovering the answers to his questions.

Mouse began drawing his knife from its sheath. He had a clear shot at either the sorcerer's throat or heart. Before the tip of the blade had cleared its holder, however, a blood-curdling cry filled the chamber, one that sounded more like the lonely cry of a panther at night than anything that could issue from a human throat, and a figure with a fiery mane blurred past him, quick as a cat launching itself toward its prey. An instant later, Mouse's discarded dagger materialized out of the sorcerer's throat, the hand-creature still clutching the cross-guard in its death embrace. Arterial blood pumped from his neck and mouth as he tried to continue his chant even as he fell to his knees and died in front of the naked girl.

Catja stared at the corpse as if she didn't understand how the sorcerer had died or why he was lying there.

Mouse took her by her hand and gently pulled her from that grisly scene.

V

Outside, he fetched a blanket from the pack and draped it around Catja's shoulders while she looked back into the gaping darkness.

Mouse stared with her.

He hadn't understood anything that Brom or Bol-lag had said to one another. He didn't think it had anything to do with the Hero's Path, though. It sounded personal, more like Brom was seeking revenge for something the sorcerer had done. Was revenge a heroic path? Revenge seemed too personal and selfish to be heroic. Was this the path Brom had him following all this time?

What if the Hero's Path was simply a story he'd made up?

But Mouse didn't feel angry. He didn't feel misled. And despite the thoughts he'd had of sneaking away, he missed Brom. It was like a piece was missing from him already, like there was a hollow spot deep in his chest. Brom wouldn't be there to tell him what to do, to help him, or to teach him. From this moment forward, everything Mouse did, every decision he made, every action he took, would be on him and him alone. He wanted to tell Catja how he felt, but he couldn't find the words. It would take time to find them.

If he ever did.

"I'm sorry your friend died," Catja finally said, seeming to somehow understand Mouse's plight.

"He was a hero," Mouse said. Maybe Brom had just forgotten that in the end.

"You're my hero." Catja tiptoed up to give him a quick kiss on the cheek.

Mouse didn't feel like one. He hadn't killed the sorcerer. And it was sheer luck he'd picked up that necklace. He lifted up the cat's eye stone to examine it. There was no doubt that it had belonged to Bol-lag and that it had protected him from the sorcerer's magic. Had Mouse known what it did, he'd have given it to Brom in a heartbeat. Instead, Brom was dead. Mouse couldn't think of much he'd really done at all.

"You came back for me," she added, once again seemingly knowing what he was thinking.

Well, maybe, he had done that. He'd tried to anyway.

Mouse shouldered the pack. It seemed to weigh more heavily than it had before.

"What now?" Catja asked, hooking his arm with hers. "Where do we go?"

SWORDS & SORCERIES

Mouse didn't have an answer. He looked away from the cave. The valley stretched north and south. Beyond the arm of forest that reached up into this hill, green pastures and a narrow stream glimmered and sparkled beneath the sun's brilliant light. In the distance, like a wall, stood a range of grey, white-topped mountains. Somewhere out there were the places about which he'd only ever heard: the fabled ports of Ming, the lofty minarets of Tomar – the so-called 'Glittering City' – and the desolate beauty of the steppes of Annasha.

Mouse smiled. There was no set path before them to follow, only endless opportunities.

"Anywhere we want to go," he said. "Anywhere we want."

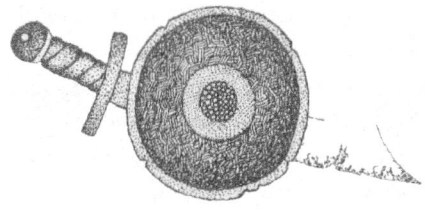

LITTLE LIVES ROUNDED BY SLEEP
Matt McHugh

"Another magnificent meal, master innkeeper!"

Tallen smiled as he cleared plates from a banquet table that could have seated two dozen but now served only himself, his daughter-in-law Mari, and their neighbours from the dairy, Ana and Kerchev. Kerchev hoisted his cup as he continued the compliment.

"You are the finest cook in the Southern steppes, perhaps the world! It's a pity you don't reopen this place."

"No thank you," replied Tallen. "Running an inn is endless work. I don't need it at my age."

"You may not have a choice," said Kerchev. "I hear that bastard Samo is on the move again, forcing local villages to feed and quarter his army."

Tallen heard Mari gasp—his own shoulders went tense—but he maintained a steady pace as he wiped a platter.

"Ale has stirred your imagination, my friend," he said. "Those are travellers telling tales to make their arrivals seem important. I'll have no more of it. Instead, let's all have custard."

The remainder of the evening lingered pleasantly until the guests bid their goodnights and teetered back to their farm, wading through grass that waved in the moonlight like a silvery ocean.

"Is it true?" Mari asked Tallen. "Do you think soldiers will come here again?"

"I've heard nothing."

"I'm worried, Dada. What if they take our winter stores? Or bring war with them?"

"What would you have me do?" Tallen snapped. "Go out and stop an army?"

Mari hung her head and Tallen regretted his tone. He took her hand and spoke gently.

"Samo is already king or kral—or whatever he wishes to call himself," he said. "We pay our levies to his collectors. He's already taken all he can from us."

Tallen's voice was edged with anger, but his heart whispered the wretched certainty he was, at least partially, to blame. He recalled the vision of Marjenko, his only child, as a young man. When Samo's horsemen first arrived—in their splendid black uniforms with gleaming silver buckles, leaping in and out of their saddles and crossing swords in showy jousts—Tallen was as seduced as any of the peasants. *Who will join us?* they cried. *Who will fight for the glory of your kral and protect your homes from the pillaging heathens?* Every young man lined up for the trials, but none excelled like Marjenko. Astride a galloping horse for the first time in his life as if he were born to it. Thundering over the field, spearing a target so squarely even the captain cheered. The pride that swelled in Tallen was like a swig of vodka that made him shudder then tingle with heat.

When the boy was chosen, Tallen did not rail or beg: *No! No, don't take him! He is newly married with a young wife and infant daughter. I need his strong arms and sturdy back in the kitchen of my inn, so I can make my money and pay your taxes. Choose another!*

Tallen said none of this. Instead he clapped the boy on

the shoulders and told Mari not to worry. Marjenko would be back soon, and draped with honours earned exclusively on the battlefield. These were Tallen's foolish thoughts of some five years ago as he watched his only child ride away, never to return.

*

"What are you doing awake, cricket?"

Tallen stood by the bed of his granddaughter, Simika, as she feigned sleep unconvincingly.

"I heard you and mama talking downstairs. Is it true soldiers are coming?"

"Complete twaddle. Grown-ups gossiping like children. Here. I have something for you."

"What is it?"

Tallen held up a mug. "Just warmed milk to help you sleep," he said, then produced a glass vial with green liquid, glowing emerald in the tallow light. "But also this. A special potion my mother first gave to me when I was your age."

"What does it do?"

"It brings dreams."

"What kind of dreams?"

"Only you can tell. Do you want to try?"

Simika's eyes went wide, glistening orbs where the single candle flame danced in double mirror. She made no sound, but nodded.

Tallen tipped a few droplets into the milk; the girl drank without hesitation. She leaned back into her pillow. Her eyelids drooped. Within a minute or two, she was swelling with the breath of sleep.

Tallen raised the green bottle and hesitated, mentally counting the years since he last tasted it. He sat on the bed beside Simika and took a sip. It was the smallest amount, only a single drop, but from long acclimation the effect upon him was profound. The potion's bittersweet tingle seeped into his blood and, without moving, he began walking along a dark passage, remembering a lifetime ago when he first followed his mother's voice into the labyrinth of shared thought.

Soon the sky brightened and grass grew beneath his feet. Simika was picking flowers on a small hill.

"Where are we, Dada?" she asked.

"In your dreams, of course."

"Magic!" she cried in delight.

"Magic is a word people use for something they don't understand. And I understand this very well."

Tallen formed an image in his mind, held it out to her like a wisp of vapor in his cupped palm. She took it, and a haze of purple blossoms erupted around them.

"Did you do that?" she asked.

"No. You did. This is your dream. Here we can exchange thoughts without even the need for words. But I can only suggest. What happens in this place is up to you."

"It is magic!"

"If that's so, then music that makes you dance is magic. Stories that bring laughter or tears, or a good stew that warms your belly and lifts your spirits, are all a kind of magic."

He took her hand and, together, they ascended, rising until they could see across the hills and forests, to the jagged mountains and the sea leagues beyond.

"This is our magic, passed down through our family. The art of visiting others in sleep to suggest images of peace and beauty." He leaned close and winked. "Why do you think we're such successful innkeepers?"

They drifted over the patchwork of farms, free as birds, slow as clouds.

"The skill is in you, granddaughter, but you must learn to use it. I can teach you how to make the green potion and how to enter the dreams of those who've tasted it. But now, I come to tell you I need to leave in the morning."

He felt the panic in her chest.

"No, Dada! Don't leave us!"

"I have to. I'll return as soon as I can. But we can still speak at night as you sleep. Because we are blood, we can commune over distance, connect in a way I can't to your mother. Will you answer when I call? Listen to what I say in your dreams?"

"I will, grandfather. I promise."

"Hold on to that promise. Make it steadfast in your heart now. In the morning, you won't remember these words. The thoughts of sleep and waking mix poorly, like oil and water. But strong feelings persist and can guide your actions, even when you are unaware."

*

Tallen set out before dawn, towing a wheeled cart with supplies. Sacks of coarse meal and fine flour. Stewed preserves and dried meat. Dozens of jars of herbs and spices. Knives and spatulas, pots and pans. A small keg of his best brown ale. And, hidden under loose planks beneath his bedroll, three bottles of green potion. His bent body and creeping age made pulling the cart a trial on the rutted road, but he kept at it. He wanted to be well away when Mari woke and found his note.

He passed other travellers. Single folk with rucksacks. Families in caravans. All moving West; he the lone

Eastbound. One even said to him:

"Don't go that way, brother. War is brewing."

He walked throughout the day. As the sun set, he saw a trio of horsemen up the road sporting the black sash and silver ring of Samo's mercenaries. They pushed into the brush and he heard the rustle and clatter as they made camp.

He dug into his cart, found some strips of dried beef. He rubbed them with safflower oil, cuts of fresh garlic and ginger. A few sweet chili flakes. He then took his cart and stomped to the encampment, calling out:

"My lords, forgive the intrusion! I fear there are robbers on these roads. May I rest near you for protection? I have no money, but can offer this."

He held out the beef strips. The men received them suspiciously, but after one sniff, their faces brightened. Soon they were roasting the sizzling meat on sticks over the fire and singing songs of praise to Tallen in their native tongue. Those songs turned to cheers as Tallen portioned out cups of ale, each secretly sweetened with a few drops of green potion. In no time, the three bid him goodnight and bivouacked on the ground. Tallen placed a drop of potion on his tongue. He closed his eyes and walked into the darkness toward their dreams.

He visited each in turn, common thoughts flowing easily where unfamiliar words would have stumbled. They were scouts, hired from the famed Eastern riders, to observe the movement of peasants, the gathering of armies, and report to Samo's generals. Tallen joked, flattered, and questioned as they revealed the roads they'd travelled, the battles they'd witnessed, and showed Tallen the direct route to Samo's fortified headquarters, unmarked on any map.

*

Tallen continued East through a second day until he approached the tents of a sprawling barracks, heralded by banners of black with a white ring. He was stopped by a pair of guards.

"Where do think you're headed, old codger?"

One gripped a sword with menace while the other began rudely poking through Tallen's cart.

"Blessings of the evening to you, officers! My name is Tallen, master innkeeper from the Great Crossroads, and I come to volunteer my service to the glorious forces of Kral Samo."

The two men looked to each other for a moment then simultaneously burst into laughter.

"Best for you to move on, uncle, before these 'glorious forces' get desperate enough to accept your offer." The one guard called to the other, rifling through Tallen's cart. "What's he got there, anyway?"

The second guard answered with a deep, lustful growl. "Food."

"Well then, you can volunteer that tribute and be on your way—and keep your scrawny ass alive."

"Gentlemen!" said Tallen as he boldly pushed past the guards. He stood by the back of his cart and began to mix ingredients in a bowl. "Would you steal brush and canvas from a painter? Chisel and marble from a sculptor?"

The men watched with fascination as Tallen chopped and minced and whisked and stirred, blending fat and flour, mingling bone broth and dashes of spice with showy flourishes. He scooped a ladleful and held it to the lips of the second guard.

"You see, I'm not here to fight, but to improve the quality of your repast."

The guard took a tentative sip, moaned, then downed

the remainder, wiping drops from the ladle with his finger. After an argument, both guards chose to embrace the risk of abandoning their posts rather than let the other take sole credit for discovering the kitchen-wizard.

The next evening, Tallen found himself overseeing the preparation of a meal for three-hundred men. Improving the quality the repast proved to be dunderously easy as the boys pressed into kitchen service had no idea how long a parsnip should be boiled or how much salt a human could tolerate. He insisted every tuber be thoroughly pulped and frosted with cheese. Waiting made the men surly, but they became models of gratitude when they received smooth flavoured mash where they expected a pickled turd. Tallen brewed batches of tea so each man got a snifterful spiked with dried fruit and a droplet of green potion. Within the hour, most of the camp was snoring comfortably.

Tallen walked among their dreams and learned where they hailed from and how they had been pressed into Samo's service. From the officers, Tallen saw their memories of maps and orders. In the West and South, wealthy landowners had formed alliances to reject Samo's rule and withhold his levies. In camps across the countryside, locals were being inducted and trained to march on the upstarts.

All this and more Tallen learned from the dreams of farmers and shepherds plucked from their fields to have sword and shield thrust into their hands. In each mind, Tallen stoked recollections of home and hearth, meadows and orchards vibrant in every season, and visions of children playing and women dancing at festivals. Wives and mothers, sons and brothers, people of common spirit spread wide across the great, rolling steppes.

*

Tallen had spent a week among the cooking pits of the training camp when a group of visitors came for the evening meal. They wore the black sash and silver ring, but also red cloaks and finely wrought vests of mail. When they removed their helmets, to Tallen's surprise, they were revealed to be women.

"Who are they?" Tallen asked an old warrior with a permanent scowl.

"Samo's private guard," he replied. "He's terrified of assassins and won't allow men into his presence, at least not unguarded by those vixens."

"They don't seem intimidating. They're quite lovely."

"Make no mistake, they have deadly arts to counter brute strength."

"Well then, I'd better see what they want." Tallen approached the red-clad entourage and bowed. "Greetings, protectors of our kral! I am Tallen, master innkeeper from the Great Crossroads and a kitchen worker of this camp. May I be of service?"

The one with the most ornate armour replied. "Greetings to you. My company and I ask for a meal, nothing different from what you serve the common men."

"That you shall have," he answered. "But I hope you won't deprive me of the opportunity to prepare a few extra dishes of greater sophistication."

"You do as you see fit, kitchen-master."

Tallen worked in a special frenzy by the back of his cart. The kitchen boys craned to watch as he sliced and stirred, pounded and chopped mysterious herbs, and tossed balls of coloured flame from a rounded pan held deep in the fire. As ladles of mush were portioned out, Tallen served the red sentries plates of flatbreads, cheeses, and puddles of dipping sauce. The women grew more relaxed with every bite and were soon elbowing one another and laughing at private jokes. As Tallen tried to clear the plates he was repeatedly intercepted by the guards' efforts to wipe up every smear of sauce.

"I'd heard rumours a genius chef had infiltrated the barracks," said the chief guard. "But I'd laughed them off until now. The court of Samo could use your service."

"Is that an order, my lady?"

"A denial would be disappointing." She yawned. "This unexpectedly good meal has left my company and I drowsy. We'll stay the night here. In the morning, I hope to have your answer."

"You will, defender of the kral. Sleep well."

*

That night, Tallen wandered through a dark maze until he found the chief of Samo's guard, sitting on the bank of a creek, dangling her bare feet in the water.

"Good evening, my lady," said Tallen. "Is this where you grew up?"

"No. It's a place I visited when I first joined Samo's service."

"How did you become a protector of the kral?"

"I was young, fast and strong," she replied, kicking her feet in the water. She stirred splashes that did not fall but hung in midair like soap bubbles. "I could beat most of the boys of our village in footraces or climbing trees. When the red-cloaked officers came looking for volunteers, I begged to join them. The training was strenuous."

Bruises appeared on her legs and arms. Across the river, Tallen saw a younger version of her, dressed only in tied linen, being repeatedly knocked down by a stout older woman wielding a long staff with frightening speed.

"But I learned," she continued. "I learned how to use skill to defeat strength. To use cunning to stop treachery."

She stood on a hill, the age she was now, her face graven with a weathered beauty. She was in her captain's armour walking through rows of guards as they rehearsed thrusts and parries. She struck those who lagged with a wooden staff until their form was perfect.

"It must be a great honour to serve Kral Samo," said Tallen.

"It was," she said. "I once saw him as a leader who unified many, who ruled with wisdom and restraint. Now all I see in him is fear and anger, like a sickness. He takes no pleasure in life and seems to hate any who do."

"Bring me to him."

"Here's so paranoid he won't let a man step within twice arm's length."

"I'm old," said Tallen. "I pose no threat. All I wish is to see people enjoy my food. Bring me to Samo. I can remind him that pleasure still exists, help return compassion to his heart."

"I almost believe you could."

"Believe it. Hold this thought and make it steadfast now. Come to me in the morning. Take me to Samo."

"As you wish, master innkeeper."

Tallen backed away, and left the captain to finish her dreams. He needed to finish packing, but had one more journey to make. He dared an extra sip of potion, just enough to extend his dream-reach, and submerged again into the darkness, calling out:

"Simika! Little cricket, where are you?"

He wandered until he saw a bubble of light, a vision within of Simika in her bed. Tallen knew the young are often so far in sleep they lay below the level of dreams. Yet, he might still reach her.

"Simika! It's Dada. Tell your mother if soldiers come, don't be afraid. Welcome them. Give them food. Let them sleep in the inn. Be generous with our stores. Hidden beneath barrels in the cellar is enough to get through the winter. Remember: welcome the soldiers!"

He repeated the message until Simika muttered, "Yes, Dada."

Tallen opened his eyes, stood up among the slumbering kitchen boys, and finished stowing his gear.

*

"Are you ready, kitchen-master?" said the red chief to Tallen as the morning sun rose behind her.

"I am, mistress," he replied.

"You may address me as Captain Strazah. Come along." She turned to her officers standing nearby and pointed. "Load to our wagons these sacks of meal and bushels of rice. Take those slabs of pork and crates of fowl as well."

The guards were loading the parcels when one of the camp's commanders pushed roughly into the group.

"What the devil is going on?"

Captain Strazah answered. "We're preparing to leave. Your cook has agreed to join Samo's court."

"And our supplies? Did they agree to join you?"

"They're needed at the kral's tent."

"You put every one of those sacks back." He stood tall, vastly overmatching Strazah in height and bulk, gritting his teeth in simmering, ursine rage.

"My authority supersedes yours, commandant."

"It's not enough you drag us from our homes to fight your wars, and now you would starve us as well?"

He elbowed his way among Strazah's guards and began slapping parcels from their hands. Instantly, he was ringed by a semi-circle of red-cloaked warriors, each holding forth one arm shielded by a heavy gauntlet, the other hand aiming a dagger. They stood ready, crouched like coiled serpents. The commandant unsheathed his sword with a wide arc and bellowed a vulgar threat.

From behind, Captain Strazah stepped up and lightly drew a gloved hand over his face. He registered an instant of confusion, then roared as four razor cuts began to bleed. He turned on Strazah and swung. She faded beyond his range and his blade bit into a heavy tent pole. Tallen felt the vibration of it through the ground underfoot.

The commandant swung wild and furious at Strazah. She dodged his blows with the grace of a dance, leaving steel whistling through air.

As the commandant blinked blood from his eyes, it became obvious to Tallen there was something more than razors in Strazah's gloved fingers. His thrusts became slower, his footing clumsy like a drunkard. When he stumbled, wedging his sword tip in the mud, Strazah swiped a dagger under his chin, releasing two fountains of blood. He collapsed very much like a sack of meal.

"Finish loading," she said to her guards. "Come, kitchen-master. You ride with me."

*

Tallen's first glimpse of Samo was inside a massive tent with carved poles and dyed silk banners. A red line of female guards formed a barrier with Samo on one side, a pair black-cloaked generals on the other. Samo was tall, gaunt, with a pallid face and bloodshot eyes. He wore a robe of purple velveteen and raked nervous fingers through his greying beard. He paced around a massive table, spread with documents and littered with scraps of food.

"The forest roads North and East are paths of treachery," he muttered. "Paths of treachery."

"Yes, my lord," said one of the generals. "We'll make sure they're patrolled."

Samo continued speaking as if to himself. "Nikita and Krylo are traitors. They build their own armies. Blue and green. Green and yellow. But their farms and beasts are weapons. Weapons! Do you hear?"

The generals exchanged bewildered shrugs. Samo aimed a venomous glare at them, but then his face went apathetic. He turned away, lying down on a couch with his back to the room.

"How long has he been this way?" asked Tallen.

"He's grown worse over the last few months," replied Strazah. "Can you help?"

"I need to know what he's eaten," Tallen said. "Let me approach now, while he's turned away. I'll be quick."

Strazah looked displeased but nudged Tallen though the row of red tunics. He carefully looked the table up and down to see the contents of the scattered plates. He went to Samo's privy bench, leaned over, and took a few sniffs. Satisfied, he started back toward the red line when he heard a voice:

"You're footsteps are wrong."

Tallen dropped to one knee. He peeked up to see Samo, still on his couch, but turned slightly toward him.

"I have crooked legs, my lord. I favour one side when I walk."

"Who are you?"

"My name is Tallen of the Woodland border, master innkeeper from the Great Crossroads."

"Great Crossroads," Samo said, rising. He leaned over the table, fingering the map. "Tell me, what's there."

"Farms, my lord. Fields of wheat and barley. Some orchards and vineyards."

"Cattle?"

"There are dairy farms, as well as ranches with large herds."

Again, Samo muttered inaudibly. Tallen raised his eyes and asked, "My lord, are you happy with your meals?"

"Are you trying to poison me?" he asked.

"No, my lord. My knowledge extends only to spices that make no one ill."

Samo waved a dismissive hand at his half-eaten portions. "Everything is dust."

Tallen walked past Samo to the table. He heard Strazah and her guards go tense. He emptied a plate then began to build it up with morsels chosen from others.

"Flavour, my lord, exists in contrasts. Sweet and savoury. Tangy and bland." As he spoke, he shredded strips of beef and venison. He shaved tendrils of apple and onion, crushed poppy and sunflower seeds with a spoon, then mingled them with flecks of clove into a bowl of red wine. He spread the ingredients over flatbread and drizzled the mixture. He curled the bread tight, cut the roll into segments each no wider than a stack of three coins.

"You," Samo said.

Tallen took one of the cuts and ate it. "Food, like life itself, loses its appeal if it never surprises."

Samo picked up a slice, chewed and swallowed. He took another. "Do what you will."

"Yes, my lord."

*

"He needs less meat, no cheese at all, and bread made only from rice flour. No wheat or rye. Tea is good, but from unroasted leaves. More fresh greens. More fish. And more wine."

Tallen stood before a trio of Samo's private cooks. One replied with disdain.

"Lord Samo favours bread and cheese. He craves red meat and despises fish."

"Not if I prepare it," said Tallen. "These are the foods he needs to recover his wits."

Outrage bubbled from the assembly. "He speaks treason!" bellowed one of the cooks.

"And stupidity," added another. "Wine recovers wits?"

"It needn't be strong wine," replied Tallen. "Juice from blackberries or beets will do as well."

The arguments spiked again. Strazah called over the din.

"I trust this man," she said. "I've seen the morale of common soldiers change after his food. I've eaten it myself, and it surpasses anything any of you have ever made. You'll do as he says. Any who object will answer to me."

*

"Simika! Cricket! Are you there?"

Tallen strained in the darkness for a glint of his granddaughter but found nothing. She was a child. Sleeping too deeply. That had to be the reason.

"Cricket, if you hear me, tell your mother I am well. I'll be home soon. I promise."

Tallen sat up on his sleeping pallet. He'd been directing the kral's food preparers for nearly a fortnight, delivering Samo a continuous rotation of small, diverse courses. His consumption grew daily, and Tallen was even permitted to wait upon him, passing unchecked into Samo's protected circle. Each time, Samo ignored him—though the generals banished to the perimeter eyed Tallen with envious mistrust.

One afternoon as Tallen assembled a tray of titbits, Captain Strazah entered the pantry tent.

"He's improving," she said. "I can see it, hear it in his voice."

"He needed variety," he replied. "Too much of any one thing puts us out of balance."

"Others tried, but he refused the changes."

"Change is easiest in increments that don't draw attention."

"Well, the legend of the kitchen-wizard has expanded again."

"I'm honoured to have helped. But I have an even greater variety of items in my cart. I was told it's not permitted to bring them here."

"That's correct," said Strazah. "No foreign items may be brought into the kral's galley."

"I've fed hundreds with my own stores—you, yourself, and your guards. You know there's nothing wrong with any of it."

"My guards have gone through your cart and found many items unknown to them. The answer remains no. I recommend you don't ask again."

Chastened, Tallen nodded. "May I take my cart to the soldiers' galley to help improve what's served to the men?" he asked.

SWORDS & SORCERIES

"I have no objection," replied Strazah. "Provided the progress you've made in improving the kral's health doesn't suffer."

*

Tallen was greeted by the kitchen boys like a returning hero. Digging deep into his cart, he portioned his every bit of seasoning and spice into measures strong enough to strike the tongue yet so miserly they covered thousands of meals. The morning porridge was tinted with anise. The afternoon borscht thickened with arrowroot and minced ham. In the evenings, braised cabbage with dill complemented a few strips of grilled meat. The day finished with tea, zested with exotic citrus and a dash of green potion.

In dreams, Tallen walked among the infantry, drawing them into a shared reverie on a wide, phantasmagorical field. Songs and good-natured jests abounded. Some lingered on the outskirts, haunted by memories of battlefield comrades who begged for life as they bled out. At Tallen's suggestion, the grieving summoned images of their lost brothers. Hands were clasped in forgiveness and farewells said in peace.

Tallen spent mornings preparing delicacies for Samo, afternoons making vats of slop palatable, and nights coaxing soldiers into seeing a world without enemies.

*

"You. Cook. Come here."

Samo called Tallen over as he brought in fresh servings. Tallen stepped onto the platform with the immense map table.

"You hail from the Great Crossroads?" asked Samo.

"Yes, my lord."

Samo pointed to the map. "And you say there is farmland here. And cattle here."

"To the best of my recollection, that is true."

Samo nodded, said nothing. His stillness made Tallen anxious.

"I do know, my kral, those lands are loyal to you. Your collectors are welcomed at each harvest."

"Yes, I've heard they are a very welcoming people," he said. He pushed an empty platter into Tallen's hands. "Bring more food and wine. My generals and I have much to discuss."

"My lord, do you plan to march on these lands?"

For perhaps the first time in their acquaintance, Samo looked at Tallen directly. Long and slow, cold and condescending.

"Go and return with more food and wine, and you will be thanked. Return with more questions and you'll be whipped."

When Tallen returned, he rearranged items to give the appearance of industriousness and listened.

"Archers with arrowheads wrapped in oiled linen can inflame the fields," said a general.

"The extra weight reduces the range of the arrows," replied Samo. "We need to set fire across a large area quickly. Have your Western scouts spread nets on trees as I ordered?"

"Yes, my lord. They report thousands of captured starlings and sparrows."

"Tie a length of twine to the leg of each bird," said Samo. "At the end, a bundle of smouldering tinder. When set free, the birds will return to their nests. In flight, the twine will burn and the bundles drop, setting off the dry grass."

"The locals may be able to beat out such small fires, my lord."

Samo shook his head. "Not if they're given no chance. Cattle driven in stampedes will clear the land."

"If the cows see or smell burning, they'll turn away."

"Blind them," replied Samo. "Gouge out their eyes and nostrils with daggers. Yoke them together then attach sleds with bales of burning hay. They'll run from the heat behind, trample anything before them, and spread more fire in their wake."

"Many may be killed, my lord."

"Quarter the carcasses and dump them into the streams and wells. Their rotting bodies will taint the water. All these lands must be rendered unusable."

"Yes, my lord."

As Tallen pretended to fill teacups, he became aware the conversation had ceased. He looked up to find Samo and the generals staring at him.

"Thoughts on strategy, master innkeeper?" asked Samo.

"Such things are beyond my knowledge, my kral."

"You said the people of these lands are loyal to me, did you not?"

"That was true when I last travelled there, my lord."

"It seems things have changed," said Samo. "My scouts report that forces bearing green and yellow banners have been welcomed throughout the villages of the Great Crossroads. Krylo and that lying bastard Alex the Lesser offer protection and decreased tariffs to anyone foolish enough to listen. Should I let such disloyalty stand?"

"I know nothing of such matters," Tallen said again.

"But, my lord, if you burn the land, destroy the farms, there will be nothing for your collectors. You'll lose wealth."

"Wealth only grows when invested," replied Samo. "And eradicating traitors is a sound investment, wouldn't you agree? Be glad you came to me when you did, master innkeeper, and left behind those treasonous lands."

"Yes, my lord."

*

"Little cricket! Where are you?"

Tallen was searching in the darkness—he had been for some time—but found no hint of Simika. He cast about as far and wide as he could, running through blackness calling to no reply.

"Simika, tell your mother to run! Leave the inn. Go South, away from the villages. Find a caravan and go all the way to the sea. You must leave the Crossroads!"

When Tallen opened his eyes, he knew he had only one option. He made his way out of the kral's compound to the barracks. The sentries, accustomed to his night wanderings, didn't question him. He found his cart—its supplies all but depleted—but still with one hidden bottle of green potion. He stowed it behind his apron and returned to Samo's kitchen.

Tallen warmed a cup of milk and dosed it with the potion. He whipped cream and egg white to a froth and layered it on top, adding shavings of cinnamon and vanilla. He pushed open the flap to Samo's tent.

As always, the red guard stood alert. Oil lanterns with silver filigree shades cast shadows throughout the pavilion. Samo lay on his couch, a bent arm resting over his eyes.

"My lord," said Tallen. "I saw the lights. Are you awake?"

"What do you want?" he moaned in reply.

"I've brought some warmed milk to help you sleep."

Samo sat up. "And what else?"

"Just milk. With some cream and flavour added."

Samo stood, walked toward Tallen.

"And are those flavours from the Great Crossroads?"

Before he was aware of what happened, Tallen felt his body driven to kneeling, guards twisting his arms into painful immobility. Samo loomed above, holding the cup of milk.

"It must worry you," he said, "that I plan to send my armies to your homeland."

"That is not my concern, my kral," replied Tallen, struggling to speak through the pain.

"You are either a simpleton or consider me one," said Samo. "Either way, I take offense. What did you put in this milk?"

"Nothing, my lord. Flavour only."

"I'll give you one chance, and more truth than you're giving me." Samo pointed and one of the guards reached behind Tallen's apron and fished out the green bottle. Samo held it before Tallen's face. "I had you followed as you left the kitchen and returned with this. What is it?"

"Just a tonic that helps bring sleep. I mixed it into the milk. It's harmless, my lord."

"We shall see," said Samo.

Tallen now found his head gripped and his neck bent back as gloved hands pried open his mouth like a baby bird. Samo tilted the cup of milk and the green bottle, pouring both into Tallen's throat. He clapped a hand over Tallen's mouth, forcing him to swallow it all. He felt himself shoved to the ground. As he lay gasping, he heard Samo say,

"If he survives, whip him and send him away."

Reeling from the quantity of green potion he'd been forced to drink, Tallen was dragged to the stables and flung into straw. When he looked up he saw several large, ugly men holding blacksmith's irons and scowling down upon him. As Tallen regarded them with no small measure of terror, Captain Strazah pushed between.

"Leave us," she said.

The men departed. Tallen remained on his hands and knees before Strazah.

"I meant no harm," he said.

"I know," she replied. "If anyone thought otherwise, you'd be dead."

"It won't happen again. I swear it, my captain."

"I know it won't. And I am not your captain."

Red guards bound Tallen's wrists and ankles and stretched his body across a low stump of wood. Tallen felt the shirt on his back cut away. Warm breath came close to his ear as Strazah whispered:

"You were warned, but you chose to make a fool of me. Now I have no choice. Be still and it will be over soon."

Tallen felt the first blow before he heard the sound. A long branch, cut from a sapling, whistled through the air and sliced into his back. For a moment, he felt relief. It could have been a steel chain or a heavy club. But as it came down over and over, every stroke freshly tearing his skin, Tallen lost any sense of being fortunate.

This has to be the last, he hoped as each blow landed. He thought of Captain Strazah. *She has to know she's made her point. This has to be the last. This has to be the last.*

Tallen lost consciousness before the beating stopped.

SWORDS & SORCERIES

*

He awoke in a ditch by the road outside Samo's encampment. Judging by the position of the moon, dawn was still hours away.

Tallen struggled to his feet and began to stagger forward. The skin on his back was raw and ripped. Blood seeped into the seat of his britches, and his shirt hung in useless shreds against the Autumn chill. Off the road, he noticed a switchback path ascending a small cliff. He began to climb, skidding on loose dirt and gravel, until he reached the crest.

The peak was not especially high but afforded a wide view of the valley. In the moonlight, he could see the formal avenues of Samo's encampment and the rougher paths of the common barracks. Peppered throughout both camps were night watch fires.

He had seen such a view many times before, not with his own eyes, but in the dreams of his son.

Five years ago, Marjenko had been quartered with the other recruits, rousted each sunrise to train with wooden swords and headless spears. At night, cold and exhausted, he would lie beneath threadbare canvas, shoulder to shoulder with his battered fellows, and try to find rest. He'd managed to keep hidden the flask of green potion Tallen had given him and, sometimes before sleep, he would take a nip.

In their shared trance, father and son would speak without words, exchange visions in the dark. Tallen felt the weariness, the disillusion in his son's heart, and he did his best to bolster it.

Courage, my boy! he would call over the distance. *Hardship summons your strength. When you return home, you'll possess a greatness of spirit others will envy.*

SWORDS & SORCERIES

When real fighting began, all the blood he saw spilled, each death he witnessed or caused, did indeed harden Marjenko's spirit. Tallen felt his son's heart become layered with scars and callous, growing less and less familiar. When, at last, an arrow pierced the boy's guts, he lay for day and a night, abandoned on a corpse-strewn battlefield. Tallen cradled his son's fading consciousness and whispered lies of comfort.

Don't be afraid. Everything is alright. I'm here. And look! Your mother is here, healthy and whole, like when you were a child. Your wife and daughter are waiting for you. Rest, my boy. We'll all be together soon. Rest.

Now, as Tallen gazed over the camps of Kral Samo with his waking vision, he trembled in shame and burned with rage. He closed his eyes, paused at the edge of the familiar darkness—then, with a howl of wrath, exploded into it.

Like a cloud of black ash vomited from a volcano, Tallen shaped himself into a nightmarish titan, astride the valley from horizon to horizon, the slumbering thoughts of a thousand fighting men glittering before him like emeralds in the mud. Whether from pain or fury or the potion Samo had forced down his gullet, Tallen felt a dream-strength beyond any he had ever known.

Reaching into wells of grief he had never before let himself feel, Tallen amplified his every imagined horror, blowing on embers until they birthed jets of flame, and—in every mind within his reach—he ignited fear.

You all will die, he whispered venomously. *Speared and slashed. Burned and smothered. Flayed and gutted. And not just you! Your wives and daughters, infants and elders, tortured because of your failures.*

Next, he spread betrayal.

Your generals and captains, your princes and kings,

trumpeting the glories of war and the will of the gods. Liars! Thieves and cowards, herding you over cliffs, stealing your lives and lands to enrich their own.

Finally, he gave them urgency.

Up! Now! Awake! They are upon you! Fight! Kill them now or die!

Tallen allowed himself to shrink, becoming again a wounded little man. When he opened his eyes, fire was already spreading in the camps below. He could hear the screams, the clash of weapons and cries of alarm, as men infused with dream-madness set upon each other and drove toward the pavilion of Samo.

Tallen lay on the ground, exhausted. When he woke, the midday sky was shrouded with smoke. In the valley, canvas and timber smouldered like skin and ribs in a holocaust pit. The silk of Samo's great tent was still aflame, its entry arch skewed and blackened. In a semi-circle nearby lay two score bodies, clad in the grey tunics of common men. Mixed throughout were hacked corpses in red cloaks. At the centre, spitted on a trio of lances, was figure in a regal purple robe. His head and harms hung down like a goat suspended over an exsanguination trough.

Tallen permitted himself one mirthless smile at the massacre he'd wrought, then once more, he lay on the ground. If there were any gods looking down, if any form of justice or mercy still existed, Tallen presumed he would never awaken.

*

"Dada! Dada, wake up!"

Tallen saw Simika beside him on the rolling fields by the Great Crossroads, the thatched roof and whitewashed walls of his inn standing out against the tree line.

"Where are you?" he asked.

"Home. Mama and I are home. Everything is alright."

As they walked through the town, Tallen saw armed men under banners of green and yellow leaning against the fences, drawing water from the well for their horses.

"What are they doing here?"

"They came days ago," Simika answered. "They offered to pay for food and lodging. They said they would protect us from the black flag invaders. All the elders welcomed them."

"You welcomed these soldiers into the village?"

"Uncle Kerchev said they stopped the war from coming."

"I see."

"When are you coming home, Dada?"

"I may not be able to, cricket."

"But you promised!"

"I'm not the same man who left a month ago."

"You said you would teach me how to make the green potion! How to share dreams. You promised!"

Simika took his hand, openly weeping. All around the landscape drained of colour, the very earth and sky speaking the language of heartbreak.

"I no longer trust myself to teach you," he answered, unable to hold back his own tears.

"I trust you," she said.

"You don't know, child. You don't know the cruelty of this world."

"Come home, Dada. Teach me our family's magic. Please."

"I don't know if I deserve to."

"Promise me."

"I'll try."

"Promise me!"

"Alright. I promise, little cricket. I promise."

Simika whooped for joy and ran along the crossroads, fragrant blossoms of colour sprouting like musical notes in her wake.

*

Tallen woke in the dark, the smouldering air pungent with death. He made his way down the hill to the road, wincing with each step. At this pace it might take three or four days to get home.

Best to travel at night, he thought. And sleep in the day to be alone with his dreams.

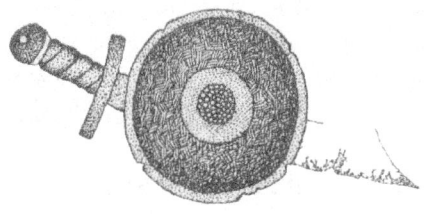

WARDARK AND THE PIRATE KING
Craig Herbertson

The fiefdom of Serpania fell to the Sudron hordes long ago, stranger. The port itself was drowned by a sea god in the age of the Monkey Lords, or so the ignorant say. Come here, girl, and bring wine for our wealthy client! Come quick! But the fiefdom is written of in books bound in human skin, a repellent practice from ancient Danresh. Come, come, I allow few people access to this room. Here in my librarium, there are many tales of Serpania but few of its forest for good reason. Why do you seek the forest? Only a fool would go there. A god might...they say one Wardark, a reiver, entered that forest in the age of the gilded swan and returned, but many tall tales are told of Wardark by the northerners...

The Inn at the port of Serpanam

The Inn smelt as though a pack of Gobeln had died and their unburied corpses lay on the straw strewn floor. It was a foetal stink, a blend of rotted fish and unwashed bodies, of putrefying perfumes, of badly cured leather and rusting steel, of sweat and pain and foul smoke. Through the retched fumes, closeted under the dark eaves of a snug, a grizzled mercenary clad in dull armour sat in huddled conversation with a whore whose oiled body reflected the dim light of waxed candles. Near the bar counter, a dwarf danced on a large table spiked with daggers and laden with the flagons of pirates who roared drunken encouragement;

a raucous revelry that drowned the eerie cries of night birds on the docks. The din suddenly ceased as the dwarf fell besotten to the floor and the pirates, tired of baiting, desisted.

There was the kind of lull that seems to fall in loud and unpleasant places at moments of unusual and peculiar significance. They are soon gone like the glimpse of a white butterfly among white flowers or a single black fly amongst a host of flies on a bloated corpse.

In the lull, a gust of wind rattled the shutters and swept under the portico where, in times past, all weapons were laid before entering the inn. To go unarmed now, in the dark days of the gilded swan, was to invite robbery or death. Neither of these prospects appealed to Scranwraith, the mad pirate king, whose leather jerkin bristled with daggers. He grinned and turned to his first mate.

"I see before me a man and a boy, and the boy does the talking. What do we make of this?" he said "The boy with his blond hair has the look of a Smaragdian or a tyke from the southern Vandergan, the man, why he stands a tumbler over my head, not a giant but well formed. Look at this hardy frame, observe these steely muscles - more like an acrobat from the southern courts. Yet the boy speaks for him?"

"I am no boy but a man!"

"A prentice sorcerer then with the man under a spell. Observe his eyes, reddened and glassy, his jaw slack; his haggard features and tangled black hair. He has the look of a beast."

"I am no sorcerer. This is my uncle, whom we call 'Deadeye' as he is simple; has been so since birth; strong as an ox though. He obeys my every command."

"And you wish to sell him? Your familial concern is touching."

"He is a burden to me. My family are all dead. His soul is dead. I have ambitions."

"Well, we will have him for a galley slave." Scranwraith turned to the first mate with a gesture. The first mate placed his drawn sword to the throat of the boy. Two more pirates had come forward ominously.

Scranwraith laughed. "Ambitious, my lad! Well, we will have you too. Welcome to your new family. You can instruct your cousin by demonstration. You need not even talk." The boy struggled hopelessly as he was grabbed by powerful arms as a sack was pulled over his head. The man with the dead eyes stared vacantly ahead.

The Inn at the Edge of Serpanam

Wardark son of Wevan threw his hand in the air to halt the six riders behind him. The only sounds were pregnant with stillness - the champ of the horses, the drip of rain and the wind idling through the thin band of trees.

Wardark had led the reivers on the Smagardian horse from the sands of the sea witch to their secret path through the hidden ravine and atop the crags to the seacrag forest where they had left the lulling waves behind with the funeral pyres and the fluttering flame-like memories of dead comrades. Down the grey scree slopes whose harsh shining stones echoed the scales of the deadly sirens, where the land flattened to low hillocks and the screams of the dying could die like ripples on a lake. Now the forest had thinned. Before the reivers, the vast wasteland of the Moersmrag marsh stretched, an eerie plain shrouded on the south by the Forest of Serpanam; a plain where the wind rippled on the marsh grass in mournful circles; where dark birds, almost too distant to see, speckled the sky, cawing like lost souls and where the far-flung mountains of Moerland seemed to merge into the bleak grey clouds.

The desolate landscape had two immediate features: the straight Smagardian road, marked by posts, built in distant ages beyond memory, with arts unknown and the equally desolate Inn, which stood in black silence a few leagues from the forest. The ruins of an outbuilding on this road were smouldering and a thin wisp of smoke struggled through the drizzle, wefting with the light wind.

From the shade of the trees, Wardark leaned forward and patted the haunch of his horse. "You have done well. That was no easy climb. You have all done well, men! This road leads to the Southwestern slopes of Mount Vander. From there, the trail over the Haken ridge is clear. Who will volunteer to return to our village with news of our quest and tell the tale of the dead?"

"I will, if no other," said Wilver. He pulled his horse up to Wardark. Typical of the Vandergan reivers, he was blonde and grey eyed, broad in the shoulder, slim of hip and long of leg; like all reivers, a well-formed man but now gaunt, thin and pale of face. He had lost two brothers in the battle with the sirens, and their evil spawn had nearly sucked the life blood from his veins on the beach. Much of his usual enthusiasm for brawling had waned.

Wardark nodded. "The sea witches say the Forest of Serpanam can only be traversed on foot. Wilver, you will take the horses if you can as a wergild for the dead. Tell our kin folk of their deeds in the Siren battle and their slaying of the corrupt Smaragdian king and his knights. Of the evils that befell us, I leave to your discretion. No wife or mother cares to hear of dark arts and sad endings."

The reivers dismounted and gathered the horses in a group. Wilver took Wardark's stallion to lead the others.

They watched as Wilver cantered across the fields towards the road and with a single wave, bid them farewell. Then, crossing the rough hillocks covered in sparse marsh grass, they came to the outbuilding. As they drew closer they observed the heads of two Smaragdian serjeants on poles before the smouldering outhouse. Below them, their rotting corpses still clad in filthy green hose and studded leather jerkins, lay in a bloodied heap. But beyond the outhouse in the kaleyard of the inn, there were other corpses, scattered where they had fallen, necks broken, bodies gnawed and savaged. Food for scavengers.

They approached, and dark birds whirred, cawing into the air. The reivers nocked arrows to their bows and spread to form a protective crescent behind Wardark as he advanced to the field. Wardark made a gesture to red-haired Vanyan and the tall reiver split from the others to make a wide sweep around to the rear courtyard where the horses would be stabled. Banen the bald ran swiftly to a well beside a low stone wall. He looked down and signalled that it was clear. His cousin, Evern, drew in at Wardark's right shoulder with his lighter bow at the ready. All eyes were on the Inn. It was typical of the Smaragdian buildings of the era of the gilded swan, a rectangular shape with a ground floor and an upper floor surrounded by a balcony adorned with wooden balustrades and the whole protected by low stone dykes. On the lower floor the large shutter on the left-hand side hung open, the other lay broken on the ground. The door too had been torn from its frame. On the balcony above, a man hung from the balustrade by the feet, his flayed skin draped from his body, a grotesque red cloak that fluttered like a limp flag in the light breeze. There were other corpses, projecting from the upper windows and laid about the balcony still clutching bows and daggers, frozen in their death throes. Three grotesque Gobeln lay dead amongst the others.

"How do you read this cousin Evern?"

Quietly, Evern replied. "The Smaragdian serjeants were slain some days ago, probably when we toppled the king; their heads have been pickled and their bodies lie unburied like thieves. The others, villagers, young, old, women, men; they were slain by beasts; an outpack of Gobeln. Their death is recent but their bodies have not been eaten." Evern paused, not taking his eyes from the open windows, the roof of the Inn. "The serjeants were killed by the villagers; the villagers were slain by Gobeln this morning."

Wardark nodded grimly. "They are near."

Dinner Hour

Raucous laughter intruded on his dreams. A beating, aching head dragged his dreams to oblivion and then he woke. The boy reached his hands up to clutch his temples and was suddenly aware with a shock that he could not move his arms. He was wet, he was freezing, he stank. Slowly, he opened his eyes. He lay in the hull of a ship, up to his thighs in foul smelling water that spilled back and forward with the movement of the ship. A single beam of light seeped in from a slit in a wooden wall and crept from the chinks in a trapdoor to the right of him. From the trapdoor a gangway descended. Naked, a spears length away and staring directly at him, was his uncle.

They were both chained to posts.

Memory returned. The Bangrel pirates had knocked him out after a violent struggle. He vaguely recalled being bounced down the gangway. It was not simply his head that ached; it was his entire body. He stared for a second at the immobile figure of his cousin until he drifted back into unconsciousness. He woke again to darkness and drifted back into horrible dreams. Then, after an indeterminable time, a glaring light roused him. Two pirates, dressed in gaudy outfits, sauntered down the gangway and approached with drawn knives. He saw their hooped gold earrings and tattooed faces grinning at him. One came so close his spice-flavoured breath tickled his face. They unmanacled him from the post but organised the chains behind his back, imprisoning his arms.

"Come now, little man. Summon your big friend and tell him to come with us quietly. If you do not," said one drawing the knife to his eye, "we will have some fun with your face. Who needs eyelids when sleep is a rarity?"

Surrounded by laughing pirates, the boy and the man were led to the lower deck. Here they saw some forty ragged men chained to their benches. The men were naked to the waist. All were thin but with muscles like raw rope and eyes of varying hopelessness. There were some empty benches as the Bangrel pirates were known to punish their own crew with a day or two on the oars. But for the moment the oars were up for refitting. At the top of the second gangway stood the mad pirate Scranwraith in all his pomp. At the foot of the gangway stood a grossly fat pirate, naked to the waist and wearing a flop hat that accentuated his single glaring eye. At his bulbous feet was a huge cauldron. He held a ladle in his hand.

"Come," shouted Scranwraith. "It is time for all ambitions to be realised. Boy! Happily, you have been promoted to barmaid. Your large friend can carry the cauldron while you serve our guests. Beware though, their hunger can occasionally erupt in vulgar manners." He laughed uproariously at his own humour as Deadeye lifted the cauldron with ease. The boy gave a reluctant signal, and the hapless Deadeye drew up to the first bench where the slaves, less than human, screaming and crying in desperation, reached out with clawed and gnarled hands for the pale soup he carried.

The Well.

Wardark stood on the balcony of the Inn. Leaning on the balustrade, his keen eyes penetrated the darkness, gazing fixedly down the road to the north. It was deep in the night. He had dozed for an hour only to be roused by Banen the bald for the watch. Sleep evaded him. The air was pregnant with forebodings. The light wind had dropped and a preternatural stillness had seeped from the earth. He gripped the balustrade. The stink of the dead permeated his nostrils. Wardark was accustomed to violence but he had no taste for it, especially the deaths of villagers, of old men and young women, of infants and children. The Gobeln outpack had taken them unawares. They had fought but the Gobeln beasts were merciless and indiscriminate. The villagers had been slaughtered in the night.

On a night such as this.

Wardark rested and stroked his left cheek, a habit when there was thinking to do. It was clear that the Gobeln were on the move. These Smaragdians were unlike his pure barbarians, the reivers of the north, but they were a simple folk deserving a simple life, not a hard death. The Gobeln had attacked the many villages of the Vandergan along the harsh Northern coasts and the outreaches of the mountains. Another man would have felt satisfaction in his part in that affair. The killing of Gobeln, his race to the mountain to set the watch fires along the mountain tops. But Wardark was not such a man. He was son of Wevan, a reiver of great renown who had travelled far across the swamps and over mountains protecting his people. He was a warrior, a hunter. Once as a boy he had trailed a band of Danresh slavers over the Moreland mountains with his father. The slavers had captured several of the women of the village to sell abroad. Three days they had followed their tracks to the edge of the Eastern desert. It was land unseen even by his father, but the need was great. They had left the bodies of nine slavers to stain the sands with their blood and retrieved all of the women. Wardark smiled a rare smile. It had been harder to bring the women back than to kill the slavers who had taken them.

Wardark recalled with a fondness his father, now a prisoner or dead at the hands of the pirate king. There were women of his village with them, if not already sold in the port of Serpanam. That was unlikely, the pirate would take the women to the fleshpots of the south, a region of which Wardark knew nothing. But like that great journey through the desert with his father, he would rescue the women, or he would die in the doing.

Wardark gripped the balustrade tighter. He looked to the shadowy figures of his warriors who had elected to sleep in the open away from the fetid air of the Inn.

They needed action.

Wardark needed action. Death inspired that desire. Action would come soon, he thought. He sniffed the air. His mind trailed back through the strange events which had brought him here: The attack of the Bangrel Pirates and the sudden invasion of the deadly Gobeln horde. He could still feel the clash of his blade against the pirate king Scranwraith. Still feel the exultation when the lit fires had summoned the Vandergan to arms. Then the despair of the sucking spawn of the sirens and his succour by the voluptuous sea witch, the death of her daughter at the hands of the Siren Queen. His killing of that monster, the death of his friend, Giant Farwood: Death, death and destruction. It lay behind him and lay ahead; so he had gleaned from the words of the Wizard Xianthus in the depths of the Vandergan mountain; those words that now seemed an age away.

As if on a mummer's cue Wardark heard a low and sibilant call. He was instantly alert. Of a sudden he became aware of a strange light a few spear lengths away from where the reivers slept. The light grew like the slow emanation of luminous fireflies in the gloaming hour.

It came from the well.

Like a cat, Wardark descended from the balustrades and down the supporting timber to the ground. Some instinct prevented him from waking his men. Quietly, he moved towards the well where the light retained a constant luminosity. His sword, reiver fashion, was slung on his back but he drew his scrim dagger and cautiously peered over the edge. The well stank. Corpses had been tossed in it, but he could not see them as the light came only two spear lengths below in the wall of the well and beyond the light was the deep shadow of the depths. There was an opening, invisible in the day, but now the light which it formed was a clearly defined ellipse. Some kind of hidden tunnel built for dangerous times. Wardark listened with ears that could distinguish between the call of a male or female marsh finch. Nothing. He listened again and looked to the rope hanging from the winch. The bucket had no doubt joined the corpses in the well. He pulled tightly on the rope. It would hold his weight.

What enchantment led him? It was as though he had no

choice. He warned none of the sleeping reivers, but instead took a firm grip on the rope and, knife between his teeth, began to descend. A spears length from the gap he thrust his feet from the opposite wall, let go of the rope and caught it again as he fell and propelled his body feet-first into the glow of the hidden tunnel. The gap was wide enough to allow him a half crouch as he landed, poised like a wild beast to attack.

Before him, in the luminous light, was a small statue of what might be a child or a gnome. The light emanated from its whole naked body but intensified in a nimbus around the shut eyelids. Wardark stared with total incomprehension. He could see nothing but black behind the luminous face. It was as though his senses were turned tapsalteerie and he stared downwards into another well instead of vertically into a tunnel. And then the hairs on Wardark's neck bristled as the statue's eyes opened and a piercing luminosity almost blinded him before fading again. To his astonishment a living face seemed to cast itself on the stone head.

It was the face of Xianthus, the wizard of ten thousand years. The eyes flickered and the mouth opened.

"Aaah, Wardark." The voice was feeble, almost beyond auditory range. "My powers are so weak here. I see nothing but I sense you near."

Wardark did not reply. He took a slow step backward and gripped his knife.

"Wardark, I sense your concern. I will not call it fear." The voice was husky and broke apart to nothingness before emerging again with more clarity. "Approach a little closer, I cannot maintain this bond. The pain of ten thousand years is no easy matter and this spirit vehicle! It is like communicating through an insect!"

Wardark took a tentative step forward. "Xianthus," he

said. "If it *is* you or not some abominable spirt of the well."

"Ahaa, Wardark. "The face overlaying the stone head broke into a cracked smile. "The spirit of the well *is* here, roused by the agonies of the recently dead, hence my mastery over it and this limited means of communication. Come a little nearer. This feeble spirit cannot harm you."

Wardark took the chance so that his face was close to the lips of the statue and its fading voice. He could see the yellowed and wrinkled face cast over the stone like a patina, the appalling pain-filled eyes of the wizard Xianthus as they searched blindly about.

"How goes our quest, Wardark? Your travel to me is like the dance of the seven veils, I see you then I see you not..." The voice faded and then returned. "...the sea, then an inn near the forest of Serpanam. How come you here?"

Wardark trusted the wizard not a whit. "The ship sank. I still venture onwards as you demand."

"Do not play, Wardark." The voice suddenly grew stronger. "I know you seek your father but forget not that I saved the Vandergan, to your eternal renown. Your way lies to the southern shore of Franken.

"I know," replied Wardark dryly. "A tomb of marble and gold beneath the sacred altar in the arch cathedral of Menolops the Gaunt. A distance apparently so far that I may die of old age on the way. As a boy, my father warned me not to talk to strangers. I did not listen."

"Ten thousand years of agony has muted my humour, Wardark," replied Xianthus through agonised lips..." The wizard began to expound on the quest which Wardark had agreed to take in exchange for the rescue of the Vandergan villages. Continually, the voice faded in and out, growing hoarse and then ratchety, at once strong and then ancient as though lips were rejuvenating and then withering like those of a dried-out mummy. "The silver chain," it intoned. "The silver chain must be taken." The voice dwindled to nothing and then abruptly roared out so loudly that Wardark drew back. "You must flee here now, now! The Gobeln come," hissed Xianthus. "Through the forest of Serpanam they will follow you. There, a broken bridge leads to the Starborn Temple of Lovers. Beware the waters of that lake, beware…for…. seek the Starborn waterfall…" And here Xianthus's voice whispered out to oblivion.

As if in dissonant reply to that tortured, unrhythmic voice, the sound of a horse, faint beyond the range of audition, came to Wardark. It was an intuitive knowledge born of his wild reiver instinct. An ordinary man, and even the best of his warriors, would not have heard it. But Wardark son of Wevan, did. And he knew the horse. With a wild shout he turned from the dimming statue, leapt from the tunnel to the rope and swung upwards.

"Rouse Reivers! Rouse!"

Vandergan Girl

Lying in the bilge water, the boy cradled the corn doll. His head beat to the sound of the shipwrights repairing the slaver's galley. It would be ready to sail to the Sudron ports in a few days. His uncle, Deadeye, stared fixedly ahead with uncomprehending eyes. Both were covered in scratches and abrasions from the gnarled, desperate hands of the galley slaves. But it was not the pain from the bruises and the cuts that troubled the boy; it was the eyes of the girl he had seen as he struggled down the gangway to the hold. Her eyes were the grey of the Vandergan. They were tear stained and red now though as she peered fearfully through a small slit. The boy had poised for a second, feigning a coughing fit and resting his hand next to the slit. As he looked up again, a delicate hand dropped the corn doll to his palm. He clasped it, then he felt the slaver's stick hit his back as he roared his annoyance. "Move boy! Sleep is a luxury here!"

The boy stumbled down the stairs quickly, hiding the corn doll in his breechclout. He heard the soft susurration of sobbing women rise above the lapping waves.

There were many captured women on board the slaver but now, in his mind's eye, he could only see one.

The Gate to the Forest of Serpanam

Wardark was the first to reach the edge of the Forest of Serpanam. Strung out behind him, the reivers of the Vandergan cast their shadows on the cobbled road as the sun rose to pierce the mist-clad mountains of Moerland. Wilver was the last, mounted on a dying horse, his head still streaming blood, his face pale and gaunt. Evern, the boy, fell to the ground, and lay on his back, his breath coming in sharp gasps. They had been running for hours.

Slowly, the older reivers gathered around Wardark as he paused before the impenetrable hedgerow that towered above him like a barrier reef between the kingdom of Smaragd and the Forest of Serpanam.

The apparently impassable mass of ancient trees, whorled and gnarled with time and supported by great swathes of prickly bushes and giant stinging weeds, was penetrated by a single odd gateway. Wardark looked bemused at the familiar pear shape. Where had he seen it last? It was made of stone, carved from a single adamantine block by some incredible forgotten art. The stone was burnished and unmarked in all but the top section where a great hole had been gouged. Then Wardark recalled the exit from the chamber of the imprisoned Xianthus in Mount Vander. The architecture of that exit was the same but there had been a burning red jewel in the apex. Clearly, at some distant age, thieves had worked a miracle to remove the jewel.

Wardark approached the gateway. Even with a pale sun now shining directly on it, the entrance was shrouded in gloom, as though something living was building a mist of material dark. As he approached, a very faint music seemed to emerge from the very centre of his being. It was a sound beyond a sound, a caged melody buried in tombs of silence, like the cold music of the distant spheres of the heavens a million miles out of reach; the tune agonisingly familiar. With its mockery of melody, a slightly musky smell drifted from the dark. It was a smell of corruption, but corruption enjoyed epochs ago and now dank and dead.

Wardark's men looked troubled as he drew back.

"We have no choice," he said. "The Gobeln come even now. Wilver speaks of many, so many that he comes wounded on a dying horse to warn us, knowing our peril. In the open we would take many of them with us to the underworld but beyond this hellish gate the sea witch told of a narrow path. We may lose them, or at least this poisonous forest will guard our flanks."

Wilver dismounted in agony and with a quiet word his horse walked away towards the marshlands. Evern rose to his feet.

Wardark faced the gate undaunted. Without a word he took a spear, a weapon rarely used among the reivers, and poked it around the massed cobwebs surrounding the mouth of the gateway, disturbing lizards and bats. With his men gripping their swords tightly, he pressed onwards.

SWORDS & SORCERIES

The Forest

On the first day Wilver died of his wounds.

The path was torturous as though designed by a madman; an impregnable forest of prickly bushes and low stunted trees dwarfed by giant and ancient quaking aspen. At times, they slashed huge, dank ferns to make a way; at others, they climbed fallen trees in darkness and then, of a sudden, they would break into a clearing where the sun shone through and stone structures would rise in tottering ruin, aged beyond the ken of man, built by people so estranged from them that their depictions on the ruined walls seemed almost surreal. At one such they piled stones on Wilver's body. The reivers drew their swords and raised them in the air, staring up at the banks of trees rising up to the west to the peaks of the seabound mountains. They left without a word, wondering at the clammy, almost living feeling of the stones they had laid over their comrade.

On the second morning Banen the bald was bitten by a bright red spider and, big as he was, collapsed in moments into a fever which threw him into delirium. All that day they took turns to drag him along on an improvised litter as the bestial whoops and cries of the Gobeln grew closer and closer. They marched on through the night and when the mist rose in the morning, Banen the bald woke. He spoke of crazed dreams where a witch of unsurpassable beauty taunted him, blinding him with a translucent blue light and then burning him in red fire when he approached her. He was weak but water from a fast-flowing mountain stream revived him, and they pressed on. The road ceased its circuitous route and became of a sudden a broadly paved path. The trees here drew back from this and even though ages had passed, something of their architected grandeur remained. To the West the forest banked sharply up the mountains to looming cliffs. To the East the forest spread like a great hoary carpet beyond their vision. Before them at the end of the large, cracked paving stones that stretched like a chequer quilted scarf, the distance showed a spherical dome that rose above the giant trees.

Wardark squinted. There were a few hours before the sun would go down.

"We must reach that patch where the forest seems to encroach on this path. There we will make a stand."

Behind them, the terror of the Eastern wastes, the guttural fetid beasts, the raving Gobeln sounded their ravening cry.

Captives of the Pirate King

A dark figure emerged from the depths of the galley, slipped up to the slave deck where huddled broken forms lay with their heads drooping on the benches. From here it crawled slowly up the gangway until it reached the halfway point. Above, under the light of the moon, the mad pirate Scranwraith stood on the gangway to the upper deck, legs akimbo, one large hand gripping the balustrade, the other a leather whip.

"Gather round, brethren!" he cried. His garishly tattooed officers leapt to his side, drawing their swords to make a fence of steel around him. The Bangrel pirates quickly formed a semi-circle, jostling to come in close, to watch as he cracked the whip in the air.

The pirates began bellowing a low chant, grunting like animals in heat.

"Tonight, we drag the obdurate headman of those barbarian villages," his voice rising. "He will not row, he will not work and so…he will die!" Each staccato phrase was met with a low grunt.

"He will be dragged, he will be keeled, he will be hauled!" The chant built, rising to a crescendo and hushed suddenly as Scranwraith brought the whip up, letting the weight of his arm fall to the natural motion of his arm and sending the whip to knock the flop hat from the fat, one-eyed pirate. The hat flew in the air to land on his head and the pirates laughed uproariously.

Scranwraith raised his hand. "And after this we will sport our captured maidens. Bring their headman, bring the captives!"

A guttural cheer rose from hoarse throats as they rushed to obey.

At this, the dark figure retreated from the hold gangway and flattened to the shadows. It was the boy who had slipped his bonds. His breath panting in hate and nervous tension, he edged a little further down the stairs to the slit and blew a low whistle. There was an agonising delay but then a girl's lips came so close he smelt the sweetness of her breath.

"Is it true?" he said.

"Yes, the mad pirate will display us for his men. He will sell us in the slave pits; all but one. That one will serve all his men unless we can kill ourselves before…"

"…No," said the boy urgently. "Never that…"

A shout of joy from Scranwraith and the sweet lips sunk back to shadow with a sobbing sigh.

"Never that," said the boy and he slipped down towards the hull.

The Broken Bridge

As one, the reivers ran swiftly along the broadly paved path with that long loping pace characteristic of the

Vandergan. Their seemingly tireless legs serving them without pause until the sun finally hit the top of the western mountains. Here they paused at Wardark's signal and gazed stoically on the volcanic mountains that drew nearer and nearer until they were a series of drooping crags nearly looming over the path. The crags withdrew like timid maidens in a semicircle to huddle around the west side of a great lake. The spherical dome, now large and ominous, rose above this lake and the giant trees like a huge half-moon, metal grey and sheened in a blue light that reflected the light of a dying sun, a great eye that stared morosely to its twin in the skies.

Wardark could see shining waters and as they drew closer, he saw that the path rose on an incline until it became a low bridge, rising half a spear length from the shimmering water. He signalled his men to retreat to the skirt of trees where the sound of water falling battled with an almost unearthly silence.

Only a few spear lengths and Wardark saw the whole vista: The broken bridge before him. A great still lake bounded on the west by the high mountains and a great carpet of forest to the east. The stillness of the lake was impossible. The waters, a clear translucent blue like a maiden's iris, lapped at the shores and the struts of the broken bridge and surrounded the strangest object Wardark had ever seen. Rising seemingly from the very waters, this enormous sphere was half submerged. It was covered with blue moss and strange violet flowers. Bizarre projections emanated at points and incomprehensible hieroglyphs were masked by the trailing vines and ivies which shrouded the sphere like a veil. It was apparently made of some unknown metal. Wardark looked again at the waters of the lake. Nothing moved on its surface. He stopped still and listened. He could hear nothing except the distant sound of the waterfall.

Slowly, he strode back to his men.

SWORDS & SORCERIES

"The bridge is broken. Only a few spear lengths separate us from crossing to the…temple." Wardark could think of no other description. "I like not the water. It has a strange cast. Go men, explore the waterfall." Wardark remembered Xianthus's words in the well. "Evern, come with me. You have sharp eyes."

The two swiftly ran to the edge of the bridge and then slowed to a walk as they began to traverse it. It was a spears breadth, enough for two men to walk together and then a good distance to where it ended abruptly. It was low set, more of a platform such as the villagers used for fishing than a bridge. It seemed only the length of a mercenary sword from the water. Wardark crouched to examine the stonework. It glistened as though an army of slugs had trailed across its surface. He looked again at the translucent water, shining bluely in the intervening space. It was unnatural. Looking up, he saw the other side of the bridge and the vague outline beneath the surface of some kind of drawbridge with skeletal struts like the ribcage of a giant beast from the elder days. The opening to the temple was a great arched and vaulted portico whose depths were obscured by hanging ivies and grotesquely coloured flowers. Again, he gazed at the water. It was hypnotic.

"No fish," said Evern. "No living creatures?"

Wardark said nothing, rose to his feet and turned. His ears had caught something, and his eyes confirmed it.

Loping down the cracked paving of the broad path in horrific silence came the Gobeln. There were too many to count. With a horrible new tactic, they had found some secret way through the trees. They had passed the waterfall unbeknown to the reivers and were now a few spear lengths from the narrow bridge.

Pale faced, Evern drew his bow and notched it.

The ravening Gobeln howled their bestial cry and, two abreast, charged with a demonic hateful cry.

Wardark grinned.

Wevan Father of Wardark

They dragged Wevan father of Wardark bound in heavy chains across the deck and cast him at the feet of Scranwraith.

Weakened by hunger and battered and bruised by constant blows, Wevan rose to his knees, defying the chains to stare with stoic grey eyes at the mad pirate king.

"Dog," screamed Scranwraith, thrashing the handle of the leather whip across Wevan's upturned face. Slowly, Wevan raised his head and stared impassively upwards.

"I have been good to you, headman. You live," Scranwraith laughed uneasily. "But I have been patient too long. Now row or be hauled."

Wevan spat at the pirate.

With a signal from Scranwraith four pirates gripped Wevan by his arms and legs as others stripped away the chains and prepared blocks and pullies. With practised ease they suspended the naked man by ropes from the main-yard and hung a great lead weight on his legs. Laughing uproariously, they drew him close up to the yardarm.

"Drop him slow lads," shouted Scranwraith. "We wouldn't want to him to die easy."

The Waterfall.

Evern dropped to his knees on Wardark's right under his sword and sent a dart flying into the eye of the first Gobeln. Before it had fallen, another had clambered on its back and its swifter companion lay headless at Wardark's feet. A second and a third fell to Evern's darts as Wardark lopped off another head and another. He grinned stoically as they fell, expecting death at any second. The Death Caravanserai was impinging on his mind like a whispering friend. A huge Gobeln stood on the bodies of its dead and roared at Wardark. Hopelessly, Evern drew his scrim knife.

Wardark took a pace forward and sliced a blow at the head, but the beast flung its arm and caught the flat of the blade. The movement threw it off balance and, arms beating the air, it fell to the water.

Then the world seemed to pause. A grotesque cry of unbelievable animal pain erupted, and the water gushed in a dizzying sulphuric explosion of vapour. Before Wardark's eyes the beast dissolved into a mess of blood that spread in exploding bubbles where it had fallen. Another Gobeln leapt on to the piling bodies and with a shout of awareness Wardark struck it heavily with the flat of his sword and sent it toppling to the left. Again, the vapour rose, and the beast thrashed wildly in agonised death. Two Gobeln leapt uneasily on the bodies. And then Wardark roared with battle rage and leapt at the two bewildered Gobeln, sending both to a terrible death with mighty blows.

A roar came from the shore. The Gobeln had all advanced to the bridge in their ravening desire but the reivers had emerged to attack them in the rear. Arrow after arrow hit them before they were aware of the new element in the game. Wardark was in full flow, lashing this way and that, pushing attackers aside with brawny arms as Evern, finding space again, fired dart after dart into the pack.

*

Leaving behind a blue lake whose shores had slowly diffused to a lurid pink, the reivers walked slowly back to the waterfall.

Banen the bald explained in his careful manner. "Vanyan took a deer path to the edge where the lake meets the cliff. It is impassable. He touched the water …"

"…and am now missing a fingertip," said Vanyan ruefully.

"But we thought to explore behind the waterfall. Then we saw the Gobeln and thinking to surprise them hid for a few moments and…" continued Banyan, "…look for yourself."

Behind the waterfall was a shallow cave where a group of men could stand freely. The dim light still revealed an iron structure like a cage at the rear of the cave; below this cage a strangely square shaft unlike any that the reivers had seen. There was a copper mine to the north where they made their weapons, but it was not sunk like this. It was a marvel of craftsmanship unknown to a barbarian people.

"You cannot see it now but the shaft is not deep," said Banen the bald.

Wardark's eyes were keener. He gripped the cage and with a single thrust pushed the bars asunder. They crumbled to rust in his hands. The others hacked away a bigger gap and then Wardark leapt to the ground. Evern joined him. The shaft led in one direction, towards the lake.

Strangely, the long straight tunnel revealed was lit at intervals by square pools of dim light. Picking his way slowly forward with his men strung out cautiously in the rear, Wardark saw that apertures above and to the side had been cut through the stone to light the way. The sun was going down and he felt the urgency both of the loss of light and the thought that Scranwraith might have fitted his damaged ship and be off to the south.

As they walked from darkness to light to darkness, Wardark glanced to left and right for traps. Peculiar hieroglyphs appeared on either side. Strange animals and beasts, great zodiacal signs and awful gods, stars and planets in portentous alignment. Sometimes the shafts caught out particular details of a compelling female face or figure, beautiful beyond conception, archaically dressed and gazing with a hypnotic beguiling smile on some distant eternity. She was a goddess, an avatar of all things beautiful with the concomitant danger of the hopelessly beautiful.

And there came a claustrophobic sense and Wardark knew that they were under the lake. The pools of light were less frequent, but they were square and the light had a bluish tinge. For a long time, they journeyed in silence as the lights began to dim and dim. With relief, Wardark saw ahead the grim outline of wide steps and then everything went dark.

The sun had dropped behind the cliffs.

"Forward," he said.

Stumbling and gripping each other's shoulders they came to the first step and felt their way blindly and slowly upwards.

A Question of Payment

To the cracking of the leather whip the Vandergan women were dragged naked, but for gold chains and collars, to the deck; their skin alabaster white under the moon, their trembling bodies like voluptuous flickering statues that sent the pirates into a frenzy.

"Back, back," screamed Scranwraith. "Only one shall be yours. The rest are for the slave pots of the south. Back I tell you!" His officers lunged forward, menacing the crew with their cutlasses. And here Scranwraith sent a pirate reeling with his eye torn from its socket by the whip. The pirates watched their comrade scrabble and scream on the deck until Scranwraith sent his cutlass through his heart. "Back. Or you will go down with this accursed village headman." Here he pointed to Wevan who dangled naked above the rising waves, his face impassive but his eyes burning with despair at the fate of his womenfolk.

In this moment of frenzied lust and barbarism, a burly docker from Serpanam strolled obliviously through the crowd. He stood before the mad pirate, his heavy muscular body like a rock, his hands black-dyed with years of pitch. "We have finished fitting your vessel, Captain, edge-joined the timbers with iron nails and caulked the planks." He then intoned the traditional seal: "With moss, with adzes, axes and awls, planes and draw knives we have fixed you. Pay us the fee and sail."

Like an actor heckled by a jeering crowd, Scranwraith was suddenly lost for words. And then he laughed. He shouted over his shoulder, "Get the shipwright his fee." It was a theatrical interval. The pirates swaying, arms around each other, humming in low voices, the prelude to the keelhauling, staring with lascivious eyes on the naked Vandergan girls as the Serpanite shipwright stood with arms folded.

Scranwraith's first mate swiftly ran to the captain's cabin, unlocked it, and emerged shortly with three bars of gold. "See here," said Scranwraith. "Three bars of gold from ancient Franken. The emperor's seal imprinted."

The Serpanite took the gold, bowed and walked back through the crowd.

"We are ready to sail," roared Scranwraith, "But first, the entertainment!"

A young girl screamed a piteous scream.

SWORDS & SORCERIES

The Temple of Starborn Lovers

As Wardark climbed the broad steps he became aware that he could make out their outlines. The dimmest of lights penetrated the dark. And slowly the light grew to a numinous glow. Gripping his sword in both hands he took the last step.

He stood at the centre of the great dome. Through a single aperture in the roof a shaft of moonlight penetrated the dust-moted air like a spear. The shaft struck the single definable object in the great structure: A huge double throne of some unknown metal which shone like new bones under water. The light cast an unearthly penumbra on this throne and then suffused to the great spaces where, beyond a few scattered square blocks, an incredible vista was displayed. In a vast circle stood catacombic chambers each with a single occupant encased in a glass-clear sarcophagus. This ring of ancient dead was like a giant's collar of sapphire-blue gemstone surrounding the semi-circle of the sphere without cessation.

Wardark signalled to his men to wait. They crouched a few steps from the top as Wardark paced over to the sarcophagi. Wardark had tasted wizardry; The throne was empty, but these coffins contained…things. Slowly, with his sword eerily glowing in the moonlight he advanced across the mosaiced floor, each step raising a cloud of dust. Trepidation in every step, he drew close to the nearest sarcophagus. A skull leered at him from the confines where it had fallen against the glass surface. Long black hair hung from an elongated skull. The next was similar but the hair was short. The third seemed to have a different ambience and a mummified body of a man, perfectly preserved, lay inside floating it seemed in some liquid like honey. It was here Wardark noted that the floor was stained, and the glass cracked on the other sarcophagi. As he walked around, gazing like a man at an exhibition, he noted a pattern. A third of those he examined were still floating in liquid; the rest, dried out husks or even in some cases, a mere pile of crumbled dust. They were all of foreign aspect with slim bodies and elongated skulls, a type of man-thing he had never encountered.

Wardark turned to the throne and approached. It was immense, two seats for a king and queen? A strange stick like structure projected between them. A coronet? Wardark was a barbarian. He had ranged further than any of his men but this whole scenario was beyond his imagination. He took a pace to the left and an eerie sigh escaped the ground. Suddenly a flickering curtain of coloured lights appeared, and an ethereal creature sat phantom-like on the throne. It was a woman of great beauty, the same face he had seen beside the hieroglyphs on the tunnel. For the space of a breath, it hovered. Its lips moved and a smile crept across the wondrous face and then it faded out like water receding from a shore.

Wardark, amazed, gave a soft curse under his breath. Damn this world of illusion. He was tired of phantoms, oppressive silence, the eerie light, and the mummified bodies. He had seen another set of steps behind the throne. They headed south. He called his men, and like children they emerged into the huge amphitheatre before scurrying across its length to where Wardark stood looking down the steps.

A dark shadow faced him at the foot of the stairs.

"Wardark," said the shadow. "Welcome to the temple of Starborn Lovers where Meredith ruled alone for many thousands of years."

"You? How did you come here?"

The Sea Witch cast back her cloak. "Under the lighthouse of Serpanam an underwater cavern leads to these accursed waters. It is known to my people. But we have little time for niceties. The mad pirate's ship will sail soon. Already the Serpanite shipwrights have repaired the bulk of it. They are greedy and extend the job a little further. If you can bluff your way on to the ship, you can take him by surprise."

Wardark crossed his arms. "Scranwraith will know me as a Vandergan reiver."

"Not when I have finished with you." She drew from her bag dark powder and other fixings. "I shall make you a black-haired man whose red eyes will be that of an idiot. The mad pirate's crew is sparse. He will take you as a galley slave. Come. Spells must be worked, and time is short."

An Ending

"Deadeye," whispered the boy. "Wake. I have worked the chains. Deadeye!"

The man opened his eyes, stared deep into those of the boy. "Wardark. I am Wardark."

He stood. He lifted the chains. His breath came in great gasps. He spoke. "Free the slaves. Do it quietly so as not to wake them…." He bunched a length of chain in his hands and began to make for the gangway. "…until you hear the screams."

On the deck Scranwraith had placed the chosen girl on a barrel where she stood, proud, making no effort to hide her nakedness. Scranwraith raised the whip and cracked it.

At the sound Wevan plummeted from sight.

The wind was rising. The gibbous moon shone through

the rigging casting a spiderweb on Scranwraith's inflamed face. The tattooed pirates encroached nearer to the defenceless girl. The ropes were hauled. The pirates turned to the starboard where the racked and bleeding body of Wevan should appear. In a single grotesque moment, the four hauling pirates fell backwards violently, and the ropes sprung upward writhing like headless snakes.

Wevan was gone.

And in the same awful moment Wardark, naked, sprang to the deck and with a great sweep of his chains to left and right, brained and smashed a dozen of the pirates. With a second sweep, limbs and heads were torn and blood sprayed in great gouts across the decks.

In the moment of senseless shock, Wardark threw the chains to the port side, wrapping pirates in a mesh, picked up a cutlass and a knife and sprang straight towards Scranwraith with a shout of triumph.

The pirates gathered some semblance of intelligence and began drawing weapons only to find a horde of slaves led by Evern rushing on to the deck in a mad frenzy. Some found themselves being strangled by the golden chains of the Vandergan women. Boarding to the port came Banen the Bald alone, swinging his axe and lopping off the head of the fat one-eyed pirate. From the stern came red-haired Vanyan with the reivers, his sword swinging in great arcs.

Scranwraith's officers, were quicker. They formed a protective shield around their captain.

Wardark was unfamiliar with the cutlass. But he was a reiver and close combat to him was not a matter of technique or craft. It was simply kill. Throwing himself at the officers he took one under the throat, the second in the heart. The cutlass stuck in the ribs. Battering the thrust of a cutlass with his bare forearm, he ripped the belly from the third and smashed his fist into the last. The blow crushed the first mate's larynx and left Scranwraith backing towards the bow.

Scranwraith was mad but no fool. All around him his men were dying in a bloody massacre. His own death was assured. Naked before him stood the object of this disaster, unarmed.

"I am Wardark, son of Wevan." Wardark folded his arms and smiled.

"Then die Wardark," hissed Scranwraith. He made to advance.

Great hands gripped his throat and, slowly struggling, the giant pirate was raised from the floor, his face purpling as his cutlass dropped and his numbing fingers clutched for the daggers on his leather jerkin. Behind him Wevan, his body bleeding from a myriad of gashes and lacerations, gave a little shake and with one twist snapped the neck of the pirate. The body dropped to the ground and Wevan pushed it away with his foot.

Behind the two men the deck was awash with blood. The bodies of the pirates were already being cast over the side. Evern was finding blankets for the girls. He seemed to be concentrating on one in particular.

Wevan gave Wardark a penetrating look.

"We had better dress, son. There are ladies present."

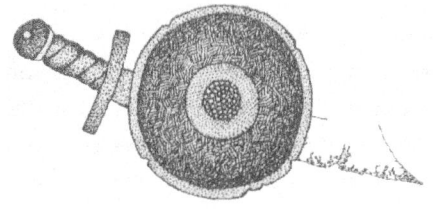

FOR THE HEART OF A SPEARSLAYER
R. K. Olson

The Spearslayer Sect was annihilated at the Battle of the Golga River by the treachery of the Three Nation Alliance. A thousand years of knowledge and the perfection of the warrior arts lost in a single afternoon. A handful survived to join the Spearslayer diaspora. Here is one Spearslayer's story.

The soaring kestrel's sharp eyes pierced the grey morning light and spied a caravan which from above resembled a multi-coloured undulating snake slithering across the rocky pine studded foothills of the Rostic Mountains.

From the ground, Portus the Slaver's open, sightless eyes stared back at the kestrel in the sky. Blood from the arrow in his chest soaked his green robe, a dark stain that blossomed on his chest.

The bandit attack was ragged and disorganized. They screamed curses and banged drums to startle the caravan in this quiet, lonely wilderness two days' ride from the city of Chenia.

The ambush and cacophony of noise panicked the two dozen merchants and tradesmen, sending some sprinting into the surrounding forest. Others, hearts pounding, huddled behind one of the seven wagons comprising the caravan. Horses and camels reared, eyes rolling and strained at their ropes and halters.

SWORDS & SORCERIES

Like locusts ravaging a farmer's field, a score of shabby-looking bandits ran in and amongst the wagons, ripping open boxes and snatching bolts of cloth, tools, spices, and all the food they could carry. One bandit was leading a horse away by its bridle.

A lean man with the sharp, angular face of a Thessite squatted next to a small pine tree with his spear held upright in his hand watching. His face was the colour of burnished leather.

Years of Spearslayer training and fighting experience taught him that the only response to an ambush is an instant counterattack. The ambushers had the element of surprise, so one needed to engage with ambushers as soon as possible. Although these bandits were inept and poorly armed, their ambush was successful.

The Spearslayer hesitated. The caravan had more men but had allowed itself to stretch too far apart. A stupid mistake. Not hiring caravan guards to save money was another mistake.

These were not his people. He had joined the caravan for convenience. If they discovered he was an outlawed Spearslayer, they would shun him or, more likely, try to take his head for the bounty.

His mind wandered back to the day the Spearslayer Sect was destroyed at the Battle of the River Golga years before. Most of the Spearslayers were slaughtered on the riverbank by warriors from the Three Nations. Spearslayer families were sold as slaves. They outlawed those Spearslayer warriors that escaped and placed a bounty on their heads.

The lean man, called Dar, was lucky. An Oceanian commander protected Dar and accepted the Spearslayer as part of his household. The Oceanian released Dar from his oath on his deathbed when Dar learned that his family might still be alive and living as slaves. Dar promised himself to find his family.

Shadow hid Dar's face as he scanned the wagons with dark eyes. He rubbed his clean-shaven jaw. Murky sunlight fought to reach the ground, casting a sombre mood that contrasted sharply with the screams and shouts coming from the caravan.

He stood up, adjusting the leather jerkin he wore over a linen shirt. In his heart, he was still a Spearslayer.

He moved forward like a panther with his spear held waist high. Seeing an opening among the swarming bandits, Dar exploded forward with hawser-like muscles snapping. An arrow whizzed by him and drums kept up an unholy racket as he dodged pine trees before bursting into the open.

Three ragged bandits turned to defend themselves and Dar's quick spear thrust ripped one bandit's belly open with the razor sharp spearpoint before he could raise his rusty sword. Dar instantly rotated his hips and swung the spear around in an arc, slicing through the neck of another ragged bandit, sending a fountain of blood pumping as the body collapsed on the ground. The third bandit dropped his bow and ran away.

Dar sensed motion to his left and saw the big, bearded Kalan that had joined the caravan at the last minute standing off to the side.

Standing six feet, five inches tall, the Kalan's burly right arm displayed the Obedience Tattoos of the Sultan of Kala. He wore his jet-black hair braided down his back in the style of a Kalan warrior. His three-foot scimitar was edged on one side and widened slightly near the tip, ending with a sharpened point. Blood was smeared on it and two arrows were embedded in his round, leather shield.

The Kalan glanced at Dar and nodded. Together, they walked toward the looters. A handful of bandits noticed the Spearslayer and Kalan walking steadily towards them and emboldened by the three to one odds, unsheathed their swords and rushed toward the two warriors.

Dar shot his spear forward in a long, fast thrust, hitting a bandit in the middle of the chest. Dar could feel gristle and tendons rip as the iron spearpoint drove forward, scraping against the rib bones.

The Kalan parried a sword swipe from a bandit with his scimitar and then sent the curved weapon whistling through the air slashing a lethal gash from shoulder to opposite hip. The bandit folded as blood pooled under him. The remaining bandits turned and ran, weaving their way through pine trees toward safety.

The attack was over as suddenly as it began. The Spearslayer and the Kalan had tipped the scales and routed the bandits.

The Kalan was breathing hard and wiping gore off his long, curved blade using the ragged tunic of a dead bandit. He smiled with big white teeth emerging from his beard, which was as black as a raven's wing. He had wielded his sword like he was playing a fine musical instrument, alternating between slashing, cutting, and parrying.

"I'll make sure our bandit friends are really leaving," said the Kalan. He took two steps and paused. Turing back to Dar he bowed slightly and said, "I am Sinie Havert, former swordsman of the Sultan of Kala."

"I am Dar," the Spearslayer replied. "You are a good sword."

Havert bowed again and added, "And you, a good spear." Then the big man turned and strode off to where the bandits were last seen.

The damage from the attack was clustered at the tail end of the caravan. Portus the Slaver and two others were dead, two horses stolen along with tradesmen's tools, silk cloth, foodstuffs and what amounted to a few handfuls of coins.

The merchants and tradesmen recovering from the shock of the attack moved woodenly as they calmed their animals and took swigs of Usmauarian brandy to calm their own nerves.

The dead were buried hastily in the soft earth. The caravan was reformed and beasts chivvied into position. The caravan started moving again.

The four dead bandits where left where they had fallen.

*

A fine layer of dust lay on the caravan as it followed a path skirting the tall, brooding Rostic Mountains. The path appeared to be only a dull white scar splitting the rocky ground. Small streams weaved through the foothills which were dotted with patches of grassy land. The mountain tops were lost in a blackness that seemed to press down on the caravan.

Dar carried his spear point down, resting the shaft on broad shoulders that flowed down to a powerful chest and into lean hips. He loosened his leather jerkin and set a walking pace that would eat up the miles to Chenia. There was a looseness to his stride as his leg muscles rolled in rhythm to his steps.

A brown-haired slave woman in a short, red shift with her hands tied slid out of the back of Portus' slave wagon and angrily stomped her bare feet, exclaiming, "Will someone please untie me!" Each stomp of her foot caused the gold bangles encircling her slim ankles to tinkle merrily.

Dar slid his dagger out and grabbed both her tied hands in his left hand to hold them steady and sliced the ropes.

"Thank Kol!" she said, rubbing her red, raw wrists. Looking at Dar with large, brown eyes, she added, "And thank you! I'm Bettia."

Her smile lit up her face and made her eyes sparkle. She had olive-tinged skin, high cheekbones and a wide, generous mouth. She ran her hand through soft, tousled brown hair that framed a beautiful oval face. Her short red shift hugged her willowy body around rounded breasts and smooth hips.

Here was a woman that understood the power of her own beauty, thought Dar. He smiled, relaxing the tension in his jawline.

"Why were your hands tied?" he asked, leaning on his spear.

"I kept trying to escape. I was sold to a Chenian warlord by Portus. He was delivering me," she said simply.

The sun was burning the murkiness away and lightening up the sky. In the advancing light, Dar noticed the hint of faint lines splaying out near her eyes. There was a barely perceptible sprinkling of grey hair amongst the rich brown tresses. A beautiful woman on the cusp of the onslaught of the ravages of time.

"I try to pluck the grey hairs out, but every time I do, two more grow back." said Bettia as she read his face adding. "I believe the warlord would have been disappointed. Portus lied about my age. I'm sure of it."

"You're free. Portus is dead. He won't complain," said Dar. Gesturing to the wagon, he added, "Are the others in there?"

"They are hiding under a rug," replied Bettia.

A rich, heady perfume with a hint of muskiness enveloped Dar as he stuck his head through the canvas flap of the slaver's wagon. He pulled the plush rug aside, scattering silk pillows and exposing four scantily dressed slave women.

Two blonde-haired slaves cowered in a corner; arms folded tightly over their naked breasts. The two other slaves, both with flowing red hair and pale skin, wore gossamer-like tops of green silk that did little to hide their ample breasts. Their diaphanous harem pants were gathered at the waist and heels. All stared at him with large, scared eyes that shone in the shadows under the canvas.

Turning to Bettia he said, "The first thing you can do with your new freedom is explain to these four what happened and that they are free now too."

"I'll tell them," replied Bettia. "Let me find my sandals and walk with you for a while." She climbed into the wagon.

At that moment, Sinie hailed him, and Dar watched the mountain of a man's long legs carry him forward. His leg muscles bulged with every step. Two merchants tailed the Kalan, struggling to keep pace.

Havert's heavy beard couldn't hide the smile on his face.

His nose was hawklike and his skin swarthy in tone. He wore a sleeveless short jacket and silk shirt that exposed his heavily muscled arms. Etched into his right forearm were the slash and cross marks of the Obedience Tattoos required of all swordsmen serving as bodyguards to the Sultan of Kala.

"Dar, listen to what these two have to say," said Havert with a soothing, soft voice, unlike his Kalan battle cry.

The older, shorter merchant of the two wore trail-scarred walking boots and a simple dark blue wool tunic and pants. The recognized leader of the caravan, he scratched his round belly before speaking.

"My father travelled this way many times in years past, as have I, and once encountered a swamp witch. The witch demanded a toll to pass through her swamp. The toll was a spoon and a bolt of cloth. That was all. I have heard tales of this swamp witch taking people as her toll payment, but I don't know if this is true. I've never seen her," he said in a whisper.

The other merchant was similarly garbed, but thin and tall. He nervously rubbed his hands together and added, "She is called the Rostic Swamp Witch!"

Havert cocked a bushy black eyebrow at Dar.

"Keep this to yourselves. Don't start any rumours. Stories of a swamp witch could be just that, merely stories shared around a fire at night to entertain," said Dar, looking from one merchant to the other with steady dark eyes.

*

The sun reached its zenith as the caravan snaked in and out of a dappled light that twisted its way down through the tree branches interlaced over the path. The sun was warm, but the air stayed cool and comfortable. A carpet of pine needles muffled the sound of the hooves. The ground was solid and the wagon wheels rolled forward smoothly to the creak of the carts.

Bettia must have told the slaves they were free, mused Dar as he watched the nubile, lightly-clothed women flit from one wagon to the next, laughing and teasing the men of the caravan.

"This is a much more enjoyable caravan now," said Bettia with a wide smile. She swung into step next to Dar, matching his stride with her long legs.

Bettia was a delightful conversationalist and very entertaining. Dar hadn't talked this much with one person in a long time.

It wasn't in his nature to share information, but Bettia drew it out of him. Dar enjoyed the attention he was getting from a beautiful woman. Her smile was infectious. Dar let the moment wash over him and relaxed.

The trail sloped downhill as it emerged from the rocky foothills and pine trees of the Rostic Mountains. The afternoon sun slanted into their eyes and slowly inched its way down the trail.

"Why are you traveling to Chenia," asked Bettia.

Dar paused. "For news of my family. They were sold as slaves and I'm searching for them."

Bettia frowned in concentration and brushed stray wisps of hair from her eyes. "How were they taken as slaves?"

Dar sighed, knowing this intelligent woman would pull his story out of him. He sensed he could trust her with his secret.

He briefly sketched his background, the annihilation of the Spearslayer Sect, his capture and aftermath of years spent as part of an Oceanian commander's household.

"Not knowing what happened to your family and branded as an outlaw?" she replied after a long period of silence. "Your Spearslayer secret is safe with me. I'll tell no one."

"The Spearslayers died on the banks of the River Golga a decade ago. For all I know, I'm the last Spearslayer," said Dar.

"Dar!" said Havert, striding forward to catch up and interrupting the conversation. "I'm told the Rostic Swamp is a mile or two down the trail. Then it's a day's march to Chenia."

Bettia stepped silently away as Havert joined Dar, noting how easily and quickly the giant Kalan moved. The big man was light on his feet.

"Good," said Dar. Pausing, he added, "What brings you to Chenia, Sinie?"

"Not pleasure, I assure you! I have a job waiting for me. I have agreed to train a Chenian warlord's troops and serve as Captain of the Guard. I'm being paid a hefty sum for my experience and expertise." Havert grinned.

"May the Gods favour you, Sinie," said Dar.

It surprised Dar that Havert didn't ask him why he was going to Chenia.

*

The downward slope levelled out, and the boggy ground became wetter with every step. Silence engulfed the caravan. The wagon masters muttered curses under their breath as the wagon wheels struggled in the mud before finally breaking free with a wet, sucking sound.

Those in the caravan with boots put them on for this muddy part of the trip. The mud, in some places, reached to the ankles.

The birds stopped singing and stayed away from the swamp. The slave women had stopped their prancing around and laughter only to be replaced by faces creased with tension. A coolness settled in everyone's bones. The wet smell of rotting vegetation permeated the moist air.

The tall, bearded Kalan and the lean, clean-shaven, brown-skinned Thessite lowered their voices and agreed to lead the caravan for the stretch of path winding through the swamp. They planned to get through the swamp as quickly as possible in the fading light.

The caravan members' colourful clothes and canvas-covered wagons seemed out of place in the grey light of the swamp as they trundled forward in fits and starts like an undulating worm.

The merchants and tradesmen slapped at hungry bugs and mumbled prayers with dry mouths to whatever God or Gods they believed in for safe passage through the swamp. Heads swivelled from side to side, constantly scanning the dripping, tangled mess of the swamp for danger.

All at once, strange, jarring shrieks echoed at intervals across the swamp, setting nerves on edge. Deep in the swamp, ancient trees in the last throes of death stretched high and barren of leaves above the stagnant, fetid swamp water. Stripped of bark and whitened by time, the tree trunks looked like bony skeleton fingers reaching for the sky. Grassy hummocks, bushes, hanging vines and half submerged tree trunks dotted the swamp and contributed to the gloom.

The swamp appeared almost impenetrable, like a wall closing in on both sides of the trail that sliced through the wetlands. The late afternoon light was sombre, creating shadows that, glimpsed momentarily out of the corner of the eye, seemed to flit amongst the dead trees and shallow wetlands.

The shrieks stopped as suddenly as they started.

Havert was recruited by a wagon master to help free a bogged wagon using his massive strength and broad shoulders. Dar glided forward, silently alert, and alone out of sight of the caravan.

Out of the corner of his eye, he caught a flicker of motion in the dead trees. His muscle memory took over and instinctively he assumed the spear-ready position of his left foot forward and right foot behind as the anchor. The spear held chest high in the short-thrust position.

The hairs on the back of his neck stood on end and he felt a hollowness in the pit of his stomach. All was deathly still. The unmistakable sickly-sweet smell of death replaced the moist breeze.

"Ho, Ho, Ho! What have we here?" cackled a swamp witch as she landed softly on a tree limb high above and in front of Dar. The witch was bent over with age to half a normal size and wore a tattered black robe. She stared out at Dar with blind, filmy white eyes underneath a tangled and greasy mop of grey hair.

She pointed a gnarled taloned finger at Dar and laughed, showing her toothless gums. "I know you and your kind. Ho, ho ho! I smell a Spearslayer in my swamp! I'm so humbled by your noble presence," she mocked.

"Crone, we mean you no harm. We will pass and continue on our way," said Dar.

The witch leaped to another tree closer to Dar, catching herself with her taloned feet and laughed, "Ho, ho, ho! How kind of you to mean me no harm, Spearslayer. But what if I mean you harm? What will you do with that puny spear, oh great Spearslayer?"

The caravan stopped in the path behind him. The merchants and tradesmen crowded together, listening to the encounter with the witch. At the mention of "Spearslayer" they whispered in surprise among themselves. Only the large Kalan and Bettia did not act surprised.

"You chatter like a monkey in a tree, witch," growled Dar. "State your business or get out of our way."

"Ho, ho, ho! Bold you are, Spearslayer! That boldness was needed at the River Golga where the Spearslayers died instead of used here against an old woman," taunted the witch, her talons digging into the decaying wood of the lifeless tree.

She leaped to a taller tree over the swamp and looked down on the caravan with rheumy white eyes.

"You may pass when I have the Spearslayer's heart," laughed the witch. "That's my toll. Pay or die!"

"I've had enough of this foolishness," grunted Havert, pulling his scimitar from his waist belt. "I'll have your head, crone!"

"Stop barking, obedient dog! Go back to your fat sultan in Kala, you fool," jeered the witch, pointing at Havert.

Havert spit in response and tried to take a step forward, scimitar in his hand. His feet felt like they were made of stone. He couldn't move.

"What this?" exclaimed Havert, "I can't move my feet! Damn you, witch!"

The witch ignored Havert and turned with a cloying smile toward Dar.

"A Spearslayer's noble, warrior heart would make good magic and have a place of honour in my collection of things," she cackled loudly. "Those people in the caravan won't help you," said the witch, nodding her head, adding, "You are all alone."

"You talk too much, witch." Dar started walking forward toward the witch perched in the tree. "Come down here and feel cold steel in your black heart!"

"Ho, ho, ho," chortled the witch, flinging her head back and rising milky white sightless eyes to the heavens. "Why would I do that? I have others to do my bidding."

Swamp water and muck near the path immediately boiled and congealed, giving off an intense, sickly rotting smell. Rising from the whirling pools of muck appeared a man-like creature fashioned from mud, sticks, leaves, and other rotting vegetation.

Dripping brown muck, it woodenly waded through the swamp. It was nine feet tall and as wide as a horse, with hands as large as serving platters. The creature knuckled its eye sockets and turned its bald head toward Dar, emitting a deep, low growl.

The witch sniggered. "Good luck Spearslayer! I'll rip your heart out with my bare hands!" She made grotesque clawing motions with her taloned hands.

Dar waited until the swamp creature was stepping from the swamp onto dry land to strike, figuring that would be the creature's most unbalanced, vulnerable moment.

Darting in low, Dar delivered a full spear thrust to the creature's groin. The spear slid smoothly in, slicing into the rotting vegetation of the creature's entrails. Dar ripped his spear back and leaped away from the swamp creature after delivering the death strike.

Only the creature wasn't dead. It staggered for a moment, but that was all. The hole made by Dar's spear closed and vanished.

"Ho, ho, ho! You can't kill it, but it can kill you!," clucked the witch, slapping a gnarled hand on her knee. She gathered up a corner of the black rag she wore and wiped spittle from her chin as she giggled.

A mist of swamp gas rolled over Dar, leaving a wet sheen beading on his brown skin and muting the late afternoon light. Dar danced away from the creature, looking for an opening to strike at the head. Feinting a short spear thrust right and low, he sent the spear point up and to the left, slicing into the creature's neck.

Its huge greenish brown head rolled freely and loosely on the creature's chest as the wound splashed buckets of brown muck on the boggy ground. Again, the wound quickly healed itself with mud and rotten vegetation.

Dar rushed in again to get behind the creature and cut the legs out from under it and force it to the ground. The creature clumsily swung its arms, catching Dar with a blow to his right shoulder, stunning the Spearslayer and knocking the spear from his hands.

The witch's peals of mocking laughter echoed across the swamp as the mist continued to thicken and darkness cloaked the swamp with the setting of the sun.

Dar crouched with his dagger gripped in his right hand.

The witch leaped to a lower branch to enjoy the fight.

"Woe is the Spearslayer!" tittered the Witch. "You can't kill something that is already dead!"

The creature lumbered towards Dar, clenching its massive, powerful hands. Havert was still stuck in place. The others were bunched up behind him, watching the spectacle with unblinking eyes and open mouths.

Dar tensed his coiled muscles and leaped toward his spear laying on the ground. He evaded the creature's arms and in one motion, plucked the spear off the ground, whirled and hurled it at the witch sitting on the tree limb.

The witch shrieked in rage as the spear burst into her chest. She tottered on the limb until the talons on her feet lost their grip and she tumbled to the ground with the spear buried in her chest. Spitting and snarling, she screeched obscene blasphemies at the Spearslayer, cursing him.

Havert, the bewitchment broken, raced forward and separated the witch's head from her body with a swipe of his scimitar, ending the noise.

"Always chop off the head of a witch to make sure she's dead," growled Havert.

The dead witch's body secreted a foul decaying stench that singed Dar's nostrils.

"She was controlling the creature like a puppet," said Dar, more to himself than to Havert. "I couldn't kill your creature, but by Kol, I can kill you, witch."

The witch's creature lay immobile on its back, seeping itself away back into the swamp.

Bettia broke free from the group and rushed forward. She hugged Dar and he inhaled her sweet scent and felt her soft hair on his face.

Tired and covered in mud and muck, he raised his voice, addressing the caravan with Bettia still in his arms.

"We have an hour of light left. Move quickly! Let's get out of this swamp before we camp for the night."

The caravan didn't need prodding. They moved the wagons, horses and camels through the swamp, giving the witch's body a wide berth. The creature melted back into the swamp.

Dar swung into the saddle of a sorrel mare tied to a wagon and pulled Bettia up behind him. He nudged the horse forward and led the caravan out of the swamp.

A short while later, in the waning light, Dar noticed an upward incline to the terrain. Soon the path reached the top of a bluff. In the distance, he could see lights winking on in Chenia below. He heard the running water of a nearby stream. He decided the caravan would camp here.

*

Dar smiled as dawn stretched rosy fingers across the sky. The air was cool and the blanket still held Bettia's scent. The sound of the babbling stream was soothing. He smiled again, thinking of last night. He entwined his fingers behind his head, satisfied with the campsite. The site was a half-day's ride from Chenia and had plenty of fresh water. The caravan had stretched out along the banks of the stream, so everyone had space to relax and refresh.

The sun was peeking over the rim of the horizon when he spied Bettia swimming in the stream. She waved to him and waded into shore. Her naked body glistened in the growing sunlight. Rivulets of water raced between her firm breasts and down long, tanned legs. Her long, dark hair was wet and slicked back. She stopped a few feet away from Dar and let him gaze at her toned, willowy body.

"Good morning," said Bettia putting her hands on her hips. "You look relaxed."

Dar smiled.

"I washed your muddy clothes. They are drying on the bank."

Dar pulled back the blanket and gestured for her to join him.

*

Dar slipped from beneath the blankets, leaving Bettia warm, cozy and asleep. He grabbed his spear, walked to the stream and slipped on his cotton pants. Sunlight poured over the stream, dappling it with shining, sparkling colours.

He washed his face and splashed cool, clear water on his body, listening to the sounds of the caravan waking up in the early morning sunshine. The birds were awake and singing. Bees buzzed about the plants growing along the stream's pebbled beach.

He had chosen this site because a slight bend in the stream afforded him privacy from the rest of the caravan. Of course, no one in the caravan wanted to be associated with an outlawed Spearslayer, anyway. The penalty for helping or being associated with a Spearslayer was death.

He leaned down, dunked his head and then took a long, cool drink. The coolness flowed down his throat and spread across his muscular chest and into his stomach. He could feel the sun's warmth on his skin and smell the wood smoke from the caravan's breakfast campfires. His hard stomach muscles flowed into lean hips and undulated as he stood and stretched.

"Dar behind you!" shouted Bettia.

He instantly dropped low to the ground, rolled across the rocky beach, and snatched up his spear just as a sword sliced through the air over his head. The reaction was instinctive from years of Spearslayer training and discipline.

"Sinie?" said a startled Dar as he peered over his spearpoint at his attacker.

The massive Kallan towered above the Spearslayer and slowly swayed the huge scimitar in his hand back and forth, locking eyes with Dar.

"I am truly sorry to have to take your head, my friend," said Havert. "I am obedient to my master, the Sultan of Kala, and he has ordered it so. I know not why. It is not my right to question. I live to honour my Tattoos of Obedience."

With a blur of speed, the bearded Kallan quick-stepped forward, slashing at Dar twice in the time most swordsmen would make a single strike. Dar danced out of the way with a newfound respect for Havert's quickness and skill.

Havert read Dar's mind.

"I am the sultan's greatest swordsman," boasted the muscled Kalan. "I finally have you alone. Now, it is scimitar against spear."

Havert exploded two quick jabs and a powerful slash that whistled past Dar's right side as he sidestepped to avoid the wicked blade.

The Kalan used his rippling, powerful arm muscles to rain jarring blows parried by Dar's iron spearhead. Each heavy strike rattled Dar's teeth, sending shock waves up and down his spine.

The Kalan leaped forward, knocking the long iron spearpoint aside and getting inside the Spearslayer's guard. Dar instantly reversed his spear, swinging it through a tight arc and smashing the butt end into the Kalan's jaw. There was an audible crack. He twirled the spear back and thrust forward, but only cut air as Havert had taken a half-step to the left. Dar pressed his advantage while the Kalan was off balance and drove the tip of the spear at Havert's belly.

This was the move the Kalan was waiting for. Havert delivered a backhanded slash, hooking the spear shaft with the curved part of his blade. A violent yank ripped the spear from Dar's hands sending the spear into the water.

Havert struck again as fast as a snake smashing the hilt of his sword into Dar's bare chest while hooking a foot behind Dar's leg and tripping him backwards into the stream. Dar sprang to his feet and reached for his dagger.

The dagger wasn't at his waist. He had left it next to the blankets.

Havert paused to catch his breath and between gasps said, "My friend, you do not fight dirty enough."

The Kalan raised his scimitar with fully extended arms over his head. The tip of the blade seemed to touch the sun.

"My cut will be mercifully quick and sure. Get ready to . . . Ahhhhh! What is this? Wench! By the Bastard Sons of Kol, she stabbed me!"

Bettia watched as Havert staggered and tried to pull the knife out of his upper back. She had buried it deep.

Dar used the confusion to pull his spear out of the water where it had fallen.

SWORDS & SORCERIES

Blood seeped through the fingers of the Kalan's left hand as he tried to stop the flow of blood from the dagger wound.

Havert pulled the dagger out with a groan, and a rush of blood cascaded down his back. His sleeveless tunic was soaked in blood. He threw the dagger at Dar and, in two bounds, reached the place where he had left his horse.

Dar knocked the whirling dagger away from his face with the tip of his iron spear. He could hear the heavy hoofs of Sinie's galloping horse receding.

Dar knew Havert would be back. Kalan warriors earned their Obedience Tattoos and were bound by a blood oath to execute the sultan's commands.

Dar hugged Bettia to his chest as the older, shorter merchant who had known of the swamp witch strolled across the stony beach, picking his way carefully so as not to get wet. His simple dark blue wool tunic and pants looked slept in. His eyes were rimmed with dark circles. He cleared his throat and scratched his rounded belly.

"I wanted to say that by law, under penalty of death, we are required to report all Spearslayer sightings. The Chenian army and bounty hunters will search the area to find you as soon as they know a Spearslayer is about."

"I will avoid Chenia," said Dar. He hated to do so because Chenia had the largest slave market, and they reported and archived meticulous records of each transaction daily. Those records might include information about his family.

"A wise move. You may have the sorrel mare. If anyone asks, I'll say bandits stole the horse," replied the merchant. "Good luck, Spearslayer."

The short merchant didn't wait for a thank you. He turned and walked back toward the growing clamour of the caravan. They were busy checking baggage, repacking and preparing for a triumphant, colourful entry into Chenia. Tonight, stories of swamp witches and Spearslayers would entertain Chenia's tavern goers.

Dar got dressed and packed his few things in a sling bag. He stepped into the saddle and leaned over, pulling Bettia up behind him. He turned and kissed her wide, generous mouth, long and hard. Then he urged the horse forward, to the north, away from Chenia. Bettia wrapped her arms around his waist and rested her head on his broad back.

The sun was inching toward its zenith in the blue cloudless sky. Its heat was bearing down and warming the ground. Dar reckoned today would be a hot day, and he had many miles to go and a promise to keep.

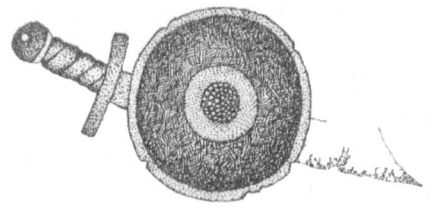

THE STONE HEADS

A Tale of Dracht Kar the Warrioress

Scott McCloskey

The sea fills my lungs like farmer's slop, fattening the hog for slaughter. With the buoyancy of my flesh lost to bloat, I dare it to drown me as I skulk along the sea floor. I cannot say how long I have walked this path, but I will not be deterred until there is reason to be. Oceans are a mere trifle.

Behind me lies the Whitewood Sands, upon which I knew freedom and purpose. As Hierarch Warrior it was mine to ferry the enemies of the Ysir to the Horsemother's Hell on the edge of my blade, which I did with same abandon used to laugh with my companions, dote upon my daughters, and make love to my husbands beneath the sunstar and Luna's silver grace.

When my life ended my sisters burned an effigy made from hair and flesh over my remains, excising from my veins the blood to seal it. It was *Orathas est Fir Gazé*; the Rite of Wind and Fire. I was bound to them beyond death, holding that I would ride again when their need was dire.

But the day of my reckoning never came.

I languished, an entombed prisoner of my own corpse, while my kin traded useless hunks of yellow rock to the Thenubrians, who used it to build upon the Verst Highlands a city of gold. Soon their greed became boundless, and megalomania beat its cadence upon the drums of war. We were the stronger, for the blood of the Horsemother is the mortar that builds towers of our womenfolk to rival foreign men. Theirs, however, were numbers and resource. The scroll used to invoke my return was stolen, and I could but sleep; my dreams plagued by the bloody gurgle of familiar throats laid open.

The Whitewood Sands, cursed by wicked shamans to perpetual deluge, became a wallowing marsh. Those of my kindred who survived the sword became the concubines of sultans, or laboured until their dying days to dig the golden city's roots ever deeper. I spit the name 'Thenubria', but there is no longer any other upon maps of my home.

I raged against my plight, but there is nothing left for me there now. With seven decades of mingled blood between my people and theirs I cannot exact the right, for their wretched flesh runs with blood of my own. I had failed my people, and so I tore down our burial cairns with my own hands, that their souls might know freedom from the hellacious swamp our home had become.

It was all I could do before I walked away. Today I walk still.

"Cap'n! Oi, call th'Cap'n up!"

Whosoever emits the mangled slur hasn't half a dozen teeth left behind their flapping lips. I am caught in a net, and through no effort of my own find myself rising to the surface. I choose not to resist; I have been alone with the plague of my thoughts too long. Besides, there are easier ways to travel the water.

My body breaks the surf, and the voices quickly multiply:

"Lookit wot th'lads dredged up!"

"See them jewels! Tha'ss a king's note! Haul 'em up!"

Varso, Blade of the Despoiler, rests upon my back. His hilt is rich and beautiful, but his barbs rip as the teeth of a giant serpent, and his curse is lethal to whomever would lay hands to take him. By right of that curse he recognizes only the owner who wins him in battle, but is now as lost as I, for the man whose hand I died by died also by my own. He fights with me because I am all he has. I sense his displeasure at every turn.

A moment later I lay flat upon hard boards, staring for the first time in days at open sky. Around me is a trawler's net. My good view is soon marred by scraggly, filthy faces.

"Drowned," a spindly seaman concludes after prodding my arm with a toeless boot. "S'ashame. Ain't every day the sea hands out swords and sluts in one!"

"I'll say," another laughs raggedly. "If she was still breathin' I'd make 'er pant fer more!"

"Should be perfect fer you, Oolger. By the time the harlots get t'you, they're so worn out the city houses are ready to toss 'em away!"

"Oi you! Say it to m'face!"

The sailors share a round of raucous laughter, broken only when a booming voice cows them to silence.

"Shaddup on deck!"

This one is large enough to command by fear, and barely clean enough for authority. He bends over me to peer through my slitted eyes.

"Y'rats, she's only got a little o'the bloat."

"So?" a hand replies. "Summa th'boys ain't seen a pretty thing in near thirty moons. Summa 'em are desperate enough that they'd even ravish this one here, so it's better she still looks nice!"

The men laugh again. The captain withers his mate with a glare. "I *mean* she don't look like old meat, y'fool. If she ain't been dead long, what's that tell ye?"

"There's...another ship?"

"There's another wreck out here for us t'trawl?" an eager man cries.

"I ain't seen no clouds in th'sky fer days," the captain says warily. "Prolly this one got the fever, and her own tossed her out. Mebbe even 'fore she died."

The men back away from me instinctively.

"Lookit that sword," one observes. "An' that muscle, too. If she's a fighter there might be a soldiers' galleon on th'hunt out here!"

"Yer an idiot, Larch. I ain't *seen* no galleons on patrol, have you?"

"Then how's she out here, still lookin' pretty?" The one called 'Larch' concludes. "Where's her ship?"

The crew glance uncertainly at the horizon, until Larch—a lanky man so grimy I cannot make out his complexion—creeps like disease along the deck by my side. "Aw who cares. I'm here fer jewels, an' I mean t'have 'em whether or not the lotta ya go off crying 'bout spears 'n sickness!"

"Hey! Captain's pref'rence!"

Larch pulls a knife and reaches towards my sword, intent upon prying free an emerald. I need not intervene. Varso can speak for himself.

"aaaAAAaaGGHHH!"

As if plunged into a raging fire, Larch's hands boil, the flesh quickly slouching from scorched bone. The doomed man writhes on the deck, black vitriol drawing the pattern of his veins on his flesh as it crawls towards his heart. The men recoil as Larch stumbles to his feet, and look on in horror as his sclera blacken and his eyes melt from their sockets. He crashes into the deck railing, doubles over it, and is taken by the swirling sea.

"Melora's mercy!" a stunned sailor cries. "It's cursed,

and the wench what's tied to it! Toss 'er over th'side 'fore we all meet the Deepkin!"

I grow tired of this. I sit up, and lance the captain with my glare.

"Gods above! She's still livin'!"

Only the captain dares approach, though I suspect his bravery is motivated by a desire to save face before his crew. Pushed by said desire to even more rash decisions, he draws his scimitar and touches the blade to my neck.

"Where's yer ship, woman? How come ye t'be here, an' what do you mean by bringing filthy curses on board?"

"I *walked* here, dog," I reply gravely. "A walk you and your lackeys have interrupted. I do not *like* to be interrupted."

"Revenant!" A terrified sailor screams. "A revenant! Kill it before we all burn with Vaal!"

I bat the captain's sword away, and springing to my feet backhand him senseless. Four foolhardy souls surround me, weapons at the ready. I can read their whole lives on their faces; two unscrupulous boys, hearts driven black by the promise of gold, and two seasoned men, stubborn and greedy as their captain. The only difference between them is the extra half-second it takes to eviscerate the latter two.

The deck is in turmoil. I have want of this ship, so I knock senseless or swat with the flat of my blade any foolish but useful oarsman who bungles into my path. Those few who offer actual resistance are relieved of either their sword arms or their heads to my preference. I walk in a straight line—as I am wont to do—towards the commanding officer, who cowers now behind a turbid wall of men. Soon my blade rests at *his* neck.

"Yer...yer not human..." he blubbers.

"And you are neither fisherman nor pirates," I mutter.

"Only vultures and worse would turn to such desperation as trawling the seafloor for sunken riches."

"G-getoff my ship," says he with a morsel of painstakingly summoned boldness. "Our souls ain't worth nothin' t'you. These here are desperate times, where lean men do what they gotta t'survive. We got nothin' a revenant would want."

"But you do," I counter. A man shatters a heavy oar over my back. I lift him by the neck, turn his head at an impossible angle, and point him at the distant shore before flinging him into the sea. "I grow tired of trudging through water. Take me east."

The captain is sweating from more than the sun. "P-passage? But revenants…they only want souls fer Vaal!"

"No revenant am I, dog," I seethe. "You look upon Dracht Kar, Hierarch Warrior of the Ysir's central tribes."

"Them horse-wenches? I heard about 'em once, but there ain't none no more. Ain't been since 'fore my granny was born."

"Then call me by the name my enemies curse: Gor Malin, the Blood of Ten Thousand."

Fear burgeons in the captain's eyes. "Th-Thenubria's ender o'the day? No…no that can't be…he's dead…"

"She will be stopped neither by death, nor the sea, nor *you.* Take me to the eastern shore, worm, and if you so dare as to associate my name with the sons of Thenubria's whore-goddess again, you will vomit out your last red breath before the final word escapes your fatted lips.

"Th-the eastern shoals ain't safe," the mousey commander warns. "There's a danger in the wind there, come up these last three full cycles o'Luna. They say the Deepkin gods are afoul of the world, movin' whole islands about an'what."

"The gods are not here. *I am*."

The captain bows his head. Quelled, the crew looks to me with the loyalty that fear brings, and the oarsmen take to their stations. I require nothing else from them, and mean to stand upon this very spot until land is in my sight.

*

I do not move until the sun has made a full cycle and is overhead again.

Nestled between blighted hills I spy a small port village in the distance. I don't ask the name, nor do I care anything about the place save that it might contain a side of salted pork and a few casks of wine. Cursed by the want of things that cannot sustain me, I seek only to burn up coin in this way until I find the means to avenge myself, my sisters, my children, my husbands, and my friends against the Golden City. Perhaps then I might return to the grasp of death denied me.

"Hold, rats!" calls the captain. As one the oarsmen cease, and our momentum coasts to a crawl.

"You have a deathwish, mongrel," I threaten. "I told you to deliver me to the shore, yet my feet still remain insulted by your rotting boards."

"We can't go no farther. I told ye, th'shoals ain't safe."

"And I told *you* of my wrath. Do you require additional persuasion?"

The captain cringes. "M-Melora's mercy, Milor—*milady*, but y'won't talk th'boys into gettin' no closer. Not even with that demon blade you got at yer back. See there."

I follow his gesture. Several young oarsmen, unable to choose between horrors, have already leapt overboard.

"That's how much this place afears 'em. Ain't none

what still has half their wits about 'em are fool enough to row these waters, an' no fish to be had besides. You c'n make threats all you want, but every man here'd sooner toss themselves over th'side 'fore they row another stroke towards that burg." He edges away from me until his back is at the railing. "Same goes fer me."

"And that village?"

"Corgrim," says he. "Dunno where you wanna go, but don't bother with 'em. They're as good as dead already."

I bring the still-distant village back into focus. A ghastly pall hangs in the air, with low-hanging clouds draped over it like a funerary shroud. The captain sidles up to me and lowers his voice.

"B'tween you an' me, you done us a service today. Too many mouths t'feed. Th'gods of the deep are up from their rest. There won't be no safe port in th'storm they bring, an' there's only so much left to eat on these waters."

I grunt. I have nothing more to say to him.

"Mercy yer way, woman. Revenant or no, ye'll need it."

I plunge into the surf, never to see the starving vessel again.

Corgrim is a bald, muddy hole, combed over with receding thatched rooves. The people are gangly and gaunt, with haunted eyes; I watch them scuttle like lice over the pockmarked scalp of their withered home. I pull myself onto a short pier, my soaked form loudly breaking the water, and am met by a piercing scream.

"The Deep Ones! They come!"

A hooded woman in a sweat-drenched apron stabs at me from afar with one finger, while two bony children, poorly hidden in her gown, mewl and weep. Two men wearing long, droopy Thenubrian moustaches cross spears at the shore to block my way. One is taller with an intimidating horned helmet upon his crown, but both are hungry nigh to sickness. I smell the fear that rattles under their mail.

"B-back, creature…!" one demands. "G-get back!"

I could pluck their heads from their shoulders as easily as grapes from a vine, did they not burn with the white-hot aura of The Rite. Thenubria's grasp reaches far, and with Ysir blood in them, I cannot harm these men so long as they are worthy of the favour of ancestors they don't even know they have. I stand fast, offering them instead a look that could kill as easily as any sword should they make good with their weapons.

"Fine hospitality, this 'Corgrim'," I sneer.

The one with the bushy beard peers at me through one good eye. "You…you've got a head. A woman's head."

I shake my tresses free of water weight and raise my brow. "And hands and feet besides, man. Do you always greet travellers this way?"

"You come out of the sea, but there's no ship at your back. From where do you hail?"

"From across the sea," I reply. I will not call Thenubria my home.

"That far? What of your ship?"

I nod at the vessel receding on the horizon. The men look at each other, then speak of me as though I do not stand right in front of them.

"She's got a head, Draf."

"Maybe, but what about the Deep Ones? She's come from the sea!"

"On a *ship*."

"So? *They* come on ships too!"

"Not a ship like that. If it were one of *their* ships it would have come right up. Whoever's rowing that one has the sense to stay away."

"But she swam that far and isn't even winded! Nobody can do that, especially a woman!"

I tap my boot impatiently. "My skins are soaked, my patience thin, and the natter in my gut demands satisfaction. Do you plan to let me in, or shall I do it myself?"

I cast them a baleful look. The other man, clearly in command, divines in my iron countenance the bleakness of his future should he stand in my way. He pulls his weapon back.

"Welcome to Corgrim, Stranger. Don't make trouble."

"An' leave that blade!" Draf croaks. I draw my sword, proffer it to him, and wait. He reaches out until a black glow shines in his eye, then wisely pulls back.

"...k-keep your damned sword," says he. "But like the captain said! No trouble!"

My sword is indeed damned, little man, I don't reply. *As am I.*

I touch down upon the beach and pause to glance over the water. I am farther now from my home than I have ever been before.

Some of the villagers glow faintly with The Rite. Most do not. All are staring. I stride through their town, interested only in staving the gnaw from my insides, until a weathered sign designates a larger hovel—but no less a hovel—as a drinking establishment.

The muscle in my chest beats one time. Campfire legends hold that the deceased can have desires so powerful as to shackle them forever to the mortal realm. I am not certain if I am truly dead, but yet nary a dram has passed my lips in four score decades. I *will* change that.

"Ho the bar!" I bellow as I hurl back the door. "Wine! Now!"

The place is little more than a log hut converted for a bar and tables. What few patrons lie therein scatter like rabbits. The portly barman moves to do the same, until I root him to the spot with my stare.

"We...we don't want any trouble, Stranger..."

"Pour the wine and you will have none," I promise.

"A-and...how will you be paying, Miss...?"

I fish a talent from my pouch, taken off the body of a dead Adzelgar lancer for better use elsewhere. Upon it is minted the sultan of the golden city; soon to be assassinated in a coup by the vizier's third daughter if it hasn't happened already. I toss it to the barman, who marvels at its golden sheen.

"Keep it coming, man."

The saffron spirits are too cheap, too sweet, and too worldly to slake my thirst. Thus I partake as a glutton, with thought only for the act of taking. When I have turned the barman's greedy eyes to worry, the door creaks open once more. I expect to hear the boots of the city guard come to challenge me, but the soft footfalls belong to a different creature entirely.

Light and bare of foot, swaddled in threadbare silks that once were rich but still match her sparkling eyes, stands a comely lass. She is either too clean for this town, or merely cleans up well. I assume the latter, for I see no escort; if this were not her home, she likely would have fallen prey to baser instincts by now. Her sun-dappled mane cascades in curls; she wears it over one eye, the other closed over but slightly in a bedchamber gleam. I drink at my table in the corner, until she floats coquettishly over to me.

"They said a man swam the entire sea to reach our pier," she observes. "Are you with him?"

"News here travels as falsely as it does fast," I mutter. "Do you *see* a man, girl?"

Her eyes widen, but she corrects herself quickly. "Such

a powerful woman. Surely of a kind I've not seen before. From whence do you hail, Stranger?"

"From the Whitewood Sands," I say without looking up. "I am of the Ysir. The horsemaidens of the plains."

She tilts her head. "...from where?"

My people are gone. My lands usurped. I grit my teeth and spit out the heathen words: "From Thenubria."

"Across the Bluewisp Sea, how enchanting! Are all Thenubrian woman so endowed?"

"Hardly."

"And your menfolk?"

I finger the cord about my neck, where rests the now sodden locks of my family's hair; husbands and daughters, all long lost. "Keepers of our hearths, and our hearts."

"Fascinating," she lies whilst inviting herself to the next chair. "I'm called Annin."

"Dracht Kar," I reply with my true name. My appellation might send the whole town into a frenzy, and I've no wish to kill in this place. Not so long as my hand isn't forced.

"Such an exotic name. Buy a lady a drink?"

"Go home, girl. Your mother's teat is too fresh to find you a harlot."

"So harsh," Annin pouts. "Your men must be quite satisfying indeed."

The girl, apparently undaunted by the man she did not find, curls against my side. She crosses her legs just so; a bit of her silks flitter away to reveal the suppleness of her smooth thighs. Her scent is like honey, and her closeness twice as thick.

"And yours must be eunuchs," I observe.

She is warm. Blessedly warm, like an unfettered night upon the virgin plains just prior to blissful defloration. I do not touch her knee, so she touches mine.

"Tell me to go away," she oozes softly.

"I've done as much already."

"But you didn't mean it, did you?"

"..."

"Wherever you come from, you're a foreigner here, no? And alone, to boot. Alone perhaps for a long time."

Her hand moves. My throat tightens.

I am a Hierarch Warrior. The End of my enemy. But among my sisters in battle were those as playful and crafty as this wench, and they were not above cahoots with my mates.

"Tell me about the Deep Ones," I say by way of changing the subject. "What does this village fear? Why am I a marvel for the head upon my shoulders?"

"You don't want to hear about that. I've a private place where we can write stories of our own. My, you're so cold..."

Cold like my people's empty cairns. When first I was brought back my stare blazed red. The hue has since reduced to a slight vermillion glimmer, but it cannot be overlooked from mere inches away. I fix her with it.

"Would you pen your story in chilled blood? I said *begone*, child."

Her eyes widen again; this time she does not recover. "You...you're not—" abandoning her thoughts on the table, she is quickly gone.

My chest thrums once more. I'm not ready for two beats a day, and so I drown them both in spirits. Gold has no value to me other than to feed my vices, and so to the barman's delight I proffer an additional talent I had since left on the table to keep me in drink. When I am done most of the day—and most of the wine—is gone.

"Melora..." the barman whispers when all is said and drunk. "Only the gods themselves can gather so many spirits!"

Beyond the confines of the lonely hovel, the setting sunstar casts a shimmering glow over the patient sea. Reds, oranges, and purples drop down the spectrum to swirl and fade across the horizon into rising blues and greens. A salty breeze catches my hair, wisping it about my shoulders. I am captivated by the spectacle, and commanded to gawk by my stupor.

"The Bluewisp Sea is a fine show at dusk," says the barman from behind. "When the lights start to dance on the water, they say you can see the soul of your loved ones what died there."

Nobody I love ever died at sea. It's just as well, for I have no need to see them more than I already do.

"Er, Miss...Milady...?"

I grunt obliviously.

"To beg your pardon a dozen times over, but...it's like this. You paid for your drinks and then a bit more and that's a fine thing, but...you've nearly drunk me clear out of house and home. I've never seen anybody what could hold their liquor the way you do, but seeing as how you've got nearly my entire larder tied up in your gut, well—you understand, I trust?"

"It is to be more gold then, miser?"

"...i-if it please."

Useless yellow rock. My people knew no such obsession and to my thinking were the better for it, but I am out among the world now, and there are those who worship differently. I reach for my purse, only to come up with nothing.

Bedamned.

I see red, and whirl upon the barman with an expression that sends him scampering back inside. "The whore in a lady's rags!" I demand. "Tell me where to find her!"

SWORDS & SORCERIES

I'm drawing a scene. Compounding my desire *not* to have to slay the guardsmen of this pitiful burg, I turn from his establishment into what passes for a street. The roads are mostly mud, and shodden as the people are, I remember distinctly the girl who glided about barefoot. An amateur mistake for a cutpurse. In an instant I am off at a run, on the tracks of game fool enough to incur my wrath.

The trail leads down a side street to a barren alley, where a single rickety door is stuck like an afterthought onto an equally rickety hovel. I grab the portal, rip it from its hinges, and toss it straight into whatever waits for me as I stomp in.

"Where are you, waif?" I bellow. "I do not know what passes for morality in this accursed stinkhole, but where I am from, there are consequences for theft! I *am* those consequences, so prepare yourself!"

The door splinters into chunks against the far wall; I hear not one, but two adolescent screeches in response. A form brushes against me on its way out. I grab it by the wrist and yank hard, with just enough clarity of mind *not* to rip the arm from its socket. In an instant my eyes are inches from Annin's.

"Rogue! Return what you have plundered before I take it out of your hide!"

The girl kicks and writhes, her feet barely brushing the floor from the height I hold her. Hers is a mask of abject terror.

"No! Monster! Revenant! Devil! Get away!"

I toss her back into the room. Looming above the crumpled child I draw and brandish Varso—I am no butcher of the weak, but I mean to have what is mine. One look at Gor Malin in all her wrath is all it takes. The girl begins to choke, then vomits up steaming panic all over the house's dirt floor.

I make a show of it, meaning to take a leg from the hovel's only table in lieu of hers, but another blade rises to parry. This other—no more than a long hunting knife—is shattered like glass on impact, and does nothing whatever to impede my progress. I take the wooden leg, and look down to find a *second* girl at my feet.

No. Not a girl. Though so similar to Annin that they can only be blood, this one is a young boy. He crouches over his dry-heaving kin, holding the destroyed knife on me as though he plans to take on the world with it.

"Away from my sister, Revenant!"

I raise a brow. "You mean to fight me with that, Child?"

"I-if you force me to…!" He stammers. "G-get out of our house or…or by my wrath, I'll send you straight back to Vaal!"

"Then return what is mine," I demand. In response, the boy produces my purse and tosses it at my feet.

"Take it! Take your filthy money and go away!"

My people have always valued the spirit of bravery, no matter how foolhardy the mind in which it takes up residence. I retrieve my purse and replace my sword, much to Varso's bloodthirsty chagrin.

"Let this be a lesson to you, brats: If you mean to knock down your enemy, make certain they do not get up. If you mean to *rob* them, make certain to leave no trace."

I turn to depart, until the boy calls out to me.

"W-wait!"

"Which is it to be, boy? 'Go away' or 'wait'? If it be the latter you'd best have something worth my time, or by the Horsemother you'll regret it."

"Are you of the Ysir?"

I stop at the door. "You listen well, but are too young to know the name."

"I do know it. I can read!" He says so with deserving pride, for I have no doubt such a skill is rare in this place. "You dress in skins and you're taller even than Captain Roth of the guardsmen. Nobody's that tall, especially women, so you must be one of them. They say the Ysir weren't human."

"Our blood is nearly yours, save for a single drop of our mother's divine grace from which our people spawned," I explain.

"That's what the legends say," he agrees. I narrow my brow.

"Take care what proofs you attribute to legend, child. You and your sister are lucky for keeping your heads today. Goodbye."

The boy rises to his feet. He barely comes up past my waist, and has little to show for himself but a gown of rags and a rat's nest for a mane. "But you can't be even *close* to human. They say you *swam* here, and your eyes...!"

"I *was* Ysir. I am more now, and in being more I am ultimately less."

The boy doesn't know what to do with that, and I don't explain.

"I'm Eldin," says he, and then pointing to his sister: "That's Annin."

"We've met."

No trace of the lascivious silks adorn the little thief, who wears instead simple peasant garb. Who knows where she got the tattered finery, but even in its current condition it is surely worth more than their entire 'home'.

"What do you know of my people?" I inquire.

"I know there are no Ysir anymore," Eldin muses. "How can you be here?"

I debate how I might put it, but am spared my quandary by a new scream from Annin; this one as person whose bowels were just cut free. Wide-eyed with panic, she rushes to the doorway and runs her hands over the frame, ignoring the splinters that embed themselves in her fingertips.

"You...you've destroyed it!" she screeches. "What have you done? They'll get in now!"

Eldin curses like an old man and rushes to tend to his damaged sister. "See what you've done! You've doomed us!"

"Who will get in?" I ask.

"They will!" Annin shrieks. "The children of the Deepkin gods! They've had enough of our meddling, our fishing and sailing! We're a disease, and they come at first dark every fortnight to cleanse us! We can't keep them out anymore! Father, then mother too...we're next!"

Eldin, crouched over his sister, looks up to me with pleading eyes. "You're strong, Stranger. Stronger than anyone here, if your blood is as true as you say. Help us. I beg of you."

I sniff. "You have lofty expectations of your robbery targets."

"I've read about the Ysir. They were death to their enemies, but they knew clemency, and they were honourable people. The kind the world needs more of. Were the stories wrong?"

History is written by the victors, and I had since supposed what the Golden Witch told me: that every tradition would play out the Ysir to be blood-drinking, infant-devouring fiends. Apparently some genuine records still survive. I owe the truth of them to my sisters, who can no longer speak for themselves.

"...your texts did not err," I reply.

The sun vanishes below the horizon, and with it all sense of sanity in Corgrim. The weak, frantic knell of an alarm gong is choked out by cries of anguish and terror that resonate from every street.

"Come!" I demand, but Annin is too traumatized to move, and her brother will not leave her. An abandoned oxcart sits by a wall in the alley—I take the whole thing up and toss it in front of the open portal behind which the children huddle. With that, I'm off into the torchlit street.

It is said that Vaal's underland has many layers. Corgrim may be one.

Whipped to a frenzy by the throes of pandemonium, the hollow citizens scatter in all directions. Some leap cackling into the sea, while others lose themselves to the predators who gather in expectation at the jungle's edge. Those who cram into the hovels for shelter swear epithets at the late arrivals, tossing them out with declarations of no vacancy.

The things from which they flee are nearly human, yet as far from it as they are close. Naked men and women, bloated by seawater that pours from boils that run up their flesh like barnacles on a hull. They utter no battle cry as they overrun the pier and rush onto the beach by the dozen, nor expressions of passion for their murderous acts. The reason is clear—each figure wears a head of solid stone upon their shoulders, carved in relief as a perfect replica of a human head. Every face engraved therein sports a solemn, peaceful face, unique to the bearer.

I watch as they disgorge in waves from a vessel moored at the harbour. The ship glows with the bluewisp lights on the tide, floating somehow upon the sea despite jagged cracks and gargantuan holes in its hull. Whatever sail it once sported is tattered to shreds, and with neither that nor oarsmen to drive it, its means of locomotion is as much a mystery to me as its buoyancy.

SWORDS & SORCERIES

I watch the stoneheaded beings at their grisly work. What few guardsmen remain slash at their faces, breaking swords harmlessly over them. Those who attack more vulnerable spots are met with inhuman speed and grace as the stoneheads parry with their solid skulls, their barnacled limbs, or catch striking blades between their bare hands. I watch one poor bastard fall before a wave of them after the first shoves its fist straight through the man's skull, pulling back bloody tissue and chunks of bone from the opposite side.

The stoneheads outnumber the inhabitants of Corgrim three to one. They spread through the village, murdering without a thought all who dare oppose them. Innocents — even children — who cannot defend themselves are dragged off screaming towards the sea.

I draw Varso as three of the creatures rush to meet me. They are strong, but I am stronger. The first is disembowelled by the Despoiler's wicked barbs, though it does not fall until I take both its legs. I remove the left arm of the second, but it ignores the grievous injury until I run it through, catch its heart on my blade, and toss the pulsing organ to the ground to crush it beneath my boot. No wound but a fatal one will stop them; I take note of this as I behead the third.

The body of my last attacker drops, and I watch its stone head roll. Tendons and bits of spine gush forth from the wound, but there is no skull beneath. The heads are neither helmets nor masks. There can be only one explanation.

Sorcery.

I bristle. A fire has broken out in one of the crowded buildings. The stoneheads wait patiently for panicked innocents to charge out, then drag them one by one towards the coast. Those already on fire are left to burn.

Cyrilia Anst Dourdan, golden witch and half-blood wretch, was the one to invoke the Rite and call me back. She called me 'Lady Berserker' in derision, but could not know how her words rang true. Dracht Kar, Hierarch Warrior, fades away in a frenzy of flesh. Twirling the Despoiler above my head, I emerge as Gor Malin, the Blood of Ten Thousand!

"Hallowed the Horsemother's Hell!"

My people's cry of amnesty for the souls of the bravely departed, friend and foe alike. I utter it now for the defenders of Corgrim, for these emotionless things have no bravery to show. I am nearly robbed of slaughter's joy by the stoneheads' lack of reaction to their own deaths, and so I count aloud each head I take. I am laughing by the time I hit two digits. By a score, I feel my lips split in thunderous cackles. The Rite has made me into something to be feared far beyond what I was in life.

Even I am afraid of me.

Luna dances freely high above; I've long since lost track of time. Crowned by her silver glow and bathed in the bluewisp lights I slaughter my way clear into the surf, taking but dim note of the wet sand that clings to my boots and crawls up my legs as I wade. The waves around me run red; I am splattered by the red-black viscosity the stoneheads' emit with their demise. I leap upon the pier, meaning to have my way onboard their vessel to destroy whatever feeble warlock controls them, but a line of them hold me back long enough for the ship to break its moorings and pull away. There are no men at the oars, yet the vessel turns on a talent and pivots its way out to sea as easily as I might clench my fist.

"Cowards!" I bellow as I destroy the remaining few left behind. "Bring your bastard children and face The End, demons, lest I bore straight through the seafloor to rip the steaming hearts from the chests of your gods!"

But the vessel is gone. I slam Varso on the pier in frustration.

"Stranger!"

Panting like a wild dog I whirl on the man, who holds up his hands in supplication.

"Please Stranger, I mean you no harm! Are you injured?"

It is the shorter of the two who met me at the pier—the one called Draf. He is lucky that his question gets through to me. I cannot be hurt, but as the witch reminded me, I can be *harmed*. I check myself over, finding all four limbs still in their places.

"Trifling scratches. What of the others?"

Draf indicates the village. The people are dousing fires with success, but mailed men and charred corpses lie torn apart by the dozen all over the beach. I see the woman who stabbed her finger at me when I arrived, weeping hysterically. One of her striplings lies motionless in the sand. The other is simply gone.

The ship vanishes on the horizon at a speed no mortal vessel could ever hope to match. I hear the cries of captives fading in the distance.

*

The morning after finds me in a scorched, sorry structure of timber and mud that passes for Corgrim's seat. What few citizens still bear a glimmer of hope have the place filled to standing room, though none dare crowd me. The sunstar sizzles us all through holes in the roof, threatening to finish what the stoneheads began.

"...and that's how it is," says Draf in conclusion. The story is an old one to them, so all eyes are on me for a reaction. Some faces scowl in ignorant fear, despite my help the night before.

"And the stone faces are those of your own people, reanimated by dark sorcery," I conclude. Draf shrugs.

"Dunno about any of that. All we know is when they come there's always more than before, and more of those gods-be-damned heads look like folks we know."

"My son almost killed me last night! It's only a matter of time before we're all like them!" someone shouts.

"Then why not leave this place?" I reason. Draf gives me a pitying look.

"You're no seafarer, are you Stranger. This is a fishing village. Our longboats would never survive the open sea, and there's no ship crewed by flesh and blood that will come around here now."

"Is this an island? What about the jungle?"

"No island, but the beasts there can smell our doom, and gather with the scent of our blood. Our ancestors came to this place *because* of that—they wanted to be left alone by the rest of the world. Now their pride will be our end, and yours too I'm sorry to say. There's no escape."

"And you expect to see this ship again."

"Every fortnight at dusk. And don't think you chased it away. It left because it was done for the night."

"It's the gods of the deep, riding a sunken ship!" declares a voice. "We angered them by taking too many fish! Now *they're* trawling for *us!*"

Draf snorts and hangs his head, indicating that while he doesn't like that explanation, he has no better one.

Nearby, hand in one another's, stand the siblings. I've seen no other youths still breathing. They may be the last.

Eldin pulls his sister towards me, pushing through adults who lack the courage to approach.

"She can help us," the boy declares.

"She ain't human!" somebody shouts.

"She's Ysir!" Eldin insists, "and...something else too! Something *better!*"

Some faces show no recognition of the word. Others back away even farther than before. Eldin is indignant.

"Didn't you see what she did last night? She destroyed six times her own without a scratch! How can you be so cowardly as to—"

"She killed my husband!" a woman cries.

"And my son!" shouts another.

"Those weren't your kin," Draf insists.

"You don't know that, Draf! What if we can break the spell?"

"You don't even know there's a spell involved that can be broken!"

"Of course you want to fight, you're just the captain's lackey!" a gaunt man spits.

"Captain Roth is dead!" Draf roars.

The gathering breaks into dissonance. I listen to them make accusations at one another, at me, and at life itself for their woes until I can take it no more, and slamming my fist on a creaking table, break it in two for their attention.

"Enough! You claim an independent history in this place, but I hear only the mewling of foals! If you do not mean to act, then march into the sea by twos and leave your village for nature to reclaim!"

"You think we haven't tried to defend ourselves?" says one.

"I have seen you run for shelter, and damn the other man who doesn't get there first."

"Many are women and children," Draf attempts.

"*I* am a woman," I riposte, then point at Eldin. "And this boy held me at bay with a broken knife to defend his home. Would you do less?"

Draf coughs, and I take the floor.

"Know first that whomever is taken by those creatures is no longer the person you knew—I have learned as much from the empty heads that roll from their shoulders. You are at war, and haven't the time to waste the sunstar on woes for yourselves. Fortify your perimeter. Gather the swords of your dead and put them in any hand that can wield them. Train your innocents. Damn the gods by dying proudly, or die *now* by your own hands, and at the very least deny your enemy their prize."

The rabble mutters amongst itself. Draf attempts to call them to order, but they do not listen. They have no respect for him.

"I will aid anyone invested in aiding themselves," I announce, "but I will *carry* none of you. If you can stand and hold a sword, you will fight. If not, another role will be found. If neither, you will *leave.*"

The people consider this hesitantly. "Who...who gave you leave to bark orders at us?" one ventures quietly.

"Listen to your captain!" Draf declares, and tosses the horned helmet to me.

"Captain Roth is returned?" one says hopefully.

"Captain Roth is dead!" Draf repeats. "Listen to Captain Kar!"

*

So begins my ascension as military dictator of a small fishing village.

Those who cannot let go of their loved ones still think me their reaper, but I have no ear for dissent. Those too old or infirm to stand at arms are set to sharpening steel, mending mail, or managing our dwindling resources, while the rest are taught to make war.

For a fortnight I put my soldiers' every waking moment—Annin and Eldin included—through vigorous training, though I know it will not be enough. Perhaps a garrison of novice spearmen might stand a chance, but making an armed camp of this muddy hole in a mere fortnight is impossible. Thus I focus upon the shield and defensive tactics, that this paper legion might hold together long enough for me to get onto that damned ship and make powder from the bones of the diabolical thaumaturge that drives it.

That is their only chance. If I cannot do it they will all be massacred, and I will wear a head of stone for all my days. In undeath, those days will be long indeed.

On a certain night when the air is crisp, I brush my locks back and look to the shining sea from behind hasty fortifications built of sharpened tree trunks.

"There," I point to the sinking colours in the sky. "A league or more out."

"It could be a privateer," Draf says hopefully, but my senses are sharpened by The Rite, and I can see clearly.

"No. It is the ship, and being three days late, it has certainly made ready. Tonight decides Corgrim's fate for good. Sound the alarm. At the speed it travels, it will be on us in moments!"

Draf raps hard on the village gong four times, then races off towards town. "It comes! Up and to your arms!"

Were I alone, I would draw Varso and damn the hordes to move me from this spot. As a leader I am a rallying point, and so make for our inner pickets to organize the defence. Most of these people will not survive, but by the Horsemother, their bravery will be rewarded in the next life to which I cannot go.

The vessel looms tall in our harbour at dusk; it has not yet hit the pier, but stoneheads are already falling over the side in a mad dash to make landfall. At length they hit the beach, and our two forces are met in a cheated lovers' homicidal embrace.

The pickets prove of value, but only to delay the inevitable. The defenders have no experience plugging gaps in a battle line, and so whatever our enemies cannot shatter with their marble craniums they simply climb over. The shield pushes them back, but the outcome of this conflict is clear.

I let the people see me, hewing down enemies in their previous captain's helm. When they are engaged and too busy with their own lives, I light out to make good my plan.

Racing towards the ocean with the wind in my hair, I kill with all the ferocity my namesake went into history for. I hack at limbs like a machete into palm fronds in my bid to cut a path through the stone jungle, being sure to add a killing stroke so that each 'life' I take stays claimed. I fight my way to the pier, taking up a torch as I speed by. When I make it to the ship my hunch is rewarded. The overconfident powers that be have thrown their armies all-in, and so there are no defenders to meet me on deck.

I board. Whoever controls the stoneheads' minds must be here. When I destroy them, Corgrim will rise with tomorrow's first light.

The planks are unsteady. My torch gleams, and by its light is revealed…

Nothing.

The melee swirls and crashes on the beach, but this place is quiet enough to rock a babe to sleep. I bob with the waves as I search the ship for a soul to pit my steel against, but no one turns out to meet me.

"Cowardly soothsayer," I rumble. "Face me, and be rewarded with a trip to see your god tonight."

Below decks is another story.

The odour of rot assails me as I descend the deck steps into the belly of the beast. My light dances over a hold bereft of cargo, and a hull so pulverized that any vessel thus wounded should have sunk below the waves faster than the crew could leap overboard. Where the bottom ought to be exists instead a richly-tiled floor of deep blue, crusted with patterns of gold and green like the flesh of a serpent. Its make is a masterpiece; the sort of groundwork reserved for imperial palisades. To the eye it appears solid like marble, but my boots do not clack when set upon it. Instead the tile yields beneath me, pulsing with a thin membrane of water. The floor shifts and writhes with my movements, forcing me to shift my weight constantly just to stand erect.

...like the flesh of a serpent.

"By all the gods of the deep—!"

Were I entirely mortal, I have no doubt the ensuing roar would have ruptured my ears in an instant. Even I am forced to cover them at least, and in so doing lose my grip on both fiery brand and demonic blade. Before either hits the strange ground the closest wall explodes, and the rushing waters of the Bluewisp Sea douse my fire forever. Varso lands point first, and digging into the floor with his wicked barbs, elicits a bellow louder than before.

The entire hold is in motion—my equilibrium is no match. Pounded by surf I am tossed around like a toy, the room crunching and creaking as if in the throes of a tempest.

Rotted boards that ought not to have held the ship together in the first place crumble to fragments, showering me with long splinters that make homes in every patch of skin unprotected by my mail. The sea pours down my throat, filling my stomach and lungs as it had the day I was fished up by the trawler's net.

There is no pain. I draw breath only because I wish it, and have nothing to fear from my entrapment on a sinking ship. If this is the best the Deepkin gods can visit upon me, they deserve nothing but my scorn.

The hold buckles as a rider on an untamed charger's back, but the ship does not sink. Instead the water gushes away, pouring back into the ocean as my view through the hole rises high above sea level. I curse black sorcery for enchanting the ship to soar like an eagle, until I realize it never left the ground. It is the scaly mound itself, upon which the ruined ship is beached, that reaches for the stars.

"The devil—?"

I recover Varso, only to have my sword arm pinned uselessly to my side. A tendril of flesh, thicker around than three stout thoroughbreds, shoots through the destroyed wall at the speed of a striking cobra to entangle me. It sports the same pattern as the tiles, and I come to understand that they are not tiles at all, but *scales*. Scales of something so gargantuan as to raise this ship stories from the surf, and so abominable as to wear it like a shell.

The tendril is all muscle; against its infernal constriction even my strength is useless. Spitting vile epiphanies through the salty water in my throat, I am pinned like a field mouse in the death grip of a boa and taken bodily from the ship.

High in the air above the harbour, I can see fires from Corgrim village. I cannot tell how many of the figures scurrying in the darkness are friend and how many foe, but the proximity of screams tell me that fresh captives have been borne alive back to the pier.

"Off me, vermin, lest I bite my way to freedom!"

My threats are in vain. I am The End of my foe, but nowhere in the Whitewood Sands nor atop the Verst Highlands did I ever encounter such an overwhelming beast. The stink of bilge overwhelms my senses, and tar-black ichor coats every part of me. Varso, insulted by my ineptitude, bites into my leg as the tentacle crushes us together.

The leviathan settles, and I plummet towards the harbour. The ship returns to its place on the waves with enough tumult to knock a dozen stoneheads and their hapless prisoners into the now wild, churning sea. I watch as a wave laps the shore far enough to engulf the fisherman's huts, smashing their unused boats to woodgrain powder.

Some of the people are crying out for their captain; others damn me for their plight. I am plunged beneath the waves, and as the ship turns away, I am pulled out to sea like a doll dragged through the mud in a careless child's grasp.

The ocean speeds by, plugging my ears and blinding me with foam. I am propelled through the water at velocities beyond the mightiest steed, my flesh scored and laid open by passing corals. The muddy, viscous juices that pass for my blood stain the water, creating jets of red-black offal that no mortal predator can hope to catch up with.

I am removed from this world by the patient lights of the Bluewisp Sea. There is no coast. No village. No surface. Should the bonds that hold me choose not to release, I will never again glimpse the grim sunstar on its wounded descent beyond the peaks. For all that I am, and all my kin made me, I can no more save these people than I could my own.

*

The sea is my domain.

I am a pupa, gestating forever in a chrysalis of stinking, oily flesh. I am deaf for the water in my ears. Dumb for the stream that violates me whenever I open my mouth. The Bluewisp Sea, so noted for its eerie glow, shines not, and struck blind by the darkness I have no idea where I am.

Varso—the only instrument I've encountered in undeath that can cause me pain—delivers a message of stinging betrayal. His curse cannot defile me for the blood in my veins stands stagnant, but my nerves remember what agony is, and they deliver his insults clearly.

"Hrrgkkk—"

I strain myself against the walls of my prison, yearning to be free. Resistance yields no fruit, so I hold my unnecessary breaths and stiffen my body as in rigor, hoping the beast will toss me away. There are none who can feign death as I can, for I am always part way there.

My cocoon opens, but slightly. I hope to force it apart, but before I can move the great tentacle rises from the water—lifting me two stories from the ground—and rears back to hurl my worthless corpse far away. For a moment I view the peaceful sky, then crash back into the abyssal depths with such force that the water might well be solid stone.

I can see the bluewisp lights again, but there is no land in any direction. I am lost at sea.

Luna's grace shines down on me, and by her children I orient myself eastward. It takes nearly two leagues of tireless swimming, but my effort is finally rewarded by the presence of two tall ships, each beached on a small scaly island.

Two ships?

For a moment, I consider swimming on. Corgrim is surely lost, and though imbued with might beyond mortal men, I have no idea how to contest even one Deepkin leviathan, much less two. If there are any villagers left with crowns of flesh, they have doubtless lost them to the hungry jungle, or taken them with their own hands before the stoneheads could do it for them.

I tire of the foibles of east and west. I will instead trudge north, swimming or walking the seafloor as long as it takes to find someplace dry to tread beneath my skins.

Before I even clear the islands, I hear the berating voices of my sisters on the waves. They violate my mind with their accusations, holding me to the word I gave these people: So long as they be willing to help themselves, they would find aid in the last of the Ysir.

"Leave me be, damn you," I mutter as I paddle. "They are all dead—there is no one left in that miserable place."

As I draw near the islands I hear the voices of captives, crying out against their impending doom.

"Damn you to Vaal, Witches," I say of my brethren as I turn back towards the islands.

My uncertain footing upon the scaly shore is made worse by the ground's constant undulations, and the strange, oily tar that the beasts constantly secrete. Across the landscape are attached a number of giant leeches, all of which are bloated to my size or greater. I remain undetected as I hike across; the creatures either do not sense my approach, or like the symbiotes they simply do not care. I find Varso glanced off a mound of scales nearly, his thirst for flesh rendered impotent by the creature's solid armour. I draw him forth, resonating with his frustrations, and stalk on.

I can hear more clearly now the laments of the damned. Entry through the hull where I was previously drawn out is simplistic. I pick my way across the blasted boards, following the sound, until I gain the deck and come across a once-regal cabin now converted to a makeshift brig. Behind rusted bars lashed hastily together, the survivors of Corgrim languish. There are no guards, but from the other ship I hear the stoic, quarter-time beat of a single drum.

"Draf...?"

The man leans languidly against his prison. His left arm is missing just above the elbow; the rag tied there is drenched in blood. He peers at me like a drunkard, uncertain of the trust he places in his eyes. Beside him, Annin's bashful lids open wide.

"You've come!" she declares.

"Silence, girl!" I reproach as I test the bars. They are well bound, to the point that it would take more than mortal strength to rend them apart. Fortunately I am not so fettered. The metal whines at my command, twisting as I bid it, until a portal to freedom is formed. Annin, ragged and marred by blood, steps through, but the rest of the rabble only stare.

"Come on then!" I hiss. "Do you not value your freedom?"

Some of them look away. Annin tugs on my sopping jerkin, then buries her face in my side to weep.

"The terrible beast...Melora's mercy..."

Draf glances sidelong at me without recognition, a haunted look on his face. I grab him by the collar and shake him into sense. "Damn you man, listen! Come with me now or never come at all!"

"T'where...?" he slurs emptily. "...s'nothin' but the sea now...sea's our grave..."

Annin holds onto me until some modicum of sense

returns to her, then manages words. "He's right. Where would we go? Would you carry us all away from here on your back?" Her fair-haired, supple modesty is barely contained beneath her swaddling rags. The shivers that wrack her are not from cold, but unlike the others she has retained her senses. My eyes ask her how.

"Eldin...I saw them take him, but he's not here. I-if...if there's any chance...he's all I have left. If not for that thought I'd be just like the others...mercy..."

I haul Draf to his feet, but the decrepit shell of the man who once was crumples back to the deck.

"Monster! Lemme 'lone! Leave me be!" he shouts, stirring the others to similar cries. He scrambles back into the cell, shoving the others as they all attempt to burrow beneath each other like so many nesting rats.

I have seen that look; known it living behind the eyes of those seconds away from death on the battlefield. These people, who were nearly at the point when first I met them, now lie broken beyond all sense of hope. Whatever shreds of meaty sanity held fast to their bones have been picked clean by scavenging terror, leaving behind dry shells barely fit to call human. I take Annin by the hand and pull her away, before the din draws unwanted attention to us.

"What of them?" she asks. I shake my head.

"There is nothing else here to save. We must go."

The drum beats from the other vessel, but this ship is deserted. If the boy still draws breath he can only be there, and so I drag his sister along to facilitate their reunion. To her credit Annin manages a skipping pace with my strides, and does not complain when I toss her from the deck to the scaly ground.

"It...it's alive..." she mutters as she shifts her weight with the oscillating ground. "...the whole island is alive..."

There's no time for a reply—at any moment the land could simply rise up and eject us into the sea. We make a timely pace to the next quivering mass, graciously touching the first, and find passage to the deck by way of fallen rigging. When I am high enough I notice not a plank of driftwood breaks the silent water, much less a dinghy. Our survival is already bleak, but if it comes to it I wonder how we will make our escape. I was born and raised on the back of a horse; Annin and Eldin's survival upon my back against the predators of the sea would be bleak at best.

We gain the deck railing just in time to see Corgrim's barman breathe his last.

The stoneheads, wearing only barnacles and peaceful expressions, array themselves like cultists of Vaal beneath the silver eye of Luna. In their clutches are held a few more scraggly survivors, some of whom are still trying to scream despite having already burnt their voices raw. One stonehead stands upon the forecastle, beating out a single rhythm on a drum stretched over by human flesh, while another retracts a broad blade from its bloody feast. The corpse of the portly barman, not yet understanding that there is no more need to breathe, writhes spasmodically against its spread-eagle bonds upon a wooden altar. The man's head, already forgotten, rolls over to us, spilling brain matter from a crushing blow by the blunt blade. The look upon his face suggests he was too delirious to scream.

"Ahh—"

"Shh!" I hiss as I clamp my hand over Annin's mouth. I glance about for a longboat we might abscond with, but as upon the other vessel find none. Neither do I see Eldin's face among the captives.

The stoneheads wait patiently for the barman's convulsions to cease, and the stain of his pumping blood to slow its spread. At these signs one of them ponderously enters a cabin, returning with a marble replica of the barman's cranium cradled in its arms. The sculpture is perfect in proportion to the original, depicting the barman's face at serene rest. The head is brought to the body, and when roughly shoved upon its bloody neck, the corpse jerks to life. Its bonds are cut, and a new stonehead rises from the altar to a quickened cadence from the single drum.

"...black sorcery..." Annin whispers from between my fingers. I shake my head. There is no warlock. No chanting. No ritual. This is nothing less than the whim of savage gods.

The barman disappears into the throng of minions, replaced by half a dozen of its mates. These new specimens show signs of wear, with chipped heads and bodies scarred more heavily than their brethren. Their flesh has since become a mottled conglomeration of sickly blue, putrid green, and desiccated grey. It is beyond my ability to fathom how long they have existed like this—perhaps they walked the land when my own lungs still stole life's breath.

The cadence quickens again, and the whole island...changes. With a crashing of waves and a shudder that bids us hold tightly to the railing, we are doused with spray as a new hill rises up from the opposite side of the ship. The far end of it is crusted by scaly hide, but that which is turned to us is a wall of soft, murky green. This wall, which rises higher than the ship, pulsates with life, as though a mad sculptor stitched together a thousand still-living bodies to create a palisade for his equally mad lord. Fleshy nodules, hung with kelp, present throughout.

"Mmmff...mggnhn..."

I tighten my grip on Annin's mouth, for such an eldritch sight is fit to drive a mortal soul instantly to madness. Though the arcane ties that bind me to this plane are proof against terror, even I feel latent pangs of human survival instinct, calling me to flee over some great subconscious divide.

I watch as the nodules expand and retract like the gullet of a bullfrog. The thin membranes they are composed of turn largely transparent when extended fully; at these moments, I can see inside. Within each, a fetally-curled stonehead exists in various stages of absorption into the mass.

Annin shoves my distracted hand away. "It…it's eating them; digesting them. We're nothing but food to it!"

I shake my head as I watch the old stoneheads being led patiently towards empty nodules. They are absolutely obedient—the stoneheads serve even unto their own loss at sea, inevitably to meet a slow, bizarre demise in these strange fluid sacks without struggle. This is a careful procedure with forethought, not a feeding frenzy.

Then I see it. From the older nodules, occupied by stoneheads of which there is little left undissolved, new tentacles grow. Miniscule creatures, coloured more lightly than the massive wall but otherwise similar, writhe forth from it like young flies from maggot casings. The heads of stone are not marble at all, but hardened mineral deposits, fit for prenatal nutrition. The rest of the body is indeed for digestion, but not by the parent creature.

The fluid in the nodules is *amniotic*.

"Breeding," I whisper. "We are not just their food. We are their *seed*."

The island quivers; the severed head rolls to my companion, its frozen eyes staring into hers. It is the last straw for Annin, who leeches life from the air around us and shatters all my thoughts in a scream of nonsensical panic. I am too slow to stop her. As one the stoneheads turn.

"Bedamned!"

I spring to the deck, Varso in hand, and meet the charging hordes. The first wave comes at me clumsily; it is a simple matter to evade and strike, or turn their momentum against them and send them crashing over the side. By the time the second wave hits I deal death freely, losing both sight of and thoughts for my charge. None of these creatures are protected by The Rite. The thirst of Orathas est Fir Gazé, that none of my well-meaning sisters could ever have understood, boils to life within me, and I take out upon them the unchecked thirst of my undeath.

"Die, motherless swine!"

These are not 'people' and so are unworthy of the Ysir call for clemency to the brave dead. Neither can they be 'killed', for they are but passionless automatons with no light of their own to extinguish. I can but destroy them — put them down like dogs — and this I do with the wondrous abandon of a gluttonous child showered with sweets. I devour them, taking their limbs as Varso shatters their heads to fragments that bite into my skin, drawing forth vile fluids that only serve to build the embers of my frenzy higher.

I charge the altar, breaking it in two as I put three stoneheads stuck upon my blade like pigs through it. I put my foot to their broken remains to free my companion's murderous barbs from their slop, dragging out their organs to crush beneath my boot. Human vitality no longer animates them, requiring me to cleave them to cold, unrecognizable chunks to put their spirits to rest. I do so with raw joy as I kick in every serene face, breaking it apart.

"*Yes!* Feed Gor Malin! Relish in your End!"

The drummer — once a simple fisherman — swipes at me. I grab his hand in mine and crush his bones to powder in my grasp. His expression never changes as I send his sculpted crown into the sea. The drum goes overboard next, just because I wish it.

They grab at me, several at a time, but I have lost myself to my thirst, and their strength is no match. They do not give way—in such a crowd, every swipe of my blade proves fatal. My heart beats up to an actual rhythm. I will destroy these subhuman things to a one, denying the Deepkin gods their revolting procreation.

'Lady Berserker'. I feel *alive*.

A great bellow issues from everywhere, and I am brained by a massive tentacle with all the force of a falling mountain. I fly against the railing, and it is all I can do to wrap myself around it to stay onboard. The desolate ship rises and falls as if in a raging storm, but I see no clouds in the heavens.

An instant later, I cannot see the heavens at all.

The original creature—the one that sacked Corgrim and larger of the two—rises from the sea to protect its mate. It blots out the moon, jealously stealing Luna's grace for the Deepkin gods. It is a thing with a thousand eyes, each larger than a mounted warrior, and enough tusks to kit a legion of pikemen. The rounded, wormlike maw bears fangs as far down as I can see, and is wide enough to swallow a watchtower in a single bite. It is a thing beyond nightmares, antithesis to mortal understanding, and I understand why it never showed its true self during the village raids. If it had, its catch would have fled madly into the jaws of jungle predators at first sight.

My hearing is taken over by the crashes it makes, and my sight is filled with its scales as it rises into the night. Its every move churns the quiet sea into raging foam, and destroys completely the tall ship it once wore like sheep's clothing. I am to the Deepkin leviathan what a roach is to all the glaciers of the distant, frozen north. To 'fight' such a thing is to sip from the ocean with the intent to swallow it all. If Annin is still alive she is surely as insane as all the others, and as such there is no one left here for me to save. If I cast myself into the sea now, perhaps it will regard me as a pest unworthy of swatting.

I could flee. If I do, these creatures will surely resume their morbid copulation elsewhere. Gods take me, but I will *not* allow it. For the first time since my purgatory began, I thank my sisters for what they have given me. Were it not for the lust of The Rite and its binding, I would not seek to do the impossible.

"Face me, wretch!" I scream into the sky. "I am Gor Malin, the Blood of Ten Thousand! The Ender of Days! I lay waste to armies with my very glance, and brook neither misshapen beast nor malformed spawn of the gods to come before me! Come and die by my hand!"

One of the creature's many appendages swipes across the deck. It is thicker than a copse of oak trees and spans longer than the whole ship, proving impossible to avoid. A mortal man so struck would be reduced instantly to pulverized flesh—I am instead hurled into the breeding wall, spared the destruction of my limbs only by its yielding softness. I crash into one of the sacks, which rips open and douses me with more thick, oily sludge.

The creature roars. I find my feet.

"Oh? Does that upset you?" I shout as I perforate another of the amniotic sacks with Varso, twisting his barbs until the sludge gushes out like a beheaded man's lifeblood. The leviathan screeches again.

"I see. Then what of *this?*"

I find another sack, this one containing the beginning tentacles of new spawn. With all my strength I dig my bare hands into the flesh wall, rip the mewling demon spawn from it, hurl it to the deck, and slam my boot down upon it, crushing it like an overripe melon. Its entrails splatter me as it mewls for its fading life.

"Your mate cannot move much while so burdened, eh?" I reason. "You bring slaves to tend to it, and these gather even more slaves to inseminate it. But what of me?" I ask as I put a hole in another sack with my bare fist. "Will you strike me down so close to your younglings? Will they survive the blow that swats me?"

With each of my assaults upon its mate's back, the creature screeches at me in rage. Murder ignites behind the leviathan's many eyes. My gambit is a desperate one, for if it decides that I am worth the lives of a few of its young, there is no way I can avoid another such strike.

The tentacles hesitate, then retract.

I have won.

Until the monster rears back and vomits upon the deck.

A tsunami of bile and sludge engulfs the ship. Everything that is not a living part of the creatures—sails, rigging, deck, and stoneheaded bits—begins to dissolve in a stew of regurgitated juices and half-digested sea creatures. I leap up, stabbing Varso into the flesh wall that I might hang onto him for support, but cannot get away cleanly. I watch as the smallest finger of my left hand turns to bone, then powder, then blows away in the wind.

Varso slips.

"...damn you, idiot steel..." I mutter at my companion as I tighten my grip, "...you can only be taken in battle...let me die here and you will live at the bottom of the sea, never to be wielded again..."

The corrosive goop proves harmless to the flesh wall and its charges. Hanging limply from my sword, I watch the beast choke itself as it prepares to bring up another volley. There's no deck to land on. Nowhere else to go.

I have spent so long doused by the creatures' oily secretions that they have become a second skin to me. Felt between my fingers, the substance is much like the animal fats my people once used to wick our candles.

Fire.

I reach one hand down to a pouch, finding there a flint I was buried with. I smash it against Varso until the first spark flashes to life, and as my sword slips completely from the wall, leap with all my might.

I fall clear of the islands, plunging into the sea at the moment the oily fluid from the leviathans comes to life in a conflagration of cleansing flames. The oil is indeed a second skin upon me — even the water cannot wash it away. I swim like mad in any direction, not looking back until I'm half a league off.

The ocean is on fire.

The howls are from beyond.

*

Corgrim is a graveyard.

The bodies of those too damaged to be of use to the Deepkin lay mangled upon the beach, or charred beyond recognition in the burned out hovels. Parts of them have already been taken for carrion, while scavenging jungle predators skulk openly through the muddy streets for more.

I have lived here for three days' time, sheltering in a lean-to in lieu of burnt-out buildings. Burying in shallow holes whatever is left, I have used the time to mind my charge until consciousness is hers again. Six hours after I found the pier, Annin floated unconscious into the harbour on a piece of driftwood. It is too much for mere fortune. Perhaps fate is not yet done with her. Varso followed soon enough.

"Idiot blade," I condemn as I retrieve him.

In the barman's hut, I find my talents. There is no grave to rob, so I put them back into a purse where they might find better use.

"Your fever breaks," I say one morning as I offer her broth made from the stock of my latest kill. "Drink."

The girl does so automatically. For the first day she did nothing but scream hysterically from sunup to sundown. When the madness of terror finally subsided her stare went out to sea, where it stayed for two days more. Only now does she look to me, her raspy voice just able to form words.

"…it is dead…?" she whispers, fearful for my answer.

"I do not know."

"…what if it comes back…?"

"There is nothing for it here anymore. This village is in peace."

"But there is no village anymore."

"Precisely," I reply.

We sit by the quiet pier, watching the sunstar decline.

"…what do I do now?"

I offer no answer. I have nothing to say.

"What will *you* do, then?"

"My way lies inland to east," I say through bites of meat from my knife.

"You have business there?"

"As much as I did when I came here," I reply honestly. "I want only to be farther from Thenubria. Nothing else charts my course."

"…you could stay here," she offers with hope, but I shake my head decisively.

"No. I may be made of death, but I will not take up with it. Besides, I am no fisherman."

"But the jungle is filled with beasts," she points out.

"I have faced the spawn of gods and am still standing."

"Can I come with you?" she ventures hopefully.

"Why?" I challenge, she pauses, uncertain how to take my reply.

"Eldin. I want to find my brother."

"Your brother is dead, Girl."

"No!" says she, springing to her feet. "I did not see him on the ship, and his body is not here!"

"Some of the remains were burned beyond recognition."

"That doesn't matter! He may have fled into the wood!"

"The jungle is filled with beasts," I repeat. I don't even feel it when she kicks me.

"Blast you, Stranger! I demand you take me with you! Take me so I can find him or I'll go in there and…and die myself in trying!"

"Good," is all I say in response. I rise, walk over to the weapons taken off the corpses I've interred, and pick out a short, sturdy blade. This I slap into her open hand.

"Know this, Annin of Corgrim: The only peace in this world is found in death. All other respite comes in fleeting moments earned between the tines of spears. If you mean what you say, you will fall upon the altar of swords and make steel your god, until you are ready to win your life back from it. If not, stay here. I may stop for a moment on the road to help a lame deer cross, but I will not babysit a mewling. Make your choice."

The last survivor of Corgrim eyes her new sword, then holds it aloft. Captain Roth's horned helm is too big on her.

This is all I need to see.

THE TROUPE
Andrew Graham

Their visit to the city of Assabarr had been a disaster. But who could have foretold the local priesthood would ban them from performing their plays on the grounds of immorality?

"They never close any of the taverns that are no more than brothels," Oswen grumbled, adding to himself sarcastically this was probably because a lot of their customers were priests. Hypocrites, the lot of them, he sulked, gazing at his half-drunk beer.

He knew what it was. The ever-grasping clerics were waiting for the troupe to offer a well-filled bag of coinage for them to change their minds. In other words extortion, he fumed, ignoring the glum comments of his fellow actors, who had joined him in drowning their sorrows in a down at heel tavern, chosen because it was all they could afford.

"We should pass the word," Oswen said, banging his emptied tankard on the bar for another beer. He was a tall man, lankily built with long, thin, fine features which somehow always gave the impression there was an offensive smell not far away. His clothes were shabby though they were originally part of the expensive wardrobe of an aristocrat whose servants sold them as cast-offs for a pittance. Shabby or not he looked after them as well as he was able, oblivious how careworn they were. To him they still lent an air of gentility.

Like most members of their travelling troupe he dressed to create an impression. Not that any of them was making much of an effort to sustain these illusions at the moment. They had spent days on the road to reach Assabarr and been confident a city this size would fill their coffers. None had expected to be visited at dawn by a bevy of berobed, po-faced priests with a written order banning them from performing their plays.

"How do they know they're immoral?" Beladeen, their principal actress, asked, "we've never even performed here yet. If you ask me it's a downright cheek." Sulkily, she sipped her wine, her bewigged hair a stunning display of gravity-defying artistry, piled high in a towering column of fake golden curls. As they would not be performing today she had not bothered to put any makeup on her face, as a result of which she looked older than she liked to pretend she was, but despondency made her just not care. After having been cheated of most of what they had made at their last stop they were in dire straits with barely enough money to cover their lodgings. Even the drinks they were supping were more than they could really afford.

There were ten of them, eight actors, with two stage crew who did most of the heavy lifting, stalwart Josanians with broad shoulders and thick, muscular arms. Ex-soldiers from the Josanian army, they doubled as bodyguards when their small party of coaches, mules and slow-moving oxcarts, packed high with all their sets, costumes, and stage equipment (including their stage) were in transit from one city to the next. Taking it in turn, one of the Josanians was with their baggage now, making sure it was safe. The other, brass-hilted scimitar sheathed menacingly at his side, stood by himself at the end of the bar, interested more in his drink than listening to the complaints being bandied around by the actors. Now and then he glanced at them with an amused air of contempt.

Fulbor, one of the principal male actors, was a small, dapper man who had an overarching ambition to play the lead despite his notable lack of height. He resented it whenever Oswen took those roles instead and was quick to take the opportunity to criticise his rival now. "I warned you, Oswen, but you wouldn't listen. Assabarr suffered a puritanical civil war in its priesthood not long ago. I knew they would be loath to risk a backlash so soon."

Oswen glared at him. "Rubbish. You might have muttered that to yourself while you were in your cups, *as usual*, old man, but you never came out and said it when it mattered."

"You wouldn't have listened if I had." Which caused some of the other members of the troupe to laugh at him.

"Gave yourself away there, Fully old fruit," Beladeen giggled.

Fulbor turned and drank his beer, ignoring the laughter, and Oswen smirked.

Remembrance of their financial quandary soon wiped that smirk away though.

"Have we enough to make it to the next city?" young Bollimarr asked. The most recent recruit to the troupe, he had a round, overly spotty face, its acne exacerbated by having to wear cheap pancake makeup on stage. It was only a year since he ran away from home to join the troupe, and still wore the same homespun jerkin and trews he arrived in, heavily patched and stretched at the joints through having grown taller and heavier since he left his parents who had provided him with his clothes to work on their farm with his older brothers.

Oswen grimaced. "The nearest city is Jakath, a mud-brick town that smells of dung. But, yes, we could get there with what we have left. Just. Whether we'd make any money off the dullards who live there, who knows?"

"Perhaps enough to get to the next city after it?" Bollimarr persisted with all the confidence of youth – and the lack of too many disappointments in his life so far.

When their coinage for drink eventually ran out a short while later the troupe dispersed to their sleeping quarters. It was while lying in his cot in the tavern's loft, shivering under the threadbare blankets provided by the landlord, that Oswen came up with an idea. It was at times like this, between wakefulness and sleep, with a bellyful of beer, his brain was at its most inventive.

The next morning, as they gathered for a simple breakfast of weak beer and boiled oatmeal, Oswen gathered his closest companions together.

Amongst them as usual were Bollimarr and Beladeen, the youth because he would agree with anything Oswen suggested, and Beladeen because they had known each other the longest even though she would quickly pick apart any jerrymandered plans that wouldn't work. Besides these Oswen included Skazaram, whose awful stage name hid his true identity. Oswen suspected somewhere around the Azure Sea he was a wanted man, which would explain why he had an overwhelming fondness for over-the-top wigs and devilish beards in the roles he played, usually a nefarious pirate or a ne'er-do-well lord. They hid his sallow, pock-marked features well. In the warmup act before the plays began he was also a skilled sword swallower. His straight bladed rapier, which he also used in whatever role he played, was completely blunt and would be useless in a genuine fight. Even so, he always wore it sheathed at his side wherever he went, which Oswen thought dangerous, though on the one occasion when someone challenged him to a fight the evil look on Skazaram's devilishly lined face as he drew the sword was enough to make his opponent back down, blathering such a profuse string of abject apologies everyone burst out laughing. The last member of this group was Mellacrenna, a tough, matronly old trouper who had been on the boards more decades than she cared to admit. If anyone hurt themselves, whether it was a bloody cut or a sprained muscle, she was the first person they would go to even before thinking about seeing a professional healer. She was also the most fearless member of their troupe and was known to climb off stage into any audience if someone was barracking them too much to floor them with a well-aimed fist, whether man, woman, old or young.

"Come on, Oswen, what madcap scheme have you come up with now?" Mellacrenna asked. "I know you're burning to get us out of the mess we're in. And get back at those meddling priests."

"*Moneygrubbing* priests, more like," Oswen said, pushing aside his half-finished bowl of oatmeal. "They make me sick."

"As well they should," Skazaram added. "I've heard some of them, those that went with the puritanical rebels a short while ago, got some of the more idiotic people in this city to throw their prized possessions onto a bonfire to prove how good they were."

The group sat in silence for a few moments, shaking their heads at the folly of the locals.

"See me doing that!" Beladeen squawked with derision.

"A Bonfire of Impurities, they called it," Oswen said. "Hard to believe, I know, but people can be barmy at times.

I'm glad we weren't here then. They'd have probably burned our costumes and props."

"Our stage too," Skazaram said. "When the madness takes hold anything can happen."

"Though it's bad enough now with priestly venality."

"What can we do?" Beladeen asked. "We've nothing to bribe them with."

"We could leave for the mudbrick town," young Bollimarr said.

"With empty pockets? And no guarantee they'll be filled there? The last time I saw it the place looked as poor as a hermit's cave."

Oswen smiled. "Why leave when we could get the locals to fund us anyway?"

Beladeen squawked again, thumping Oswen on the arm. "And why would they do that, dear? Those priests won't let us perform our plays. If we try the watch will lock us up, then boot us out, stripped of what cash we have left."

"Who said anything about performing plays?" Oswen asked.

"What else can we do?"

Oswen cast his eyes conspiratorially around his companions. "If the priests won't let us do our plays, why not join them instead? Why not set up our own priesthood?"

More than just Beladeen squawked with laughter this time.

Oswen waited till it had died down, then said: "I'll bet there is no shrine or temple for the god of thespians here."

"I didn't even know we had a god," young Bollimarr said.

"Neither did I," said Skazaram. "You're making this up, aren't you, Oswen?"

Their leader shook his head. "Of course not. We've a

god all right. Alas, most of us neglect to acknowledge the little fellow which is why perhaps he doesn't lend us that much help, but he's real all right. Pallafravex is his name. I saw a shrine to him once in Oriaska. It wasn't much of a thing, and I think he had only three or four priests, all retired actors. They managed to scrape a few offerings now and then, mainly from passing troupes like ours, just trying to get some extra luck."

"But who'd give us offerings?" Mellacrenna asked, joining in for the first time as she folded her sturdy, butcher's arms in a look of disapproval. "It's even more madcap than the usual schemes you dream up when you've been drinking late."

Oswen cocked his head to one side. "Madcap maybe, but it would give us the opportunity to work. I'm sure no one, even amongst the priesthood, knows what the rites for Pallafravex are. Whatever we do who could dispute it?"

"What do you mean?" Skazaram asked, sounding intrigued. A born anarchist there was nothing he enjoyed more than being disruptive, especially if it hurt or embarrassed whatever elite was in charge somewhere.

"We build a statue to Pallafravex and turn our stage into a shrine. Our rites for the god of thespians is to perform our plays in front of him. If the people in this priest-ridden city happen to be close by and watch what we're doing and, furthermore, enjoy what they see so much they throw offerings to us…"

"You're mad," Beladeen said, grinning. She slapped a hand on the table, startling other customers in the tavern who were still eating their breakfasts. "But I like it," she added.

"Unless we get bundled off to jail," Mellacrenna said, unconvinced.

"Would we be worse off if we were?" Oswen asked.

So it was, having finished breakfast, they set off for where their wagons were stored, still guarded by one of the Josanians, who was only too pleased to take the opportunity while they went about their work to snatch some extra sleep.

It took them all day but by the end they managed to cobble together something that they hoped would pass as an idol. Ten feet tall, it was mainly made of wood covered in some of the sailmaker's canvas they used for backdrops, painted to look like a robed figure. Because it was meant to be the god of actors, they chose to stand it in a dramatic pose, one hand raised above its head in an expository gesture, the other loose by its side. For the head, they joined two large papier-mâché masks that were originally meant to be giants in one of their performances, facing fore and aft like a two-faced god. ("That's different," said Mellacrenna sarcastically, who had never heard of such a thing.) They filled in any gaps between the masks with plaster which, as soon as it dried, they painted. It was a crude construction, but as no one had ever seen a representation of Pallafravex, they were agreed all it needed was to look grand enough. Their final touch was to find an appropriate wig.

The idol completed they went on to build a wooden altar, which they painted red.

When they had finished they retired for something to drink in celebration. The remaining members of the troupe, who had not been let in on the scheme, were aghast to find out what their comrades had been up to. Oswen could barely restrain himself as he explained their plan. "Tomorrow," he said, "Assabarr is in for a shock."

Even before the sun rose above the city walls the troupe was out in force, including the Josanians, whose strength would be needed to help put together the stage at one side of the market, before they slid the idol of Pallafravex off the oxcart onto it. The giant masks they used for his head were possibly fiercer than Oswen would have preferred, but there was no denying they looked dramatic. The last touch was to push the altar onto the stage in front of it.

Oswen said that one of them would have to be high priest with at least two acolytes. He nominated Fulbor for the role. For once his diminutive height would be an advantage: he would make the idol appear taller than it was. For good measure he added two other smaller members of the troupe, the twins Inkmay and Rasmay, neither of whom were particularly good actors in any case and would not be missed in their productions. As high priest it would be Fulbor's role to announce the plays they were to perform in homage to their god.

Satisfied that everything had been done, the only thing left was to decide which plays to perform. Peeked at the behaviour of the priests, Oswen chose a scurrilous farce of bed-hopping in a brothel involving several priests, a high priest and a clutch of magistrates, all pillars of the community. Mellacrenna was not sure about the wisdom of his choice and told him so. "You're poking them in the eye," she said. Which Skazaram, true to form, was delighted with.

It was midday when the market square was at full throng, filled with stalls, merchants and customers, that the stage was unveiled for all to see. Even above the hubbub, for all his lack of height, Fulbor's stentorian voice boomed out and heads everywhere swivelled round to see what was going on. Dressed in resplendent robes Fulbor and his acolytes made obeisance to the idol of the god Pallafravex, before turning to the crowd that had been drawn by curiosity towards the stage.

"We revere the god of thespians everywhere, the

magnificent Pallafravex. In homage to Him we present to you a modest offering." He swept his hands to either side of the stage, from behind whose curtains Oswen and the rest of the cast skipped out, dressed in their costumes and full makeup. Oswen, whose voice was almost as loud as Fulbor's, recited the rhyming couplets of a play about the misspent activities inside the "Boisterous Brothel."

It was a lewd verse, which amused the crowd who laughed at the image of licentious priests cavorting with the "ladies of delight". The plot rested on the high priest's determination to root out and shame those who, he had been told, frequented it, not realising many of his own clerics were chief amongst them. The clownish attempts to disguise themselves or hide from him led to all sorts of ridiculous situations, which the crowd loved.

Oswen was pleased how things were going and was fully expectant that when they finished this ludicrous farce the "offerings" to Pallafravex would be abundant. There was nothing like laughter to make an audience loosen their purses.

But that part of the proceedings was never reached. With only a few minutes to go before the cast would cavort about the crowd with baskets for them to fling in their coins a squadron of the city watch armed with bludgeons and protected by shields forced their way through and formed an impenetrable line around the stage.

"You are under arrest," the sergeant in charge of the watch growled, silencing dissent with a thrust of his mace of office into the stomach of the nearest member of the audience to protest, who doubled over and fell to the cobbles, gasping for breath.

With impressive speed the watch gathered the actors together, including their "high priest" and his acolytes, escorting them away so quickly even Oswen, who had expected some sort of attempt to stop them, was taken by surprise.

It was clear the authorities were prepared to act fast. Instead of being taken to the cells where miscreants usually spent days on end waiting for judgement, the troupe were escorted straight to the magistrates' court, which was situated inside an impressively pillared building not far from the market square. Bundled up the broad steps that led up to it, they were all but frogmarched inside, down marble corridor after marble corridor till they found themselves in one of its principal chambers, forbiddingly faced in black granite. Crowded into the dock, they had to look up to the magistrates' tiered thrones. On the highest sat a richly dressed man who regarded them with pursed lips. Portly, his face was covered with a sheen of perspiration which he dabbed at with a lace fogle.

An official called the court to order. "His lordship the Magistrate Khassan Ushari will hear the case of the Osweni Troupe of Actors who have broken the ban imposed upon them by the City's Priesthood to perform their licentious and lewd plays."

"Licentious *and* lewd," Skazaram whispered to Oswen, still wearing the oversized leather dildo which was part of his costume as a libertine priest.

"My lordship, I object," Oswen spoke up in his best, most forthright voice.

The Magistrate Ushari scowled at him. "You object to the accusation that your play is licentious and lewd?"

"I object that it was not a play we were performing today, but a rite in homage to our god Pallafravex."

The magistrate frowned. "Who?" A court official came over to him and whispered in his ear. Shaking his head, he said, "We will call in a senior priest to clarify matters. I have never heard of this god of yours."

A short while later a priest wearing dark red robes with a tall conical hat embedded with sparkling jewels, mainly emeralds, was ushered into the courtroom. He glanced disparagingly at the huddled actors, then stood before the magistrate, his stance one of confident superiority.

Magistrate Ushari asked if there was such a god as Pallafravex.

"There are one hundred and sixty gods listed in the rolls of the temple. Of these there is indeed a god of that name. He is a minor deity. We do not even have an idol for him in the temple. No one in Assabarr has worshipped him in centuries, if ever. Of course we have no resident actors, only transients such as those arrested today."

"Well?" Magistrate Ushari asked, turning towards Oswen. "What do you say to that?"

"Knowing how neglected our poor, benighted deity is, we have our own idol of Pallafravex, which travels with us."

"But what has this to do with you being in breach of the ban on performing your lewd play?"

"Lewd and licentious," whispered Skazaram sarcastically.

Ignoring his colleague, Oswen said, "We were not in breach, my lord. That was not a performance. It was a rite in homage to our god."

The priest shook his head and laughed. "Rites indeed! Since when did the rites of priests include such bizarre antics as those displayed by your players today?"

"They are appropriate for our god, who looks upon them with beneficence."

"Beneficence!"

The Magistrate Ushari spoke up. "Would the

priesthood have records of all appropriate rites for all the gods in our pantheon? Would they be able to ensure that what the defendant claims is true and accurate?"

The priest frowned. "We would have to make a search. Pallafravex is an obscure god. There may be gaps in our records for suchlike."

"But we must ensure that we know. How can I find against these people if we cannot determine that what they claim is not true? I admit their rites for this peculiar god of theirs are bizarre but, without proof to the contrary, how can I deny them the right to perform them?"

"They are nonsense," the priest stuttered. "No god would have such rites."

"Pallafravex is a whimsical god," Oswen called out. "It is quite fitting that he has whimsical rites. He finds them amusing and fitting."

"Pah!" retorted the priest, but the magistrate looked far from sure. Giving a wrong judgement could easily go against him politically, Oswen knew. Where in doubt, prevaricate. That would be the wise thing for him to do and was exactly what the actor had been relying on.

In the end, the case was put on hold till verification could be obtained from the priesthood's records. "And if not from there, perhaps from one of your fellow priesthoods in neighbouring cities," the magistrate suggested placatingly.

Which was all Oswen needed to hear. He and his co-defendants were released immediately afterwards.

"A shame we lost getting any cash from our performance today," Skazaram said as they left the court building.

"But there's always tomorrow," Oswen said. "And after what happened today there'll be even more people interested in seeing our play then."

"Till the priests dig up some record of Pallafravex's rites. Then we'll be sunk," said Mellacrenna.

"It will be days before they can find anything, even if they have anything to find. I would lay good money on them never having had anything in their scrolls about Pallafravex. He was never popular with priests, just as actors have never been popular with them either."

On the strength that tomorrow they would be in funds, the landlord at their lodgings was willing to let them eat and drink their fill, though the interest he was charging was stiff. Still, Oswen was in too good a state of mind to care. Today had gone better than expected, and he was sure they would have another three or four days in which to reap even more from their performances. After that discretion would see them on their way before the priesthood had time to find out something about their god and his genuine rites. If that happened whatever cash they raised would be swallowed in fines. Or worse. He did not fancy the idea of being condemned to the stocks. That had happened once years ago and the smell of rotting cabbages and other nasty vegetables, fruits *and worse* took him weeks to wash away, never mind the humiliation.

As anticipated their performance the next day went without hitch, and the audience, perhaps encouraged by the way in which they had successfully cheeked the priesthood, was one of the most generous they had ever known.

"Another couple of days like this and we'll be well-nigh wealthy," Beladeen preened, well into her cups even before the sun set, her high-flying hair in jeopardy of tilting beyond the point of no return.

"Perhaps not wealthy," Oswen corrected, "but comfortable at the very least. Which is a better position than we've been in for quite a while."

Even Mellacrenna was enthusiastic over the way things had gone. "Though we don't want to push it too far," she warned, echoing Oswen's thoughts. "Even gods like Pallafravex have no time for human pride."

"Raise them high, knock them low," Skazaram rejoined, as drunk as any of them. "That's the gods for you, pompous asses."

"Shush!" Mellacrenna warned. "It's never a good idea to disparage the gods. They have long arms and short patience, so the saying goes."

Which may have been why, Oswen thought to himself sometime later, they were wakened in the early hours of the morning by one of the Josanian bodyguards, stammering about a fire.

By the time Oswen and those still in a fit condition to climb out of bed arrived at the scene the blaze was over. Only glowing ashes remained where the stage had stood a few hours before. As for the idol, that was no more than a blackened stump.

"How did it happen? Weren't you and Kassarder on guard?" Oswen demanded of the Josanian who had roused him. But even Josanians, it turned out, could be overwhelmed, which was exactly what happened when more than a dozen masked men caught him off guard, clubbing him senseless before setting fire to the stage and the idol. Both being made of wood they burned well, especially when tar was added. Its noxious stench still reeked as Oswen stood by the embers.

"Well, that's it." Mellacrenna shook her head as if this was what she half expected all along.

Not that Oswen could contradict her. "Those bloody priests, they must have hired thugs to do this for them. Those moneygrubbing clerics wouldn't dirty their fingers doing something like this themselves. But their money will."

"I say we scrape together what's left of today's earnings and leave Assabarr," Mellacrenna said. "I wouldn't mind boxing a few of those priests' ears, but what's the point? You know we're outmatched. We'll get nowhere trying to beat them."

Which riled Oswen, who hated to be outmatched like this.

The next morning he gathered all the money they had left and headed into the city. There was only one place he was interested in – the Street of the Apothecaries. If he couldn't win by one means; he'd win by another. Fair or foul were one to him now.

Though most of the people he talked to were wary of his enquiries Oswen could be remarkably persuasive and it did not take him long to find who amongst all the shops along the winding, cobblestone street was more than just a common apothecary. He knew from long experience that far more potent savants in the sorcerous arts chose to hide as nothing more than healers and apothecaries and sometimes both to avoid prosecution by the priesthood. Such men were discreet in what they did. But discreet or not, if you knew the right questions they were not always difficult to find when you needed one.

Thus it was that by mid-afternoon, his feet sore and his throat parched from too much talking, even for him, Oswen found the man he needed.

"You realise that creating something in the image of a god could anger that god." The man was tall, thin, with a shaven head, about the crown of which he wore a strange contraption made up of leather and thin steel bands on which an array of highly polished lenses were attached, two of which were positioned in front of his eyes.

Having been reluctantly admitted into his private quarters high above his shop, Oswen was impressed by the strange contraptions that filled it, from an amazingly intricate astrolabe to bell jars containing strange creatures that floated in oily liquors. The man, Ossani, was dressed in dark blue velvet robes embroidered with finely wrought gold designs.

Having shown the man all the coins he had, Oswen said that if they could perform tomorrow and the day after that there would be more.

"Money is not everything," Ossani said in a gentle, somehow soothing voice. "The priesthood is aware of my... *other* activities, besides those of being an apothecary and sometime healer. Fortunately I have been useful to them in the recent past as they have some rather drastic penalties at their disposal for sorcery, which is forbidden in Assabarr, punishable by flaying. Which, believe it or not, is a potent deterrent." He smiled disarmingly. "Nevertheless, I would not wish to antagonise them needlessly, however tempting that might be."

"You cannot help me?" Oswen said.

"I did not say I can't help you. But what help I give must be oblique. I would prefer it if the priesthood had no knowledge of my involvement. Though, if an idea I have works they will not suspect me at all and it would do much to discredit them. The weaker they are in Assabarr the better it is for those like me who might one day have to feel their wroth. They are too meddlesome and should confine themselves to those matters for which they are best suited, such as carrying out the rites required for their various gods."

Ossani told the actor to come back to his shop that evening when he would give him something that would help. "But let no one, even your closest associate, not even your wife – or your lover – know you have been to see me. I will know if you do." Oswen had no doubt, from the keen look given to him through the thick lenses of the man's peculiar optical device that it would woe betide him if he did. For all his suave urbanity, the healer was not someone to take for granted. Oswen nodded enthusiastically. Leaving the bag of money on the chair in which he had been sitting, he got up and left, relieved to breathe in the air of the street outside.

By dusk he was on his way back, eager to see what the healer had prepared in the meantime. The sad sight he had left behind of the burned-out wreckage of the stage and idol when he passed through the market square filled him with anger. Whatever help the healer gave for some sort of revenge against the interfering zealots of the priesthood he would gladly use.

The Street of the Apothecaries was deserted by the time he reached it, swathed in shadows between the infrequent flambeau. Glad of the anonymity the gloom gave him he was about to knock on the healer's door when it opened and Ossani ushered him inside. Shutters closed for the night, the shop was lit by lanterns, highlighting the many differently coloured bottles of portions lined on its shelves and the dried herbs hung from the stout wooden beams that crossed the ceiling. Ossani waved to a stool for Oswen to use while he picked up an earthenware pot, its lid copiously sealed with wax.

"It is most important – most important indeed – that this vessel remains closed," Ossani warned. "Do not drop it or feel tempted to peer inside. Some things it is better not to see. Do you understand?"

At the intense scrutiny the healer gave him Oswen

swallowed then nodded. "I'll do exactly as you say."

"Pray do," Ossani said. "I am here to help you, not damn your soul." He smiled disarmingly, though Oswen found little reassurance in his words. "When you return to the market square use a knife to dig out a hole in the side of the burned idol as close to its base as you can reach then place this vessel deep inside. When you are done cover the idol with pitch. I have a tub of it here for you to use." Oswen nodded as Ossani pointed to a large bucket full of the black viscous substance. "When you have finished, set fire to what's left of the idol and leave. Do not linger. Go away from there as fast as you can."

"What then?" Oswen asked.

"Nothing more. When you return after sunrise all will be complete." As Oswen picked up the earthenware pot and tucked it under his arm as gently as if it were a newborn baby, Ossani said, "And remember this: say nothing to anyone about me. I am not involved." When Oswen said that his lips were sealed, Ossani nodded, then added, "I am a skilled divinator and will know the instant you break your word."

With this warning running through his mind Oswen picked up the bucket one hand then left the apothecary's shop. His arms aching from carrying the two loads he hurried to the market square. No one, not even the city watch, were about and he managed to bury the pot deep inside what was left of the idol easily enough. He then doused it with as much of the pitch as would pour from the bucket, careful to avoid getting any on himself. That done, he ran to the nearest flambeau around the perimeter of the square, lifting it out of its iron socket. Using this he eventually managed to set fire to the pitch. As soon as it had caught he returned the flambeau to its place then ran as fast as he could back to his lodgings without looking back, already hearing the crackle of flames as they filled the market square with a luridly tinted incandescence.

Despite knowing the light cast from the fire was far brighter and more peculiarly coloured than the pitch should have created, Oswen resisted the temptation to see what was happening. There were strange sounds too, such as high-pitched screams like demons in pain. They sent shivers down his spine – and more speed to his heels.

Back at their lodgings he stole upstairs to the loft, hot and flustered. He was surprised to come across Beladeen in her grey flannel night gown. Without her high-towering wig on, she wore a cotton cap to cover what Oswen knew to be the greyish white tufts of hair that covered her scalp.

"Where have you been at this hour, Oswen, you old rogue?" she said, peering at him in the dim light of the candle stub she carried in one hand.

"I needed to think," Oswen said, still panting from his exertions.

"Is that why you're out of breath and sweating so much it's dripping off your chin?" She laughed sarcastically. "Pull the other one, Ossie. What was it? It was either a woman or you were thieving."

Too exhausted after all he had been through tonight, Oswen pushed her aside. "You'll find out soon enough tomorrow," he told her over his shoulder as he threaded his way to his cot.

He was late getting up in morning and had to be roused from his bed by some of the others, though he cursed them to the seven hells before immersing his head in a bowl of water to freshen up.

The rest of the troupe were still in the bar, despite having finished their breakfasts hours ago. Even the two

Josanian bodyguards were there, though unlike the others their faces were inscrutable.

"Well?" Beladeen asked. "What were you really up to last night?"

Obviously primed by her the others echoed her query.

"Have you thought of something to get us out of our fix?" Skazaram asked. "I know it won't be for nothing you were up half the night."

"Nor was I," Oswen conceded, as he tucked into his cold oatmeal and lukewarm beer.

He wouldn't say anymore because he had no idea what Ossani had planned and was sure he would be as surprised as everyone else at what they would find when they went to the market square, though that something astonishing had happened there was soon obvious long before they arrived a short while later. The excitement amongst the crowds they walked through was palpable. It was more than that, it was infectious.

When they reached the edges of the square some of the crowd, recognising the actors from when they performed there before, gave vent to cheers of support, which astonished them all, including Oswen, who could not wait to find out what had happened.

Soon the crowds between them and where their stage had stood before it was burned dispersed before them, revealing a radiantly glowing, towering statue of flaming gold. Although its face was different to the crude idol they concocted before, Oswen knew it was the god Pallafravex in all his glory, standing twenty feet tall, one hand raised in a dramatic gesture, the other hanging by his side, just as they had originally made him.

Instinctively Oswen and the rest of the troop, including the Josanians, fell to their knees. Many onlookers did the same. Oswen could not help thinking this was probably the most homage Pallafravex had received in umpteen centuries anywhere around the Azure Sea.

Soon, though, practicalities returned to Oswen, and he told the others to rush and get their costumes, they had work to do. Soon, with Fulbor attired once more in the guise of high priest with his two acolytes, the rest put on what was intended to be a whimsical farce. It was a slipshod, on the spur of the moment production which they adlibbed their way through, but for the awestruck spectators, who spent most of their time gazing up at the radiantly glowing face of the idol, it was more than enough. As proof of this, the coins they collected were even more generous than before, overspilling their baskets and weighing them down so much the women struggled to keep hold of them.

That night the whole of the troupe celebrated in style, no longer in the rundown inn they had used before but in one of the best in Assabarr, where they hired a private room.

"I don't know what you did last night, Oswen," Beladeen said, "but I know you must be responsible for what's happened in that square. How did you do it?"

Recalling Ossani's warning, he said, "My lips are sealed. Please don't ask. Regard it as a miracle. Pallafravex has taken his revenge on those who desecrated his idol. Will that not do?"

"For children, maybe," Skazaram said.

"Then you must behave as if you are children." Oswen laughed.

The voice of sobriety as usual Mellacrenna said, "Say what you will, the priesthood will not be pleased."

"What can they do in the face of a miracle?"

"I don't know, but whatever created that idol in the market square maybe closer to blasphemy than a miracle."

"Unless it really is Pallafravex," Oswen insisted.

Unlike the others Mellacrenna was not convinced. "I never heard of him manifesting himself like this elsewhere. Even the greatest of the gods have done so only in myths and legends."

Oswen laughed again. "I'll be accusing you of being a disbeliever if you go on like this."

"Maybe one of us should be. Don't poke the priesthood too hard, Oswen. You don't want to face their inquisitors. This smells of sorcery."

Which had a sobering effect on him. After all, he knew deep down it was sorcery that created the idol - and sorcery was outlawed in Assabarr, with dire consequences for those who used it.

Inevitably, the following day the square was visited by a large group of the most senior priests, accompanied by a squadron of armed guards, who cleared a space in front of the idol, which stood glowing as radiantly as before.

The priests gazed up at its lustrous face then immediately started to call out numerous chants. Oswen, along with the rest of the troupe, was stood to one side, barred by the guards from going any closer. He suspected most of the chants were exorcisms against demons and suchlike. Just as Mellacrenna had forecast it was obvious the priests suspected sorcery, but none of their efforts had any effect. The idol still stood as tall, solid and eerily effulgent as before, defying the priests' best efforts. Realising what they were up to many in the crowd began to snigger, while others made sarcastic catcalls. Some even had the temerity to mimic the priests' chants, adding ludicrous squawks. The situation was beginning to get out of hand, before the guards closed ranks around the priests, locking shield to shield and brandishing their viciously pointed spears towards the crowd, who were quelled by them.

"Sooner or later they'll find the right words," Mellacrenna whispered in Oswen's ear. "You know that as well as I do. And when they do, and that is exposed for the fraudulent lump of sorcery it is, we're for the high jump. And the high jump for sorcery in Assabarr is the flayer's knife."

Oswen knew she was right. They had done what they could in this priest-ridden town, now it was time to leave while they still could. If they lingered too long the trickery behind what he had helped to create would get them into more trouble than they could handle.

Oswen spoke to the rest of the troupe and told them to load their possessions onto their various wagons and oxcarts as quickly as they could; they would be leaving Assabarr later today. Urging them to waste no time, it was not long before the entire troupe were sat on top of their vehicles, which trundled towards the nearest gate. Soon, the open road lay before them, first stop the town of mud brick houses and the smell of dung. After that, with a plentiful supply of coins in their well-filled coffers they would head for Oriaska, the richest city hereabouts.

Sitting atop the foremost wagon, Beladeen beside him, Oswen felt elated. He had saved the troupe from financial disaster and was inordinately pleased with himself. He had shown yet again how fitted he was to be their leader. No one else could have achieved what he had managed. From disaster to triumph and all in one day.

Beladeen leaned against him and said, "Now we're free of Assabarr why don't you whisper in my ear just what you did? You can't keep secrets from me, you old rogue."

Oswen glanced at her, then gazed back at the city as it receded into the far horizon, its walls no more than a diminishing line in the distance. Ossani was only a memory now, he and his strange, mysterious, arcane magics. None of them seemed threatening anymore, not with the whole world stretched before him, basking in the sun.

Feeling inordinately proud of what he had achieved, it did not take much persuasion from his sometime lover before Oswen regaled Beladeen with the full story, especially his part in it, which he shamelessly embellished.

When he had finished his face had a look of inordinate pride and self-satisfaction, which lasted for just a few precious, swiftly gone seconds before a ghastly expression of sheer horror took their place. It was a change that shocked Beladeen so much she instinctively shied away from him on the seat they shared at the front of the cart.

For what seemed endless moments Oswen gazed transfixed at the road ahead of them, sweat dribbling down his strained features. To Beladeen it was as if whatever he saw was something only he could see. Then as suddenly as it had afflicted him, whatever paralysis gripped his body released its hold and Oswen shrieked in mortal terror, before throwing himself onto the road where he lay grovelling, his fingernails scraping as if they were claws into its sunbaked rucks.

So it was Oswen died, a mumbling, moaning wreck of a man, whose need to boast had finally got the better of him. Beside him, stricken with grief by what had happened, Beladeen realised that whatever Oswen had been telling her before he collapsed she had completely forgotten, as if something had wiped it from her mind.

*

Ossani shook his head with sadness. He had genuinely

hoped the thespian would stick to his word, but few ever did. He should have known, though he had warned the man. What more could he do?

Even so, as he went about his affairs that day Ossani did pause to wonder if he had been wise to give the help he had. Satisfyingly, he knew the idol of Pallafravex would irk the priesthood for many days before it finally fell into dissolution when the demon's secret name was included in their exorcisms and its true self was revealed to them all.

Although he knew the priesthood would not be able to lay any blame on him for the idol, there would be some amongst them who would suspect. But he was already aware his days in Assabarr were coming to an end and sooner or later he would have to leave. In the meantime, he thought with a grim smile of satisfaction, he had badly embarrassed the priesthood one more time.

Which for the moment was more than enough for him.

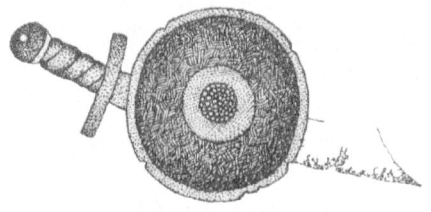

LAIR OF THE MUTANT KING
Adrian Cole

The world has fallen to the Kaizen, ferocious warriors from another world who have poured through the Hell Gate they have opened and trampled Man beneath their feet, for the most part enslaving humanity. A few pockets of resistance remain, and from them rise lone challengers to the alien empire, among them Estarziel, the Crimson Warrior, who bears the Burning Blade, a powerful weapon to aid her in her desperate fight to reclaim Man's world.

*

Skarrack leaned on the prow of the small sailing craft, which was little bigger than a fishing smack, its lone sail drooping, of scant use in this calm air. He was not a tall man, though his body was well muscled and scarred with wounds he'd received over his thirty years of life, a life spent in a bitter contest with the elements of his unforgiving world. Sea fog swirled listlessly about it as it had done for days since the boat had left the islet port of Mamnos. Skarrack studied the blankness ahead, certain he could see through the shifting murk to where something much darker loomed up and ever up, cliffs groping for the sky. He and Estarziel, the warrior for whom he acted as squire, had almost reached their destination on this silent, lonely voyage. Turning, he saw her metal-sheathed figure beside the mast, watching patiently, face obscured by the tight-fitting helm and its mask. The armour, a dark crimson, forged in demon fires, gleamed in spite of the dim light. The other occupant of the boat was Krennel, a sour-faced, weather-beaten sailor who had been the only inhabitant of Mamnos prepared to take Skarrack and the warrior into these eastern waters. They were sluggish but calm, though they swarmed with legends, none of them savoury. Krennel bent his back, working the oars, saying little. He had been well paid for his exertions and was content.

"I must visit Landhanga," Estarziel had told Skarrack. "The Kaizen have not yet polluted it and crushed its people, as they have almost everywhere else in our beleaguered world."

It was easy in this cloying fog and the stumbling hours to mull over earlier conflicts he and the warrior had fought. She had been a Fire Witch, one of the coven of sorceresses serving the last kingdom of Man on the island of Vallamarza. When the alien Kaizen swept in, the king had used the Fire Witches to summon demons, the Crimson Warriors, also from realms beyond this world. Even their terrible powers had not been enough to better the Kaizen, and as a last desperate resort to sue for peace with the invaders, the king had betrayed the Fire Witches and the Crimson Warriors. This terribly misguided act had backfired disastrously. The Kaizen swarmed, destroyed almost all of humanity and now ruled, unchallenged and omnipotent.

Skarrack's companion had escaped the annihilation. Now she followed her own private trail of vengeance against the Kaizen, using the powers of the Crimson Warriors invested in the blade she carried and the demon armour she wore. The first time Skarrack had served her, he saw many men die winning back some of humanity's lost ground and pride. Afterwards he had a simple choice: go back to being a pitiful member of a downtrodden, defeated slave nation, or break free and become the Crimson Warrior's squire. His spirit had not been altogether broken and he had chosen the latter.

"What is in Landhanga for us?" he'd asked.

"It has a king, Finnwalder. Word is he yet retains a small army, high up on the plateau. Last night I heard from the watermen. It's true. Finnwalder and his retainers have been ignored by the Kaizen – for now. I must get to him before they do. Between us we can form a battalion of resistance and possibly make Landhanga a fortress of our own. I need a base." Her eyes had blazed. Skarrack had never seen such single-mindedness in anyone, a bleak determination to which all Estarziel's other emotions had been sacrificed.

He again peered into the shadows. Surf broke against rocks along a line from port to starboard, marking the foot of the immense cliffs. White shapes flapped overhead like brazen ghosts, sea birds shrieking their anger at having their realm disturbed. Some dived, wings blurring, but they swerved away as the small craft bobbed closer.

"I can only take you in so far," Krennel had growled. "Them rocks are like teeth. They'll rip the guts out of my craft. You want to get ashore, you'll have to take to the water." His tone suggested his passengers were demented even to think of such a thing.

Skarrack ignored him. Others would think the same, almost certainly the Kaizen, too. Only the mad would attempt to get ashore here, and then climb.

She was beside him, silent as a phantom, her green eyes fixed on the now revealed cliffs and the foaming seas beneath them. "Are you set? As ever, Skarrack, I absolve you of any commitments. There's no need for you to risk your neck."

"We've fought Kaizen together, and lived. This is a lesser challenge."

She nodded, turning to wave Krennel away. Then, without another word, she dived over the bow and into the white swell. Skarrack followed, the water claiming him. Krennel shook his head, quickly using his oars to turn the craft and manoeuvre it back into calmer seas. In moments the fog enfolded him. By nightfall he'd be back in Mamnos, spending some of the outrageous fee he'd received, the two strange travellers forgotten.

Skarrack kicked out against the pull of the tide, which ripped its way along this barbaric coast. He was a strong swimmer and was used to the cold, northern waters, where, as a youth, he had pitted himself against the waves of the coast of Skullabar. The great ice cap of the north fed those seas with their melt-waters, so he was used to the bitter grip of a freezing sea. He could hold his breath far longer than men unused to a cold swim, and did so now, until he was able to propel himself upwards, out of the spume, to where he could grasp at a rock and utilize the next surge of the sea to lift him on to a low shelf. He braved himself and defied the surf's efforts to drag him away again. After that it was easier and he clambered closer to the cliffs. She was there before him, already assessing the climb.

Neither of them spoke: their words would have been torn away by the roar of the waves and their thundering across the rocks. She unstrapped the backpack that had been moulded to her and undid its buckles, pulling out a cloak, donning it quickly. As he did the same, she pointed upwards to where a wide cleft in the stone formed a natural chimney. Her meaning was clear and he nodded. They re-strapped their backpacks and she began the climb, agile as a spider, he following. Again the sea birds dipped and dived, but they lacked the courage of eagles and other birds of prey.

It was a slippery, dangerous ascent, and more than once Skarrack felt his heart lurch as he almost lost his grip or footing. Ironically the challenge became exhilarating and he warmed to it, intent on matching the extraordinary climbing skills of the warrior. Whether or not she had supernatural powers to aid her, he simply focused his steely resolve. Overhead, the fog remained, if anything thickening, so it was impossible to know how far they must ascend. It was probably just as well, he told himself. The sight of too mountainous a challenge could well crush his will to meet it.

Twilight had stolen the world by the time the two climbers reached the ridge at the top of their climb. Beyond it the fogs had dispersed, revealing a bleak sky, partially lit by moonlight bleeding through passing clouds. Sounds of the sea and its exploding waves had receded, and the sea birds had long given up their attempts to dislodge the couple, packed on the many ledges of the cliff for the night. Skarrack and the girl heaved themselves on to the ridge, ducking to avoid a sudden buffet of wind – they were several hundred feet above the water.

The warrior unsheathed her blade, which shimmered in the moonlight, spells dancing lightly around it, quiescent until the powers locked within the steel were summoned. By the sword- glow, the two figures could see some distance around them. This was the apex of the Landhanga landmass, a huge peninsular jutting out from the eastern lands, and a once powerful kingdom. The ground sloped steeply into distance like a solidified mud flow. Tufts of thick grass studded it and occasional rocks jutted from the wind-scoured soil like cracked teeth.

"Is it far to the city?" Skarrack asked.

"We'll be there before dawn if we hurry. Mind your footing. The ground is treacherous." She would have said more, but there was movement on either side of them, shadows coalescing in the night.

Skarrack pulled out his own blade. It was a well-crafted weapon, taken from the fallen body of another warrior, far from here, and although it lacked the magics of the Burning Blade, it was reliable in a fight. Enough blood had been spilled by it to convince him of its durability. Beyond the two figures, more broke from the mist. Huge, clad in thick armour, with long swords and pikes, these were no ordinary men.

"Kaizen!" gasped Skarrack. They were here after all. Either spies, sent to scout this remote place, or outriders of an army that was spreading from the main continent, seeking further conquests. Either way, there was no time to consider the possibilities. The Kaizen attacked.

Skarrack faced a group of three from one side, while the girl was confronted by a larger group. A dozen Kaizen in all, which should have meant impossible odds and a swift end to the puny humans. Skarrack swung his blade in an arc and moved with practiced agility. He had spent many hours trained by the girl since becoming her squire, and although he had always been useful with a weapon, she had toughened him and given a finely honed edge to his skills as a warrior. His speed saved him from the initial thrusts of the Kaizen, matched against their brutality and sheer force. They wore typical black armour embossed with golden sigils, its segments fitted to their massive forms, giving them the appearance of large insects. Their grotesque steel helmets resembled the heads of some wild god of the night and their long, curved weapons hissed as they split the curdled air.

Skarrack knew he had no hope whatsoever of downing even a single one of them. Against three, he was helpless. If they meant to pitch him over the cliff, it would be no more than moments before they did so. His companion, however, blazed arcs of white light around her and as the first of her opponents stepped confidently in to disembowel her, she brought the Burning Blade upwards in a sweep that tore through his armour and almost took his sword arm off at the elbow. The Kaizen emitted a shriek of agony that echoed around the clifftop.

Back-to-back, Skarrack and the girl kept the Kaizen at bay, realizing now that there were at least a score of them. Others, who must have been watching the cliffs further along, had joined the affray.

It's a betrayal, thought Skarrack. *Someone has tipped them off. Why else would they be here on this remote headland? They can only have been watching for us.*

"Get ready to move when I give the word," whispered the girl but he caught her words clearly. "Inland, fast."

Swords clashed once more, sparks dancing as the Kaizen powered forward. When the girl told him to move, Skarrack shifted, sprinting away from the cliffs, turning to cover his back, the girl beside him. He watched as she raised her blade and plunged it down into the earth as if dispatching a fallen enemy. The Burning Blade glowed a deep red, as if pouring crimson energy into the soil. Thick serpents of smoke curled up into the air around them and the ground shook. Before the Kaizen could react, two fissures opened on either side of the weapon, gradually widening. Skarrack and the girl were thrown backwards as the gap became a deep rift.

The nearest of the Kaizen to it lost their footing and abruptly toppled into the yawning darkness, while the remainder tried to stagger away from the danger. The girl pulled out the blade and a great chunk of the cliff sheared off and fell away into the drop beyond, taking a dozen Kaizen with it. The remainder, seeing what had happened, tried to leap to safety, but another thick slice of cliff peeled off and collapsed. In moments the entire pack of Kaizen killers had disappeared, plunged outwards and away, dropping like boulders far, far down on to the sea-smashed rocks at the foot of the cliffs.

"I doubt they'll survive a fall like that," said the girl. "And Kaizen don't care much for the sea. If any of them do survive, the waves will drown them." She re-sheathed her sword, her eyes smouldering with the grim pleasure that made Skarrack shudder.

He watched the surrounding land, but it was empty, no other Kaizen appearing. "They were expecting us," he said. "Someone blabbed."

She nodded. "Human spies, eager to win favour with the Kaizen. All too willing to be slaves to the invaders."

Skarrack watched the night for any signs of more Kaizen. She was right. Humanity was on its knees, grasping at straws to survive. The will to continue the fight had left many. He himself had come close to a final despair.

They began the descent down the long slope, made more difficult by the darkness and the fickleness of the moonlight. A long time later, his muscles protesting, they reached an outcrop of rocks with a natural sheltered overhang away from the stiff breeze. Far down beyond the edge of the eastern slope, a city had been built into a natural depression, its lights dimmed, surrounded by dark stains of forest.

"Get some sleep," she told him. "I'll keep watch, though I doubt if there will be any Kaizen here."

He prepared his bedroll. "Who do you think betrayed us?"

"Probably a spy in Mamnos. Word of our bloody work in the west may have spread. I daresay the Kaizen have set a reward on our heads."

"In future we'll have to disguise ourselves better."

"If Finnwalder will take us in, we may not have to."

"Is that the plan? To rally to his standard?"

She nodded. "Yonder city, Moonvale, is remote. Somewhere to rebuild our rebellious army. Finnwalder was once allied to my father, Attras, the commander of the king's armies on the royal island fortress of Vallamarza. They fought the Kaizen there. Finnwalder was one of the few men who escaped the slaughter. He swore vengeance before returning to Moonvale. His hatred of the Kaizen burns yet. Rest, Skarrack. Soon after dawn we'll go down."

*

She studied him, curled up in his blankets under the overhang, sleeping, exhausted by the climb, the conflict and the long trudge to this small sanctuary. Not for the first time she marvelled at his willingness to serve her, something most men would have shied from, seeking an easier existence in this downtrodden world. Yet he saw in her a beacon, a cause to rally to, embodying the desire to defy the invaders. She needed more like him. The Kaizen were not invincible. There were ways, and powers, to kill them.

Skarrack snored softly, his rugged features contorted, his thick mane spread around his face and over his shoulders. He had once had a wife and children, she knew that from brief conversations he'd shared with him. Details of their fate, like that of so many others, wasn't something he had shared, but they were lost, killed in a raid, or another aspect of the war. Their deaths were part of what fuelled him.

She went back to her watch, satisfied the land around them was empty. If another group of Kaizen attempted to trap them, they had nowhere to disguise their approach. Far below, Moonvale's lights glowed, obscured by thick, drizzling mists, and their colours were strange, not the vivid glare of torches or beacons. They had a dull, phosphorescent glow, like something found in deep underground caves, spawn of its fungi. The city offered hope, but the lights made her uneasy.

*

Skarrack woke an hour after dawn, the landscape in shadow, a miasma rising from the earth, cold and unhealthy. He furled his blankets and belted them tight, drawing his cloak around him. The girl was on the rock crest, wedged between jutting stones, out of sight from above, well camouflaged. She had been dozing, but jerked awake as he approached, her reactions remarkable. She had taken off her helm and mask, revealing her face and mass of jet-black hair. There was a faerie beauty about her features, hardened by the cold gaze which rarely softened, her eyes icy.

In moments she was up and ready to move on. "We'll use the morning mists to shield us."

He nodded. She got by without having to eat much, but he felt his belly complaining.

"If you're hungry," she said, her helmet restored, "there'll be food in Moonvale."

Is she reading my mind? he asked himself. It was something he'd often wanted to ask her, but he decided he'd rather not know.

They moved on downwards, the mists dissolving quickly. The flat, empty grassland sloped even more dramatically, like a huge ship keeling into a deep trough of ocean, and the vista beyond Moonvale opened up. The land sheared away there and Skarrack realized the Landhanga peninsular had broken free of the mainland in some geological cataclysm and become an island. One, moreover, ringed by cliffs, jutting up like a vast mesa in a desert of churning foam. Maybe it was fortunate. Surely the Kaizen's main forces would have little time to explore it.

Skarrack was finally able to satisfy his appetite when he used his short spear to bring down a young deer. He and the girl were obliged to eat its meat raw. As they went onward, several gullies ran down like huge claw marks towards the forest ringing Moonvale, until the two figures were swallowed by one of them, ducking under the clawing branches of wind-blasted trees. They were in a place of shadows again, a cold, forbidding zone, where the ground underfoot was choked with roots and fallen boughs, treacherous and inhospitable. If this was the approach to Moonvale it would deter anyone investigating the place, possibly even the Kaizen. Why should they spend time and energy in such a forsaken place?

Skarrack said as much.

"I imagine it's why Finnwalder came back here."

"Do you think we'll still be hunted?"

"We've killed Kaizen," she said. "That marks us."

Soon they'd reached the base of the gully, where a stream trickled over slippery stone into the forest. It reared up suddenly like a great beast, its moss-hung boughs and masses of leaves whispering in a strong breeze. This offered no comfort, but plenty of cover. They crossed a brook and searched out a path through the tangled undergrowth.

Skarrack studied the plants and trunks, surprised at their nature. Many were oddly bleached, as if sucked dry of energy, and he soon saw why. There were clotted banks of fungi beyond, pale and sickly, growing into the trees, in some places taller than a man, with wispy fronds dangling, hair-like. He and the girl avoided them carefully, as they would have spider webs of such size.

There was a path, strewn with rocks that resisted the burgeoning progress of the undergrowth, and the two figures worked their way along it. Birds flapped away from their progress, crows or something like them, carrion birds that cursed their passing in a unified, bleak chorus. The distance to the city was deceptive, for by the end of the afternoon they had still not reached its outer walls, although there were many old buildings scattered about, isolated and rotting.

"Perhaps," said the girl, "we should camp for the coming night. Safer, I think."

He nodded agreement. The forest ahead promised an ugly reception. He had known for some time it was stirring. There were sounds and the suggestion of movements, as if something hostile slunk through the bushes. It would be difficult to travel without a torch, and light would only serve to attract whatever lurked ahead like moths to a candle.

They found one of the collapsed buildings, a roughly rectangular block that might once have been a store. It had low walls and no roof, but its stones had conveniently piled up in one corner to form a rough stair up to the high point of the wall, a makeshift tower which provided a reasonable place to bed down, affording as it did a view of the immediate surroundings. They ate the remainder of the deer meat, again uncooked, but the girl did not complain. Soldiers in the field took what they could get.

She agreed to let him have first watch and settled herself in the makeshift battlements. He watched the trees, knowing the forest life was teeming, apparently more alive as the sun fell beyond the invisible horizon and night's darkness swiftly smothered everything. Now the sounds intensified. Bizarrely they were like voices calling to one another, but these were no human voices. Apes, perhaps? Though apes were not normally night creatures. Gradually he realized whatever was out there was moving closer, ringing the broken tower. Feral eyes gleamed in the darkness. When an abrupt silence dropped like a curtain, Skarrack knew an attack was imminent.

The girl was already awake, sliding her sword from its scabbard, its entire length glowing softly. "I know," she said. "I heard them in my sleep."

They braced themselves at the top of the makeshift stairway as the explosion of noise came and bodies erupted from the trees, a swarm of thick-skinned humanoids, bent over like simians, their twisted faces grotesque in the flickering light, their rows of sharp, yellowing teeth wet with saliva. Snarling, long-nailed hands reaching out like weapons, they rushed forward, the first of them leaping up the stairs. The girl met the first pair and scythed them apart at the waist, her Burning Blade lighting up like a firebrand, its energy ripping through flesh effortlessly. Bursting into flames, the two creatures toppled off the stair, immediately replaced by two more.

Skarrack saw others clambering up the sides of the wall and placed himself above them, driving his blade downwards, chopping viciously into their skulls, spattering the stones with blood and gore. He ran back and forth, stemming the climbing horrors, who seemed hell-bent on reaching him and the girl, oblivious of the bloody defence, as though madness spurred them on – that, or something else drove them, a supernatural force, typical of such blighted lands.

Skarrack would have been confident of repulsing the massed ranks of the creatures in spite of the wild abandon with which they attacked, as he had seen the fiery power of the Burning Blade at work before, incredibly annihilating scores of Kaizen, with as little effort as a foot crushing ants. Yet in this conflict the sheer weight of numbers of the ape-things made victory uncertain. Hundreds were pouring out of the forest, clearly intending to swamp Skarrack and the girl, burying them under a huge pile of bodies, regardless of losses. For a long time the pair restrained them, but even their unusual energy was beginning to flag. The fighting had become automatic, instinctive, yet as the defenders knew their strength was slowly ebbing, they also knew the creatures were maintaining their level of assault, careless of the withering fire with which the Burning Blade hosed them.

Behind the press of snarling ape-things, a fresh chorus of screams and shouts mingled, though this was not directed up at the defenders. A new element had entered the contest. Torches blazed and more forms appeared from the trees, swords flashing as they began their own bloody work, carving paths into the massed ranks of the ape creatures. Skarrack paused briefly to peer out into the glowing firelight and saw men there, armoured and helmeted, chopping into their foe.

Abruptly the assault on the tower ceased as the wild creatures turned and hurled themselves at these armed warriors. Skarrack and the girl were breathing heavily, almost drained, their arms tiring, as they watched a fresh battle blaze ferociously below them. Although outnumbered, the warriors ringed the creatures and tore into them in what could now be seen as a series of unequal contests, steel against flesh and bone. Bit by bit the warriors carved a path through the ape-things, driven like machines, automatons that fought at a single, devastating pace. The first group of them made their bloody way to the foot of the stairs and prevented the beast creatures from climbing them.

It ended when the creatures made a wild break for freedom and as one their entire company loped back into the forest, taking to the trees, which swallowed them up quickly, leaving a sudden punctured silence behind them where the maimed and injured had fallen. One of the warriors, apparently their leader, cautiously climbed up the stair, kicking aside several corpses as he did so, his blade dripping.

"I am Agar, servant of King Finnwalder. I am to take you to him." He spoke in a flat, unemotional voice, and again Skarrack was reminded of a machine, the ultimate fighting man, locked into his orders.

The girl studied Agar suspiciously, in spite of the fact he'd saved her and Skarrack's life. But she nodded, though the Burning Blade yet fizzed and hissed like a live thing.

"Word had reached the king you were here on Landhanga. He knows you were attacked by the Kaizen. They are his enemies, too."

"Where is Finnwalder?"

"In the city, Moonvale. We go there."

The girl and Skarrack climbed down to the Agar and his men. The last of the ape-things had gone and the warriors formed themselves into a fresh defensive unit, ready to march. All this was done in relative silence, perfect military precision. Skarrack met only stony, indifferent gazes.

"I am Estarziel, and this is my squire, Skarrack."

Agar nodded, as mute as his men. He studied the forest cursorily, giving orders for the march to begin. A few warriors held brands, making the tangled path more visible, and with barely another word, the party moved away from the grisly scene of battle. All around them, out in the pitch darkness of the forest, the ape creatures called and hooted to one another, and there were other sounds, deep growls and savage snarls, as of larger predators, beasts poised to attack.

"What else dwells in these forest deeps?" Skarrack said to Agar, pressed shoulder to shoulder as they wormed their way deeper into the interior.

"Things you would not want to see by daylight. The old wars poisoned Landhanga and spawned new life forms, corrupting many others. The Upanti, those we fought, are descendants of a race of men who were once proud masters of the kingdom." Agar's voice was clipped and indifferent, as if he was spouting facts written on a sheet of parchment, bare and minimal.

"Who rules them?" said Estarziel, close behind them.

"A rival to Finnwalder, who would overrun our king and become master of all Landhanga. He is Nunnazad, and has allied himself to the Kaizen. His spies are abroad across all the kingdom, some say beyond it in the islands."

The girl tapped Skarrack on the shoulder. "There you have our betrayers."

Skarrack grunted and Agar motioned for silence.

It was beyond midnight when the party reached the walls of the city. High up on its walls the guards recognized the returning warriors and a door opened in the great gate. Skarrack wondered if the forest creatures would launch a final, desperate attack, but none came, and the party threaded through the doorway and into the torch-lit passage beyond, where armed guards stood like statues, gazes fixed on the night. Agar took Skarrack and Estarziel up into the city and to a large, domed building where there were rooms that may once have been opulent, but which had fallen into sad disrepair. There were beds, however, and bathing facilities, so that the two guests were able to clean up.

Agar clearly had no mind to volunteer any further information and withdrew. Skarrack, in his room, collapsed on to a wide bed and was soon asleep, utterly spent.

*

Estarziel called on Skarrack soon after dawn, and he surfaced from a deep, dreamless sleep. Sluicing himself with cold water, he followed the girl down a series of corridors where several guards stood rigidly to attention. This must be a wing of the palace, he assumed. Agar met them and led them out on to a narrow balcony overlooking the city.

"Wait here. When Finnwalder is ready, I will take you before him," he told them, leaving more guards by the door.

The sun had risen in cloudless skies, where hunting birds followed the thermals, high up and circling out beyond the city walls and over the now silent forest. It had become a deep green mass surrounding the city like an eager sea. Skarrack leaned on the parapet, studying the blocks of rectangular buildings beyond. By the stark sunlight many could be seen now to be in a state of disrepair, not much better preserved than the ruins beyond their walls, and most of the towers leaned, in some cases dangerously, being gradually dragged down by groping tresses of ivy. Where the towers withstood the excesses of the vegetation, their stone was pocked, their colours bleached and stained as if some repellent disease had claimed them. Skarrack caught glimpses of metal, evidence of ancient machines, rotting like the bones of fallen creatures from far back in time, and there were thick pipes and twisted tubes crushed between walls and collapsed masonry.

"The Kaizen may not have been here," he said to Estarziel, "but time has done their work for them. This city is a mausoleum, no different to others we've seen."

"If it has nothing to offer the invaders, they may ignore it. That would be to our advantage."

"Yet if they pursue us -"

Agar had returned and called to them. They followed him out into the corridor and along another, wider one, where efforts had been made to clear away any rubble and cut out any of the ubiquitous weeds that threatened every part of the city, even this palace. Agar opened a small door and took them inside a great hall, with a high, domed ceiling the dimensions of which were lost in shadows. No natural sunlight had been allowed into this vast space, and a score of wide braziers burned their coals around its walls. The place was almost empty, its dusty air quivering, its flagstones echoing to the footsteps as Agar led his guests to the edge of a wide, circular pit.

Skarrack gasped as he looked beyond its rim. Inside the pit, shapes coiled and twisted, like immense serpents, slick and gleaming in the wavering light, spreading out sinuously to reveal a central bulk, which heaved itself gently upwards. In utter amazement, Skarrack found himself being observed by two moon-like eyes the size of plates. They were set in a sagging face in a swollen head as large as he was, a bloated, bald globe supported by wide shoulders that sloped away into shadow, neckless and glutinous, as if it had risen from a mire. A long gash of a mouth opened and a black tongue slid about inside it.

"Finnwalder greets you," boomed the voice, the words amplified by the emptiness of the chamber. The eyes had a gleam that suggested misery, the grotesque features twisted in what must have been pain. "Does my appearance shock you? Of course it does. I was once a man, like you, Skarrack of the northlands. And in that form I fought alongside your father, Estarziel. Fought and lost, fled here, to this cursed city. Have you seen it? How it festers and rots, pulled down by the disease of the ages, the poisons that seep down to the very roots of Landhanga."

Mutated, thought Skarrack. He'd seen much of it in his travels. But this was beyond anything he'd encountered previously, an extreme distortion of humanity. His horror increased as he watched the elongated arms of the king caressing the serpents as they coiled and twisted around him, seething like immense maggots, sending oily ripples across the surface of the viscous pool in which he wallowed.

Skarrack glanced at the girl, who had not donned her helmet for this meeting. It dangled at her side, her scabbarded blade strapped there. Her face, normally so stern, her eyes cold, for once had softened, her sympathy for the former ally of her father undisguised.

"Don't waste your pity on me," growled Finnwalder. "All of mankind is to be pitied now. Soon it will be over for all of us. The Kaizen will scourge the world of us. Nothing can stop that."

"Are they responsible for this?" asked Skarrack.

The vast head shook. "No. Man's own rashness unleashed the broken sorcery, the mangled science, long before the Kaizen came. Who is to say that it wasn't the cataclysmic damage of the old wars that paved the way for the Kaizen Hell Gate to be opened? I am a product of Man's stupidity, as is my shattered city."

"The Hell Gate is closed," said Estarziel.

"Too late! So many of the invaders have poured through it. Their final harvest has begun. But tell me, daughter of Attras of Vallamarza, why are you here?"

Estarziel had composed herself, stiffening, her face again a mask of controlled anger. "The world must marshal its resistance. I had heard Landhanga was a potential base for this. And that its king would yet stand against the Kaizen. If so, I will lead others here, more warriors for your army. An army that would eventually go out and break the Kaizen stranglehold."

Finnwalder laughed, a deep-throated growl that had more contempt than mirth in it. "As well attempt to command the ocean to retreat. And besides, your wild designs are known to your enemies."

Estarziel scowled. "They knew I was here. They were *waiting* for me on the cliff top. How did they know?"

"That sword you carry, the Burning Blade of legend, is it? Yes, it is sought by the Kaizen, ever since you displayed its powers so insolently in the western lands. It is a beacon to them. They fear it. They have set every spy, every twisted ally they have to seeking it out. Whenever you draw it and expend its fires, it summons them."

"Are more of them here, looking for me?" She smiled in a way known to Skarrack, a way that warned of her eagerness to oppose the Kaizen.

"They'll come, and soon, I think."

"What of you? Will you fight them? You have good men in your city. I've seen them fight."

"Yes, they'll fight."

"And the forest beast men, the Upanti" said Skarrack. "What are they? Who controls them?"

A curious look spread across the features of the king.

"Like me, they are cursed, doomed to wander the forests until my warriors can root them out like weeds and exterminate them. By day we seek their haunts, but by night we stay in the city, where it is safe from their crazed assaults. In time we will rid our land of them."

"When the Kaizen come," said Estarziel, "will they seek to control these creatures?"

"They are beyond control."

"Even an ocean can be turned, if enough power is wielded against it."

Finnwalder's gross features creased in a smile. "Of course. Fight the Kaizen alongside us and we will secure your safety from them. Your Burning Blade can then help us destroy the forest vermin. Between us we can make Moonvale a haven from the invaders. You would make me your king?"

"There must be other bands of men, lost warriors who would come to Landhanga, to a unified banner."

"Humanity needs such a banner, and a home. When the next Kaizen hunters come here, we will be ready for them. Stay within our walls, and be patient." With that the king slowly subsided, gathering fresh shadows around him. Abruptly the audience was over.

Agar gently ushered Estarziel and Skarrack from the chamber, taking them to new quarters that were a little more salubrious than the ones in which they had spent the night. "I have scouts out around the perimeters of Landhanga," he told them. "As soon as we get word of the Kaizen, we will gather."

Left alone again, Skarrack and the girl ate sparingly and drank a little of the fresh water provided. He sat while she paced restlessly, deep in thought for some time. Finally she turned to him, speaking quietly. "Do you sense the atmosphere in this haunted citadel? A feeling of menace?"

He had been uneasy since waking, his instinct warning him against some unfathomable force, an invisible miasma of malevolence. He spoke softly to her, trying to frame his gut feelings. "Perhaps I'm being unduly cautious."

"Something's wrong. This city is like a tapestry, with segments missing. Something I've misread, vital knowledge. Finnwalder consented to my requests too easily."

"Could it be a trap? You think he may be an ally of the Kaizen?"

"It's not safe to remain here. For the rest of the day we'll go along with whatever is proposed for us and appear to be satisfied guests. But tonight, when they will be concentrating more on the Upanti, we'll leave, even if we have to cut our way out. Otherwise I think you're right, Skarrack. Finnwalder is going to hand us over to the Kaizen. I was being naive in coming to him."

"No, it must have been a shock to you, as it was to me, when you saw him."

"He spoke to us as the king I knew. Yet beneath his apparent acceptance of my suggestions lurked something far darker, a devious energy that controls him. And it's that that's at the heart of my misgivings. Yes, we leave tonight."

*

They knew there were guards outside their chambers in the corridor. They had been housed in a tower, where the only safe way out was through its single door, escorted by the guards back down into the palace. There was a small balcony, and as night took hold, they stood on it, bathed in moonlight. Like other towers, this one had several thick strands of ivy and other creeping vegetation working its inexorable way up to its flat upper reaches. With their backpacks strapped to them, they clambered lithely over the parapet and took a firm grip on the vines, and moments later were swinging down into the shadows. The city spread below was silent and lightless, moonlight shimmering along strands of ancient cabling, relics of a bygone era, that fanned out from the wall of the lower tower, lost in other clumps of knotted branches and vegetation.

"We'll make our way across as many rooftops as we can," Estarziel whispered to Skarrack. "We should be able to get close to the outer walls. We'll hide somewhere until dawn and then go back through the forest."

He was nodding, his eyes searching for the best place to swing off the tower, when a sudden movement below snagged his attention. A heavy shape, larger than a horse, was pulling itself out of the matted ivy and on to the metal strands. Its joints creaked and gleamed, metallic and polished. Its orchestrated movements identified it as a machine, and one dedicated to a single purpose. Even in this poor light, the impression it gave was unmistakable: it had the look of an immense arachnid. Skarrack cursed, knowing the way down was blocked by this sentinel. Worse, the thing was intent on rising, undoubtedly to challenge them.

"We dare not fight it here," he told Estarziel. "We'll be discovered."

"And this time put in chains," she agreed. She also studied their position. There was a narrow window not many yards from where they hung and she climbed across to it, Skarrack following. He could hear the scrambling creature below. It would be upon them in minutes. Estarziel reached the window and pulled herself into its black slit, turning to wave him to her. He followed, barely able to squeeze through, and once inside he dropped down to a corridor beside her, wreathed in darkness. Outside he heard the scraping of the creature's many legs as it sought to gain ingress. One long appendage entered and poked at the internal darkness, but the creature's bulk would never gain entry.

Estarziel moved down the confined corridor. It was dusty, evidently unused, for webs hung down like small curtains, living spiders shrinking back into the clefts and hollows of the walls, not eager to investigate. A little moonlight speared in from the slit window, where the creature without had abandoned the pursuit. There was enough light to see ahead. The corridor became a stair, leading downward, and as the two figures descended, vague light from below lanced off a confusion of numerous pipes and metal spars. Some were little thicker than wires, tangled like undergrowth, others were fatter than a human body, rusting and slowly disintegrating. The two figures were swallowed up in what appeared to be a vast machine, something that had operated in the haze of years gone by, the intestines of some huge organ of energy, long redundant. The war-ravaged cities of the world were choked with such mechanical debris.

Undisturbed heaped dust and detritus suggested no one had trodden this tormented region for years. Skarrack and Estarziel remained silent, an instinctive agreement; they were awarded for their caution when sounds came up from below. They squeezed between two segmented ducts and found another corridor, creeping along it towards soft light and the sounds. There was an inner window, again a narrow cleft, opening to a chamber, which they surmised must be below ground level and under the base of the tower. Looking through the opening into the torchlight beyond, they saw they were somewhere high in the dome of this chamber. It was not disused, its walls hug with rich tapestries, its columns scrubbed, etched with strange hieroglyphs and sigils, many statues spread around the base of a slickly maintained great hall. The polished effigies harked back to the great ages of Man, when this city had been far more ostentatious, a royal seat of power. It was filled now with human movement. As Skarrack and Estarziel gazed upon it, they shuddered in amazement.

At the centre of the hall, there was another wide pit, identical to the one beside which they had been introduced to Finnwalder. The monarch spread himself in this one's muddy embrace, the countless serpent-like entities surrounding his bloated form gleaming in the bright flames around him. As before, he caressed them sensually and they writhed over his shoulders and across his expansive bulk. Numerous guards, combined with other men, dressed in robes that proclaimed them to be officials, probably priests, surrounded the king. Kneeling at their feet were a score or more warriors, wearing nothing other than a breech-clout, their hands chained, their heads bowed in the abject misery of prisoners. Estarziel and Skarrack took all this in and exchanged a brief glance, not needing words to confirm what they both understood. It was the other groups beside the columns that stunned them. They were comprised of the Upanti beast men of the forest. Yet they were not aggressive, their savage faces inanimate, their bodies relaxed, and Skarrack wondered if they had been drugged.

"Like hounds," Estarziel whispered. "They *serve* the warriors."

As they watched, mesmerized, they heard the chanting, taken up by everyone below apart from the prisoners, until the sound swelled into an unholy chorus, deep and unsettling. Finnwalder's expanded face broke from the surface of the pit, his huge eyes opening wide, and in them now was little vestige of humanity. This was something beyond that, something from another dimension, a horrifying energy, speaking only of pain and distress. The prisoners stirred under that baleful gaze, immediately trying to wrest free of their bonds, but the warriors around them held them and brought them to heel with swords.

Gradually, undulating to the rhythm of the chanting, the serpent-like things slid out from the pit and across the slabs towards the prisoners, who were now desperate to free themselves, screaming in terror. Yet there was no avoiding the writhing, faceless horrors, whose tips opened up like undersea plants, each revealing a mass of tiny, wriggling tendrils. These clamped over the heads of the human victims, tangling with their hair, penetrating their ears, locked in place, seemingly feeding.

Skarrack and Estarziel were rooted, appalled at the transformations that were taking place, for as the serpent-things fed, so each captured human slowly morphed, until, released, they slumped down, faces and bodies converted – into beast-men. This was how the Upanti had been formed! This was no accident of poisoned genetics over time, it was a biological process controlled by these reptiles from the pit. And the expression on Finnwalder's face proclaimed his joy at seeing the foul work of the things that obeyed his will. Around the chamber, the warriors stood unmoving, as if their minds had been switched off, their vision blocked: they were like men dreaming, unaware of the nightmare enfolding.

"We have to destroy Finnwalder," Estarziel whispered to Skarrack. "He means to turn all the men of this city into the beast creatures."

"And doubtless us with them."

"We must return to our chamber, if they haven't realized we left it."

Quickly they climbed back up the way they had come until they reached the window where they had entered this part of the tower. Estarziel pulled herself up on to the ledge and looked out. The spider guardian was gone, and as she went out on to the tangled ivy, she saw no sign of it. Skarrack followed her and they climbed upward to the balcony of the room they'd been housed it. Dawn was yet some distance away and deep shadows flooded the city below.

Inside the chamber there was nothing to suggest the guards had entered. It seemed likely that their brief absence had not been noticed.

"All that happened in the forest was a *sham*," said Estarziel. "The fight, the killing of the Upanti. Staged for our benefit! Yet there's nothing to suggest Finnwalder will be aware we know the truth of his perfidy," said Estarziel. "When we're taken before him again, we must act. Somehow he controls the minds of all his men, both the Upanti and the warriors. No wonder they behave like soulless machines!"

"If we kill him, it ends. With their minds freed, they'll not seek to enslave us."

"He plans to keep us here, unaware of his treachery, until the Kaizen come. And his prize for handing us over will be the Kaizen sanctioning him as ruler here, a satrap in a land they have little use for."

"So we maintain the deception. Let's hope we don't have too long to wait before he summons us."

"We can be sure that when he does, the Kaizen will be getting closer."

*

Their frustration at being confined was tested to its limit, but by the onset of the next evening, word came they were to be taken before Finnwalder. They were gambling on his not knowing about their near clash with the arachnid guardian below the tower, and that it had not presented a report on their movements. As Agar took them down into the palace, Skarrack and Estarziel mentally reviewed the course of action they had planned. It would rely on timing and conviction. They would be surrounded by the guards, and once they launched their plan, the warriors would no longer be complacent. Both Skarrack and Estarziel had been allowed to carry their sheathed weapons, to allay any doubts they had of his friendship.

In his pit, Finnwalder observed them with a twisted smile. "The Kaizen have sent another party of troops to Landhanga. My spies inform me they will be at our gates this day."

"How many?" said Estarziel.

"Thirty of their finest warriors, powerful beings that expect to take what they want. We must prepare to fight." The great eyes blazed.

Estarziel and Skarrack stood close to the edge of the pit, where the serpents writhed and churned. Behind them a score of the warriors had arranged themselves in a semicircle, watching with their usual bland indifference, machines awaiting instructions. They were all armed, but their weapons were sheathed.

"I presume," said Finnwalder, "that you will use your Burning Blade against them. That, combined with my own elite corps should be enough to bring them down."

Estarziel, again not wearing her helmet, carefully watched the serpents, which had edged closer to the lip of the pit, as if scenting her. Beside her, Skarrack had his hand on the hilt of his sword. He sensed a tautness of the atmosphere, a gathering of energy that seemed tainted, oppressive. Estarziel's face, he saw, reflected her fanaticism, her zeal for the quest written starkly there, her eyes like jewels, bright and terrifying.

She nodded.

"It must contain unimaginable power," he said. "I am deeply intrigued. Draw it and let me see its glory."

Skarrack felt a pulse in the air around them, a living thing, and knew instinctively that Finnwalder was exercising his own power, as he did over his servants. It quickly strengthened, a firm grip, difficult to resist. Skarrack knew that Estarziel also felt it. They must strike now, before the moment was lost. She seemed to catch his thought, drawing the blade, which sang as it was revealed, a white glow suffusing its steel.

"Wonderful," said Finnwalder. "Marvelous engineering." The serpents slid over the lip of the pit, slitted mouths opening in unison. "I wonder – could I hold it for just a moment? Just to feel that power, the thrill of it." He dipped his long arms in among the writhing bodies.

Estarziel turned the blade so that she was holding it in both hands, an offering. Skarrack wanted to shout a warning: this was too much of a risk. If Finnwalder got a grip on the sword, he would never return it. Skarrack and Estarziel would be his first victims. As he opened his mouth, Skarrack found he could not utter a sound. Whatever mental sorcery Finnwalder had conjured would not let him. Skarrack was paralyzed. He stared in horror at the serpents as they rose up from the pit, and as they did so, Skarrack understood their true nature. They were not serpents at all, *but appendages of the king, part of that blasphemous body, controlled by it.* Finnwalder wielded them now, reaching out with them eagerly to take the Burning Blade, his eyes reflecting its blaze of light, a lascivious smile spreading across those gross features.

Skarrack's thoughts were in turmoil as he was forced to share something of what was going through the monarch's mind. With the sword he would be omnipotent! He and his warriors, beast-men and humans, would slay the oncoming Kaizen and consolidate their place here in the lost peninsular. The world outside would lose its champion, the Crimson Warrior, and Landhanga would be left to rot and crumble, as the last days of Man drew ever closer.

Estarziel held the blade out, a few feet from the grinning face, apparently as powerless to act as Skarrack. Yet something flared in the sword, an abrupt emission of vivid light. For a few seconds it bathed the girl and in its aftermath, she suddenly swung the blade around and gripped it with both hands, the full fury of her determination and wild dedication to the cause burning anew, incandescent. Finnwalder was dazzled and before he had an opportunity to react, she plunged the Burning Blade into the space between his eyes and drove it in to flesh and bone, up to the hilt. It was one with her, an extra limb. The monstrous visage shook, the eyes filling with agony, and smoke flowed up from the point of entry.

Skarrack felt a weakening of the grip that held him and he drew his own sword. He used it to slice into the nearest of the serpentine arms, cutting off its open-mouthed extremity. Around him the guards were jerking to life, pulling their blades out in readiness to chop Skarrack to pieces. Finnwalder was writhing from side to side in his pit, throwing up great gouts of muck, his appendages flinging this way and that in a maddened, blind rage. The face became horribly contorted, like that of some demon from the darkest pits of the nether worlds, the true visage of the entity that had possessed and so corrupted the king.

Estarziel clung on to the blade's haft, refusing to let its victim tear itself free. The warriors converged on Skarrack, but one by one they fell to their knees, gazing about them dazedly, mouths working like those of beached fish. Skarrack paused as the many arms of the king flopped from side to side uselessly, life seeping from them. He would have leapt forward to assist Estarziel, but a sudden change in Finnwalder's face held him back.

The former king's face had sloughed off the nightmarish visage of whatever demonic power had reshaped it. Instead it was an old, human face now, riddled with pain, tears streaming from rheumy eyes, jaw sagging. "Don't spare me," the old man gasped. "You have cast that thing back into its deepest charnel pits. The power in the Burning Blade has charred and maimed it. Kill me, too. It can never return to usurp my body."

Around the fallen king, the mass of serpent appendages had grown still, life eradicated. He sagged further down as Estarziel pulled free the Burning Blade. She held it up and gradually its bright light subsided to become a dull glow. Slowly the warriors shook themselves, coming out of their daze like men aroused from a deep sleep. When they saw Estarziel standing before Finnwalder, they were confused. Was she friend or foe? The king shuddered, as if being shaken by something, the last dregs, perhaps, of the thing that had possessed him. His eyes blazed in sudden desperate fury, a final surge of defiance. Estarziel again plunged the Burning Blade into the face and it began to melt, the features merging, the flesh sliding from the head in thick rivulets, the entire hideous body convulsing and sinking under the lifeless forms around it.

Estarziel pulled the blade free and again held it high. At once, all the swords of the warriors flared brilliantly. Every man holding a blade dropped it, staggering back. Slowly the fire in the swords faded. "You are slaves no more," Estarziel told them. "Whatever had hold of your king has perished. Take up your blades. You will need them when the Kaizen arrive."

*

Skarrack leaned out over the broken battlements. In the forest he could hear the sound of horses approaching, a small party. There were beast-men in the trees, several score of them, but they held back, waiting the commands of their new masters, for the death of Finnwalder had scourged something from them. They answered to Agar and his warriors now.

"They're here," said one of the men on watch, leaning from a low tower above the wall, indicating the forest trail.

Beside Skarrack, Estarziel again drew the Burning Blade. She had donned her helmet for this encounter, but her eyes yet blazed with the obsessive desire to defeat the invaders. Skarrack knew she had been a Fire Witch, and there was an element of them which was not human. Maybe such grim powers were needed in this conflict.

"Since they've come for us," she said, "then let them take us, if they can!"

Moments later the Kaizen riders nudged their huge steeds out from the trees and arranged themselves in a semi-circle, looking up at the battlements and the force opposing them. One of the Kaizen, a typically massive warrior, came forward and he raised a battle axe in mock salute. "We have come at the invitation of King Finnwalder. He has something for us."

"The king is dead," Estarziel called. "But your prize awaits you. If you can take it."

The Kaizen warlord recognized her and let out a bestial growl that his fellows took up, all lifting their weapons. There were no more words. It was to be a fight, and one which the warriors of the city would never have expected to survive. However, as the Burning Blade flared anew in Estarziel's grip, so too did their blades, feeding on it, and as one they leapt from the battlements on to the scree below, racing down upon the Kaizen. The invaders were bemused for no more than a few minutes and goaded their war steeds forward. Light and fire roared as the fighting began.

Skarrack had experienced this exultant use of a blade ignited by Estarziel's weapon before, so when he sliced open the armoured belly of a Kaizen warrior and watched the being crash to the earth, blood soaking the ground, he shouted encouragement to Agar and the others. Many fell, for the Kaizen were immensely strong and were not easy to bring down, but the sheer weight of numbers opposing them, coupled with the power of the swords, beat them back. In the forest the beast men had formed a huge battalion and although they used no more than tooth and claw, they poured over the Kaizen like ants in an endless stream.

In less than an hour it was over. The Kaizen, who had come here thinking to take command of another city, chaining the will of its king to their own, were ripped to pieces. Estarziel stood over the corpse of the last of them.

"They'll come again," said Agar, dripping blood from his own wounds and those he had opened in the enemy. "Next time in force. This is a great victory for us, but we may live to regret it."

Estarziel shook her head. "It's me they want. And this

blade." She studied it. Its light had faded, drained in the battle.

"What is wrong?" said Skarrack.

"It spoke to me. Unless I find a new source of power for it, it will be just another simple sword. We will have to leave Landhanga and go south. We'll find what we need there." She turned to Agar. "You'll be safe for a while. The Kaizen will ignore you, in spite of this bloody work. They'll be seeking me." She laughed, a bitter, caustic sound. "And I will be ready."

Skarrack felt the power of his own sword fading, and with it the sudden burst of killing lust, an emotion that had shaken him to his core. Is that what it was like for her? Perhaps it would strengthen the bond between them, and reduce her isolation, the bitterness that made all men, including him, forever strangers to her.

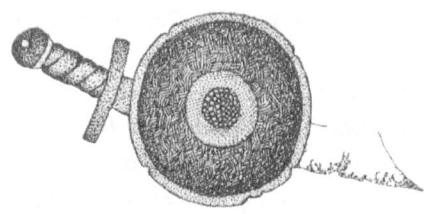

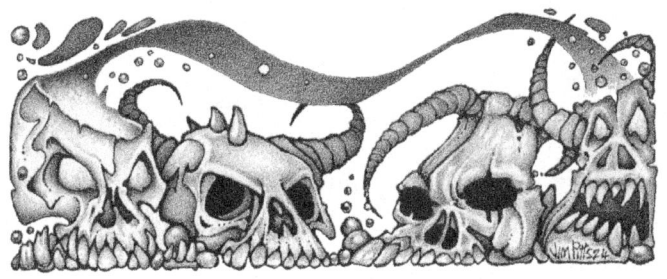

ALSO AVAILABLE *from*
PARALLEL UNIVERSE PUBLICATIONS

Carl Barker: *Parlour Tricks*
Charles Black: *Black Ceremonies*
Benjamin Blake: *Standing on the Threshold of Madness*
Mike Chinn: *Radix Omnium Malum*
Ezeiyoke Chukwunonso: *The Haunted Grave & Other Stories*
Irvin S. Cobb: *Fishhead: The Darker Tales of Irvin S. Cobb*
Adrian Cole: *Tough Guys*
Adrian Cole: *Elak: Warrior of Atlantis*
Andrew Darlington: *A Saucerful of Secrets*
Kate Farrell: *And Nobody Lived Happily Ever After*
Craig Herbertson: *The Heaven Maker & Other Gruesome Tales*
Craig Herbertson: *Christmas in the Workhouse*
Erik Hofstatter: *The Crabian Heart*
Andrew Jennings: *Into the Dark*
Samantha Lee: *Childe Rolande*
David Ludford: *A Place of Skulls & Other Tales*
Samantha Lee: *Childe Rolande*
Jessica Palmer: *Other Visions of Heaven and Hell*
Jessica Palmer: *Fractious Fairy Tales*
Jim Pitts: *The Fantastical Art of Jim Pitts*
Jim Pitts: *The Ever More Fantastical Art of Jim Pitts*
David A. Riley: *Goblin Mire*
David A. Riley: *Their Cramped Dark World & Other Tales*
David A. Riley: *His Own Mad Demons*
David A. Riley: *Moloch's Children*
David A. Riley: *After Nightfall & Other Weird Tales*
David A. Riley: *A Grim God's Revenge: Dark Tales of Fantasy*
David A. Riley: *Lucilla – a novella*
Joseph Rubas: *Shades: Dark Tales of Supernatural Horror*
Eric Ian Steele: *Nightscape*
David Williamson: *The Chameleon Man & Other Terrors*

www.paralleluniversepublications.blogspot.com

SWORDS & SORCERIES
TALES OF HEROIC FANTASY

PARALLEL UNIVERSE PUBLICATIONS

Crimson Quill Quarterly
Volume 2
April 2024

Featuring the Talents of:

Mike Adamson
Alexander J. Azwell
T. M. Bosley
Deborah L. Davitt
Teel James Glenn
J. Brice Odom
R. K. Olson

Coming in 2024
The Elak of Atlantis Trilogy
by
Adrian Cole

Adrian Cole's
Elak of Atlantis Trilogy

Elak - Warrior of Atlantis
Elak - King of Atlantis
Elak - Sea Raiders of Atlantis

Three collections of tales
from the fabled
Atlantis of Elak - warrior and king

Illustrated by Jim Pitts

To be published by
Parallel Universe Publications in 2024

Swords & Heroes

An Anthology of Sword & Sorcery

Edited by Lyndon Perry

Childe Rolande
The Myth and the Legend

Childe Rolande, Hermaphrodite and Freak, is born into the fiercely matriarchal society of Alba at a time when the fabric of the nation is crumbling.

Rolande fulfils all the technical requirements of an ancient Prophesy which promises that one day a 'Redeemer' will arise who will be 'the one and the both', and who will sweep away the age-old tyranny of Alba's female rulers to 'bind the nation together in peace'.

The hopes and dreams of Alba's downtrodden males are centred on this mystical being, whose eyes hold the wisdom of the ages and who can reputedly change into an eagle at will.

Can Rolande live up to their expectations, wrest the antlered throne from the Warlord of the Clans, drive the evil Sorceress, Fergael from her stronghold in the Dark Tower, and unite the polarised Kingdom?

A seething dark fantasy set in a dystopian Scotland in the far future, where myth and magic are alive once more, *Childe Rolande* is a gritty, no holds barred story of bloodshed and mayhem, of betrayal and brutality.

Optioned to be filmed as a TV mini-series, Samantha Lee is already at work on a sequel.

Available as a paperback and a kindle e-book.

PARALLEL UNIVERSE PUBLICATIONS

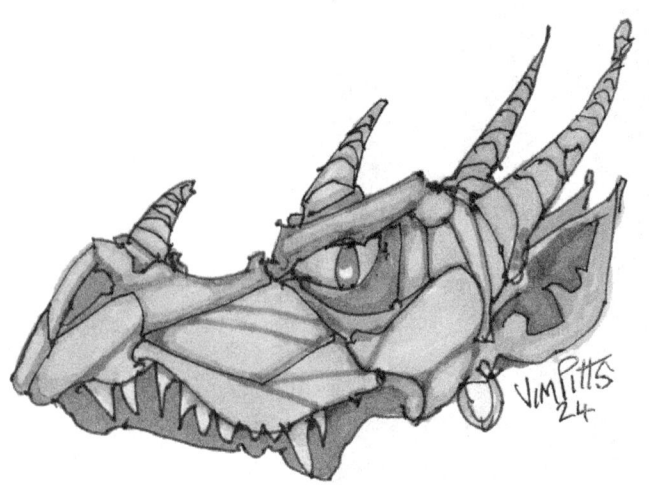

Made in the USA
Coppell, TX
02 June 2024